Listen up!

"In the next few days you will be getting ready for your training. Listen to your officers and noncoms. They aren't here merely to harass you but to save your lives. Their methods may seem rough, but they are no rougher than the enemy in combat. Keep that in mind. You are preparing for combat. The enemy will not be there to assist you. He will be there to kill you..."

SEEDS OF WAR

KEVIN RANDLE
& ROBERT CORNETT

ACE SCIENCE FICTION BOOKS
NEW YORK

To

Wilson Tucker, Joe Haldeman, and Clarence Andrews
for their help

and
to

K. Kadrmas
just for the hell of it.

This book is an Ace Science Fiction
original edition, and has never been
previously published.

SEEDS OF WAR

An Ace Science Fiction Book / published by arrangement with
the authors

PRINTING HISTORY
Ace Science Fiction edition / August 1986

ISBN: 0-441-75878-9

Ace Science Fiction Books are published by The Berkley Publishing Group,
200 Madison Avenue, New York, New York 10016.
PRINTED IN THE UNITED STATES OF AMERICA

TELEX
START

The following combat record tapes were selected from the 201 files of the individuals listed below:

 FETTERMAN, Anthony B. First Lieutenant, Seventh Ranger Company, SCAF. "The only way to get killed in combat is to make a mistake."

 KADRMAS, Karen. Lieutenant Colonel, First Armored Corps, SCAF. "There is no glory in war, only death."

 KISOV, Vasili Illiyavich. Major, Third Aviation Company, SCAF. "Never walk when you can ride, and never ride when you can fly."

 MASTERSON, Lara. First Lieutenant, 358th Training Company, SCAF. "All your noncoms, however, are combat veterans who have passed the acid test of warfare. They have survived."

 MCALLIF, Steven M. Private First Class, First Pathfinder Brigade, SCAF. "There was no retreat from there, only extra duty."

Initial background information has been compiled from official video-tape records of the Executive Board for the meeting held 6 June, 2146, in Washington, D.C., the United Americas and from the private tape files of the officers in attendance.

1

June 6, 2146

The activity inside the pressroom of the White House had the
urgent look of ordered confusion. David Pierce, floor director
for station WBN, hated surprise press conferences because he
never had the time to check the equipment out properly beforehand. After fifteen minutes of trying, he still couldn't get
his headset to work. Disgusted, he tossed it to the assistant
director, pulled the set off the assistant's head, pressed it against
his own ear and keyed the mike. "Coming up on the minute
mark, stand by. Stand by in graphics."

"Graphics is ready."

"Stand by on the sound."

"Sound is ready."

"Stand by on playback."

"We've got a hold on playback."

"What's the problem with it?"

"It's not working."

"I figured that. What's wrong with it?"

"I don't know. They're working on it."

"Well, get it fixed for Christ's sake. Stand by in lighting."

"Lighting is ready."

"Sound, have you got a level on the President's voice?"

"The President isn't here yet."

"Well, where the hell is he?"

"He's coming now."

"Coming up on thirty seconds. Get that voice level. How we doing on playback?"

"Playback is ready."

"Stand by on tape."

"Tape is ready."

"Roll the tape. Static shot on the super. Key the announcer. Take tape."

"Ladies and gentlemen, the President of the United Americas."

"Dolly in. Key the President, and lose the super."

"As President and Commander in Chief it is my duty to the United American peoples to report to you tonight that hostile actions against a United American exploratory ship in free space in the vicinity of the Tau Ceti star system have today required me to order the military forces of the United Americas to take action in reply.

"The initial attack on the manned scientific probe *Star Explorer* on August 2, 2134, by an unknown, hostile force, has left little hope of survivors. Radio telemetry from the unarmed scientific vessel, which was on a purely peaceful mission, indicates that the *Star Explorer* had achieved synchronous orbit about the fourth planet of the Tau Ceti star system and was peacefully engaged in taking scientific measurements of the planet, when it was suddenly and viciously attacked, without any provocation whatsoever.

"Before radio contact was abruptly broken, a personal message was received from Colonel Zech, the ship's captain, stating that the vessel had suffered heavy damage, with great loss of life. Colonel Zech reported that the attack was believed to have originated from the planet's surface and that the pressure hull of his vessel had been breached.

"The performance of the commander and his crew in this engagement is in the highest tradition of the United Americas

Corps for the Peaceful Study of Outer Space. This act of violence against the peaceful representatives of the United Americas must be met not only with alert defense, but with positive reply. That reply is being initiated even as I speak with you tonight."

The President glanced up from the prepared text of his speech and surveyed the surrounding cameramen, sound technicians, and waiting journalists to gauge their reaction. Their faces were masks of stunned disbelief.

"In the larger sense this act of aggression aimed at our unarmed scientific mission, brings home to all of us the importance of the struggle for peace and security in outer space. Aggression by terror against the scientists aboard the *Star Explorer* is an open aggression against the United Americas themselves.

"The determination of all Americans to carry out our full commitment to the free and peaceful exploration of outer space will be redoubled by this outrage. Yet our response, for the present, will be limited and fitting. We Americans know—although others appear to forget—the risks of spreading conflict. We will seek no war.

"I have instructed the Secretary of State to make this position totally clear to friends and adversaries. I have instructed Ambassador Kuber-Ross to raise this matter immediately and urgently before the Security Council of the United Nations. Finally, I have today met with the leaders of all parties in the Congress of the United Americas and have informed them that I shall immediately request that Congress pass a resolution making it clear that our government is united in its determination to take all necessary measures in support of freedom and in defense of the peaceful uses and exploration of outer space."

The President stared soulfully into the camera.

"I have been given encouraging assurance by the leaders of all political parties that such a resolution will be promptly introduced, freely and expeditiously debated, and passed with overwhelming support."

The President's voice seemed to catch and he cleared his throat.

"It is a solemn responsibility to have to order even limited military action by forces whose overall strength is as vast and awesome as those of the United Americas, but it is my considered conviction, shared throughout your government, that firmness in the right is indispensable today for peace. That firmness will always be tempered with mercy. Its mission is peace.

"I will now entertain a few questions from the distinguished members of the press."

After several seconds of shocked silence the assembled journalists rose as one, clamoring for recognition. The President stood quietly behind the podium, blinking into the klieg lights, surveying the pandemonium before him. When the noise had subsided, he singled out a familiar balding head.

"Let's start with Mr. Zima of the Chicago *Tribune-Times*."

"Mr. President, how far away is this star, and does this mean that our scientists have succeeded in developing a way to exceed the speed of light?"

"I am informed that the Tau Ceti star system is 3.7 parsecs from Earth, making it approximately twelve light years distant," the President replied. "As for your second question, we're into a technical area here. I'll defer for the moment to Dr. Paul Simons, director of the Ames Research Center. Dr. Simons is in charge of Project Star Listener, the scientific team put together to search for and monitor signals from the *Star Explorer*."

The President was joined on the podium by a hulking ape of a man who looked more simian than scientist.

"The answer to your question is no," he said. "The *Star Explorer* was powered by a standard form of ionic propulsion, advanced for its day, but not too different than what we use on interplanetary runs now. If I may anticipate the next question, it took the crew nearly thirty-five years to reach the Tau Ceti star system at sublight speeds, although the time span would have seemed only about ten years to the explorers, because of the time dilation consideration of relativistic travel. The radio signals we picked up last night were, of course, beamed back toward the Earth a dozen years ago—August 2, 2134, to be exact. And it has been nearly fifty years since the *Star Explorer* left Earth orbit."

There was a mixed muttering of confusion and apprehension from the press corps. The President indicated a man he recognized as a member of the electronic media.

"Mr. President. Roger Gribin, World Broadcasting Network. The probe was launched before the Exchange?"

"That is correct. The *Star Explorer* was a United States spacecraft at the time of its launch. It was redesignated a United Americas vessel five years ago, to bring it in line with current policy. The project originated with the last elected President of the United States, the Reverend Dr. Charles Jager, who was largely responsible for the Exchange. Jager, as you know, was a highly unstable religious fanatic elected by a coalition of welfare and religious minorities that regarded the destruction of anti-Christian groups as a holy crusade. The project was mounted in strictest secrecy, and stemmed from Jager's twisted efforts to prove the existence of God, whom he believed lived on Tau Ceti."

"Why haven't we heard about the *Star Explorer* before, if it was launched fifty years ago?" demanded Gribin.

"Shortly after the probe was launched, the Exchange began. The Exchange was followed by worldwide famine, acute economic depression, and the terrible epidemic of Martian Plague— brought back to Earth by the survivors of the Russo-American Scientific Survey team. With those problems to worry about, along with the deaths of Jager and his key personnel at the hands of a revolutionary tribunal five years later, the *Star Explorer* project was quite understandably forgotten. Just a few years ago references to it were discovered on computer tapes at the old National Aeronautics and Space Administration's central files storage facility in the ruins of the Manned Space Flight Center in Houston, Texas. An immediate radio telescope search for the probe got under way, and a few months ago we began receiving valuable telemetry from the vessel."

As Gribin sat down, other newsmen leaped to their feet. The President pointed to the middle of the room, but instead of the reporter he indicated, a young woman with long blond hair shouted, "President Putnam, there are a number of questions about the recent charges that your Internal Security troops have openly fired on crowds of unarmed workers in São Paulo."

The President stared as two security officers began moving toward the woman. The cameras remained on her, and he signaled the security men back to their positions. "The purpose of this conference is to discuss the destruction of our probe, and questions will be limited to that subject. If you'll hand a written question to the press secretary, I will see that you receive a written reply."

The woman clearly didn't want to accept the answer, but other newsmen jumped up shouting for attention. The President made a note to have the woman's White House press credentials revoked. The President pointed again, this time with the expected results.

"Jacques De Beirs, *Le Monde*. Exactly what sort of military action is the United Americas planning on taking?"

"As I pointed out in my prepared statement, I will go before Congress tomorrow to ask for a resolution empowering me to take whatever steps may be necessary in the name of the United Americas to protect her citizens and property from wanton acts of aggression, wherever they may occur. I have conferred with the Joint Chiefs of Staff, and it is their considered opinion that a punitive force of sufficient strength and resource can and should be immediately mounted for the express purpose of extracting reasonable retribution from the ruling governments of Tau Ceti Four."

"Mr. President, that still doesn't give us an idea about the magnitude of the military action you're planning to take. What would this punitive force be composed of?"

"As I've indicated, this punitive force would be composed of sufficient military combat and support personnel and equipment to engage in and carry out protracted conventional warfare against the ruling governments of Tau Ceti Four, without benefit of normally existing lines of supply and communication, should such action be necessary. We will, of course, pursue all possible diplomatic channels that might lead to a peaceful resolution of this crisis, but we must not let ourselves be caught unprepared, should war be necessary."

"Mr. President. Heinrich Zegler, *Die Stern*. Is the United Americas planning to move unilaterally?"

"Of course not. All nations will be invited to participate in this great adventure. As I mentioned, I have instructed our ambassador to the United Nations to propose a resolution before the Security Council, and then the full body of that organization, calling for immediate sanctions against the Tau Cetians.

But it was a United Americas probe that was attacked and American citizens who were killed, and it is our responsibility to move against the Tau Cetians."

"But doesn't any action taken by the United Americas implicate the entire planet, whether or not all nations agree with your action?"

"Not necessarily. The hostile strike against the *Star Explorer* may have been the action of only one government among many on Tau Ceti Four. If so, we will deal with that one government. If we do not hold an entire planet responsible for the actions of one of its governments, there is no reason why the Tau Cetians should."

Before anyone could say anything, Putnam added, "Ladies and gentlemen, we are facing the greatest challenge that has ever confronted the people of Earth. We're talking about our way of life. If the Tau Cetians are allowed to believe they can attack us at will, there will be no stopping them. We must, for our security, carry the challenge to the enemy. They must learn that we will not tolerate unprovoked assaults. Once we have resolved this conflict, we will extend the hand of friendship.

"As always, we will meet new people and new challenges with peaceful, good intentions, but we must not allow those who would destroy our way of life to take advantage of those good intentions."

There was a sudden outburst in the back of the room. One of the pool cameramen ripped off his headset and leaped in front of the cameras. "Don't any of you understand what's going on here," he shouted. "This is the first contact mankind has had with intelligent life anywhere in the universe, and he's talking about blowing the suckers away!"

The cameraman grabbed for one of the microphones set up for use by the journalists, but was tackled by Secret Service men and wrestled to the floor before he could use it. As he was dragged from the room, he shouted, "Don't you people realize this is a declaration of interstellar war!"

The door to the pressroom closed, shutting out the disturbance. There were several seconds of awkward silence, then the President self-consciously cleared his throat.

"Let me say first that I am deeply moved and concerned with the comments made by this unfortunate and obviously overwought young man who evidently does not understand the full ramifications and seriousness of this situation. He nevertheless has raised a valid point which deserves a response. In fact, the conditions for interstellar war already exist. They were initiated, not by us, but by the Tau Cetians. We didn't attack them, they attacked us. This government seeks no wider war. What we seek is a peaceful resolution to this grave situation. But it would be an act of the greatest foolhardiness not to prepare ourselves for military action, particularly given our previous experiences with Tau Cetian diplomacy. No one abhors war more than your President, but if war is necessary to ensure the peace and security of our great peoples, then we must be prepared to take the necessary action.

"We have time for two more questions."

"Grace Stevens, the Denver *Post*. Mr. President, you said that the space probe had been attacked. How do we know this for certain? And how do we know where the attack came from?"

"I stated earlier that we had received a coded message from the commander of the *Star Explorer*." Putnam picked up a sheet of paper. "I will read the message exactly as it was received.

"This is Colonel Zech, commanding the *Star Explorer*. Our vessel is under attack by spacecraft of unknown origin. We have suffered heavy damage. Our main engines are out, and our life-support systems have been crippled. The main pressure hull has been breached, and we are rapidly losing atmosphere. We have three dead and five injured. Believe attack to have originated from the planet's surface. We will attempt—

"The message ended abruptly at that point. In my prepared statement I noted that the *Star Explorer* was in orbit about the fourth planet in the Tau Ceti star system. This fact, along with Colonel Zech's message and previous telemetry indicating that life existed on the planet, leads us to the inescapable conclusion that our space probe was attacked by the inhabitants of Tau Ceti Four."

"The message said three dead and five injured. How large was the crew of the *Star Explorer*?"

"There were eight scientists and four navigation, engineering, and flight specialists. We must conclude that there were no survivors.

"There is time for one more question."

"Mr. President. Richard Cash from the Des Moines *Register*. The figure twelve years has been mentioned a number of times. Am I correct in assuming that this hostile action you're speaking about happened twelve years ago? Isn't it a bit late to be worrying about it now?"

"It is never too late to be concerned about the safety and well-being of our citizens, or the protection of United Americas property, Mr. Cash. Nor is it too late to be concerned with the freedom and peaceful uses of outer space.

"Also, though it's true that the attack on our spacecraft occurred nearly a dozen years ago, it was only yesterday that we learned of it. You must keep in mind the built-in time lag caused by the enormity of stellar distances. The appropriate time for a reasoned, measured response is now, immediately upon our learning of the outrage.

"An unprovoked, vicious, openly hostile attack on a United Americas space vessel engaged in peaceful scientific investigation in free space must not be allowed to pass without reprimand, irrespective of where or when such an attack occurred. We cannot sit idly by and allow any enemy to destroy several billion dollars worth of United Americas property anytime they might feel like it, and murder United American citizens with impunity, simply because they are too far away, either in terms of distance or time."

The President swept together all the papers that he had spread on the podium and tapped them into alignment.

The senior press correspondent, Lee Dennis of the Tampa *Tribune* said, "Thank you, Mr. President."

As the journalists filed from the pressroom, Roger Gribin turned to Bill Zima. "Well, Bill, what did you think?" he asked.

"If you really want to know, I think we're in it for the tin and the tungsten."

2

Kadrmas, Karen
Major, Armored Corps, SCAF

"*TANK*—a heavily armored, self-propelled combat vehicle embodying the basic military characteristics of firepower, mobility, and crew protection. They are designed for many different purposes, and may be used as part of large infantry units, as a separate striking force (such as an armored division), or for reconnaissance."

It was a quote from a microfilm copy of the *Encyclopedia Britannica* over a hundred years old. It was an accurate description of the combat role of the tank then, and still is now. I suppose it will be accurate in another hundred years as well.

The first Kadrmas died in a Sherman tank in October 1942, at the battle of El Alamein. The second died in a Centurion in the Gaza Strip on June 6, 1967. The third Kadrmas died in a Chieftain in Syria in 1983, as did the fourth in the Pan-African War. Before the twelfth Kadrmas went off to fight, he took his fourteen-year-old daughter aside, had a quiet talk with her, and read her a paragraph from T. E. Lawrence.

"All men dream; but not equally. Those who dream by night

in the dusty recesses of their minds wake in the day to find that it was vanity; but the dreamers of the day are dangerous men, for they may act their dreams with open eyes, to make it possible."

He told his daughter never to forget the dream of a free Israel, an Israel that could one day live in peace, and then he kissed her and gave her a copy of a cracked and yellowed book that had belonged to the Kadrmas in 1942. It was *The Tank in the Attack* by Erwin Rommel. I still have that book.

I don't know exactly what I felt when the orders came; perhaps nothing. I've been a soldier too long and fought in too many battles to get sentimental over the friends I would never see again. I hadn't that many friends anyway, and no relatives. I think that it must have really been easy for me. At thirty years of age I had lived a fairly full life, had three love affairs—none very torrid, or suggestive of something more permanent, just sort of fun, and I guess satisfying in a detached way. I'd fought in two wars, a conflict, and four police actions—to use the phraseology of the Tel Aviv parliament—and been wounded once. The wound wasn't serious, and anyway, it was in a place that didn't show. Life on Earth had been fun, and grim. I was going to miss it, but not that much.

I didn't go off cheerfully or with any misguided ideas about making the world safe for democracy, you understand. I thought the whole mess smelled—flying off to attack a race we'd never seen and that probably didn't know we even existed. So they blew up an exploration ship launched more years ago than anybody could remember. So what? It wasn't as if they had nuked the moon or the Martian Colony. The Tau Cetians—assuming of course the ship had been destroyed by them—weren't even close to being in our neighborhood, and it would have been a terribly good piece of detective work for them to be able to figure out where the *Star Explorer* came from. But orders are orders are orders, and a good soldier's duty is to follow them—so long as they're "lawful," whatever that may be—and if there's one thing I am, it's a good soldier; a fact apparently recognized by SCAF's personnel selection computer, which had decided to expedite my promotion to major and give me command of an armored battalion.

I can't say I was terribly impressed with Baltimore. To be

fair, I never have liked large cities much, except for Tel Aviv, which hardly qualifies compared to the cities of the American eastern seaboard, even though the population is about two million now. Except for the central metroplex, the area around Baltimore is still mostly waste. They had to rebuild the whole thing after the Hanafi Muslims blew it up with a bootlegged hydrogen bomb forty years ago. Business never quite returned. Oh, there's some industry, but the principal part of what used to be the city of Baltimore is mostly taken up by the spaceport now.

The spaceport itself forms the hub of a half wheel surrounded by the Baltimore seaport and five feeder airports, the largest being the David Froiseth Memorial. Froiseth, it seems, was a hero of the Exchange. He disobeyed orders to launch his missile wing, and held until after the initial attacks were over. When the other side had exhausted all their weapons and thought the Americans had done likewise, they started massing their conventional forces for the invasion. Froiseth surprised them with the 129 missiles that were still combat ready out of his original 150. They were all MIRV of course, and after they fell, there wasn't enough left of the enemy combat forces to worry about. Despite the fact he won the war, he had disobeyed orders, and was court-martialed for his efforts. There was some talk by the Air Force of shooting him, but President Jager vetoed the idea, and after a few years Froiseth was eventually restored to full honors in the military, and proclaimed a national hero. It seems he had never even visited Baltimore, let alone lived there. But when they were rebuilding the place, someone suggested naming the spaceport after him. He lost that honor to Robert A. Heinlein, and had to settle for the principal airport.

All this I gleaned from the loudspeaker in the reception shuttle as we were conveyed from one of the outlying terminal hubs to the main terminal complex. I got off the monorail at the west-end station of the terminal, retrieved my two flight cases from luggage dispersal, and prayed that the rest of the things I'd shipped would make it into the right shuttle at the spaceport. It was mostly small personal belongings—books, clothes, odds and ends. I'd sold my furniture and terminated the lease on the apartment in Elat. Having my things put in storage for fifty or sixty years seemed pointless.

I made my way to Customs and Immigration, where my pistol caused a few raised eyebrows, though not because it was a pistol. Almost everyone carries small arms in America nowadays, though I understand that at one time, during the height of the gun control madness seventy or so years ago, mere possession of a handgun was a capital offense. The interest was caused by its age. It's a Browning 9mm semiautomatic that belonged to my great-grandfather. It uses ammunition with a cartridge case. They don't make that kind of ammunition for handguns anymore, except for special commemorative firearms. I've always liked the old guns, however, and do my own reloading.

It took me a while to convince the officials that it was a family heirloom, and not a collector's model for resale. They finally let me in with it after I agreed to pay the collector's import duty of fifty dollars New American, or about ten pounds Israeli. They wouldn't let me bring in my twelve-pack of Coca-Cola, though. They told me there was plenty of it available at a dollar a bottle, and that you could buy it for half price at the USO club on level three.

I was four days early, and wanted to find a hotel room and get a shower. But I was thirsty, and decided to try out the half-price Cokes. If I could pick up some to take with me, so much the better. I took the escalator up to level three, parked my suitcases in a couple of lockers, and made my way to the club.

I found the bar, got a Coke, and discovered that carryout was not available. Then I started looking for a place to sit. It was pretty crowded, and there didn't seem to be any seats. Finally I spotted an empty chair at a table already occupied by a short, stocky man with dark hair and a light mustache—it might have been red or blond, it was hard to tell in the dim light. He was wearing a flight coverall, and I thought I recognized the insignia as being that of an RAF major, or a squadron leader, as they call them. I noticed he was drinking Coke instead of a mixed drink, walked over, and asked if I could join him.

"Please do, lass," he said. "The name is Pete Peterson—still officially of His Majesty's Royal Air Force, but soon to be of SCAF. You are, I perceive by your dress and appearance, an officer in the Israeli Defense Force, Armored; and quite beautiful, though I confess, your rank escapes me."

I think I blushed slightly. I've been around, and I know I'm pretty fair looking, but I'm not used to people calling me beautiful. His direct statement caught me off guard.

"Major Karen Kadrmas," I said, smiling and extending my hand. I ignored the breech of military protocol. Hell, I couldn't see any point in us majoring-and-squadron-leadering each other to death. He surprised me by rising and kissing the back of my hand, rather than shaking it.

"Pleased to meet you, Major. I've just about finished my Coke. How about you? May I buy you one?"

I started to say no, then shook my bottle, realized it was already half empty, and said, "Sure, why not? And Karen is fine. No use in getting title happy."

He held up his Coke bottle in one hand and two fingers of the other. The girl behind the bar nodded, and sent the Cokes back with a waitress.

"Tell me," he said, "are all Israeli tankers as pretty as you? If so, I've been living in the wrong country for the last thirty-five years."

"Only the women are as pretty as I am," I replied. "Some of the men are quite homely. Now you tell me, are all RAF fighter pilots as direct as you are?" That mammoth mustache of his, which I now saw was bright red, twitched. I thought that he was smiling somewhere behind it, but the light was too dim and the mustache too huge to be certain.

"Ah, well, now, I'd say not by half. Besides, a fighter pilot I am not. I used to be, but I've been in Intelligence for the last five years. Hard to believe, isn't it?"

"What?"

"That anyone so handsome as meself could have anything to do with Intelligence."

"All right, then, is everyone in Intelligence as modest as you?"

"Only me. It's me one great fault. I've been trying to overcome it."

"Oh, brother! Good luck. Anyway, if you're not a fighter pilot, what are you doing in a flight suit with strike-command markings?"

"Ah, as I said, I used to be a flyboy. I've got five days

before I have to report to SCAF, and I volunteered to ferry the last surviving Shrike out to the new air museum at Albuquerque, New Mexico. I figured it might be the last airplane I ever get to fly. But I might be willing to delay a day if you'll have dinner with me. What's a lovely like yourself doing in a pit of a town like Baltimore anyhow?"

I hesitated before answering, then almost burst out laughing at the ridiculousness of it. The whole solar system might technically be at war with another star, but that didn't mean that everyone you talked to had to be a spy. Even if the Tau Cetians were among us and could pass for human, a pretty farfetched idea, I couldn't for the life of me see how a knowledge that SCAF was recruiting armored personnel would do them any good, especially if it took a dozen years for information to reach the Tau Ceti system.

"I'm here to link up with SCAF also. Like you, I'm early. Four days. I don't suppose there's anything to do in this town?"

"Not unless you want to take me up on that dinner invitation."

"You are persistent, aren't you?"

"One of me best qualities."

"What did you say you were doing, running around in that flight suit?"

"Ferrying the last of the Shrikes out to its final resting place at Kirtland Air Force Base. It's a tactical support fighter, though the one I'm flying is the B model, a two-seat trainer version. But I perceive that you are ducking the issue. If you're hoping I'll forget I asked you to dinner, you're wrong. You know I'm persistent."

"Supposing I were to say yes, then where would you be? You've already said you were on your way to New Mexico, and as it's only, let's see, ten-thirty Baltimore time, I hardly think you'd waste the entire day here just so you could take me to dinner. Or did you mean lunch? Besides, where would we eat? You already said there's no place to go in Baltimore."

"How about Denver? A friend told me there's a place there called Casa Bonita that serves fantastic Mexican food, and comes complete with wandering musicians and cliff divers."

"You must be mad."

"Quite. All Englishmen are. I'm also quite serious."

"I find that hard to believe."

"I assure you it's true. Look, I've got to take this fighter to Albuquerque anyway. Nobody cares what route I take, so why not go by way of Denver? The plane's a two-seater, so there's room for both of us, and it's been fitted with a cargo pod on the center pylon for luggage. Even with my stuff, I'm sure there's room enough for yours, unless you're traveling with a trunk. Anyway, we can leave anything that won't fit here, and pick it up when we return."

"Look," I said, "I can't just go charging off across the countryside. I've got to report for duty."

"You just said that you didn't have to report in for four days. We can be back in plenty of time."

"How?"

"Elementary. They run two courier flights a day from Kirtland to Andrews Air Force Base, which isn't that far from here, and we can hook a ride back on one of those. Personnel traveling under SCAF orders have priority. We could soak up some sun for a day or two and then fly back. I promise it won't cost you a cent."

"It's an interesting notion, but not very practical. Besides, my orders say travel from Tel Aviv to Baltimore, not Tel Aviv to Baltimore to Denver to New Mexico to Baltimore again."

"Begging the Major's pardon, ma'am, but I'd be willing to bet those orders don't say how you're to get from Tel Aviv to Baltimore. Oh, look, Karen, I know what you're thinking. You're thinking, 'Here I am in Baltimore, for Christ's sake, where I've just met this perfectly insane Englishman who's suggesting I run off with him for three or four days to New Mexico. The man must be mad, and I must be mad too, if I say yes. Anyway, I don't even know him.' Well, you're right, of course. I'm absolutely stark-raving unhinged, and you are too, if you say yes. But we've both got orders to report to SCAF Baltimore, and if you are in a combat arm, which you are, that can only mean you're slated for the big jump to Tau Ceti. I am too. So the only real question you've got to answer yourself is if you'd rather spend your last few days on Earth soaking up sunshine in the American southwest and getting occasionally inebriated with a mad Englishman you hardly know, or staring out of some hotel-room window in Baltimore, alone."

I really think I'd planned to say no right up until that point. It was, after all, a pretty ridiculous suggestion. But there was something about the image of sitting alone in a Baltimore hotel my last few days on Earth that made me feel cold and hollow inside, and instead of saying no, I said, "I'll think about it. Let's go get some lunch somewhere."

We had lunch in the restaurant on the fortieth floor, overlooking the western end of the airport. There wasn't much to see. It was raining, the water coming down in great, gray slanting sheets buffeted about by the wind. It was the kind of rain that wraps a heavy wet blanket of silence around your head, and threatens to suffocate you until you want to scream to see if you'll be heard or if you can hear yourself. It depressed me, and reminded me of another rainstorm, one that had turned the sand and clay into gumbo mud, clogged the drive bogies and made the tracks slip tractionless, while hot, spent 12.5mm brass lay thick in warm young blood on the steel floor. In the morning, when the rain was gone, the brass and the blood and the mud were still there, but a few good friends were not. I knew then that I really didn't want to sit alone in a Baltimore hotel room and watch the rain for four days and wonder if the screams from the nightmares would wake up the people in the next room. I looked across the table at those thick black eyebrows and that big red mustache, and I said, "I don't have a helmet, or an oxygen mask."

"Not to worry. The cabin's pressurized, and I've got a headset in my flight case. Only one parachute, I'm afraid."

"You're not very confidence-inspiring."

"You can have it if it makes you feel any better."

"Pete, I want you to understand one thing. Just because I've decided to go along doesn't mean I'm going to sleep with you. I might, but I don't know yet. I haven't decided."

"And I haven't asked you . . . yet."

"Fair enough. Just so we understand each other. When do you want to leave?"

"About fourteen-thirty local time, if the weather boys are right. According to the latest weather info this mess ought to diminish into light showers by then. These old birds don't have as fancy nav aids as the newer ones, and I'd prefer to wait till things slack up a bit."

"We'd better go claim my suitcases so I can change clothes."

"Going to cover up those nice legs of yours?"

"Afraid so."

I had one set of battle dress in my luggage, and a pair of combat boots. One thing the IDF taught me is never trust all your boots to be shipped separately. Not if you value your feet for walking on. By the time I'd changed and we'd caught the shuttle to the proper terminal, checked the weather again, and Pete had run his preflight, the weather was lifting. We loaded the luggage, climbed in, and headed west. I was sensible enough to keep my mouth shut until we were clear of the weather, somewhere over West Virginia.

"Tell me," I said, "what did you want to be when you were a boy?"

"I never was."

"Oh, come on. Everyone was a little boy once."

"You were a boy?"

"Of course not."

"See. Not everybody was a little boy."

"Well, you were. You must have been."

"Nope. Always been me handsome self."

"Oh, I give up! The question I was trying to ask was whether or not you always wanted to be a pilot."

"Nope. I always wanted to be an evil medieval prince and keep beautiful young maidens like yourself locked up in pillories in the dungeon, to have me way with when I pleased."

"Not me. I'd escape and run away."

"You already tried it. That's why I had to lock you up in the pillory."

"I see. Have you always been in the military, or did you write fantasy fiction for a while?"

"Never a writer, but I did edit sex manuals for a time."

"Know a lot about sex manuals do you?"

"I know what goes where and why."

"I don't believe you."

"Don't believe I know what goes where?"

"Don't believe you ever edited sex manuals. You made that up."

"True. But it's a good story, don't you think?"

"Aren't you ever serious?"

"Not if I can help it. I was serious once. It didn't agree with me."

We landed at Stapleton, or rather Buckley Naval Air Station, which is on the east edge of the Stapleton complex now. I understand they used to be separated by Colfax Avenue, but that was a long time ago. Nowadays Colfax is just another rapid-trans tube cutting under the runways. We checked into adjoining rooms at the Holiday Central and I finally got a chance to strip and take a shower.

Casa Bonita was all it was advertised to be. According to the menu the original business was well over a hundred years old. It had been enlarged and expanded four times since, and was a maze of cavelike tunnels and balconies set on rock cliffs. It had four bands of terraces, and six waterfalls employees would dive from, into pools about 30 meters below. *Impressive* seemed an inadequate description.

We ate well and got slightly drunk, then went back to the hotel lounge, where I got totally drunk, blabbed my life's story at Pete, and managed to find out between jokes and tall stories that he'd wound up in Intelligence because of a background in tectonic physics. When we finally gave up getting drunk around three, it seemed natural that I should tell him I'd decided, and that the answer was yes. He smiled, and reminded me he hadn't asked yet.

"Not tonight," he said. "You're drunk, and I won't have you accusing me of taking unfair advantage. Tomorrow, or rather this evening, when we get to Albuquerque, I'll ask."

He did, and the answer was still yes.

The morning after, in Albuquerque, I ached all over. "You sly bastard," I said. "I'll bet you really did edit all those sex manuals."

"You're being greatly unfair in crediting me abilities. I'm a self-taught man, I am."

"Tell me, Mr. Self Taught, do all Englishmen have the same fascination with butts that you do?"

"Well, now, I cannot say for all Englishmen."

Well, that basically was it. We spent two days soaking up sun and two nights soaking up each other, and then it was over. We caught the courier flight back to Andrews, took the shuttle to Baltimore, and said, "Good-bye, it's been fun."

I reported in at 1300 to a Nordic-looking type who turned out to be more German than Scandinavian and didn't particularly care for Jews.

"My grandparents were Jewish," I told him. "I'm an Israeli." Then I turned and started to walk out.

"Don't you salute superior officers when you're dismissed?" he yelled after me.

"Not unless they're combat rated. Besides, I don't see anybody around here who's superior."

I looked at my orders and had to laugh. I was billeted aboard the assault transport *Erwin Rommel*. I wondered if it was somebody's idea of a joke.

I caught the first available shuttle up and was digging around in the pile of luggage for my bags when I heard a familiar voice say, "I believe these are yours." I turned, and there were those same black eyebrows and that same red mustache.

"I don't suppose you'd care to explain what you're doing here," I said.

"Let's just say I was too fascinated with your butt to forget about it for the next twenty-five years, and let it go at that."

I did.

3

Masterson, Lara
Recruit, SCAF

The government letter had been sent to my father, but it was clear that it should have come to me. And it was clear that I had to go to Baltimore, if only to take a physical. In school we'd studied conscription, but it was something from the past—it had nothing to do with a modern society. We were free to come and go as we chose. That's what I told my father, and he said there was nothing we could do about it, free society or not. If I didn't go voluntarily, they would draft me anyway, and send him to prison.

At first I didn't mind, because I didn't have to go until June, which was months away. Sometimes, when my little sister was obnoxious or I had a lot of homework, I looked forward to the trip, if only as a way to break the monotony, but as June approached, I began to get scared.

The night before I left, I couldn't sleep. I hoped that I would fail the physical or wouldn't pass the written tests, but knew that I would. There was nothing wrong with me, so I knew that I'd become part of the force being formed to crush the aliens on Tau Ceti. I didn't want to do that, because I had nothing against the people there.

Oh, we'd all heard about the *Star Explorer,* but I thought it was some kind of mistake. Still, we armed and planned and scheduled for the invasion. The only thing missing from all the planning and arming was the people who had to go, and I was one of them. Nearly everyone who lived near us had one or two children who had received the Letter.

I looked toward my father as the mono-bus arrived at the station in downtown Baltimore. I thought his eyes were shiny, and I was afraid he would cry. I'd never seen him cry, and it scared me more than anything else that I might see it now. He looked away quickly, as if he'd found something fascinating to study out the window. But I saw him rub his eyes, and knew why.

The conductor announced the station in a hushed voice that suggested he knew why the majority of the passengers were on the bus. I stood up and tried to say, heartily, "Here we are," but it came out in a high, tight voice. Father merely nodded.

We collected my baggage and walked down the ramp to one of the lower, sidewalk levels. I'd been ordered to report at 1400 hours, which Father said was two in the afternoon. I didn't think much about it, but he wondered why it was so late in the day, and as we strolled through Baltimore, we found out. There were thousands, hundreds of thousands of people who had been conscripted, and the only way to process them all was to stagger the times throughout the day.

The building where I was to report wasn't far from the bus station. We were ten minutes early, and stopped outside it. I didn't like the look of the place. The walls were made from old stone, apparently salvaged from the bombing, and the architecture was nineteenth century. It was massive, with no delicate lines anywhere. The windows were large, and the doors larger. There were twenty or twenty-five steps leading up to them.

"Should only have thirteen steps," I heard my father say.

I asked about it, but he just mumbled, "Never mind."

For a moment we stood staring at each other, then he pulled me to him and hugged me tightly. "I'll wait," he said. "Maybe you won't pass or they won't need you, so I'll wait in case you get to come home. If you need anything, I'll be here."

I didn't know what to say, but I did know he was saying all the things that would make it easier on me. I clutched him as hard as I could. Behind me there was a noise as they opened the massive doors. Then some of the people standing near us started up the steps while their parents and brothers and sisters and friends waved to them.

Father was now openly crying. He told me to be good and that he would stay close for the next few days. I kissed his cheek—noticing that it was rough, like he hadn't shaved in a long time—then fled up the steps, following a group of boys who were laughing as if starting a great adventure. Father waved once. I didn't know it then, but it was the last time I would see him or any of my family in person.

I entered the Induction Center with the group of boys. At two o'clock, as we stood in the giant, cold hall, a uniformed man closed the big doors. Our orders had said to be there at two, and if we'd been even a minute late, we would have received our first lesson in military life.

Another man in uniform had us line up along the walls— girls on one side and the boys on the other. That was the last segregation by sex they would make, and it was only because the physicals given to the girls differed from those given the boys. The girls would have a nodule implanted that would prevent pregnancy for six years. I spent most of the afternoon sitting on the stone floor with nothing to do except wait my turn.

About dinner time, after I had finished my physical, they herded us into a cafeteria and gave us something to eat. It wasn't particularly good or well cooked, but it was something. Then we were shown where we'd sleep that night. Since they weren't going to turn the lights out until ten, and we still had a couple of hours, they gave us a bundle of papers to fill out so that the processing would move faster in the morning.

The next few days were a repetition of the first day. We were prodded, examined, tested, and classified. We were stripped of our civilian clothes, which was almost like stripping us of our civilian identities, and given new clothes—given our uni-

forms. Our hair was cut to fit regulations, and we were given
preliminary training so we wouldn't be lying around all day,
wasting time.

One evening, after one of the boys had packed and been
sent home, we were given orders assigning us to specific units
that would be forming in the fleet in the morning. As I read
the first line—that damning first line—I began to cry, because
I knew it meant I wasn't gong to get to go home. "Congratulations," it said. Congratulations for what? For not getting to
go home? I didn't want to go to Tau Ceti, and I didn't think
many of the others wanted to go, and yet they were congrat-
ulating us as if we'd won a privilege.

After dinner that night I went to find a visiphone. Father
had given me his hotel number and told me to call the moment
I had some news. I didn't want to call him, because I'd have
to tell him what had happened, and by putting it into words,
it would suddenly become real. Yet I wanted to tell someone.
I punched the buttons and watched as the screen swirled until
the connection was made. As his image solidified, I began to
cry again, and almost couldn't talk.

"Daddy," I said quietly. "They're going to make me go."

He didn't say anything. He only stared at me, the muscles
in his jaw tightening.

"Can't you do anything?" I demanded.

Through my tears I saw him rub his eyes. In a shaky voice
he said, "I'm sorry, baby, there isn't anything I can do. I've
tried. God, I've tried. I've called everyone I know or can think
of, but no one will listen or seems to care. I'm so sorry, baby."

I sniffed and tried to square my shoulders, but felt as if I'd
just been sentenced to death. "Tell Mom and Joanie I said good-
bye," I said bravely. "I have to leave tomorrow."

"Can we get together tonight?" he asked, a little too quickly.
"A Coke, or maybe something to eat?"

"They won't let us out tonight." Then it seemed like just
one more cruel and arbitrary rule. I realized later that it was
to prevent us from going AWOL at that last moment.

Neither of us spoke for several minutes. We just stared into
the phone. Neither of us wanted to say good-bye, but we knew
we couldn't stay on the line forever. Finally I said, "I'd better
be going. There are others who want to use the phone."

He nodded. "Okay, Larie. I guess I'll go home tomorrow. Write before you take off."

That seemed a little abrupt to me, but then what could he say? What could I? "I'll write," I told him, then added, "Someone said they might give us furloughs before the fleet leaves."

"That sounds great!"

I knew he didn't think they'd let us come home, but he tried to sound cheerful about it.

"Good-bye, Larie. I love you."

"I love you, Daddy." I didn't want to say good-bye or disconnect or anything else. I just wanted to sit in the booth for the rest of my life and pretend that the next minute would never come. I felt the tears running down my face, and tried to say something else, but the words wouldn't come and all I could do was stutter.

"Larie, be careful and hurry home. We'll wait for you. I promise that. Please let us know how you are." He reached for the phone as if to touch my cheek. "You'd better go."

"Good-bye, Daddy," I said again, but I couldn't push the disconnect button.

Maybe he sensed that. He said, "Good-bye," snapped it out in one short word, and his face suddenly dissolved. I stood staring at the blank screen for a moment, then heard someone pounding on the door.

"Come on! Come on! You're through."

The following morning we were told to pack everything and get ready to board the shuttles. We were told that all civilian items should be packed separately because they were going to be left behind and stored. They couldn't afford to waste space on the ships for unnecessary civilian clothes.

When the packing was done, some maintenance people came through, loaded all the civilian packages, and took them away. We were left with only our new military gear, waiting to be told what to do next.

Although they told us to hurry, they didn't tell us why, and we ended up standing around, waiting for something to happen. I was surprised by the inefficiency of the whole thing, but would soon learn that all of SCAF operated that way. I had always thought that government services ran smoothly.

We were informed that we would receive lunch on the shuttle

so we could pack our mess kits, but at about eleven; a sergeant showed up and said we'd have lunch in the Reception Center and that we should unpack our mess kits. I'd put mine on the bottom, out of the way, just as I had been instructed.

It was late in the afternoon before we were finally taken onto a shuttle. We left our military gear on the dock so someone else could load it, because we wouldn't do it right. At least that was what we were told.

The inside of the shuttle looked well-used. The carpet was stained, and ripped, worn and so dirty that I couldn't tell what the original color had been; the seats narrow and close together; and there was almost no leg room.

As we entered, we were told to take the first empty seat we came to and to store our personal gear either under the seat or in the racks above us. Once seated we were told to remain quiet and buckled in until the signs above the front cabin door said we could move around.

It wasn't long before I felt the engines rumble to life, and there was a momentary shock as the shuttle began to lift off. But it wasn't like the forces the first astronauts had had to withstand. Finally the sign said UNFASTEN YOUR SEAT BELTS.

There was a mad rush for the bathrooms, and there were lines for nearly an hour. I sat back and tried to read, but couldn't concentrate. All I could think of was that we'd finally started, and that my family was at home wondering and worrying about me. I took a deep breath and forced myself to stare at the SCAF Basic Training manual, but the words meant absolutely nothing to me. I realized that I'd read several pages and couldn't remember one word.

I was surprised when the cabin attendant came out of the galley and started serving us dinner. She was a real cabin attendant, working for American SpaceLines. She wore their standard uniform and had long blond hair that hung down her back, as current fashion dictated, but in direct violation of all the grooming regulations that had been explained to us at great length. As I looked around, I saw several attendants, male and female, preparing and serving meals. I had thought the flight was going to be short, so I asked the guy sitting next to me.

"From what I understand," he said, looking up from the magazine he'd smuggled on board, "we'll be on this thing for about twenty-four hours. The fleet is being assembled as far from Earth as possible."

"Twenty-four hours? You've got to be kidding."

"No. It's all right there in the training schedule," he said smugly before turning back to his dirty pictures.

I sat back and tried to remember where I'd put my training schedule. Not that it made any difference, but I was surprised to hear that they would stick something like our flight into the training schedule.

We had just finished dinner when one of the cabin attendants announced that we should turn out the overhead lights. There was a movie they wanted to show us. I assumed it was another hygiene film suggesting how we could avoid getting VD or AIDS or something worse, but it turned out to be a real movie. It lasted two hours, but seemed much shorter.

While the attendants distributed a snack after the movie, the sergeants told us to find something to study, now that our fun was over, but no one did. Finally, seeing that we were ignoring them, they said it was time for lights out and that we were to go to sleep. That wasn't easy, because the seats didn't move, so we had to sit upright. There wasn't enough room for my legs and they began to ache. All I wanted to do was stand up for a few minutes. I walked to the latrine, then went to the galley to get something to drink, and tried to find several more excuses to walk around. But one of the sergeants yelled at me to "sit down or else."

That night seemed to last forever. I was awake for more of it than I was asleep. Each time I woke up, I'd wonder if I had really been asleep, because I wasn't sure. Time seemed to pass, but so slowly that I thought the night would never end. I know I feel asleep once, because at seven someone shook me and told me it was time to eat breakfast, whether I wanted it or not.

Now my whole body screamed for sleep, and since I wasn't supposed to be sleeping, I could hardly keep my eyes open. They seemed to be filled with sand. I had to close them just to rest them. I didn't know how often I would feel like that in the coming months.

After a cold breakfast that was as tasteless as damp cardboard, one of the sergeants started to lecture about the ship we were going to serve on. He was trying to tell us where it would be, how it would act, and what our training would be like. It was a mishmash of topics thrown together to occupy the time. I thought it would be better if they just let us sleep.

It was almost twenty-four hours to the minute after we boarded the shuttle that it docked with our training ship. We were told to stand up, pick up the stuff we'd brought with us, and move into the aisles. NCO's joined us, split us into small groups, and escorted us off the shuttle. We were taken to a large room where we recovered the military gear we'd packed the day before.

Then we waited. Finally an officer carrying a clipboard entered. She read off names, pointed at NCO's, and had us form lines behind them. Once a squad was completed, they moved out double time and counting cadence. Halfway through the list she came to my name.

We had only enough time to put our gear on the floor near the bunks that stood empty and stark in the brightly lighted room that would become our squad bay. An announcement was made over an internal PA system that would become a part of our life. It said we were all to report to the reception center to be officially welcomed. Our squad leader, a buck sergeant who had been sitting on one of the bunks waiting for us, told us to form up, then marched us out.

4

Fetterman, Anthony B.
Sergeant First Class, SCAF

After six years of fighting and advising in small countries, never having an opportunity to advance very far because one side would lose quickly and the mercenaries would no longer be welcome, a chance to be in a big campaign with a real army was exactly what I wanted. I didn't have a lot of personal items that I needed to take with me; never had a chance to gather much. Just a couple of things that I'd acquired and learned to love. My orders said I should report to Baltimore's Spaceport Induction Center on Tuesday the twenty-third. I was four days early.

There wasn't much of a military nature to be done in Baltimore. Oh, there were the normal bars and taverns and clubs that always spring up in military towns, places that only wanted to separate the lonely soldier from his or her money with as little effort as possible. I toured a couple of them, seeing a lot of women dressed in very little or nothing, followed by men dressed in very little or nothing. I really didn't want to spend my time buying extremely expensive and very weak drinks for a tired girl who only wanted to go home, so I reported to the Induction Center almost as soon as I hit town.

An officer looked at my records, flipping through the pages slowly, as if it was a great work of fiction. He nodded as he read the section that detailed my commando training, smiled as he read the pages outlining my combat experience. He said there was a shuttle leaving in an hour or so, and if I had seen enough of the Baltimore nightlife, I could catch it and join the fleet immediately.

The shuttle wasn't quite full at lift-off. I didn't see anyone I knew, so I ignored them all, even the cabin attendant who tried to force a magazine on me. I kept my eyes closed so I wouldn't have to talk to anyone.

Twenty-four hours later the shuttle docked with a massive ship and we were taken into it through the airlock. We were informed that our personal baggage would be stored for us, were to report to the ship's reception center and were there for nearly half an hour before anyone came to talk to us.

We certainly weren't receiving the royal treatment—the man who finally arrived to welcome us to the fleet and SCAF was only a sergeant. Since nearly all of us were sergeants too, he knew we didn't want to hang around too long. He took enough time to tell us that because we were all experienced in combat, we would be assigned as instructors. When he finished, another noncom took his place and called off our names from a computer list, assigning us to various training companies being formed.

A corporal who wasn't bad-looking, except for a mild case of acne, asked me to follow her.

"Have you been here long?" I asked her.

She kept looking forward, as if to hide her face from me. "I arrived about two weeks ago," she said.

As we continued down a long corridor, I asked, "What do you do?"

"I'm a clerk-typist. We're almost there. You'll probably be the sergeant assigned to one of the training platoons. Captain Simms will brief you on your duties."

"When do the troops arrive?"

"Not for a while. We're trying to get everything set before they get here so there won't be any wasted time."

She opened a door and stepped back so I could enter first. The room looked like a hundred other orderly rooms in a hundred other places. There were three desks—one for the clerk, one for the admin specialist, and one for the first sergeant. There were the mandatory posters on the walls explaining how to dress like a soldier or what the badges of rank meant or how to wear any ribbons you might have.

The corporal pointed toward the first sergeant's desk. "Sergeant Jenkins will be back shortly. He had to run up to Battalion, but as soon as he's back, he'll take you in to meet the captain."

"Thanks." I sat down in one of the chairs and watched the corporal. Her legs were almost perfect, and her skirt was as short as regulations allowed. I figured she was attempting to draw attention away from her face by displaying as much of her legs as she could, and I approved of the tactic. But once her face cleared up, I wondered if the legs could compete, since there was great potential in the face. I also figured that if I was very nice to her now, it could pay off in the long run.

She was bent over the bottom drawer of a filing cabinet that had to be there only for the atmosphere, because microfiche and computers were more efficient, and her skirt was hiked way up. When she straightened and turned, I could see that she was blushing.

"Say, corporal," I said, "you never told me your name."

"It's Judy. Judy Dumont."

"I'm Tony. What are you doing for dinner tonight?"

"You work pretty fast, Sergeant," she said coyly.

"There's no work involved," I explained. "It's just that I hate to eat alone, and if you were a man, I wouldn't hesitate to ask, so I decided to ask."

She sat down and leaned on her desk, her face nearly hidden behind the computer terminal. "I'm not sure that's a very flattering way to ask me to dinner."

"What do you want?" I said, shrugging. "I thought it would be nice to have company for dinner and that you might make interesting company."

Now she smiled. "That's a little better. But I don't know."

"Oh, come on, Judy. Be a good troop and eat with me."

Before she could answer, the first sergeant walked in. Conditioned by hundreds of other orderly rooms, I'd expected something that looked like it had escaped from a horror film. But this man looked like a marshmallow. He was short, skinny, and balding, but his uniform fit perfectly and his boots gleamed like black mirrors. His voice was something else entirely. It was full and rich and sounded like it came from the bottom of a well a thousand meters deep.

"You Fetterman? I'm Jenkins. Captain Simms will want to meet you."

"Anything you say."

He turned toward Judy. "Is the captain in?"

"I don't know." She pulled the keyboard toward her and tried to look very busy, as if frightened by Jenkins.

Jenkins knocked on the door, heard a muffled response, and opened it. "New man here."

"Send him in."

The voice was my first clue, but I still wasn't ready for the captain. She was better looking than Dumont and didn't have any minor problem with acne. I wondered about this company and SCAF, and decided that I would enjoy being in it. We wouldn't need any pin-ups because they were already assigned to us. I stepped toward her desk and saluted as smartly as I knew how.

"Sergeant First Class Anthony B. Fetterman reporting as ordered, ma'am."

She returned the salute and stood up so that she could shake my hand. I glanced toward her legs, but she was wearing pants.

"Sit down and tell me about yourself."

I ran through my background, talking about jump training in Argentina and fighting in South Africa. She nodded occasionally and made one or two notes. She smiled through most of it, then said, "Looks like we finally got some real experience."

She explained that we would be training new recruits in the art of warfare. I almost laughed when she said "art of warfare" because I knew there was nothing artistic to it. Oh, you could make some real artistic plans and back them up with beautifully drawn maps and diagrams, but once the operation started, the art of it ended. Someone had once said that when the battle began, the plan ended, and everyone scrambled to stay alive. It was the historians, months or years after the battle, who explained it in terms that could be described as artful. But the fighting itself was just a mad scramble for survival.

Captain Simms told me that a syllabus had been written and we would follow it during the training of the recruits, but we would be allowed a great deal of latitude. She said that Jenkins would give me a copy, and that I was expected to read it, several times, before the troops arrived.

"I expect we'll have a good tour," she concluded, holding her hand over the desk so I could shake it. "Glad to have you with us."

I stood, shook her hand, and saluted as she dismissed me. In the orderly room Jenkins told me where my bunk was and pointed to a pile of suitcases on the floor.

"Those yours?"

"One or two of them."

"Good. They got it right for once. I'll give you a hand storing them, then we'll catch a bite to eat while you tell me about being a war hero."

I glanced at Judy, who tried to hide a smile that said "Too bad."

During the next several days I was kept busy with briefings, classes, and equipment inspections. They wanted to make sure the instructors were competent before they handed the new recruits over to us.

The briefing I enjoyed the most was the one explaining our mission. As we all knew too well, the *Star Explorer* had been destroyed by creatures living on Tau Ceti. Our mission was to move into that system, secure an operating base there, then deal with the creatures. If they were hostile, we were to invade, destroy their war-making capability, and occupy their planet. If they accidentally destroyed our ship, we were going to extract retribution for that. Until we discovered the nature of the aliens, we were working under the assumption that they were hostile because they had apparently attacked the *Star Explorer*.

Judy and I managed to grab a couple of dinners together, but I soon lost interest in her because she was looking for something more than I was willing to give on such short notice. She didn't let things develop naturally, but tried to force them because she wanted to get engaged and married, and she wanted to do it right away. All she talked about was marriage. I decided it wasn't her complexion that was the problem, but her attitude.

Finally the troops, the new recruits, were brought on board. I stood near one of the arrival ports to watch. They were all young; so very young. Not many of them were fifteen, and I suspected that the majority were lucky if they had seen their fourteenth birthday. They were all bewildered, and left the shuttle like cattle being led to slaughter.

The squad leaders were there, trying to guide the recruits to their areas, but there was massive confusion. Men and women were yelling contradictory orders at the recruits, who bounced around like Ping-Pong balls in a high-speed game. Each shuttle was supposed to have specific people assigned, and each was supposed to use a certain port so that the already designated units could be formed. It didn't work that way. The right shuttles got to the wrong ports, and all the computer-generated lists were wrong. No one could find anyone they were supposed to, and it was made worse by the continuing flights of shuttles from all over the Earth.

Finally I could take it no longer, and left for the company area where I could drink a cup of coffee while waiting for the mess to be straightened out, if it ever was. The solution was so simple that I couldn't believe no one had thought of it, then realized it was so simple that SCAF would never use it: Just keep the troops that arrived on each shuttle, and update the computer.

During the next few days, as we continued to orbit the Earth and the recruits and supplies continued to arrive, the squad leaders were busy trying to teach the recruits some basics so that the real training could begin soon. Many times we found that whole squads had been assigned to the wrong company. They had to then be shuffled so that everything would agree with the computer listings. Stupid. Stupid. Stupid. But it made the paper planners happy.

When everything was finally straightened out, the supplies had all been received and the last of the recruits had boarded, we blasted out of Earth orbit. The whole fleet's engines fired at once, lighting the sky on the dark side of the Earth like no fireworks display ever seen. Slowly the mass of ships moved away and crossed the orbit of the moon as we continued to build speed for the twenty-six-year slide to Tau Ceti.

Shortly after that, as if to begin the whole program fresh, we were ordered to reception for the initial briefing. I arrived early so that I could watch everyone else come in. I knew this was going to be a disaster because there were too many people who were new to the military. It was an even bigger boondoggle than the arrival, and looked as if it were going to keep getting worse, until a huge noncom walked to the center of the stage in front of the hall and bent to the microphone. He kept saying, over and over, "Ten-hut!" until the noise evaporated and everyone was quietly standing at attention.

A young officer stepped to the mike as the noncom faded to the rear. "Be seated," he boomed, and waited as the rustling of a thousand recruits rose and then died. When everyone was seated, he shook his head and said to the men standing behind him, "God, what a mess! How do they expect us to do anything with it?"

It was a cheap trick. He was telling the recruits, without really speaking to them, that there was a lot of work to be done. He was hoping that his statement, supposedly overheard accidentally, would make them work harder to prove that they weren't a mess.

He spoke for a few minutes, welcoming the recruits to SCAF and the ship and telling them that he hoped they'd find the experience interesting and rewarding. He then introduced the division deputy commander, Brigadier Johns Umpanda.

Umpanda strode to the microphone, towering over it. He didn't slump forward so that the mike would be closer to his lips, but stood tall and straight. The brass on his collar gleamed, reflecting the lights from overhead. His uniform was perfect, the trousers holding knifelike creases and the shirt perfectly starched. Everything about him seemed to suggest soldiering and discipline and devotion to duty.

"Ladies and gentlemen," he said and paused. "I can call you that because at the end of the voyage, you will be. You will also be soldiers—the best-trained, best-equipped soldiers in the universe. You will be the beginning of an Earth empire that shall one day spread over the known galaxy.

"I have little to say to you today because you don't really want to hear me speak. You are more interested in what is going to happen to you during the next five years, wondering if you will be able to meet our standards and if you will let your friends and family down. Do not worry about it. You have been selected from the people in our solar system. You are the best and the brightest, and none of you will fail.

"Our mission is going to take us to Tau Ceti Four. The voyage will last over five years of ship time. During those years you will train, and retrain, and then train again. By the time we land you will react through instinct. You will make lightning-fast decisions, and you will discover that you were right.

"The commander of SCAF and the commander of the fleet have asked me to welcome you to the SS *Erwin Rommel*. We are glad that you are here, and look on it as an honor to serve with you. We will do everything we can to make sure that you survive the campaign. But we need your help. Learn your lessons, and you will stay alive.

"In the next few days you will be getting ready for your training. Listen to your officers and noncoms. They aren't here merely to harass you, but to save your lives. Their methods may seem rough, but they are no rougher than the enemy in combat. Keep that in mind. You are preparing for combat. The enemy will not be there to assist you. He will be there to kill you."

He slowly folded his notes. "I have nothing more to say to you, except welcome aboard. Are there any questions?"

I hoped that no one would be foolish enough to ask anything. Umpanda didn't really want questions. He was alerting the others that he had finished his remarks. He turned toward the men on the stage with him and said something I couldn't hear. As he walked from the stage, a noncom stood and yelled, "Ten-hut!"

After Umpanda was gone, along with most of the staff officers, a noncom crossed to center stage and began a speech about the training. I didn't listen because I'd heard it all before, not only here, but in a hundred other locations. I let my mind drift, ignoring the recruits and squad leaders. When they finally called the recruits to attention for the last time, I straightened and watched them herded from the hall. The real job was about to start.

5

McAllif, Steven M.
Recruit, SCAF

While the tall black man was speaking, and most of the non-coms were watching the stage, I took a few moments to get my bearings. Since I had arrived on the *Erwin Rommel*, there hadn't been time. We'd been driven from the docking area to a squad bay, then immediately brought here for our welcome-aboard speech.

He wrapped up his talk by asking us if there were any questions. We said nothing. He turned to those behind him on the stage and said, "I can see that you people have a lot of work to do." He walked away without looking back.

From the stage someone shouted, "AH-ten-HUT!"

Without having a chance to think about what I'd just heard, we were ordered out of the hall and back to the squad bays. The squad leader, who told us his name was Marquette, took a couple of minutes to say we had almost no time to prepare for the first inspection. The squad bay, a large room containing twelve bunks, was piled with newly issued equipment, more uniforms, and our bedding. I grabbed a blanket and tossed it on the top bunk that had my name taped to it, then turned toward my bunkmate, tapped her on the back, and held out my hand. "Name's McAllif," I said. "Steven McAllif."

She turned from making up her bunk, a completely bewildered look on her face, and almost absentmindedly said, "I'm Lara Masterson."

I was glad that she was my bunkmate, because she was pretty cute. She was at least as tall as me, about five feet five, and had short brown hair with bangs that came almost to her blue eyes. I had never seen eyes so blue.

"What do you think so far?" I asked as I tried to make my bunk according to military regulations.

She flipped the pillow to the head of her bed. "I don't know. All I've done so far is to leave home for the Induction Center and then go to the staging port and then up here."

"I know what you mean. No one tells us anything. If I hadn't been in the Junior Marines, I think I would be completely lost."

She left the pillow where it was and sat on the edge of her bunk, trying to align her shoes, boots, and sandals under it, as she'd seen some of the others doing. "You've had some military training," she said.

"Not much, but enough to get me by for a while."

She didn't say anything then, she just stared at me. I wanted to talk more, but we had an inspection coming, so I reached up and dragged the sheets out of the pile of bedding. I began to make the bed, pulling the sheet tightly by reaching up under it and stretching it behind the springs. She was watching me.

"What are you doing?"

"Making the bed tight. They like to see coins bounce on the top blanket, and the only way to make them bounce right is to have the blanket pulled tight."

She glanced toward the people next to us and saw that they were doing the same thing. She sat down again and let out a long sigh. "How am I supposed to know that?"

One of the girls on the other side said, "Ain't war hell?"

"Watch me," I said. "It's easy." I took the sheet away from her, snapped it out, and let it float down. I tucked the end under and folded the corners so they made a forty-five degree angle. Then I fitted the blanket and did the same thing. I finally took the pillow, put it at the top of the bed, and folded the other blanket over it. When I was done, I said, "That gets you started. Now hang up the clothes, and store your gear in the top of the locker. But hurry. We don't have much time."

While she was fixing her bed, I arranged my uniforms in the wall locker. I quickly folded the duffel bag and set it on the bottom. I pointed all the shirts the same direction and tried to space the hangers. I almost had everything finished when the inspection team walked in. Lara was on her knees, pushing her duffel bag into the bottom of her locker when someone yelled, "Inspection *post!*"

We all snapped to attention where we stood, but I could tell that we had done something wrong. Marquette yelled, "Inspection post," again, but none of us moved.

"Well, Sergeant, I see that you haven't gotten them properly trained yet."

The sergeant mumbled something I couldn't hear, but the reply was plain enough.

"I don't give a shit if they only got here this morning or what they were supposed to have learned at the embarkation center. It's your job to make sure they know what they need to know, and if you can't do it, I'm sure we can find someone else for the job."

Marquette stepped to the center of the squad bay stiffly, as if he had both legs in splints, and told us what he wanted. We leaped to the new positions in front of our bunks, and kept quiet. The inspector started with the people next to me. He didn't stay there long, saying, "Very nice," as he moved toward me.

It was a disaster from there. Lara hadn't had enough time to sort out everything and put it in her locker. She'd left some stuff on the floor. Her bunk wasn't tight enough, and the inspector ripped it apart. He looked into her locker, stepped back, and dumped the contents. Next he kicked her shoes and boots from under the bunk.

He inspected my locker quickly, then stepped in front of me so his face was only two inches from mine. He looked only seven or eight years older than me, but he was trying very hard to appear older.

For a moment he stared straight into my eyes, breathing on

me with his bad breath. He looked away for an instant, as if checking his cue cards, then pointed to Marquette. "We have an individualist here, Sergeant. He was too busy with his own gear to help his buddy.

Lara spoke up brightly. "Oh, no, Lieutenant, ah, sir, he was—"

He spun toward her, his gig stick slashing through the air, smacking the bunk near her ear. Lara flinched as the lieutenant roared, "No one told you to speak, recruit." He said *recruit* as if it were something dirty.

"Sergeant," he continued then, "see that she has two days of extra duty. And see that the individualist has one for not helping his bunkmate."

The rest of the squad fared no better. Demerits flew for nearly everything that could be imagined. The lieutenant dumped more lockers, kicked more shoes, and ripped apart more beds. When he was finished, it looked as if nearly every locker and bunk in the bay had exploded. He stopped momentarily at the door, to admire his handiwork, then left without a word.

As soon as he was gone, I swung on Lara and shouted, "Thanks a lot. You should have kept your big, flapping mouth shut!"

She stood with her hands on her hips and yelled back, "I was only trying to help you!"

"I don't need your help. Especially when it gets me extra duty. I wouldn't have gotten it if you had just shut up."

She raised her voice again and shouted, "All right. I'm sorry. So kill me, for crying out loud."

"Hey! You two knock it off before you get the rest of us in trouble," one of the others broke in.

Lara stooped down and started to sort through her clothes. One of the other squad members brought over her shoes and put them under her bunk. He looked at her and said, "My name is Mark Leupin. Let me give you a hand."

The girl who had said that war is hell came to help Lara too, and introduced herself as Wendy Martinez.

Before we had a chance to do much, Marquette returned. He said, "Those of you who were assigned extra duty, please come with me. The rest have free time until zero-four-thirty hours tomorrow. But instead of sloughing off, I'd spend the time getting ready for another inspection. If you feel you have that wired, you'd better pull out one of the manuals and have a look at it."

Lara and I walked slowly to the front of the bay and waited for our instructions. Marquette pointed at me and said, "McAllif, you'll be a server in the Officer's Mess tonight. After you've cleared the tables, you'll be released to come back here and get your gear squared away. Just keep your mouth shut and your ears open. Move out."

As I started through the door, I heard him telling Lara that she would be in the galley cleaning it up after everyone was fed the evening meal. Until then she was assigned general KP.

It was nearly three when I felt the bunk shake as she climbed in. I peeked over the edge and looked down at her. She smiled up at me and sat there for a moment, the light from a safety lamp casting strange shadows, her hands clasped between her knees. She said, very quietly, almost inaudibly, "It wasn't so bad."

At four-thirty the overhead lights snapped on and a whistle blew. I hated the lights coming on like that, shining right in my eyes. I rolled over so I wouldn't have to look at them, my face buried in the skinny pillow SCAF provided, then forced myself out of bed. As I swung my feet over the edge, I almost kicked Lara in the head.

We all headed for the shower room to wash up and brush our teeth. One or two of the braver souls tried to take showers, but I was afraid there wouldn't be enough time for that, getting dressed, and making the bed before we had to fall out for breakfast.

When I came back from the shower room, Lara was standing next to her locker in her underwear, looking dazed, trying to get the Velcro on one of her coveralls open so she could get it off the hanger. As I grabbed mine, I whispered at her, "Leave that one and get into another. You don't have time to screw around."

She frowned at me, but did it. Just as she fastened the last of the Velcro, Marquette put in his second appearance of the day and hollered, "Fall out!" We formed a single file, minus the people still in the shower.

Breakfast went quickly, too quickly, and before we were herded out, one of the noncoms informed us that we had just finished our last easy meal. None of us knew what that meant, but we couldn't speculate on it as we marched back to the squad bay.

Before he disappeared, Marquette told us we would have another inspection that morning, to be completed while we were out at classes. He told us that we would eat "square" meals, which meant we had to pick the fork straight up, then make a square corner and bring it straight to our mouths. We had to put down the fork after each bite. There would be no talking at the meals, and meals would be limited to fifteen minutes.

He stepped to one of the bunks, glanced at the blanket as if to make sure it was clean, then put his foot on the edge of it. He leaned an elbow on his knee before saying, "In a few minutes we will attend the first of the classes. From this point on you will be responsible for all the information given to you. In other words, there may be tests, and you will be expected to know anything that has been told to you from now on."

The classroom was nowhere near as large as the auditorium we'd been in the day before. We stood at attention, waiting, then were told to sit down and listen closely because the briefing we were about to receive could save our lives.

An officer walked to the center of the platform. He was a member of the ship's company—one of the engineers, I think. Behind him was a swirling, colored mass of the holograph display tank, which slowly solidified until it was a rotating view of the ship. As the officer set himself behind the podium, the lights dimmed. He turned on a small lamp on the podium, unfolded several sheets of paper, looked at the screen behind him, and reached for the laser pointer.

When he had everything adjusted the way he wanted, he began. "Good morning, ladies and gentlemen. I am Lieutenant junior grade Ralph Hodges and I will be conducting this class in ship orientation. It's a two-hour block of instruction that will show you the workings of the ship, locations of various activities, and your battle stations in the event of attack. At the conclusion of this block of instruction you should be able to find any of the main cabins, compartments, and storage areas, and be able to move to your battle station from any point of the ship."

He looked up from his notes before picking up the laser pointer and flashing it into the holograph. A flaming arrow appeared over part of the front of the ship. "As many of you know, this fleet was designed so that it could utilize the available interplanetary freighters and passenger ships. These gigantic vessels, some over a thousand meters in length, were originally designed for movement of supplies among the planets, and for colonization. The engines were fine for interplanetary travel, but not efficient for interstellar flight.

"By linking three or more of these vessels, we've been able to create ships such as the one you're on now. The center is a colonization ship capable of carrying nearly a thousand people. One outside ship carries munitions and war material, and the other holds food supplies and gardens. In many cases a fourth has been added as a simulator for training."

He continued, telling us about converting the ships to interstellar drive. It was mainly a question of replacing one power plant with another, he said. The only problem was the hydrogen gas in space. As the speed of the fleet increased, it was bombarded with more hydrogen atoms, which created a radiation problem. However, a screen was developed that dragged part of the hydrogen with it, which was then used to augment the fuel. The effects of the radiation were dissipated by the screen and kept away from the ships.

It was dark and warm in the hall, and the topic wasn't all that interesting. It was hard for me to stay awake, and I'd had several hours of sleep the night before. I didn't know that Lara had fallen asleep, but one of the noncoms caught her. He stood grinning at her as she snapped awake, an astonished look on her face.

"Masterson," he said to her, "you have two more hours of extra duty tonight."

"But I haven't finished the duty I got after the inspection."

"Well, gee, I'm sorry as hell, but if you open your mouth once more, I'll make it ten hours. Now try to stay alert."

She didn't look too happy, but then, none of us were. I

began to hate the sergeants more than I hated SCAF or those damned people on Tau Ceti who blew up our lousy ship, getting me into this mess. I figured Lara probably hated them more than I did, but she did stay awake after that.

6

Kisov, Vasili
Captain, Third Aviation Battalion, SCAF

I could not quite see Brown seated across the table from me. My eyes still hadn't made the adjustment from the harsh briefing lamps to the normally subdued light of the Officer's Club.

Brown said that it was his turn to buy the drinks. I wasn't sure about him. His gold bars were so shiny that it seemed he'd just taken them out of the wrapping. Already he was getting loud, and once or twice the air coordinator had turned toward us.

"Take it easy, Brown. You'll get us all thrown out of here," I said.

"Screw you Kissoff."

"The name is Kisov, Lieutenant."

"Leave the kid alone. He's been in training for so long that he's forgotten how to be human."

I was about to say something when Brown pointed at the door and told us to take a look. One of the Israeli officers was walking in. She was wearing the standard uniform of miniskirt, khaki shirt, and knee-high boots. Her hair was much longer than regulations said it should be, but I didn't notice anyone running to tell her about it. She looked around carefully, then took a seat at the bar.

"Boy, that's my kind of major."

"Brown, shut up."

Brown signaled the cocktail waitress and ordered another round. As the drinks were delivered, Brown said, louder than necessary, "There I was at fifty thousand feet, when the rotor blade came off. The automatic pilot jumped out with the only parachute on board. All I had was a silkworm and a sewing machine. Busy, boy was I busy."

"Okay, Brown, you've entertained everyone here. How about keeping it down?"

"Yes, sir, Captain Kissoff, sir."

We all talked quietly for a while. I glanced over at the Israeli now and then, and noticed that she was glancing at us.

"I believe the good major is lonesome," I said to no one in particular.

"I believe you are right, Captain," said Bradley. He was one of the lead pilots.

"Maybe you should invite her to join us."

"Go ahead, Kissoff. It's your move."

Instead of doing anything, I just stared in her direction.

"Go on, coward. She doesn't bite. At least they're not supposed to anymore."

Finally I stepped to the bar beside her and leaned on it with both elbows. But I didn't look at her. In the mirror I could see the others waving at me. I turned slightly, studying her long hair and her profile. She was concentrating on her drink, doing her best not to look at me.

I thought about giving up, since she wasn't going to help me, though she knew why I'd walked up. The bartender came over and asked what I wanted. My drink was only a quarter gone, but I said, "I'll have another of these."

"What's wrong with that one?"

"Nothing. Nothing at all. I just didn't want to have to get up later."

He walked away shaking his head.

I turned toward her and said, "That's not the real reason that I came up here."

She smiled.

"No. There was another reason," I said. She continued to stare, making it very hard. "We noticed that you were here all by yourself, and felt that a fellow officer should not have to drink alone."

"It's only a Coke."

"Ah, well, there you have it. You obviously need some guidance here. We can help you learn the ropes."

"I already know them."

She really wasn't going to make this easy. "I was wondering, that is, we were wondering if you would—since you are alone—if you would care to join us for a drink?"

She nodded at herself in the mirror. "I don't know. I'm waiting for someone."

"Of course. We knew that you wouldn't be alone for long, but we hoped you might join us until the rest of your party showed."

She picked up her drink. "I can only stay for a few minutes. When my friend arrives, I've got to go."

"No problem. Like I said, we were only worried because you were alone and we didn't think that anyone should be alone on a night like this."

"What kind of night is it?"

"Dark."

She laughed. "Right. Dark. Lead the way."

At the table I introduced the others. "The ugly one with the big head is Dominick, next to him is Williams, here's Bradley, then Stanhope—if you can believe that name—Pierce, and last, the youngster is Brown."

She nodded to each one. "I'm Karen. Kadrmas."

For a moment, as everyone wondered what to say so that he could impress her, the conversation seemed to die. She watched us squirm as we tried to think of something clever.

"Why don't you go on with your war stories. I heard the one that the young lieutenant told."

"We weren't really telling war stories."

I picked up my drink and looked at it carefully. It was now about half gone. "I was. I remember the time back in aught-five in the big Sino invasion. We were fighting it out with Mig-47's."

"Shut up, Kissoff. We don't want to hear that piece of crap."

"Now, Williams, Brown might be interested. Give him some pointers. Anyway, I managed to down two of the jets before one of them sneaked up behind me. I didn't know that he was there or I could have taken some evasive action. Hell, with a helicopter I could have stopped in midair, and in seconds he would have been miles in front of me.

"He caught me with a burst from the 20mm cannon and took out the engine. No real problem because all I had to do was an autorotation. On the ground I checked the copilot and crew chief. They were okay, but among us, all we had was three rounds. Out of the trees swarmed about half a company of Chinese soldiers whooping and hollering about death to the Imperial Russian swine. I fired the three rounds." I stopped and drained my drink.

Brown snapped. "What the hell happened?"

"We got killed."

Brown stared at me as everyone else at the table disintegrated into laughter. Brown wasn't sure what to do or say.

The cocktail waitress reappeared. "You guys need anything?"

I looked up. "I'll have a sloe screw."

Karen looked at me. "Good luck."

From there we began telling each other real war stories. The pilots talked about flying in China. Karen, a tanker, told about parking her tank at the base of the pyramids in Egypt. She hadn't stayed there long because her unit moved deeper into Egypt. When the war was over, Israelis controlled most of that country but withdrew, according to the peace agreement. They occupied a strip 50 kilometers wide on the Egyptian side of the Suez.

The conversation then degenerated into a discussion about the relative merits of helicopters and tanks. Karen claimed that tanks were better because they "were safer" than helicopters.

"Yes, but they aren't cool. At least we're not bouncing around the desert in a hot box."

"They're air conditioned now. Besides, the armor gives us some protection. What do you use?"

"Skill and daring," I replied.

"I see that your skill and daring has earned you three Purple Hearts."

"Those were times that my daring exceeded even my fantastic skill."

"I'll give you one thing—you certainly are modest. I don't know when I've met a group of more quiet and modest people."

Stanhope picked up the ball. "You know, I believe that's one of our biggest faults. A lot of people have told us that, and we're trying to overcome it."

Karen began to laugh. "Well, I wish you luck." She looked up as another major walked in. I hadn't met him, but had seen him, and thought he worked in the Intell section.

Karen finished her drink. "I've got to go, gents. It's been surreal."

I started to get up. "What went wrong?"

"You don't have a mustache."

"I could draw one from supply."

She touched my arm. "Do that and give me a call."

"Well, at least there's a light at the end of the tunnel."

"What does that mean?"

I took a deep breath. "The way things have been going lately, I figured they would eject my room into space, and when I opened the door, I'd step into nothingness."

She smiled. "I've got to go. I'll look for you gentlemen later."

We all watched her head out the door with the Intell major. Brown looked as if he wanted to cry. "What's he got that we don't?"

"Karen."

"Good point."

7

McAllif, Steven M.
Trainee, Training Platoon Alpha, SCAF

After several weeks we were taken to the arms locker and given rifles, but no magazines for them. We were told the rifle was our responsibility and that it was to be with us at all times. We couldn't leave it behind to go eat or take a shower, and it had to be within easy reach when we slept.

The morning sessions were taken up with classes about our rifles. We were told it fired 7 x 60mm caseless ammunition, expanding hollow point, boat-tail, that the overall length was 102cm, and that it weighed 3.01 kilograms. One of the noncoms stood on a raised platform and tore one apart, cleaned it quickly, and reassembled it. He then did it step by step as we followed his lead. When we had them reassembled, we were told to tear them apart and reassemble them again. We kept it up until lunch.

We lined up by squads at the doors leading from the training hall. A noncom asked us questions about the rifle, which we had to answer correctly before we were allowed out. They then gave us a cartridge and told us to fire it. The cartridge was little more than a primer, but it did indicate whether the rifle had been reassembled correctly. Lara's misfired and she was sent to the end of the line, to field strip her rifle and repair it.

After lunch we were sent to the squad bay to change into PT gear. Lara was already there, having missed lunch because she couldn't get her rifle to fire. A noncom finally showed her that one of the gas cylinder plugs was in backward. She was sitting on her bunk, staring at her rifle.

Wendy stepped to the bunk and shook her, but got only a blank stare. She turned toward the center of the room and said, "Say, some of you had better help us over here."

She pushed Lara off the bed and forced her to stand up. Susan Norton, the girl who had the bunk next to ours, straightened the blankets. She reached into Lara's locker and grabbed the PT uniform. "Someone had better help her change and then straighten her gear."

Wendy shook her head. "The kid is shot." She pulled the zipper on the coveralls and tried to force them off. Lara pushed her away and pulled up the zipper.

"Come on. We have to hurry." Wendy stepped across the bay to her locker and changed into shorts and a T-shirt. The rest of us were ready to go. I was lacing my tennis shoes.

Lara just stood, not moving. Susan was pulling on her knee socks. The others were trying to straighten the squad bay in case there was an inspection. I jerked Lara around and slapped her, turning one cheek red. She took a half-hearted swing at me, but her eyes focused.

"Get into your PT gear."

She changed quickly and was pulling on her shoes when Marquette came in. "Let's move it." He saw Lara struggling with her shoe, but seemed to ignore it. When we were lined up, he marched us into the corridor.

The other squads from the platoon were already there. We stood against one wall. Leaning against the middle of the other was the platoon sergeant, Fetterman. He told us to stand at ease.

"This corridor connects with another that circles the outside perimeter of the ship. By following that corridor around the ship, we have a track of almost two kilometers. Various studies have shown that running is one of the best exercises available.

It strengthens the legs, builds the lung capacity, improves the circulation, and helps the heart.

"Today we begin a program designed to help you. We will run. We will run together, as a team. And I mean as a team."

He called us to attention, told us to face to the right, and said, "Forward, march." We stepped out and had taken about three steps when he yelled, "Double time."

It was easy at first. We jogged down the corridor, made it to the outside and turned. Slowly the platoon sergeant increased the speed so that it was more than a jog. We were taking long strides, running as hard as we could. One of the men in the first squad stumbled and fell. The others jumped over him, leaving him gasping for breath. Another fell and then another. Lara stumbled once but stayed on her feet and kept going.

I could feel the pain building in my shoulders and working its way toward my lungs. My mouth was dry, making it hard to breathe. My chest burned and I wanted to stop. But I thought that the pace couldn't last much longer, so I pushed myself.

Lara stumbled then and fell to one knee. I stopped behind her and Mark stopped behind me. For a second we panted, trying to catch our breath while the rest of the platoon ran away from us.

"We're going . . . going . . . to have to . . . get . . ."

"Help me," Lara said. I grabbed her arm and tried to lift her to her feet. Mark didn't move, but Susan did. I hadn't seen her stop.

"All right . . . let's . . . go."

We pulled Lara up. She shook her head, some of her hair falling onto her forehead and sticking to the sweat. Susan shouted at her. "Get moving . . . you . . . dumb . . . bitch."

We started to run again, dragging Lara with us. She slowed us down, but at least we were moving. The rest of the platoon was not too far away. Mark pushed Susan away and grabbed Lara, forcing her forward. Wendy grabbed her arm as I let go. She gasped something, but I didn't hear it.

The platoon had slowed the pace, and we managed to catch up. Two of the other squad members took over for Wendy and Mark. We all fell in, trying to keep the squad together. Only about half the platoon was still there. The rest were scattered along the corridor trying to breathe and hoping they would die so the pain would go away.

Fifteen minutes after we started, we were back in the center corridor. Two different members of our squad were carrying Lara by now. The platoon sergeant stared at them for a minute, but they held onto her. He told us to sit down to wait for the others. Lara sank down, closed her eyes, and started to fall to one side. But Susan kept her sitting. She was obviously asleep.

When the rest of the platoon straggled in, Fetterman called us to attention. By that time most of us had caught our breath. What we needed was something to drink so we could get the cotton out of our mouths. The sweat had dried from our skins but our clothes were still soaked.

"I'm not pleased." Fetterman glared at us. "I said that this was to be a team effort, yet I saw people jumping over their squad mates. This will be noted. You have twenty minutes to get ready for your afternoon classes."

That class was a snap. All we had to do was stay awake while we were learning what constituted a weapon. We learned that we might find ourselves in a hostile area without a rifle or knife, but that there were always weapons. A noncom held up the pop top from a beer can and was explaining how it could be used to kill.

Juan Lopez stood and said, "I really don't expect to find such a terrestrial invention where we're going."

The noncom paused for a moment, then seemed to swell. "Well, trainee, I see that SCAF is wasting you here. Obviously, with your intimate knowledge of the enemy, you should be in Intelligence. Why don't you brief us on what we *can* expect to find?"

Lopez didn't move and didn't say anything for a few seconds. "I thought—"

The noncom waved at him. "You didn't think. If you had thought, you would have realized that we can't make any assumptions. And you would have realized something else. I'm not here to teach you to use a beer-can tab as a weapon. I'm here to teach you to improvise. Remember, there are no dangerous weapons, only dangerous men."

Lopez sat down. It woke some of us up. To that point so

much had been thrown at us so fast that a lot of it was getting by. Now I decided to pay closer attention.

When I got back to the squad bay after dinner, I saw Lara sitting on her footlocker wearing only a pair of flimsy bikini panties and reading one of the manuals.

"I missed you at dinner."

She looked up. "I didn't go. I wasn't authorized a meal tonight."

For a moment I didn't say anything. "You mean because you couldn't remember how the cyclic pulse rate on the laser kept the rate of fire constant."

There must have been too much arrogance in my voice. She slammed the book shut and stared at me. "I suppose you remembered it all, but we'll never know because no one *asked* you. They always *ask* me."

I stepped back and sat on the railing that ran across the foot of the bed. She seemed close to tears. "No," I said softly. "I didn't remember any of that, and I was glad they asked you."

"But they always ask me. Every time we have a hard problem in class or a tough exercise in the field or a thorough inspection, they ask me the question, tell me to participate, or give me the roughest inspection."

I studied her closely. I knew that she wasn't complaining without some justification, and wondered if that could be called complaining. I didn't know what to tell her, but felt I had to say something. I glanced at the floor, then looked at her bare feet. "Why is that?"

"Oh, God, I wish I knew. Maybe if I had the answer I could do something so they wouldn't be on my back all the time. If they'd only give me the chance to catch my breath, but they don't. Every time I finish one tour of extra duty or one study assignment or one problem, they give me two more."

I thought I had the answer, but I didn't say anything because I didn't see how it would help. She had come to the attention of the instructors on the first day by telling them I hadn't been ready for the inspection because I'd helped her. If she'd kept quiet, they wouldn't have learned her name. It was always easier to call on someone if you knew their name.

I remembered a fellow in junior marines summer camp one year who had practiced that rule very effectively. Since he was new to our section, he was made acting executive officer. Several days later an instructor going down the list of those who had to recite some part of a lesson came to his name and asked who he was. No one could believe he was the exec because he'd done such a fine job of remaining unknown.

Lara was studying the book again. I watched her for a few minutes. She reached and scratched her bare knee. Finally I broke the silence, "You want to go to the rec center? They're showing a film tonight."

"I don't think I'd better. I have to study this in case we get survival training in the morning."

I reached over and pulled the book out of her hand. "We're not going to have survival tomorrow or anytime this week."

"How do you know?"

"Because I'm on the detail to clean the company offices, and I've seen the schedule for the rest of the week. We're going to begin some classes on the weapons systems employed on the helicopters and the tactics used by them in close air support."

"You're sure?"

"They could always change the schedule, but I don't think they will."

She picked up her book and flipped it open. "The way my luck is running, they will, and the first question will be asked of me, and it will be the hardest one they'll ask all day. I'd better stay here and study." She leaned back against the wall and crossed her legs.

"Look, Lara, you're not supposed to sit here every day and study everything. For Christ's sake, we've only been going two months, and we have five years to go."

"But I won't last five years if they don't leave me alone, and the only way they'll do that is if I know the answers to every question they throw at me."

Her eyes were shining as if she was going to cry. I wondered how many of us would crack under the strain. She had to be close. I could always tell Fetterman about it, but I didn't know if that would help. It might make them rougher on her, make them figure they should get rid of her as soon as they could rather than waste any more time training her. Maybe they'd decide she would be better in some kind of clerk's job.

"Lara, the chances of them changing the schedule are very remote. Survival has to be scheduled weeks in advance, and they can't just zip into it."

"How do you know?"

"I was talking to the clerk in the company office. She was saying that each unit has to schedule the training so it doesn't conflict with the schedules of the other units."

"You really mean that we won't be going to survival tomorrow?"

"I really do."

She looked uncertain. "I suppose I know most of this stuff well enough."

"Sure you do. You'll have plenty of time to read that later. Right now you should throw on your coveralls and go to the film."

Still she hesitated. "I don't know if I should."

"Look, you've already said you've done your extra duty and missed your dinner. No one said you couldn't go to the rec center for a couple of hours."

She slammed the book and stood. "How long before the film starts?"

I glanced at the clock above the door of the squad bay. "About ten minutes, according to the schedule."

"Wait for me." She tossed the book into the top of her locker and grabbed a pair of clean coveralls. She started for the latrine, but turned. "You'll wait, won't you?"

The rec center was almost full when we got there. We had to take seats in the back, which made the screen hard to see. Just as we sat down, Lara said, "I'm hungry. Couldn't we find something to eat?"

"There were a couple of candy machines outside." As I said it, I realized that it seemed like an awful waste of space on the ship. Candy machines served no useful purpose, except that they made it seem more like home. Maybe the psychological effects of the machines outweighed the space they took, I thought.

"Save my seat," she said. "I want to get a couple of candy bars. You want anything?"

I shook my head. "I had a big—" I almost said dinner, but didn't want to remind her, and tried to cover it. "I'm not very hungry."

She returned just as they were playing the SCAF anthem. We all stood at attention, staring at a screen that showed flags waving and our ships in flight. As they switched to the film, Lara slipped into the chair beside me. She tried to quietly strip the paper from the candy bar, but failed. It rattled as if she were blasting it open. When she finished the candy, she looked at the screen and laid her head on my shoulder. I put my arm around her and was about to say something when I realized she'd gone to sleep. I hadn't known she was that tired.

Just before the movie ended, I tried to wake her. She didn't move for a second, then mumbled something. I shook her arm again.

"God damn it, I'm awake you stupid son of a bitch."

Around me I heard people laughing, and someone said, "Hey, McAllif, you so interesting that you can't keep her awake?"

That brought another burst of laughter.

I whispered, "Lara, come on. We've got to go."

The lights came on, and she sat up suddenly and looked around wildly, as if trying to figure out where she was. Finally she looked at me and seemed to relax.

"We've got to go now."

"Was it a good movie?"

I shrugged. "It was all right, I guess. If you like war films. We're actually on a great crusade, you know."

She smiled. "I had heard that."

"The film made it all clear. We were shown how the *Star Explorer* was ruthlessly attacked by creatures with four arms and three eyes. Our side fought heroically, but the beasts finally overwhelmed them. We're going to avenge their deaths."

We followed the crowd out of the rec center. Lara stopped at the candy machine and eyed several of the items.

"We're not allowed to have candy in the squad bay."

"I know, but I'm so hungry."

"You want to have another reason for them to be after you? Go ahead and take something back."

She hesitated, then shook her head. "Let's go. I want to go to bed."

"Sounds good to me."

"Alone. I'm tired."

"How could you be? You slept through the whole film."

"That's the most sleep I've gotten in two weeks. I thought that I would go for the record, or something like that. The Rip Van Winkle Memorial Sleep Award."

The next day I found out I was wrong. They could change the training schedule when no one had scheduled the survival area. No one had it scheduled. I'd assumed it wouldn't be changed and that Fetterman had told us to study survival as a trick.

I found out just after breakfast, when Lara came screaming into the squad bay. She tossed her hat at me and shouted, "Way to go McAllif, you dumb son of a bitch." She stopped right in front of me. "Don't worry, Lara. They can't change the schedule, Lara. Go to the movie, Lara.'"

"What the hell is wrong with you?"

"Figure it out genius. We're scheduled for survival training and you didn't let me finish studying."

For an instant I was confused. Then it filtered in, and I couldn't think of anything to say. I knew that almost no one had studied anything because we had all known how the schedule worked.

Fetterman walked into the bay before I had to say anything, and someone called the room to attention. We all fell in and waited while Fetterman walked from one end of the squad bay to the other. Marquette waited by the door.

"The uniform of the day will be warm weather, tropical. You have five minutes to change and fall out with survival gear." Both he and Marquette left without another word.

As the door shut, Lara spun toward me. "See? See, you idiot? And you know what's going to happen? They're going to ask questions, and they're going to ask me most of them, and I'm not going to have the answers and I'll miss dinner again and have more extra duty." She sat back on her bunk, pulled off one of her shoes, and tossed it at my locker. "God damn it, anyway."

I didn't say anything, just started to change. I pulled the short-sleeve dark green shirt from my locker and buttoned it.

"God damn it, Steve." She tossed her other shoe at my locker, but missed. It caught me in the ankle.

"All right. I made a mistake, but you don't have to carry

on like that. Everyone is in the same boat."

"Yeah. We're probably all in the same boat because the great Intelligence man told us that they couldn't change the schedule." Her voice was icy.

"You can stop now. You've made your point. I was only trying to help you. You needed some time off and you got it, so just shut up."

She stared at me for a moment, then jerked at the collar of her shirt, ripping it and popping the top two buttons. She looked at it, then at the buttons bouncing on the floor, before turning toward her locker. She didn't say anything else.

I finished changing, grabbing my survival kit from the top of my locker, and stepped past Lara. She didn't even look at me. As I neared the center of the squad bay to wait for Marquette, Susan walked up.

"Looks like we blew it, Steve."

"Sure does. I really didn't think they could change the schedule like that."

"I heard someone say that they probably did it on purpose so they could catch us with our pants down."

Lara finished lacing her boots just as Marquette came into the squad bay. He told us to form a single line, weapons ready, and to move out. Susan took the lead and Lara brought up the rear. Although this was survival training, there was a possibility that we would be attacked, so we tried to stay alert.

We were led into one of the simulators. Dense foliage was everywhere, except for a narrow path. Fetterman halted us just before we entered the forest.

"Normally you wouldn't want to follow any trails made by either intelligent creatures or by animals, because the enemy would probably be watching them or have them mined. Today, however, the training is survival and not squad tactics, so we won't worry about attacks."

Fetterman plowed into the trees and bushes and we followed. I grabbed one of the leaves, but instead of popping off, it slipped out of my hand and sprang back into place. The whole forest was made of plastiform.

The winding trail seemed to last forever. In the trees we could hear animals screaming and hooting and calling, and we could hear things crashing out of sight. I felt shivers up and down my spine, and began to watch closely where I put my feet.

We finally entered a semicircular clearing where there were bleachers. Two noncoms stood at the foot of the bleachers, watching us. They pointed, and we all moved to find a place to sit. I tried to get next to Lara, but she moved away, so I found a place near Susan.

Susan looked toward Lara, then back to me. "What was that all about?"

Before I could answer, Fetterman yelled, "If we wanted talking we would have let you know about it."

We sat quietly and waited for the class to start. One of the SCAF instructors flipped a cover up so we could see the first page of a chart on the easel next to him. He said, "Good morning. My name is Sergeant First Class Meyer, and I'll be conducting this block of instruction."

He pointed to the other person. "This is Technical Sergeant Martha Hernandez, and she will be assisting me.

"The first thing to remember in survival is that there will be plenty to eat and drink, if you know where to look. You can't run out to the corner grocery, but there will be plenty if you just keep your head."

Meyer looked toward Fetterman and said, "Does anyone know the biggest killer in a survival situation?"

No one moved. I glanced at Lara. Fetterman did the same thing, and she stood. "Panic."

Meyer nodded. "Right. Panic. If you panic, you will forget everything you've been taught, and you will die. If you remember this block of instruction, you will survive."

Meyer pointed back to the easel. "Now, during this block of instruction we will cover..."

I tuned him out. I knew what he was going to say because it was written on the easel. One thing about SCAF, they tried to cover all the bets. They hit you with audio and reinforced it with video and then tried to ensure that you remembered it by asking questions from the instruction before you got to the end. It was a giant system of constant rewards for being right and punishment for being wrong.

Lara was sitting almost by herself, carefully following

everything being said. The air was hot and oppressive, and I was wringing wet. Since this was a tropical setting, I figured the humidity was at least 99 going to 100. I wondered how good this training was going to be, since we didn't know a thing about the planet we were to invade.

It seemed the instructor read my thoughts. He was saying, "... ask yourselves what value this is. We don't know a thing about the environment. However, a few generalizations can be made. Since they did attack our probe, we know that there is intelligent life, and it stands to reason there will be lower orders present. Therefore, much of this will be valuable...."

He faded again. I looked around. There was an impression of sunlight filtering through the trees, but I knew that it was the lamps overhead. The air seemed to smell clean or different, and there was a hint of coolness to it, like an early morning dew, but it was still hot. I finally identified the cool as a very slight breeze from the air conditioner. The humidity made everything sticky.

Meyer had flipped to the last page of the charts and was carefully looking around. He asked a question and Fetterman called a name. When the person he called couldn't answer, Fetterman asked Susan, then Lara. Lara was able to give a quick and concise answer. Fetterman nodded his approval.

That went on for a few minutes. Fetterman asked everyone in the squad a question, and each time it was Lara who answered. Finally he stepped to the front and roared, "What the hell is wrong with you people? Don't any of you ever study? Only Masterson seems to know anything. Everyone has two hours of extra duty tonight except Masterson."

We were given a ten-minute break. Even though we'd screwed up, SCAF had discovered that people learned better if the blocks of instruction were broken into small segments. We wouldn't be punished by having our breaks denied, because that would be counterproductive.

I walked over to Lara, who was drinking from her canteen. She wasn't too neat about it, and was letting some of the water dribble down her chin and neck.

"See," I said, "you didn't need to study last night."

She put the cap back on her canteen and stowed it carefully

before she looked at me. "We've just about covered everything that I studied last night. Before too long I'll be on the extra-duty list, thanks to you."

"I wonder what it's like?"

She looked up. "What what's like?"

"To be perfect, of course. I see now. You were only leading us on, and you really know everything because you're perfect."

For a moment she looked at me, then smiled very sweetly. "Fuck you very much, asshole."

I turned and headed back to the rest of the squad. Susan drifted my way and we talked for a few minutes. Fetterman called us back to the bleachers and we went into finding food in a jungle environment. While Hernandez talked, a bowl of insects and bits of snake, among other appetizing items, was passed around. We were supposed to eat some of it so we would learn that things other than soybean meal were edible.

I didn't hear much of Hernandez's lecture. I did hear her tell us to be careful with the grasshoppers. Their back legs had tiny spurs on them, and they could get caught in the throat. "It's not good practice," she said, "to try to sneak around the jungle while coughing and hacking all over the place."

In the afternoon we were paired and led to different parts of the simulator so we could try to make our way back to the entrance. I tried to link up with Lara, but she ignored me and picked someone else.

Fetterman said that if we made it in under an hour, the extra duty would be removed. If it took over five, we could count on a couple of extra hours tacked on to what we already had.

Lara made it in forty-seven minutes. Susan and I did it in two hours and thirty-four minutes. When we finally moved to the squad bay, one pair was still out. They had been wandering around for over seven hours, and Fetterman was preparing to find them. The flora may have been plastiform, but the fauna weren't.

After the extra duty I was tired. They'd kept us out late, then came up with more things for us to do. The only one who didn't have to worry about that was Lara. When we came into the squad bay, she was asleep.

Fetterman turned on the lights and told us we had twelve minutes to get ready for bed. That included time to take a shower, and I knew we all needed showers. The humidity in the jungle school had made us sweat, and the sweat dried slowly, leaving a sticky, itchy residue all over our bodies.

As I pulled off my shirt, I looked at Lara. She opened her eyes, stared, then rolled to her side.

"Hello," I said.

She didn't move. I didn't know if she had gone back to sleep or if she was still angry about the survival training. I finished undressing and grabbed a towel and some soap.

I made it in just under twelve minutes. I tossed my towel into the locker and slammed it. Lara jumped at the sound, and I knew she was awake.

"I said, Hello."

She rolled over and looked at me. "So what?"

"Look, you don't have to continue this."

The lights went out suddenly, and Fetterman yelled, "That's it. Go to sleep. We have some surprises for you tomorrow. There will be two less for breakfast."

"Lara, I don't know why you're acting like this."

"Lights out, McAllif. Time to go to sleep." Her voice was cold.

I shrugged at the wall locker. "Fine. Act like a baby. See if I care."

She said, "Ha," and rolled over again.

When they turned the lights on the next morning, Lara was already up and gone. I wondered where she was and what she was doing. Maybe they'd needed volunteers for something last night, and since she was the only one around, had volunteered her.

Susan strolled over and looked at Lara's empty bed. "Where's your friend?"

"Who knows? The high command probably needed her advice on something and sent a colonel down her to escort her to the flagship."

"My, my, aren't we a bit touchy?"

I turned toward her. She was smiling. "You know what, Susan? Sometimes you are a real horse's ass."

"Thank you, dear. That's the nicest thing that you've said to me all week."

"I'm sorry, Susan. There was no reason to jump on you."

"So okay, let's go get some breakfast."

I pulled on my boot and tied it. "Fine. I could use some."

After duty that day we attended the funeral for the non-survivors. When it was over, Susan and I strolled back to the squad bay and talked quietly. Lara was there, supposedly studying a manual, but she kept peeking over the top, watching us, so I tried to give her something to watch. She ignored me as I got ready for lights out.

8

Masterson, Lara
Trainee, Training Platoon Alpha, SCAF

This class was an unpleasant surprise. So far all the classes were about subjects that could be called military. There had been weapons familiarization, small unit tactics, and all-environment survival. Now we sat in a class with a large holographic display of our part of the galaxy in front of us while one of the navigation officers explained the situation to us. We were told that this was to be one of those nice-to-know classes and there would be no tests on it. After it was over, I knew why.

The navigator, a lieutenant colonel named Freestone, had a way with words. Everyone listened closely. In fact he commanded our attention so well that everyone would have passed a test easily, if one were given.

Freestone pointed into the holograph and said, "Earth and our solar system are rather out in the boondocks, when speaking about the galaxy. We are in one of the spiral arms, and as you know, our closest neighbor is just over four light-years from Earth. It's interesting to note that close to galactic center, the stars are separated by small parts of a light-year, and we begin to talk about distances in light-weeks and light-days."

That might have been interesting, but I didn't see what relevance it had for the rest of us. It didn't take Freestone long to make it clear.

"We are now traveling at about three quarters the speed of light—give or take a couple of thousand miles a second—heading toward Tau Ceti. Now the faster we go, the slower time becomes for us. I'm sure that you have all had this in school on Earth, but I'm going to take a moment to elaborate."

I suddenly had a sinking feeling in my stomach. I knew where he was going to take this, and knew I wouldn't see my family again. An icy hand grabbed my stomach and started to massage it.

"According to Einstein, the faster we go, the slower time becomes for us. Earthside, the time we take to get out to Tau Ceti will be something like twenty-five or twenty-six years, but on the ship it will only be four or five years, depending on a number of factors. Of course, the return trip will also take twenty-five years. I don't know how long we'll be on Tau Ceti, so we're talking in the neighborhood of fifty years for the people left on Earth."

I felt the blood drain from my face and was suddenly light-headed, dizzy. I tried to look around, and saw that those near me were as stunned as I was. Some still hadn't realized what Freestone was saying, but it was all too clear to me. SCAF planned a mission that would last only ten or twelve years, and that was what they kept saying: "You'll only be gone ten years, and think, when you return there will be ten years of accumulated pay for you." The deceit made me sick.

I had entered the ship thinking that ten years would pass. A lot could happen in ten years, but the odds were that my family—my mother, father, and sister—would still be alive, and waiting for me. Now we were told that it would be over half a century before we returned, and the odds were that they would be dead or too old to remember me. I felt the tears start then, but I didn't care.

Freestone continued as if he were announcing sunny weather for the rest of the week. "As our speed increases, the time dilation will become more acute. This means that the discrepancy between us and the people of Earth increases."

I stared into the holograph, but it was hard to see because of the tears. Earth was marked in bright red, and Tau Ceti in green, and I thought the colors were reversed. A yellow line connected the two, and a large blue dot showed the approximate position of the fleet.

"Our latest calculations," said Freestone, "show that we'll begin decelerating in another two years, six months, and four days. We estimate that we will arrive about two years after that. On Earth over twenty years will have passed."

He kept stressing the time dilation, and one of the boys finally shouted, "We know that now. You've made it abundantly clear." The hostility in the voice was unmistakable.

Freestone put a hand to his eyes as if staring into a bright light and searched for the source of the voice. He said, to no one in particular, "My job is to make sure you understand. I didn't know that you were being brought on ship without fully understanding the ramifications of time dilation. I was only asked to clarify the situation."

For another few minutes Freestone continued to clarify the situation. He explained that flight routes and the times involved made precise calculations about the dilation effect difficult. He asked for questions, but everything was so obvious that no one had anything to ask. Then we were dismissed and told we could take the rest of the afternoon off.

Back in the squad bay no one had much to say. I think most of us were wondering why we hadn't figured it out before. Now it made no difference because there was nothing we could do about it. That's probably why SCAF waited until we were in deep space before telling us.

I heard McAllif hit his locker door with his fist and say, "Of course they're paying us for actual time served, not total time passed."

"What does that mean?" I asked, figuring it was just another of McAllif's sarcastic comments.

"It means that if fifty years pass on Earth but they're only paying us for the ten years we'll have served on the ship, as calculated by the ship's clocks, they save a lot of money."

As if that weren't bad enough, Mark almost shouted, "Look at it another way. If they wait for us to return to pay us, they save more money. If you're killed, they don't have to pay you at all."

"Wait a minute," I interjected. "They'll have to pay your family."

"Yeah?" said Mark. "What family? What they just said means that our families will probably be dead before we can get back. Leave it to SCAF to figure it out from all angles."

That killed the conversation. No one wanted to talk about it. We had all been told that our families were gone. They weren't dead yet, but they would be before we could get back. A few younger brothers and sisters might survive, but the majority of us were being told we would never see our families again.

Dinner came and went, but most of us didn't go. We were trying to adjust to the idea of being temporal orphans. I didn't know what to say or do. I thought of writing home. SCAF claimed that a mail ship left the fleet each month with microfiched letters, but I no longer believed it. They wouldn't waste so much money or effort.

Fetterman came in about twenty minutes before lights out. He didn't give us one of his usual pep talks. He merely informed us about the training schedule for the next day and told us to be ready. He hesitated for a minute, almost as if he wanted to say something more but didn't know what. He turned and stepped out.

9

McAllif, Steven M.
Trainee, Training Platoon Alpha, SCAF

Tuesday morning's training schedule called for desert warfare practice in the simulator ship. The tactical situation was an infantry holding action against an armored thrust. Having learned their lesson, neither Lopez nor any of the others asked how we knew that the enemy had tanks.

At 0530 hours we fell out in the uniform of the day, which was khaki shorts, shirts, knee socks, and a cleatless track shoe. Naturally we were required to bring full web gear and wear our body armor. All the weapons, including the antitank rockets, had been replaced by laser training aids. The beam would actuate a sensor on the tank that would cut out the ignition system, stopping the tank. We wore film badges that could be discolored by the tank's lasers and that scored hits and kills against us.

But before we even made it to the middle of the "Israeli Desert," the noncoms had a surprise for us. Someone had decided that we could use some practice in urban warfare, and not having a city handy, we were going to assault down the corridor connecting the *Erwin Rommel* to the simulator ship.

Susan, the acting squad leader, was simulated-killed immediately, which wasn't a very good move because those killed during the exercises had extra duty that night. Command fell to Lopez, who lasted about twice as long—maybe ten seconds. There was no one to advise us, and the only rule of the day was to survive. We couldn't get into the corridor because the enemy fire was too intense. They could see us as soon as we stepped into the doorway.

Lara solved the problem. "If they can see us, why don't we fix it so they can't."

"What are you going to do, turn out the lights?"

"No. We'll wait until dark."

"Listen," I said. "I don't think it's such a dumb idea. Why don't we roll a smoke grenade down the corridor and run through the smoke?"

Wendy grabbed one of the grenades and said, "Okay, but I don't think the noncoms are going to like this. It'll screw up the ventilators."

"So what? They're all at the other end, and they won't know who threw it."

Wendy pulled the pin and lobbed the grenade around the doorway. "How long do we wait?"

I shrugged. "Don't know. About fifteen seconds should do it. Got to give the smoke time to spread." I looked at my watch until the time had passed, then said, "Let's go."

Lara grabbed my arm. "What about masks?"

"Masks?"

"Gas masks. The corridor is full of smoke, remember?"

"Oh, yeah."

I stepped into the doorway and waved my arm. The entire squad followed, with Lara bringing up the rear. After five steps I hit the wall for the first time. Someone bumped into me. The smoke had done its job. When I figured I was about halfway down the corridor, I opened fire. It was returned immediately by dozens of ruby-colored pencils stabbing through the haze. My film badge discolored and buzzed. I was simulated-killed. Cheating a little, I tried to get to a wall so I wouldn't be stomped on by those behind me. It didn't work. I bumped into someone and we both fell down.

As the squad pushed past me, I could see the bright shafts of light from the lasers, normally invisible, now clearly reflected by the smoke. Less than a minute later there was a bright flash and the firing stopped. The corridor cleared almost immediately. The vents worked better than we thought.

Lara was the only survivor. Apparently she had crawled down the corridor underneath the laser fire and tossed a flash grenade. It had discolored all the noncom badges.

Fetterman had two paragraphs of praise for Lara and twenty minutes of critique for the rest of us. "Your first mistake was getting killed. Your second mistake was trying to come down the corridor without smoke. Your third mistake was trying to come down the corridor a second time without smoke. Your fourth mistake was coming down the corridor standing up. Your fifth mistake was coming down the corridor instead of using your grenade launcher from the other end. Your sixth mistake was firing your rifles in the smoke and giving your positions away, except for Masterson, who exhibited the tiniest inkling of common sense by using a grenade instead of her rifle. Your seventh mistake was all bunching up like a herd of cows and not dividing into fire and maneuver elements. And your eighth mistake was all getting killed. With the exception of Masterson everyone has earned an hour of extra duty—no, it was such an exceptional performance, we'll make it two."

The simulator was essentially a freighter of the largest class. Except for small compartments for the engines and the crew, the entire ship's interior consisted of a lot of space that could be arranged to create various terrains. Today the astroturf had a rust-brown color, with just enough sand sprinkled on top to get into your shoes. Overhead were all the heatlamps in the world. The temperature in the simulator was 42 Centigrade. Near one end, about a third of the way down, some simulated passes had been constructed from poly-foam.

We joined with the other squads, that had already made it through the corridors, and got our orders. Three fourths of us were assigned to defend the closest pass and the others were to support the tanks. If we were overrun, we were to fall back to the second pass and defend it. There was no retreat from there, only extra duty.

Fetterman gave us the assignments. Pickett, from the first

squad, was made company commander. Heiniken from the second squad was the exec, and Susan, from our squad, the first sergeant. Heiniken was to command the first and second platoons, in this case twelve men each, and hold the first pass. Susan would command the third, a mobile reserve, while Pickett and the fourth platoon dug in at the second pass. All in all we had about forty-five ground troops against three light-armored fighting vehicles and a dozen infantry.

I was busy trying to complete a foxhole when Lara came over and sat down beside me. I looked at her. "What's up?"

"Steve, I need some help. After all that Fetterman said, I couldn't ask him." She pulled her rifle off her shoulder.

"Why not?"

"I don't know how I did it, but I didn't throw the grenade. I was trying to run down the corridor without getting hit, and I tripped. I dropped my rifle and it slid across the floor. I lost sight of it, and just as it disappeared in the smoke, there was a flash. I think I broke something in it."

I stopped chopping at the poly-foam. "Well, son of a bitch. Let me see it." This was the first time in a week that we had spoken. Suddenly we were friends again.

I looked at the rifle closely, but couldn't see anything wrong with it. "Have you tried to fire it?"

"It doesn't."

I shook my head. "It must have overloaded or something, and exploded when you dropped it. I can't see anything wrong with it."

She stood up and brushed the sand off her shorts. "What am I going to do?"

"Since there aren't any serial numbers on these, I'd just turn it in at the end of the day and hope that someone discovers it's broken so they can fix it. I certainly wouldn't tell anyone."

We hadn't heard him come up, but we heard him when he got there. "What the hell are you two doing?"

I started chopping again. "Nothing, General Heiniken, sir. We were just—"

"Never mind." He turned to Lara. "Have you finished digging in?"

"Pretty close."

Heiniken took out a map. "Okay, pretty close. I want you

to move down about a hundred meters and dig in near the bottom and on the north side of the slope. You've got picket duty. If you sight anything, you identify it, report it, and then fall back to here."

"Yes, sir." Lara trotted off toward her foxhole, gathered her gear, and began working her way down the slope.

"As for you, wise guy, I want you to move fifty meters out in front so that you can cover her withdrawal."

"But I've just about—"

"No buts or just abouts. Move. Intell claims that the attack will come in less than an hour."

The attack came much sooner, of course. I didn't think they would let us get everything ready. I heard the tanks before I could see them. Over the top of a small hill I could see a cloud of dust. Since there wasn't much sand to kick up, I figured it was another of the simulations to add authenticity.

When I saw that, I flattened myself into the shallow hole I'd dug, staring forward. Apparently Lara hadn't seen or heard anything, because she was still chopping away. I waited for her to look up or stop and listen, but she didn't. I thought about shouting to her, but was afraid it would give away my position, and that could leave half the company unguarded.

The tanks finally appeared and I saw Lara dive for cover. She watched for a moment, and looked back toward me, but I don't think she saw me or knew where I was. I saw her grab her rifle and then stand up suddenly, dropping it. Three people moved in from the side, having outflanked her. I hadn't seen them because the hill had been in the way.

I set my rifle on the small mound of poly-foam in front of me and aimed carefully. I squeezed the trigger and saw one of the people fall. I fired a second time and scored a second hit. The rules said that each casualty had to fall, for the added realism.

The third person grabbed Lara and shoved her toward me, using her for cover. He fired several times, but the shots were wide. I didn't move, hoping he would give me a better shot, but he didn't. I watched him lash Lara's wrists behind her, then put another rope around her elbows, drawing it tight so that they were only inches apart. It gave her a strange, stiff posture.

Just as he finished, I got the third shot and dropped him. I

stood up and yelled for her to run toward me, but she didn't
move. I yelled again and started forward, but stopped abruptly,
skidding on the sand. It was obvious there was a fourth person
down there, hidden by the slope. I turned and ran back toward
our position.

"Heiniken. They're on their way."

"Where's the other guard?"

"She was captured."

"And you did nothing?"

I took a deep breath. "What the hell was I supposed to do?
I managed to shoot three of them, but there was a fourth and
I couldn't get a clear shot. I figured it was better to have one
captured and you alerted than to have two killed and you surprised."

Heiniken peeled off his helmet and wiped the sweat away.
He glanced at the small radio transmitter in the helmet and
frowned at me. I knew what the question was going to be.

"I don't know why she didn't transmit. I didn't think of it."

Heiniken nodded. "All right. I guess there is no way for the
noncoms to know. If the enemy was monitoring our frequency,
they'll think that they managed to kill you and capture Masterson without any word getting back to us."

Sitting behind us was the tent used by the noncoms. They
sat there watching and critiquing everything we did. Heiniken
was right. They would have monitored Lara's capture on their
TV, and would have seen me trying to rescue her, but they
wouldn't know that I hadn't used the radio because I'd forgotten. If Heiniken backed me later, we could tell them we
were on radio silence for some reason.

Naturally a mistake like that was supposed to be reported,
but the prevailing attitude was "cooperate and graduate." That
was the one flaw in the system. There was no way that they
could make us report the mistakes of the others. I wouldn't
forget about the radio again, so there was no reason to report
it. The downtrodden and the underdogs always stick together.

I took my position in the center of the line. Someone had
been detailed to finish my foxhole for me. I was one member
of the rifle team. Our job was to take out the infantry thrown
at us, making sure they didn't get too close. Behind us, set
near the top of a ridge so they could withdraw quickly, was

the antitank squad. If it looked bad, they were to withdraw to the second hill to make their final stand with the Headquarters Platoon.

As we had figured, the tanks tried to come straight up the draw. They were in a triangle formation. Behind them, trying to use them for cover, was the remainder of the infantry. I couldn't see Lara, so I assumed they'd either left someone behind to guard her or had killed her.

As soon as they were in range, we opened up. All of us were trying to hit the infantry because our rifles would have little effect on the tanks. I saw one of the enemy fall and then another, but they kept coming. The tanks, with their pulse lasers firing much like an old Gatling gun, raked the slope with a heavy fire but did very little damage. The main battery of the tanks were firing occasionally, but they hadn't gotten the range of our antitank unit or hadn't spotted it.

At what seemed the last second, the antitank squad opened fire, destroying a tank with the first shot. The infantry dropped from it and the crew sprang from it, but we managed to shoot them as they scattered for cover. Suddenly, as the tanks and their infantry tried to destroy our antitank people we became unimportant. The shooting was over our heads, and there was little for us to do. We tried to hit some of the enemy, but they were too well concealed.

A second tank was hit but not destroyed, only damaged. It reversed and started backing away from us. Some of the infantry tried to get out of the way, and we picked them off. One man slipped, tried to get up, and slipped again, sliding back to the tank. They couldn't see him and there was a high-pitched scream, almost like tires on cement. A second later the body was pushed from under the treads. It was mangled almost beyond recognition, the blood staining the sand and poly-foam.

For a second the fighting stopped. The tank kept backing away, the crew unaware that they had run over someone, but the infantry gathered near the body. One noncom charged from the tent screaming at us to "Keep firing, the battle isn't over." At one end of our line a few lasers opened up, raking the men near the tanks, but they seemed unaware and unconcerned.

A yellow flare broke overhead, near the heatlamps, signaling the end of the battle. Fetterman ran from the tent, waving for us to follow him. We formed a ragged line near the body, most of us trying not to look at it. Using a hand set Fetterman recalled everyone, including our reinforcements and headquarters. Lara, her hands still tied, was pushed toward us by her guard. We stood and waited.

Fetterman flipped a hand at Lara. "Someone untie her, for crying out loud."

After a few seconds the other noncoms put the body on a stretcher and carried it away. Fetterman said, "What the hell happened to you people? You were in the middle of a battle, and suddenly everyone stands up and stops."

"But Mead had just been—"

"I don't give a shit about Mead or what had just happened," Fetterman roared. "You people were in a battle situation. The defending troops won because you jerks down here just quit."

The commander of the enemy said, "But we had a real casualty. Mead had been run over and we—"

"God damn it to hell, how can I make you understand? If you make a mistake, you're going to get killed. I'm sorry as hell that Mead got killed, but he made a mistake. You could see the panic after he slipped the first time. If he stayed calm, he could have gotten out of the way. Hell, he could've rolled under the damn thing so that it passed over him, but instead he panicked and got mashed by the threads. He made a mistake."

"Sergeant, I was—"

"Shut up. We have told you dummies that making mistakes kill. You've just had a practical demonstration. Not only did Mead get himself killed for real, but many of you were simulated-killed by your stupid reactions. We are not playing games here. Soon we are going to be in battle for real, and people are going to be dying for real, just like Mead. Unless you learn your lesson, large numbers of you are going to be dead."

For moments we didn't say anything. Most of us stared at the stains in the sand and poly-foam, glad it hadn't been us but wondering about the cruelty of the noncoms. They weren't going to investigate or say kind things about our fallen comrade. They called him stupid and almost seemed glad he was dead.

Fetterman shook us awake. "We have work to do. We start

the exercise again. Everyone killed has an hour of extra duty. Masterson has half an hour since she was only captured and because her partner ran off and left her. Tankers, move your vehicles back to the starting position."

Pickett and Heiniken took a few minutes trying to decide how to defend the pass again. They didn't think the tanks would be coming the same way. While they talked, Lara came over to me. There were bright red rings around her wrists and near her elbows, where the rope had bitten her flesh.

"Sorry about leaving you."

"Wasn't much you could do. There were another six people waiting down there. They hoped you would try to make a grandstand play."

"I started to help."

She rubbed her wrist. "I know. You were right, though. If you hadn't been, they would have given you extra duty."

During the next battle they tried to outflank us. They sent two tanks up the center with very little infantry, and spaced them out, trying to make us think all three were there. The other tank was trying to climb the hill to one side of us so that it could fire down on us, but it didn't make it. Apparently it was supposed to appear just as the other tanks did so that we would be confused and lost.

They ran into our reinforcements. The Headquarters Platoon had seen the tank and ordered the reinforcements to take it. The battle began about halfway up the slope, and our troops were slowly pushed back until they were on the crest. As that happened, the other tanks began a dash toward us, confusing some of us and causing a breach in the line.

Heiniken, seeing the troops on top of the ridge and the tanks coming at us, called a hasty retreat, leaving the reinforcements alone on the hill. As we pulled back, the third platoon was surrounded and slaughtered and simulated-killed. The tanks and infantry rejoined, chasing us across the valley floor, toward the second pass.

If Heiniken had held his ground, we would have won the battle right there with very few casualties. The retreat cost us troops and supplies. We spread out at the second pass and held it. When the battle was over, half the company was dead—

mostly from Heiniken's mistake—but we had captured one tank, destroyed the other two, and wiped out the infantry. The victory was clearly ours.

We spent the rest of the day fighting different situations on different sides. Each of us had a chance to be with the tank company so we would get some experience as armored infantry. Periodically the commanders were switched so we would have more people gaining that experience. In Heiniken's case, he was relieved because he'd been responsible for the third platoon being wiped out.

Somehow I made it through the day without getting killed again. I had only one hour of extra duty. Those who'd been captured, and several had that misfortune after the first battle, had a special extra duty. Lara told me about it later that night.

She came back late, after I'd been in bed for what seemed several hours. She climbed onto the railing. I rolled over and asked what was happening.

"I wanted to see if you were awake."

"I am," I replied. "Now."

She reached out and touched my hand. "Steve, I'm sorry I acted the way I did after the survival training. I was just so damned—"

"Forget it." I wanted to tell her that I thought she'd acted like a little kid and we were supposed to be grown up, but I didn't have the energy or the desire at that time.

She nodded. It was hard to see her in the dark. She said, "I just got back from the POW course."

"That's what I thought." I hadn't had the honor of attending the course yet. You were selected for it by being captured during one of the exercises, and it was assumed that everyone would be captured eventually.

I wanted to go back to sleep, but I could tell that Lara was on a talking jag, and since I'd only recently gotten back into her good graces, I didn't want to do anything to upset her. I said, "What was it like?"

Lara hesitated. "You don't really want to know, do you?"

"Certainly. I wouldn't have asked if I didn't," I lied.

"Well, I'm not going to stand here and tell you. Either you have to come down and sit on my bed or I'm coming up there."

I pushed my blanket back. "I'll come down. It'll be easier that way."

She pushed her pillow against the post that held my bunk up and leaned back. "I'm sure I don't want to play that game again. The first thing they did was tie us and leave us in a big room. They tied us so that it was almost impossible to move. All we could do was sort of roll around. No one seemed inclined to do anything, except one guy. He rolled toward his friend and they whispered for a moment, then rolled back to back. For a few minutes they didn't seem to be doing anything, then one of them sat up. He untied his friend and they both started to untie the rest of us. Before they got too far, the noncoms came back. We all had to stay for the rest of the training, but those two guys got to go. Not because they were successful, but because they had at least tried something."

She stopped to take a breath. She'd taken off her coverall and was wearing only her panties. I didn't have on much myself, and felt a deep affection for her, but figured it was only because she was so close and so scantily clad. I felt a little guilty about it, but didn't want to do anything to spoil the mood.

"Then they separated us and made us walk up and down one of the corridors," she said. "They left our hands tied behind us, and my shoulders began to ache, but there wasn't much I could do. One by one they took us into a room and closed the door.

"Inside there were a couple of the other people. Three noncoms were yelling at one girl, screaming that if she didn't sign the paper, they would put her into the pit with the snakes. When she didn't sign, they opened the pit. When they closed the trapdoor on her, she began to scream. When the doctor finally took her away, she was still screaming."

I watched Lara as she told me this. I could see that it bothered her. "I was next," she said. "They tried to get me to sign, and when I refused, they said that I would be put into the pit. I'd already seen what had happened to the other girl."

"Bloody sadists," I said.

"After a while, when nothing happened, they pulled me out, and I figured that the first girl had put on an act to frighten me."

"You're probably right, Lara." I found it hard to believe that she'd been that quick. It would have been two or three days before I figured it out, if someone didn't tell me sooner.

I moved closer to Lara and took her hand. She didn't pull it away, and in fact I thought she squeezed it slightly.

"They tried a few other things. They tied my hands in front of me, then I was hung by my wrists. In just a few seconds it seemed that my whole body ached. Finally they let me down, pushed me toward a table, and told me to sign a paper. If I signed, they said, I could go. When I didn't, they said I could go. That was the test. If I had signed, just to come back here, I would have been given extra duty and been reassigned to a second POW course for a week. Since I didn't, I was rewarded."

When she finished talking, she leaned forward, bending at the waist and pushing on her back. "God, I'm sore."

I took the cue, if that's what it was supposed to be. "Want me to give you a back rub?" She hesitated, and I said, "Come on, it'll do you good."

She slid down and rolled to her stomach. "Go ahead."

I straddled the back of her thighs, feeling her cool, dry skin against my own thighs. I knew that I was going to be in trouble quickly if I didn't take control of myself. I rubbed her shoulders, working my way down to the small of her back and then along her sides. She muttered, "That feels good."

I kept at it for a long time. Finally I slid backward and began massaging her thighs. I couldn't believe how soft and smooth her skin was, or that she didn't say anything to me. When I reached up to peel off her panties, she lifted her hips so I could pull them down. Once they were off, she rolled over and pulled me close, holding me tight and kissing me.

I slipped a hand between us, sliding my fingers over her. Still she said nothing, but held me tighter and kissed me harder. Finally I pulled away, more to catch my breath than to do anything else.

Lara said, "You're not going away are you? You're going to stay down here aren't you?"

"For a while. I'll have to go back to my bed later. What will the others think?"

"Probably the same thing you thought when Mark and Wendy were seen in the same bed . . . or maybe you're worried about Susan?"

Her voice wasn't much above a whisper, but it carried a lot

of hostility. I shook my head. "I'm not worried about Susan, only you."

Apparently it was the right answer because she pulled me to her and started fumbling with the waistband of my shorts, trying to slip them off. The next morning no one said anything to us.

10

Fetterman, Anthony B.
Sergeant First Class, Training Instructor, SCAF

"Good morning. For anyone who cares, the time is zero-four hundred. For anyone foolish enough to forget, or who hasn't learned it, my name is Fetterman and I am your platoon sergeant. For the next five years plus the duration, I will remain your platoon sergeant, unless you are either reassigned or make a mistake. If you are reassigned, you will have another platoon sergeant. If you make a mistake, you will be *dead*. The only way to get killed in combat is to make a mistake. Remember what we teach you, and stay alive.

"We now begin a fourteen-hour block of instruction designed to help you stay alive. This is a basic introductory course on tactical category weapon systems employed by SCAF to accomplish its assigned wartime tasks. By the end of today you will be familiar with the functioning and use of each of the weapon systems discussed, and will have had an opportunity to test fire most of them. You will not be expected to be proficient in their use—that will come later. By the end of the voyage, you *will* be proficient.

"This morning there will be eight one-hour blocks of instruction on seven new weapon systems. The first hour will
consist of a review of a weapon system with which you are,
or had better be, already familiar. The SCAF basic assault rifle,
the M-4. At twelve hundred we'll break for a field lunch of
type-two field rations. At twelve-thirty instruction will resume,
covering six different weapon systems in one-hour blocks. We
will finish at eighteen-thirty, and you will report directly to the
mess hall for dinner.

"For the purpose of this fourteen-hour block of instruction,
the simulator ship has been divided into fourteen separate areas.
As you finish in one area, you will be instructed as to which
area to report to next. We will now start with instructional
block one—review of the SCAF basic assault rifle M-4. You,
Masterson, tell us what you know about the M-4."

The girl looked a little uncertain, then stood.

"Sergeant, the M-4 is the basic SCAF assault rifle. It is the
result of a finalized design designated originally as the trials
rifle M-3-1A, which was the winner of the SCAF assault-rifle
competition held two years ago in Zurich. The design was
developed and refined by New Springfield Armory of Geneseo,
Illinois, the United States of America. The weapon is currently
manufactured by New Springfield Armory; by Armalite of Costa
Mesa, California, and Kobie, Japan; and by the Finnish firm
of Valmet. It is a gas-operated recoil-dampened selective fire
weapon employing . . ."

I listened with one half of my mind as the girl went on
detailing operating procedure, immediate and remedial action
stoppage drills, stripping and maintenance. I'd had some doubts
about Masterson. She hadn't seemed to get it all together at
first, but lately she'd been doing better. There was something
about her I couldn't quite put my finger on. As I thought about
it, I realized that I hadn't expected her to make it this far. She'd
surprised me by hanging in there, and I'd unconsciously reacted
to the situation by making things tougher on her. It was the
old self-fulfilling prophecy syndrome. I didn't think she'd make
it, so I'd been making it impossible for her to make it. The
squad leaders had picked up on the situation and started leaning
on her too. For a minute it made me mad at myself. Not that

I particularly felt sorry for the kid. If there was anybody in the platoon who couldn't make the grade, I'd rather find out now than in combat. It was just that I realized my behavior had been unprofessional, and that irritated me. I made a mental note. There'd be no overreaction, no slackening of training discipline, but I'd do my best not to make her the platoon goat from now on unless she deserved it. My job was to make these kids into good enough soldiers to keep them from getting themselves and their buddies killed while neutralizing the enemy, not to break people completely. That sort of thing was the province of the sadists in counterintelligence. Nobody was unbreakable. If I spent the next five years trying to break everybody in the platoon, I wouldn't have any troops left to fight the Tau's with. Counterproductive action was more than stupid, it was a mistake. A soldier can't afford to make mistakes.

Masterson was beginning to wind down, so I asked a few specific questions and then quizzed the rest of the platoon, making sure that each one had an opportunity to foul up. Three did and received a half hour of extra duty for their efforts.

After fifty minutes of review I gave them a ten-minute break and shuffled them over to the next area for familiarization with the SCAF light automatic weapon, M-K. I was already acquainted with the Israeli-produced submachine gun and knew it to be an effective and reliable weapon, as far as submachine guns go, but except for house to house fighting, I'd take a good assault rifle over a machine pistol any day of the war. If you can take a target out at six or seven hundred meters with one shot, you don't need a squirt gun. I knew the K in M-K stood for Colonel Yitzak Kalan, the weapon's inventor, but I'd yet to figure out why SCAF had given it a letter designation instead of a number, like all the other weapons. A tech sergeant was briefing the troops, and I tuned him in as he twisted a 25cm silencer onto the overgrown automatic pistol in his hand.

"... the Kalan fires 9×25mm caseless ammunition from a forty-round staggered box magazine. It is capable of semiautomatic fire, or of automatic fire with a cyclic rate of either 700 or 1400 rounds per minute. Adjustment is by the thumb safety. The first notch is safe, the second semiauto, third 700, and fourth 1400. The last position is a five-round burst selector."

I tuned him out again and went over to the NCO station at the main hatchway to get a cup of caffeine. As I was sipping the stuff, Captain Simms came in from the corridor. She was wearing fatigues that threatened to explode in any of several locations, and I realized for the first time what a good-looking gal she was, even if she did seem to prefer wearing pants to wearing a skirt. She slid down against the wall and motioned me over, unbuckling her helmet and dropping it on the floor.

"Tony, I've been looking over the report on the desert exercise. It doesn't look too good."

"I know. I'm afraid if these kids had been the crew of the *Titanic*, it would never have made it away from the dock."

"I know what the report says, but is it really all that bad?"

"It's considerably worse. I've tried screaming and cursing, I've tried extra duty and PT, I've even tried reasoning and logic. I just don't know what the trouble is. Some days they almost seem to realize what this is all about. Other days . . . well, you've seen the report. Lopez standing up in the middle of a cross fire after being stung by a sand beetle, Mead managing to get himself run over by a tank—the list goes on. I'm about at my wits end. If they were consistently screwups, I could accept that and write the lot of them off as unfit for combat. But they aren't. I just can't seem to reach these kids."

"If you can't find out what's wrong, maybe one of the other platoon sergeants can."

"I never said I couldn't handle my job, Captain. I'm sure they'll shape up okay. They just need a little more time."

"Fine, you've got fifty-five months and a wake-up to get them into shape. That's probably more training time than any other army has ever had. I'm told that during the first American civil war they were sending men into battle who had never even fired a rifle. Stop by my quarters tonight and we'll discuss the situation some more."

The rest of the morning was spent in familiarization with the P-35 personal defense weapon, a fancy name for pistol, and with hand and rifle grenades. I was familiar with them already, of course, though a few new grenades had been added that I hadn't known about. The most interesting things were the new mines. There was a new lightweight radar-doppled Claymore, and a geophone-triggered ultrasonic one with a ten-meter clean-kill radius, which the instructor said was completely safe at twelve meters and inaudible to the human ear.

I made a mental note to suggest to Simms when I saw her tonight that all noncoms be required to attend the weapon familiarization classes with the troops, then rejected the idea. We'd all get the full treatment from the experts during proficiency training, and the NCO's had enough to do as it was. I would, however, suggest that the appropriate manuals be placed in the NCO library so we could all be brought up to date on any new systems we didn't know about.

We finally made it through combat flame weapons and wrapped up the morning on the Stoner general purpose machine gun, M-100GL, with attached 40mm grenade launcher. It came in the standard version, which I'd seen before, and in a chopped and bobcatted version with hinged butt stock, for use by pathfinder personnel, which I hadn't seen.

We broke for lunch, and I gathered my squad leaders beneath a plastiform maple tree so we could run over the schedule for the rest of the day and tomorrow. I tore open the field ration kit, poured the packet of freeze-dried coffee into my canteen cup, and half filled it with water. I pulled the heating tab on the ration container and set my cup on top of it. There was a hissing noise from the cup, and thirty seconds later the tab popped up, indicating that the meal was ready. I'd lucked out, getting carrots and peas, mashed potatoes and margarine, apple crisp, and fried chicken. The chicken was all textured soybean meal and seaweed, of course, and most of the rest of it was too, but at least it tasted fairly close to the real thing, and the color was about right.

We started out after lunch on the general purpose SCAF missile, the man portable M-219. The weapon was a single-shot, self-homing missile in a sealed, self-contained disposable launcher. To operate, one simply removed the end caps and safety and firing covers. This activated the infrared television camera in the nose of the missile. When the target was framed in the sight brackets, you depressed the safety lever, which achieved a lock-on target. Pressure on the firing stud would then launch the missile, which would track the target until impact occurred. It could be used against fortifications, armored vehicles, or low-flying aircraft. The results of the warhead were substantial, and the hit probability exceeded ninety-nine percent.

We moved to the next area and were shown the SCAF standard Point Air Defense System Mark III, which consisted in the main of a compact high-speed computer, a battery of detection and targeting systems that included over-the-horizon radar, and a high-energy charged-particle beam weapon. I won't pretend I understood why it worked. The physics was considerably beyond me. But the operation was simple enough. Once in place and switched on, you just left it alone. Any incoming aircraft, missile, or cannon shell was instantly vaporized. Supposedly it could discriminate between enemy vehicles and SCAF vehicles. I decided I wouldn't want to test it.

Eventually we came to a system I could understand—the 155mm LCSRW, or Large Caliber, Soft Recoil Weapon. Basically it's a howitzer of advanced design capable of handling semitelescoped rounds with either conventional, nuclear, chemical, or biological warheads.

By late afternoon everybody was beginning to drag a little, including the instructors. We expanded the break period to twenty minutes and let the troops have some coffee.

We were given a firing demonstration of the Gatling, M-97 Series 1200—a multibarreled design typical of modern high-fire-rate weapons, chambered for 7×60mm assault rifle cartridges. The principal difficulty with it, now that heating problems had been overcome, was keeping it supplied with ammunition. It had a big brother—the 35×150mm M-100 Series 1200, which was intended for use by aircraft and armored vehicles. Some clever person, reputedly a design engineer but more probably a helicopter pilot, had dubbed the 7mm gun a minigun after its ancestor, and in a fit of humor, tagged the 35mm a maxigun.

"Helicopters are *the* aircraft of SCAF. Officially they aren't called helicopters any more, they are called Close Support Craft. But they still have rotor blades, they still work like helicopters, and they still look like helicopters, for the most part anyway."

It was the next to last session of the day, and the captain standing next to the machine was a Russian named Kisov. I call it a machine because that's what it looked like to me. It may have been a helicopter to Kisov, but it was like no helicopter I'd ever seen. The shape was more like that of a lifting body, and it had two sets of very stubby fins which couldn't really qualify as wings but seemed to be trying to. As far as I could tell, any resemblance it had to a real helicopter stopped with the landing skids and the rotor blades, but then I'm not a pilot.

"The specially designed rotor system and the aerodynamics of the craft make it suitable for use in either extremely dense or extremely rarified atmosphere. The aircraft has independent environmental integrity and will float, giving it the capability to operate from water as well as land.

"The Type One can carry a wide variety of weapons to fulfill its assigned wartime tasks. These include mini- and maxi-guns, air to surface rockets and missiles, air to air missiles, bombs, napalm containers, and 40mm grenade launchers.

"The Type One has a crew of only one, who must pilot, navigate, and be the offensive and defensive systems officers. He is, fortunately, aided by several high-speed computers and a greatly simplified fire-control system. In addition to fulfilling its primary wartime tasks of providing close air support and air superiority umbrella for SCAF ground troops, it can function as a light utility and transport or rescue craft. The Type One will carry up to fifteen combat-ready troops at speeds up to one thousand kilometers per hour. Range is not a serious factor since a nuclear-fueled sealed turbine system is employed for propulsive power. Now if you will follow me in groups of six or so, we will take a look at the inside."

The final item of the day was a look at the tanks. They're called armored fighting vehicles now, of course, and they come in two varieties—light and heavy. The light-armored fighting vehicle is a tracked, high-speed, nuclear-turbine-powered vehicle with five centimeter impervium plate. It weighs about fifteen tons metric and has a crew of three. Armament consists of a turret-mounted minigun and a 105mm low-pressure gun. There are twelve 40mm tube launchers located on the turret, which can launch smoke, gas, high explosive, or canister rounds. The commander's cupola is fitted with a Stoner GPMG and a Honeywell-manufactured fire-control system linked to the main battery. Maximum speed over level terrain is one hundred kilometers per hour. It has independent environmental integrity, floats, and "swims" at twenty kilometers per hour. It functions primarily in the role of infantry-support gun.

The heavy-armored fighting vehicle weighs forty tons metric and would probably have been considered a medium tank in earlier times, were it not for its fire power. The turret mounts four principal weapon systems: a 35mm maxigun for defeating aircraft and lightly armored vehicles and fortifications; a 105mm low-pressure gun of the same type as used on the LAFV; a battery of eight wallaby missiles with low-yield tactical nuclear warheads of about .5 kilotons each, useful on heavily fortified and wide-area targets; and perhaps the most important piece, a Gatling laser of gigawatt power. The commander's cupola mounts a minigun. If the five-man crew were to decide to take on a star-fleet-class destroyer, the odds would be just about even. It can be taken out, of course, but you've got to hit it in the right place, with the right punch, and you've got to *hit it*. And I mean first.

After the evening meal the squad training sergeants took over the troops and I went back to my cabin to get cleaned up. It had been a long day, and I would have preferred going to bed had I been given the choice. But I still had my meeting with the captain to attend. I took a shower, and after studying my face in the mirror, decided I needed a shave whether I felt like one or not. Since I didn't know if I should expect a constructive suggestion and discussion session or another ass reaming, I put on a class two uniform, psyched myself up to take a verbal slap in the face, picked up my notebook in case things broke the other way, and walked over to Captain Simms's quarters.

As I said, I was prepared for either eventuality, at least as much as I could be. I was not, by any stretch of the imagination, prepared for what greeted me at the captain's door. Simms was wearing a long white chiffon dress slit clear to the waist on both sides with a deep veed neckline. Her feet barely peeked out from under the bottom, and I could see she was wearing velvety-looking black shoes, fastened with a Velcro strap around the ankle, that had sort of squared-off toes and a three-quarter heel. She'd done something with her hair, and it fitted her like a fluffy battle helmet with red-gold bangs lazily hanging over her eyes. Cute, I thought to myself, but what I said was, "Sergeant First Class Anthony B. Fetterman, commanding Training Platoon Alpha, reports as ordered, Captain." I wondered who she had a date with.

She smiled and said, "Come on in and sit down, Tony. We're informal here tonight. I didn't mean what I said this morning to be taken as a direct order, it was merely a suggestion. I am glad you decided to come on over though."

Friendly suggestion, hell. If I hadn't showed up, she'd have nailed my ass to the bulletin board first thing in the morning. One thing I'd learned about Simms since I'd been in her company—everything she said was an order. If the gentle captain said "shit," you'd better start crapping. She might be a damned good-looking woman, but she was no cream puff. Her approach to combat training was strictly no-nonsense. So what if she looked good enough to be a silicone sister centerfold? Put a dagger in that young lady's hand and she was a real fool-killer. I knew that from personal experience because she did the hand to hand classes herself, and she'd dumped me on my butt more than once during the NCO preparatory sessions we'd had before the troops arrived. And I've killed more people than most folks have friends.

She waved me past her and I walked a few steps into the room, then turned around to watch her close the door. The dress fastened behind her neck, leaving her arms free and her back bare to the waist. It was a good back, I told myself—slim, well-muscled, with a nice light-brown tan. I wondered how much time she put in under a heatlamp to keep it looking that way. I had a pretty permanent tan from all the time I'd spent under Latin American and African skies, but even it was beginning to pale a little by this stage of the mission. Most of the troops were positively pasty white by now, except for the ones with the new cases of sunburn from the desert exercises. Her shoulders were flecked with freckles overlaying the tan, and I ran my eyes down her back and over her bottom. Very cute indeed. Nice ankles too.

She pointed at the couch and said, "Sit. Get comfortable. Can I get you a drink? You take bourbon and water, three to one, over ice, I believe." It wasn't a question, but I couldn't remember ever having drunk in her presence before. Someone must have told her.

"Thanks, Captain, I'd like one very much."

"I told you we were informal here tonight." She smiled. "I appreciate your sense of protocol and discipline. I'm especially fond of your sense of discipline, Tony. But as long as it's just the two of us, call me Lydia." It wasn't a request.

"Yes, Lydia, I'd like a drink," I said. I wondered what the hell she was up to.

She flashed a big smile and said, "That's much better."

I watched her walk over to a little cabinet set against one wall. Her walk was terrific. I studied her butt for a minute while she fixed the drinks, then took a quick glance around her quarters. Being a platoon sergeant, I didn't have a roommate, but I only had one room and had to share my shower with another platoon sergeant. Officers, I saw—or at least captains—got two rooms. I wasn't surprised that rank had its privileges, even in the Retribution Army, but I was surprised that SCAF would waste so much space. I suppose the idea is to make living in a ship for five years at a stretch tolerable, if not comfortable.

As she came over, I laid my notebook down on the coffee table in front of the sofa and took the drink from her hand. She sank down in an oversized red beanbag chair across the table from me. The front part of her dress fell between her legs, baring both of them to well up her thighs. She had great legs—slim, but not skinny. I suppose they would have been a bit too muscular for most guys I know to really have enjoyed them, but I've always been turned on by those kind of legs. You know the type. The kind a dancer or a pro tennis player or a track star has, or in this case, I reminded myself, the kind a soldier has. The way that dress molded itself to her made it obvious she didn't have anything at all on underneath it. She was wearing a shade of frosty silver-pink lipstick, not the deeper red that I preferred, but it went well with the freckles around her nose, gave her a little bit of a girlish look. I decided that whoever had a date with her tonight was one lucky son of a bitch.

"Tony," she said, "I trust you won't mind if I speak frankly.

This isn't for the record. Everything said here tonight is strictly between you and me. Is that clear?"

"Yes, Captain."

"I told you before, call me Lydia."

"Yes, Lydia."

"All right then. I've been watching you quite closely, Tony, and I must say that in these six months we've worked together, I feel I've come to know you quite well. Perhaps better than you know yourself."

Here it comes, I thought. After all this informal nice guy banter, I'm about to get my ass reamed anyway. If she's tried so damned hard to prove to me it's nothing personal, she must be getting ready to relieve me of my platoon. Well, fuck her, legs and all.

"What I'm trying to say, Tony, is that I like you, and I like your style—especially your style."

I like your style, but . . . I said to myself.

"I've observed that you are a strict disciplinarian, Tony. That's a philosophy I totally agree with. An army is nothing without discipline, and a soldier is not a soldier until he learns both to accept discipline and to discipline himself. Don't you agree?"

"I believe so," I said. I wondered where all this was leading.

"Good. I was sure you'd agree. Oh, God, Tony, you don't know what it's like trying to run a training company. With a combat unit it's different. At least there most of the NCO's and staff officers are professional soldiers. This outfit . . . well, if it weren't for you and Jenkins, I don't think I could keep it going. Do you have any idea what I've got to work with? My exec, First Lieutenant Cadin's chief claim to fame, is that he is an excellent administrative specialist. He has a combat record, but it is totally without distinction. Of my section leaders, only Second Lieutenant Vieta has seen combat. He was in on the Panamanian incursion, if you can call that combat. More like riot control I'd say. All he managed to do was earn himself the purple durple. Second Lieutenant Halladay is so fresh from the officer's academy, he still thinks of himself as an upper classman. Oh, he tries to hide it, but his squeaky new jump boots give him away, despite his best efforts to junk them up. Did you know he actually tarnishes his jump wings with candle smoke to dull the finish? You see, Tony, except for you and Jenkins, I simply don't have any professional help."

She paused and looked at me, apparently expecting some kind of response. I said, "I can see where it does put you in a difficult position, Lydia."

"Exactly. Here, let me get you another drink."

"Thanks, but no. Tomorrow's going to be another day, and besides, I'm keeping you from going somewhere."

"Nonsense," she said, picking up the glass. "I need another drink, and I don't like to drink alone, so you'll have one too. Besides, you're not keeping me from going anywhere."

She walked over to the cabinet and started to mix the drinks. Then she turned around and flashed me another of those dazzling smiles. Jesus, what teeth.

"What's more, I'm not expecting anyone either. No, Tony, I'm not going anywhere, and neither are you. Not just yet anyway."

She walked back over and sat down next to me on the sofa, crossing those wonderful legs of hers and pulling her knees up on the cushion as she handed me the drink.

"I think it was your professionalism that first attracted me to you, Tony," she said. "I really do admire professionalism. I've studied your 201 package, and you really do have an outstanding combat record. You got a Decoration Militaire and a Croix de Guerre for your services with the Belgian paras, and the Castle of Good Hope Decoration from the South Africans. The American government gave you a Distinguished Service Cross, a Silver Star, and two Bronze Stars, for, I believe the terminology was, various acts of service rendered. How did you manage to collect so many medals at your age, Tony? You must tell me sometime. I was rather disappointed to see, however, that you managed to get yourself shot up twice. How did that happen?"

"I made a mistake."

"And the second time?"

"Different time, different place, different mistake."

"And after the second mistake?"

"I didn't make any more. I decided it was healthier not to."

"Good. I like that answer. I trust you won't be making any mistakes here. Now about that problem you've been having with your platoon. I've decided that your basic approach is sound, but I think you need to toughen up the discipline a little. As I said before, I'm a very strong believer in discipline. These people we're dealing with are mostly thirteen and fourteen years old. They're still basically children. When a child is naughty, you've got to spank him. If you've got one who is causing you some particular problems, make an example out of him or her, maybe it'll whip the others into line."

"Are you suggesting that I publicly spank one of my troops?"

"Why not? If he deserves it? Though I suspect a flogging would be more in order. The Uniform Code of Military Justice still provides for corporal punishment in time of war, and we are in a state of war. If you've got one that's particularly recalcitrant, I'll be happy to administer the punishment myself. That way it'll be clear that it's being received for misconduct rather than as any personal vendetta you might have against the trainee."

"If that's what you wish, Captain."

"It is, and stop calling me Captain. In public I fully expect us to Captain and Sergeant each other to death. In the privacy of my quarters I expect to call you Tony and I expect you to call me Lydia. Now that we've taken care of that business, there's just one more thing to take care of. I've decided that I was unduly rude to you in our conversation this morning. I will not tolerate unnecessary rudeness in my company. Not even from myself. It detracts from discipline and is counter-productive to achieving training goals. Anyone guilty of such behavior must be disciplined. Severely. Do you understand me, Tony?"

"Uh, I'm not quite sure that I do, ah, Lydia," I said, though I had a hunch that I was beginning to understand her all right.

She reached behind the end of the couch for something, and then moving closer, laid it in my lap. I looked down at it. It was a black leather-covered riding crop.

"I've locked the door so we won't be disturbed," she said. "Discipline me, Tony. That's an order. And Tony, don't make any mistakes."

11

McAllif, Steven M.
Private, First Pathfinder Brigade, SCAF

Many of the assignments had finally been made, and all but four of our squad had been selected as pathfinders. The main reason was the cohesiveness and logic that we had displayed time and again. For example, we had carried Lara during the first run, all of us pitching in to help her. But during one of the hot weather training sessions, I'd gone back to the unit rather than rescue her, because the whole unit would have been in jeopardy if I'd tried to save her. Another time two squad members were left behind because the whole company would have been lost if we failed to capture a specific target. It showed judgment that was necessary for a recon squad to survive, that we could determine the best time to stick completely together, and that we knew the mission came first.

The new squad members were Richard Patterson from South Africa, Mary von Ehrlich, Daniel Flying By O'Rourke and Linda Zalaznik. Each one of them had demonstrated a certain resourcefulness required of pathfinders.

The final training mission called for cold weather warfare

practice in the simulator ship. The tactical situation was a
pathfinder team sent to find a suitable base camp and establish
a perimeter until a reinforced company could be landed. As
soon as the base was established, we were to make raids against
a fortified enemy. We could expect attacks against our base at
any time.

At 0530 we fell out in the cold weather gear which consisted of thermal underwear, a small battery-operated heating
suit, and white coveralls. Since the temperature would be
about −40 Centigrade, a light helmet had been provided. It
was not a space helmet, because it didn't keep the oxygen
in. It kept the cold out. Again we were using the laser training
aids.

We moved to the corridor that would take us into the simulator. As always, we expected an ambush. Rather than risk a
casualty, we used smoke on the corridor, fired a High Explosive
simulator grenade down it, and followed with the squad. We
made it to the other end, secured it as the ventilators drew the
smoke out, and formed for our briefing. Susan had been made
the permanent squad leader now, with Sergeant Marquette becoming her advisor. O'Rourke was the assistant.

The cold air almost knocked me flat when we entered the
simulator. Even with the thermal suit and the helmet, it was
like walking into a wall of ice. A wind whipped through,
carrying small white pellets that looked like nuggets of snow—
not the flakes of relatively warm snowstorms, but small pellets
that reminded me of hailstones.

The poly-foam was white. I could see some trees not far
away, but with difficulty because the helmet kept fogging. I
knew I wouldn't have that problem once we'd spent some time
in the simulator.

We fanned out, spreading across the frozen ground until we
could barely see each other. That way, if one of us was captured,
the rest had a better chance of getting away. We weren't supposed to get into any fights, and had been instructed to retreat
at the first sign of trouble. We were to find a base camp, not
engage the enemy.

Patterson came over the radio. "God damn it's cold."

"Knock off the chatter."

We moved into the trees, drawing together because we

couldn't see as far in the forest. We all stopped on the edge of a clearing, staring into the center of it, studying it but not moving into it. Susan waved at me and I slid over to her. She pointed to the left and made a circling motion. I began to move out. She sent Zalaznik in the other direction.

We met on the other side and crouched down, flattening against the hard, cold ground. There was still no movement in the clearing, and it was obvious there were no ambushes set around it. I stepped out of the trees and waved. A moment later the others came forward, avoiding the center of the clearing.

As she walked up, I looked at Susan and she shook her head no. The clearing was too perfect, and since Marquette had said we could expect resistance since they knew we were coming, it stood to reason they would know which area made the best base camp. That ruled out the clearing.

We moved forward again and found another. It wasn't perfect, but it was adequate. We moved into it the same way. There was no evidence of ambush or booby traps.

Half the squad broke off and set up a perimeter in the trees while the rest of us spent a few minutes setting up camp. Using the pieces of nylon we'd brought with us, we constructed a low, camouflaged tent. Without saying a word, Susan pointed to me and Mark, indicating that we were to work our way back toward the reinforced company.

In less than two hours we had the whole company assembled in the clearing, pickets established, and a dozen tents with heaters set up. As soon as we were warmed, we were sent out to locate the enemy.

Once again we spread out through the trees, moving slowly and carefully, aware that booby traps, land mines, and enemy sentries—any of which might be real by this stage of our training—could be near. The plan called for us to move 250 meters and then close in. When we regrouped, one of the new people, Mary, had disappeared. We could only assume she'd been captured.

Susan signaled that we were to retrace our steps, carefully looking for any sign of a struggle. It didn't take us long. Normally we wouldn't have pursued the enemy, but our orders called for us to locate them, and the easiest way to do that was to follow them. We separated into parallel lines, one following the trail and the other guarding the first unit from ten meters. By keeping low and moving slowly, we were able to find the enemy. Several of us wanted to attack because we could see Mary tied to a tree near the center of their compound. Susan shook her head, and we withdrew quietly.

Inside the base tents we could remove the helmets and talk. Fetterman was with us now, and we told him what had happened.

"Instead of making an immediate move, I felt we could do more by coming back, but I would like to hit them as soon as possible," Susan said.

Fetterman shook his head. "We're not concerned with your missing troop."

"But there is no reason to delay. A platoon should be able to take that compound."

Fetterman came close to smiling. "So you think you could take it, do you?"

"Of course. As I said, there were only three tents, and each of those was fairly small."

"All right then, you've got it. Take the first and third squads with you. There will be complete radio silence. Report back in one hour."

Susan was on her feet. "Let's go. McAllif, tell the squad leaders we move out in five minutes. We don't have any time to waste."

At the enemy camp Susan detailed one squad to attack each tent. One person from each squad was supposed to break off and try to get to Mary. We separated, set up, waited five minutes, and moved as one.

It went bad from the very first moment. They had been waiting for us. As we rushed the tent, I realized why Fetterman had smiled. Just because the structure on the ground is small doesn't mean the inside is small. Apparently there was some kind of underground system. The enemy poured out of the tents.

We fired as fast as we could, but the squad members were dropping quickly. I heard Susan gasp, "withdraw" and then fall. I turned and ran for the trees as she spoke. They stopped me less than a meter away. Mary had been simulated-killed in the very beginning.

At our base camp Fetterman seemed delighted. "You were getting a little too cocky. Everything had been going your way for so long, you forgot that you can make mistakes. Norton, you were so sure of yourself, and all you accomplished was the destruction of three squads. In a combat situation you would have destroyed the effectiveness of your platoon and hampered the ability of the company. You let emotion color your thinking."

"All I did was assume—"

Fetterman roared, "You assumed too damn much! You never assume. Did you think to check the surrounding terrain? Did it look as if more than a few people had been in the area? A unit the size of the one you encountered would have left a hundred traces, but you missed *all* the signs!"

The tanks came during the night. We had been told that the enemy wouldn't have tanks, but they were rolling up the left side of the perimeter almost before we knew they were there. One of the pickets had been able to trip the signal, so we knew they were coming, but we didn't have much time.

The flashing light inside the tent woke us. We rolled out of bed, slipped into our gear, and moved out. We didn't know who was coming or with what, only that the enemy was near.

I filled my position, about twenty-five meters from the tent, hidden near the trunk of a tree. Dead brush nearby concealed me, and I could hear someone moving toward me. He wasn't very good in the woods, making enough noise for a platoon. I didn't look directly toward the sound but to one side of it, because night vision works better that way. Vaguely silhouetted, I could see a man-sized shape moving slowly toward my tree. By the way he moved, I was sure he didn't know I was there.

Slowly he approached, looking around, trying to spot me or anyone else. I drew my knife, leaned against the tree so that no one could sneak up behind me easily, and waited. It didn't take long. He pushed the barrel of his rifle into the bush and I grabbed it in my free hand.

"Son of a bitch," I heard him mutter. He pulled again, trying to jerk it free. "Are you believing this?"

I wondered who he was talking to, but didn't hear anyone respond. I was hoping the enemy would think his rifle was caught in the branches of the bush. He slid his hand along the barrel, and when I felt him touch my wrist, I grabbed, pulling him off balance so that he fell forward. As he went down I simulated-killed him with the knife.

To the right I saw a laser rifle flash once, and it was answered by three more flashes. Firing suddenly erupted on the right, the lasers lighting the ground with their dim ruby glow. Another shape was coming from that direction. I flipped the lens that would illuminate the identification triangle on the suit of those on our side. We were all equipped with them, and unless the right combination of lenses was used, the triangle wouldn't show. It was our means of identification at night.

The shape came forward, moving toward me, apparently unaware of me. There was no identification triangle, so I flipped the lenses out of the way and waited. The new intruder tripped over my first victim, and as he fell to one knee, I simulated-killed him also.

Ten minutes later the lights overhead blazed, signaling the end of the exercise. When the two I simulated-killed stood up, I found that one of them was a member of our company. She had forgotten to attach the ID badge before she moved out. Later I discovered that Fetterman and the noncoms had told several of our people to circulate without the badges to test us. One or two of the pickets had refused to kill without seeing who it was if they came from the direction of our compound. I was commended for my ruthlessness while the others were given extra duty.

We had broken up the attack with very few casualties. The only mistake we made was not killing fast enough. We were told that we shouldn't wait for identification in the situation we were in. The ID badges should have been enough, and when they couldn't be seen, we should have killed.

The rest of the exercise went equally well. We were able to uncover one of the enemy's camps and destroy it quickly. At the end of forty-eight hours, the exercise ended and we formed in the corridor leading from the simulator. Everyone from both units was supposed to be there, and the noncoms made a quick head count. Three people were missing.

One was found in his bed. Unfortunately for him, he had been one of the first out of the simulator and hadn't waited to hear instructions. When searchers failed to find the other two, the heat in the simulator was turned on and sensors started sweeping the entire ship. It took nearly thirty minutes, but the bodies were located. Both had frozen to death, apparently because their suits had malfunctioned. Fetterman seemed to think it was their fault because they hadn't checked their equipment well enough.

As we were leaving the simulator, we received word that we were very close to our destination.

12

Masterson, Lara
Private, First Pathfinder Brigade, SCAF

We were in the rec center for what seemed like the millionth briefing we'd had. This one was different though—it would be the final Intell briefing before the invasion. The officer behind the lectern wasn't a very tall man, around 1.7 meters, but he had a stocky, solid look about him. He had dark hair, brown or black—it was hard to tell—and thick bushy eyebrows. The rest of his face didn't quite match somehow. Maybe it was the bright red handlebar mustache, I don't know. I wondered how he could ever coil it up inside a field protective mask, or even a space helmet. It wasn't until quite a bit later that I thought to wonder how he got around the grooming regulations.

"Good morning, troopies. Today's Intell briefing is brought to you by Peterson, and he is me. This thing on the wall behind me here is a three dimensional holograph of the entire universe, suitably narrowed down to the single insignificant planet we are concerned with. We received it by narrow beam transmission from one of our recon ships about an hour and fifteen minutes ago. So this is the latest info we've got. It's the good stuff you're getting. After the briefing feel free to ask questions or talk about it among your friends. We were going to classify it, but who are you going to tell way out here? All seriousness aside, let's get on with it, shall we?"

A withered old lifer looking like a zebra with all his stripes was seated on the stage to Peterson's left. He groaned audibly and shook his head.

"The photographs show no large oceans, but there are numerous lakes and several inland seas, probably the remains of the oceans we can't find. There are no mountains, but a lot of foothills, again apparently the remains of past ranges. There are some forests, but not many. We can see large deserts, but the majority of the surface is dry savannah, verging on desert, indicating that there may be some ground moisture.

"There are seven major cities, if that is the proper term, with at least a dozen minor ones surrounding each major one. Our sensor probes, strangely enough, do not show large biological concentrations in the city areas. This may be the result of some sort of shielding effect of the domed structures that seem to make up the cities, but we can't be sure. The size of the cities indicates that our bio readings are far too low. No real evidence of industrialization that we can see, though there are some indications of mining operations. We theorize that whatever industry there is, is housed within the major city domes. Of course, the outlying domes we think are smaller cities may actually be industrial complexes. No way to tell for sure until you get there.

"There are huge agricultural complexes surrounding the city domes, apparently sustained by irrigation, which would suggest a structured society based on the hydraulic theory of civilization development. In other words, somebody had to dig the damned ditches. But, of course, this is all guesswork anyway.

"For you night owls, I'm afraid there won't be much night. The planet appears to have a moon nearly as big as itself. The two revolve about an epicenter and keep each other well lighted. I'm afraid the best thing you can hope for is a total eclipse, which doesn't seem likely. In short, you commando chaps won't be sneaking up on anyone in the dark because there will be no dark, just an occasional twilight zone.

"Now for the sun worshipers—you're going to be getting plenty. Not only will it be light all the time, but there won't be much cloud cover either. Our probe indicates an occasional cumulonimbus, but they're few and far between.

"The temperature ranges from a toasty forty-seven degrees Centigrade at the equator to a positively frigid forty-two degrees at the poles. That's above zero, not below. The mean surface temperature is a balmy forty-five degrees, which is about as mean as you can get. With a polar temp of forty-two, there is, of course, no ice or snow, and we haven't been able to figure out where they get the cubes for their scotch. So unless they have air-conditioning, when you chaps and chapettes get to the city, there'll be a hot time in the old town.

"The big thing that bothers us is that there are no indications of surface transportation, no highways, roads, railways, obviously no significant rivers, not even a cow path, or a cow for that matter. Worse still, we've no indication of aerial transport, can't find any airdromes or landing fields, not even a helipad. One of my cohorts in crime theorizes that such facilities are concealed beneath the domes, or possibly under camouflage netting, if they're expecting us.

"Are there any questions at this point?"

I had fifteen or twenty I could think of, ranging from poison gas to poison snakes, but before I could speak a young second lieutenant in the back of the room stood up and shouted, "You sure we got the right place?"

"Fucking aay, tweety. The recon ship found the wreckage of the *Star Explorer* drifting about the planet, complete with a dozen well-frozen bodies."

"What about fortifications?"

"Who knows? We can't see any obviously identifiable fortifications. The domed cities may be fortified, or they may be nothing but forts, if this is some sort of outpost planet. We can't see any gun barrels or missile silos, but that doesn't mean they aren't there."

"I'm a little worried about sweating to death. Can't the cold weather suits be modified into cooling suits?"

Peterson started to speak, but the zebra stripes stood up. "I think I can handle that one, sir. I'm Chief Senior Master Sergeant-

Major Mifflin, the fleet armorer. There are some very good technical reasons why we can't make such a modification. The big one is that the heating elements in the suits are a series of electrical wires designed to generate heat, not cooling tubes designed to carry heat away. Even if they were, the heat exchanger necessary for such an operation would weigh about fifteen kilograms. You people will have more than enough to carry without it. Besides, while it's awfully easy to freeze to death at forty-five below, very seldom does anyone die of sunstroke. Be sure both your canteens are full and remember to take your salt tablets and you'll be okay."

"I sort of hate to ask this, but what about diseases?"

"We have some microprobes aboard the recon vessel and hope to be able to answer that one for you before insertion. I think that—"

Peterson was interrupted by someone who handed him a note.

"Well, I guess we won't be having those microprobe reports after all. The recon vessel has just ceased transmitting. We assume it has been destroyed. As for diseases, that'll be for the pathfinders to catch. If they live, fine. If not, we'll have to figure out something else before we send the rest of you in. The key thing, now that they know we're here, is speed of action. Everyone report back to your squad bays and pick up your gear. Pathfinders go to your transport stations and stand by. Pathfinders off in thirty minutes, the first wave will follow in one hundred thirty-five minutes. Well, boys and girls, the balloon goes up starting now. Good luck and good hunting."

Good God!

We were called to attention, the officers left, and we ran for our squad bays. I pulled my coveralls off and threw them on the bunk, figuring what the hell, they can gig me *if* I get back. I considered changing underwear but decided that with the desert uniform, web gear, and body armor, I'd be warmer than I wanted anyway, and opted not to wear any underwear.

"Jesus," I said. "I wish we had more time to prepare."

"Shit."

I turned and saw Steve holding a broken shoelace in his hand. Disgusted, he heaved his shoe at his locker door, then realizing he was going to need it, picked it up and started digging in his gear for a spare lace. He paused just long enough to glare at me.

"What the hell do you want more time for Lara, you've had five years?"

"I know. It's just that they sprung it on us so suddenly."

"Five years is one hell of a long spring."

"Oh, shut up. You can't even find a shoelace. Here, take one of these."

I made a quick weapons and equipment check, knowing we'd make at least a dozen more before the drop. I think I dreaded the drop the most. The high-speed shuttle ride pulling a lot of gees would probably be rougher physically, but somehow I'd never convinced myself that it made good sense to abandon a perfectly good aircraft in flight. We'd each made over two hundred jumps in the simulator ship, but somehow I knew the real one would be different.

We formed at the door and Susan made a check of everybody's equipment. Satisfied, she marched us down to the transport bay, where we picked up our parachutes. We buckled up, checked our jump-buddy's gear, and were told to mask up by Senior Platoon Sergeant Bocker. It seems somebody had decided that since we didn't know for sure about the diseases, it would be prudent to wear our field protective masks. Besides, they'd help protect our faces when we punched out of the shuttle, and the planning staff had decided it would be a good idea to dust the drop zone with CS. If the local populace had a physical system similar to ours, the irritant would help keep them busy while we were on our way down.

Sergeant Bocker was an old pro. He'd been in the service for close to thirty years. He was an ex-paratrooper, ex-ranger, ex-special forces, ex-everything from the old U.S. Army before it became part of SCAF. He'd fought as an "advisor" in South Africa, Uganda, Kuwait, and the Argentine, and had more combat jumps than the rest of us had total. After the final weapons and equipment check, he made sure everyone's mask was on tight enough that it hurt. He didn't want any dead bodies because of some Tau germ, and he didn't want anyone losing their mask when their chute popped and coming down wheezing into a CS filled DZ.

Finally the last checks had been made, the bone induction receivers and throat microphones of the helmet radios checked for the last time. We strapped into our individual ejection seats, made sure all the restraints were tight so we wouldn't lose an arm or a leg when we punched out, and took the D-rings firmly in hand. Bocker made the final walk-through and strapped himself in. After that there was nothing for us to do except sit in the darkness and watch the red light over the cabin door, waiting for it to turn yellow, and then fifteen seconds later green as the order came, "Eject, Eject, Eject." One and a half seconds after that we'd be blown clear of the shuttle by the explosive bolts and hydraulic rams under the seat rails, whether we were ready or not. We sat there, all sixty-six of us, waiting for that stupid light to change color. I remember thinking, "There's nothing left to do but pray," but I just couldn't do it. I guess I'd forgotten how. Then I felt the bottom drop out from under the ship, felt the shuttle's engines roar to life as a weight resembling an elephant rolled slowly down over my head and sat on my lap, and knew we were on our way.

13

McAllif, Steven M.
Private, First Pathfinder Brigade, SCAF

Instinctively I jerked at the D-ring to open my chute as I plummeted through space, almost forgetting the lessons I had learned in the simulator ship. If I had been unconscious or injured, an altimeter would have activated it at five hundred meters to keep me from smashing into the ground. The curtain of black that had fallen over me as I was ejected slowly raised, and I inhaled deeply, my lungs screaming for air, as I tried to clear my vision.

Below me there wasn't much to look at. Off far to the right was the checkerboard pattern of cultivated fields, and beyond them, the shining of a city dome. Directly below was nothing except the brown of dead vegetation and dusty sand.

Over me the parachute canopy was almost invisible. It was camouflaged so it would be hard to see from the ground, and the effect was so stunning that it gave me the sickening feeling of being suspended in the air by nothing. Around me I could see the other members of the recon platoons and pathfinder squads. Some were yanking on their shrouds so that they were swinging about, becoming hard targets. I was content to drift downward, less worried about being a target than of hitting the ground hard enough to break a leg if I were oscillating. Besides, I couldn't see anything moving, and no one was shooting at us. The planet didn't even seem inhabited.

As I approached the ground it was like dropping into a blast furnace. The hot air, whipped by a hotter wind, sandpapered my bare skin. My arms and legs broke into a sweat, and the sand clung to them like mud. The eyepieces of my mask began to fog because it wasn't seated right, and I lost sight of everything except what was close to me.

The sand was soft and broke my impact as I rolled to my shoulder on touchdown. The wind tried to fill my chute, but I was able to collapse it and gather it up before it dragged me away. I pushed the harness lock on my chest and felt the rig drop off, then picked it up, moving with it toward the center of the DZ so I could toss it on the pile already there. Without a word to Susan, or from her, I trotted to the perimeter to help with security. Most of the others were already down, but a few were still airborne, caught in the thermals and strange air currents that plagued our descent. I watched one trooper drift away from the DZ, suddenly seem to zoom upward until he was nearly out of sight, then begin his descent again. He finally hit the ground fifteen hundred meters away, out there alone where he could be an easy target for the enemy. If the enemy learned the actual size of our force, they might attack at once and overrun us with ease.

I keyed the mike on the short com and reported, "One down, bearing 255 degrees, one-five-hundred meters, approximate."

"Roger. Monitor progress."

While I stayed on the perimeter, watching for the enemy and the SCAF trooper trying to reach us, one squad of pathfinders was regrouping near the pile of parachutes in the center of the DZ. From there they headed north, found a flat, hard-packed area that could support shuttle landings, and requested that the remainder of the advance force join them. When they radioed their instructions to us, half of us moved forward. The trooper who had fallen so far away was making good progress and would probably reach the DZ in time to join the last section as it evacuated.

At the shuttle landing site we dug in. There was some light

scrub brush on the northern edge, and I took a position there, scraping the sand out of a tiny depression, deepening it. I widened it slightly and then crouched down. From there I could see over a click.

Ten minutes later I heard the sound of the first shuttle as it whooshed out of the sky, deafening me as it slowed and then rolled to a stop. Combat engineers swarmed out of the back carrying and pushing their equipment. As the shuttle lifted with a roar, they took over the duties of preparing the landing strip.

The sun was miserably hot, without mercy. The protective mask made the whole situation worse; it was becoming unbearable. My eyes stung from the sweat dripping from my forehead, and with the mask on I could neither wipe them nor my forehead. If I hadn't been afraid of a fatal disease, I would have stripped the mask and thrown it as far as I could.

As Susan made her way around the perimeter, telling us that we no longer needed the masks, the sun dropped lower in the sky. I had hoped that it would signal the beginning of a cool evening, but the heat was not dissipating. In front of me the flat plain shimmered as the sun continued to bake the sand. There was no movement now, as even the blast-furnace wind died.

Behind me more of the shuttles touched down, each bringing equipment, people to assemble it, and a few to add to the defense. We now had nearly five hundred troops surrounding the airhead, guarding the twelve hundred assembling equipment.

I'd been studying the landscape with its dried-up bushes and stunted trees for almost two hours when Susan came around again. She crouched near me, staring into the distance.

"You can take a break for some chow. Make sure you take some salt tablets," she said.

I didn't speak, just got to my feet, and keeping low, jogged toward the mess tent she'd pointed out.

Several squad members were sitting in the shade of a gigantic packing crate, eating. I sat with them, drinking half my water ration in one hasty gulp and immediately regretting it as knifelike pains stabbed through my head. As the headache faded, I tried to pull my wet shirt away from my skin, but it clung to me.

Lara peeled the skin from a fresh orange and shoved about

half of it into her mouth. Juice dribbled down her chin and onto her shirt, although she was already so wet that it didn't make any difference. She chewed quickly and gulped as she used the heel of her hand to wipe her chin.

"So far so good," she said as she forced the other half into her mouth.

I pushed the white mass that was supposed to be potatoes out of the way so that it wouldn't contaminate the rest of my food. "What does that mean?" I asked, not really caring.

"It means," she said, "we're down and set up and there's no resistance yet. If they wait much longer, we're going to own this place."

Mark folded his mess kit and put it away. He scraped at the sand so he could bury the food he hadn't eaten. "I hear there are six other airheads, and they're all in safely. This could really be a piece of cake."

"I wish they would hurry. I'd like to get back to the air-conditioning in the fleet," I said.

Lara laughed. "The man does enjoy his comfort." She slipped out of her body armor, unbuttoned her shirt, and took it off. She tried to wring it out but failed. She put it back on, but left it unbuttoned. "This is one miserable place," she said. "The asshole of the galaxy."

As I finished eating, Susan walked up. "I'm afraid we're going to have to remain on the line all night. They're going to continue to push to build up the airhead, so everyone is pulling triple duty. Tomorrow night we should have some tents up and be able to get some real sleep."

I'd barely reached my foxhole as the sun disappeared below the horizon. As the darkness closed in, I began to worry. In the twilight I couldn't see more than fifty meters, and I began to imagine movement just at the limit of my vision. It was never anything big or sudden, only a hint of movement, like someone trying to sneak through the brush. I strained to hear the dry crackle of leaves, but there weren't dry leaves to crackle and the only sound was the blood rushing through my veins.

Apparently I wasn't the only one who was jumpy. To the left I heard the bolt of a machine gun slide home, followed by the abrupt rattling of fire that died as quickly and unexpectedly as it started.

About that time the sky stopped darkening and began to lighten again. Far to the east, toward the horizon, there was a bright glow that made me think the sun was about to rise. Then I remembered the huge moon the Intell officer had told us about. It was gigantic, as he'd said, and in minutes it was almost like day again—a very cloudy day. I could see several hundred meters, and it was clear no one was out there.

A patrol of seven wormed their way through the perimeter, heading out to see if the machine-gun crew had hit anything or if there was anything for them to have hit. The rest of us stayed put, hugging the ground, waiting and watching.

After four hours on the line Susan came around again and relieved us. We were going to get a break of one hour, then have the easy duty of guarding the people assembling the tons of equipment being unloaded by the endless flow of shuttles.

Once again we all—that is all the people from my squad—got together at the large packing crate. I couldn't tell if it was the same one or not, and didn't really care. I found a cup of iced tea, declined the sugar, and then wondered where in the hell they had gotten the ice. Almost everyone was drinking it, or ice water, and we all avoided the beverages that contained sugar because that would eventually make you even more thirsty.

I rubbed my head and leaned back, closing my eyes. Lara sat down beside me and stroked my arm. "Steve, was that you firing?"

"Don't be stupid. It was a ways off from me, and it was a machine gun, not an assault rifle," I said, peeking at her.

Lara brushed sand from her knee. "Susan said that someone saw something."

"I figured that out all by myself."

"I told her I was surprised that whoever fired didn't get into more trouble because we're supposed to be quiet, but Susan said that since we were down and well established, it didn't make any difference, and besides, if the enemy didn't know we were down by now, a couple of shots weren't going to clue them."

"Are you planning to carry on a running dialogue, or are you going to be quiet?"

"I was only making a little conversation."

I closed my eyes again. "Well, make it somewhere else."

Not long after that I was told to guard one of the crews trying to assemble a helicopter brought down in three pieces that could be put together quickly. Then the rotor would be attached, which would take a little more effort because if they made a mistake it could spin away, leaving the helicopter hanging in midair.

Both the men and women of the assembly crew were stripped to the waist, and all were sweating heavily. Six of them swarmed over each helicopter, but once they got rolling, it didn't take them long to finish.

Almost as they completed the aircraft, a pilot ran out, inspected it quickly, and then cranked, its blades spinning faster and faster until it leaped into the air. Two others, which I hadn't seen built, joined it. They circled the perimeter once and then split up, heading across the savannah.

As scheduled, I was put back on the perimeter at 0400. The moon was beginning to set and the shadows closed in again, but with the helicopters overhead and the lights behind, I wasn't seeing movement near every bush. I watched them all closely, hoping for something to break up the monotony.

The sun reappeared shortly after 0500. The sky brightened slowly while the ground stayed wrapped in darkness. Then, almost as if someone had turned on a light, the ground lit up. As that happened, Susan came around again, telling me I'd be relieved in twenty minutes or so and should report to the mess tent.

When I got there, Susan was sitting on the ground, rubbing some kind of salve over her arms and legs, which were bright red with sunburn. She smiled self-consciously because of the stupid mistake she'd made. We had been warned a dozen times that the sun would burn us if we weren't careful, and she had forgotten. She ignored my question about it and told me to find something to eat because we had a new assignment.

One of the helicopter pilots reported that he had seen something about three klicks south of one of the domes. It hadn't been much, just a flash of golden hide as the creature disappeared into a shriveled forest. We were to locate the creature and determine if it was intelligent.

Quickly she told us we would be using standard squad tactics, then went on to explain what that meant, until Lara pointed out that we already knew standard tactics. Susan stood then, brushing the sand from the seat of her shorts.

"I want to stress one other thing," she said. "So far no one has made any contact with the enemy. This is the first report we have of any creature of any size. I want us to be very careful."

"How much local life has been found?" asked Mark.

"I'm not sure," responded Susan. "The only thing I've seen so far indicates that all the life is fairly small and stays underground to escape the heat of the day."

We disposed of our trash and walked to the perimeter. Before moving through it, we had a weapons check. Susan gave us the order to put the silencers on the assault rifles because at the airhead we didn't have to worry about the enemy hearing our gunfire, but we didn't want to advertise our location while on patrol.

The point man, Mary, trotted off, and when she was about a hundred meters away, the rest of us followed. The flankers were out about twenty-five meters away. We tried to keep to the little cover available.

The sun had climbed high into the sky and was heating the ground rapidly. The blast-furnace wind we'd run into yesterday began to blow again. The shimmering sand and bright light hurt my eyes, and I flipped down a filter to cut the glare. I couldn't smell anything in the air, or hear anything, except for a single bird cry. It was just us, the sand, the dried vegetation, and the sun.

Susan cut to the north, heading almost straight for a dome that hid one of the minor cities. At least that's what Intell told us. Moments later we caught Mary, who was crouched near a bare tree, staring into the forest. We fanned out around her while Susan formulated her plan. She sent half of us around the perimeter of the forest, circling the woods to the south and to the north as a blocking force to cut off the retreat of anything we flushed, unless it was a very large unit. The rest of us would move straight into the trees.

When the other half of the squad disappeared, we advanced slowly, entering the trees almost like the beaters in an African jungle film. We were spread fairly thin, moving slowly and quietly. The bushes, with their few brittle leaves rattling in the hot, dry wind, covered any sound we made.

About halfway through the woods we came to the others, crouched under the bushes and behind the trees, watching our progress. Since we hadn't found the golden creature, Susan decided we would continue our search.

When it finally broke cover, we weren't quite ready for it. I caught a glimpse of golden hide from the corner of my eye and dropped to one knee, spinning. I raised my rifle but couldn't get a clear shot. I heard a quiet, muffled snap and saw the creature fall forward, roll once, and stop.

It almost had to be the same creature the helicopter pilot had seen from the air, or its twin. The color was right, it was medium size, and it moved with the grace of a well-oiled machine. But it wasn't intelligent—at least we didn't think it was, because it looked like a large cat. I wondered if our built-in prejudice may have caused us to overlook the obvious because we'd been conditioned to expect humanoids as the intelligent life forms. This thing had run on all fours, didn't have any hands with opposable thumbs, as we expected of intelligent life, but did have paws. Susan checked the body carefully to make sure it was dead, then suggested we take it back to the airhead for the biologists in the fleet to examine.

We tied the creature's feet together and dropped it over O'Rourke's shoulders. "Yeah, let the dumb Indian carry the load," he grumbled.

"You killed it. You carry it," said Susan.

By mid-afternoon we were back at the airhead. The change there was amazing. It had expanded in all directions and the number of people in it had grown by thousands. The amount of equipment had easily tripled. Helicopters were flying in and out rapidly, kicking up huge clouds of dust and sand. Near the center of the airhead, off to one side of the runway now surfaced by the combat engineers—who'd used a reinforced Fiberglas to harden the strip—was a tent city.

Although Susan told us to grab some chow, most of us headed for the tents. Each of them was large, and since they all had the flaps down, I expected it to be sweltering inside. But it wasn't. Someone had set up an air-conditioning system, and it was surprisingly cool. That seemed to be the trigger, because we all exploded into laughter. We pushed one another aside, as if fighting for the best cot or to clear a space, several of us collapsing to the nylon floor, rolling around.

There was even a system where we could field bathe. It wasn't as pleasant as a steaming shower, but it did get the sweat and grime off. I suspected that we wouldn't have had the luxuries if there had been any resistance, but since no one had even seen the enemy, the brass topside was cutting us some slack.

After a quick shower I sat back on a cot, letting the cool blowing air dry me, watching Lara toweling herself after she had washed. I shouted at her, "Looks like I got my wish. You can thank me now if you like."

She walked over slowly, rolling her hips in a way she must have thought sexy. She tossed her towel to the side, letting the last droplets evaporate.

"I guess you did," she admitted reluctantly. "I've got a couple of other things I would like before I go handing out thanks. You think you could wish them up?"

"What's in it for me?"

She leaped on my cot, landing on her hands and knees. "I'm sure that we could work something out if you succeed."

"How about working it out in advance?" I said, rubbing the inside of her bare thigh. "I work better under pressure."

She laughed and slowly slipped away, then stretched out on my cot. "I never thought war would be like this," she said. "In all the exercises, we were always on the go, always being attacked or maneuvering or attacking, and so far all we've done is basically kill a kitty cat." She looked at me and said, "You're certainly not acting like yourself."

I was relishing the cool air, the dim light, and the comfort of the cot. "What does that mean?"

"Not much. Only that you've been awfully quiet, and more than a little irritable."

"So?"

"So nothing. You want some?"

I looked around. Almost everyone else was asleep or working on going to sleep. My body ached, and yet I felt good, except for my eyes, which felt as if they were filled with sand. "I don't know," I said carefully. "Let's sleep for a while first. We go back on duty in only a few hours."

After I said it, I was sorry that I had, but I didn't brood about it very long because I quickly fell asleep. Lara had beaten me to it, so I guessed she wasn't very upset about it either.

Although we'd been scheduled to go back on the line at 0400, they waited until 1000 to wake us. The schedule had been shifted several times during the night as more people poured into the airhead. We were to the point where there were almost too many troops and too much equipment for the airhead to function efficiently. Before we had to fall out, we were given new, clean, modified uniforms.

Going outside this time was worse than walking into a blast furnace. I shivered once or twice as my body tried to acclimate itself to the sudden temperature change.

After eating, and a briefing that told us we would be scouting the approaches to Lesser Dome 1-6, we spent the time cleaning our weapons, learning the lay of the land from a series of aerial photographs the pilots had made, and studying the maps created by computer. Susan attempted to brief us on the terrain and what to expect, although no one had really seen any of it yet. The dome had protected the city from photographs, and apparently from any of the other sensors the fleet had, so we were still operating without anything concrete.

Just before we left, we had a quick meal and there was one more weapons check. Always another weapons check! When we were ready to go, we were issued several hundred extra rounds of ammunition, and that stirred a lot of speculation. We didn't like it, afraid of what it meant, but were told it was only a precaution. So far we had been on the planet's surface nearly seventy-two hours and had found no sign of intelligent life, except for the domes and cultivated fields.

We started out about two hours before sunset. According to what we had been told, at least seven other pathfinder squads were moving at the same time for seven other lesser domes. About an hour behind us, following our path, was a company of rangers. If we made it to the dome without contacting the enemy, we would hold there and wait for the rangers. Once they were in place, we would enter. If we got into trouble, the rangers would be there to provide immediate help. Not far behind them would be a Para Amphibious Infantry maneuver battalion. They would occupy the dome once it had been cracked and secured.

On the way we saw nothing, heard nothing, and stirred up nothing. I wondered how a planet that didn't seem to have much life, either intelligent or not, could destroy our space vessel and then a recon probe. There had to be something we were overlooking, but I couldn't figure out what it was.

The dome loomed ahead of us, reflecting light onto the surrounding terrain. There was a slight rise to one side and we worked our way up it. Once we were near the top, we halted. The flankers moved in and the rear guard caught up.

Susan knelt in front of us and spoke quietly, almost like the coach trying to arouse the team before the big game, finishing her speech with, "We'll form our perimeter here."

It seemed she wanted to say more, but couldn't think of it. She just added, "The rangers will be here shortly."

It was just before sundown when Susan creeped to my position to say, "Be ready to move out in ten minutes. We're going to look at the city."

"Where are the rangers?"

She nodded behind her. "They're down there. Once we move out, a platoon will fill in here. The rest will take up positions defending this rise." Without another word she left to alert the others.

14

Kisov, Vasili
Captain, Third Aviation Battalion, SCAF

The first thing I noticed was the bright light filtering through the hatch of the shuttle after it had landed. The second thing was the heat. It struck me almost like a physical force. Sweat sprang onto my forehead, and my shirt was soaked in seconds. Silently I cursed the safety officer because he had decreed that all helicopter pilots would wear long-sleeve shirts to prevent bad burns in the event of flash fire. I fumbled for my sunglasses with one hand as I shaded my eyes with the other.

There wasn't much for me to do while they were unloading my helicopter and before they began the process of assembling it. I watched some of the troops setting up and expanding the perimeter, and envied them their short sleeves and shorts, but they were all wearing body armor, and that had to be more uncomfortable than my flight uniform.

The crates containing the pieces of my aircraft were off-loaded and stacked away from the airstrip. I walked over to examine them. There was no apparent damage, since the outside of the crates seemed to be intact. I considered prying the lid, but didn't have the tools to do it.

"This one yours, sir?"

The man was one of the combat engineers. He wasn't wearing a shirt and had taken off his knee socks, and still he didn't look cool.

"Yes. It's mine."

"We'll get on it right away." He turned and waved to several others. "Let's go."

The rest of his crew came over at a trot. I couldn't believe they could move that fast in the heat. Even the women were wearing the absolute minimum, only their shorts. I wondered about the logic of that, for either sex, because of the real possibility of attack, not to mention the probability of sunburn. But the troops on the perimeter were supposed to give the engineers time to get to their body armor and weapons, and the sunscreen issued was supposed to prevent sunburn.

With their help, it didn't take long to get the helicopter put back together. I checked the control cables carefully, the engine-mounting bolts, and the oil levels in the transmission. Once they were completely finished, I climbed up on the head and examined the rotor system minutely. If I lost that, there wasn't a whole lot I could do to recover.

We pushed the helicopter to the side then, and I sat in the shade of it to wait for the next move. The sun went down, the sky darkened slightly, and the moon leaped up, bathing us in a new, bizarre light.

The first flight meeting was called at 2300. We were told we would fly recon and that each of us would be assigned a specific section of land to search. Then we were handed computer maps showing our assigned sectors.

I didn't pay much attention after I found out what was going on. Most of these briefings, even when we had an idea of what the ground and enemy looked like, were ridiculous. They had even brought in one man to give us a weather briefing, as if we had studied enough of the planet or the weather patterns to be able to predict anything. But we had to sit there and listen patiently because he was a colonel.

Of course, we didn't have to listen quietly. Brown began

the opposition by asking the time of official sunset.

"There is no merit to that question, Lieutenant," he was told, "because it is light all the time."

I decided to pick up the ball and run with it. "Excuse me, but I believe the lieutenant was wondering if we could expect a severe change in thermal air currents after sunset and if moonrise would create different cooling problems."

The weatherman turned to me. "Ah, yes, I see. I didn't understand the question."

He rattled on, trying to answer Brown but unsure of how to do it. The more he talked, the more we realized that he didn't have any idea of what he was talking about. I thought about asking all kinds of questions, but decided the kindest thing I could do was let the subject die a quick and natural death.

The weatherman was followed by the mandatory safety officer. I wondered what the brass was thinking about. The safety officer wasn't even a pilot, and he was going to tell us how to be safe pilots. I noticed that no one seemed to be paying attention to him because he was only a lowly lieutenant.

I checked the helicopter once more before take off. I wanted to make sure the filters were still clear, that the control linkages were still tight, and that the engine deck was still clean. Since we had no real schedule—simply get up as soon as possible— I delayed long enough to find an assault rifle. Our equipment list didn't call for one, but I wanted it anyway.

It was uncomfortably hot when I finally cranked. The outside air temperature meant that I had to be careful not to overheat the turbine during the run up. I lifted off, climbed steeply while circling the camp once, then turned to the north. If there was anything of interest moving anywhere, I figured it would be close to the dome.

Just being at the controls, watching the ground slide under the helicopter, and listening to the sound of the blades whipping the atmosphere seemed to relax me. Earth was no longer several light years behind me, but seemed much closer, almost below me. There were no lights on the ground other than at the airhead, and the moon was a hell of a lot bigger than it should have been, but I didn't care because I was flying, and not sitting in a ship in space while someone else did the piloting.

Far in front of me, three or four clicks away, was a city dome. I didn't want to fly close to it until I had to. We didn't have any idea what kind of antiaircraft defenses the enemy might have, so I tried to avoid finding out by staying clear. I turned to the east and slowed, so I could watch the ground better.

I flew outbound for several minutes, turned to the south, back toward our base camp, then banked to the west to make another sweep. I passed over a scraggly forest with nothing moving in it and only a few real trees. There were no animals hiding among the trees or near the dome or in the desert, and certainly nothing with any intelligence. That bothered me, and I wondered if there had been some kind of disease that had wiped out all the animal life; and if there had been, I wondered if it was still potent enough to kill us.

Below me something flashed and I kicked the pedals, turning abruptly so I could get a better look. I slowed, then lowered the collective so I could get closer. At the edge of the forest I saw a golden creature, but couldn't tell if the gold color was hair or tanned skin as it ducked under a bush, apparently to avoid me.

Just as I passed over the bush, the golden creature broke from its cover and raced deeper into the forest. As it had begun to run, I jerked back on the cyclic, trying to stop all my forward motion. I shoved the collective to the stops and kicked the pedals hard, trying to get a better look, but the being had eluded me. I had the impression that it ran on all fours, but I wasn't sure.

I dumped the nose, adding power, then started a slight climb, and once it was established, pulled a light pencil from my pocket. I had to let go of the collective to do that. Using my left hand, I made a mark on the electronic map display fastened to the holder strapped to my thigh, so I'd remember where I had seen the golden creature. Since there had been only one, and since I wasn't sure if it was intelligent, I went back on patrol.

For another hour I flew back and forth over the desert areas, working my way toward the airhead. I didn't see anything else on the ground, but I did almost hit a bird. It wasn't very large, and the colors ranged from a dirt brown to a muddy brown, but it was a bird. I chased it for several minutes, but it dived into a tree and I decided it wouldn't be wise to follow.

The moon began to drop toward the horizon and the ground to blacken. I turned back toward the airhead, then remembered I was supposed to take video of the dome. If there was any intelligent life on the planet—and the domes, among other things, suggested there was—the best time to find it would be the darkness before sunrise. Maybe they would turn on some lights. I knew that a match could be seen at five miles on a clear night at sea.

I dropped the collective and dived for the ground. I leveled at one meter, used the night-vision goggles which turned the twilight into green and eerie day, and banked to the north, heading straight for the dome.

As it popped into view I scanned it, but could see nothing behind it. Just as I came to it, I yanked back on the cyclic and climbed up the side. Looking under me, I could see only the dull shape of polished metal gleaming at me. There were no lights visible through it. Maybe the entire population went to sleep at dawn, or maybe the dome was opaque.

My orders only called for a quick sweep for photographic purposes. Although I couldn't see anything, maybe the infrared camera could. The cameras and sensors came on automatically, recording everything as I flew over.

When the photography and surveying was done, there wasn't anything left to do. I climbed to two thousand meters for the return flight, so there would be little chance of the enemy knocking me down with small arms, assuming their weapons had the same range restrictions as ours.

I still didn't understand the whole thing. We had yet to encounter anyone or anything. We had found plant life and scattered evidence of animal life, and the domes suggested intelligent life, but so far there was no rock-hard proof.

Ahead I saw the lights of our base camp. Even that now looked strange and out of place. Not only were they the only artificial lights I'd seen, but you normally didn't advertise your presence with a bunch of high-intensity work lamps. But, then again, we hadn't seen anyone, and we'd been on the ground for quite a while.

I entered the bludgeoning traffic pattern and landed. After

shutdown and check-in with the people in operations, I went over to the chow tent. Most of the other pilots were there already, drinking tepid coffee. I found a cup and sat down.

Brown stared at me. "Where the hell you been?"

"Out and about. You see anything?"

He smiled. "Only for a moment or two. Thought I saw someone moving through the brush, but he or it was gone before I could get turned around and back to him."

I took a swallow of the coffee and made a face at it. "That's about all I saw."

Brown pushed his cup away. The day was already getting uncomfortably warm, as if it had ever really been cool. "I'm going to get some sleep," he said.

I watched him walk away. "I wonder if they want us to go up again soon?"

Dominick stared into his cup as if he had found something alive and interesting in it. He said, "If you're smart, you won't ask. You'll wait for them to come and get you."

15

Masterson, Lara
Private, First Pathfinder Brigade, SCAF

We did a preliminary EM scan of the dome area, but the sensors didn't indicate any concealed weaponry. That didn't mean the place wasn't surrounded by all sorts of nasty stuff, just that if there was anything there, our instruments weren't calibrated for it. Susan ran through a last check with Marquette, and we waited for the sun to drop below the horizon. The darkness fell like a curtain, and we flipped down the passive night filters and moved cautiously toward the dome.

The advance was a success, as far as it went. Nobody stepped on a mine, nobody stumbled over a trip flare, and nobody fell in a pungi pit. Unfortunately, when we got to the dome rim, nobody could find an opening either.

Since we only had forty minutes until the moon lit up the landscape, we didn't have time to recheck the entire dome to see if we'd missed the door. It was probably just as well since it would likely have been guarded or booby-trapped anyway. We tried digging underneath the dome, but after fifteen minutes it became apparent that wasn't going to work. We settled for melting a hole into the dome wall below ground level with thermate—thermal putty.

The building—if that was the right word—that we'd cut into, seemed to be one huge room. We figured it would be about right to open the dome just below ground level, but we were wrong. There was a faint glow of light from the walls and ceiling, and even without the night-vision filters we could tell that the floor was about seven meters below us. After the rim of the hole cooled, we dropped a rope through and Mary, who was point, dropped down it. She sank into the floor up to her waist.

"The whole damned place is full of grain," she said. "It's some kind of storehouse."

Susan looked at Marquette. "What do you think, governmental stockpile?"

"Hell, I don't know. It could be a civilian storage bin, a governmental stockpile, or maybe we've stumbled into the back room of a bakery. We don't even know if they have a government, or a civilian populace for that matter. That's what you and your squad are here to find out, Corporal."

We dropped three more people down the rope, and sent a sample of the grain back for analysis with one of the guys from Beta squad. Three minutes later Richard Patterson came back to the rope to report finding a ventilation grate and a recessed area in one wall that could be a door. The rest of us dropped down the rope, and Gamma squad moved up to the hole.

We did a scan on the door, but found nothing. If this had been something simple, like a combat assault, we'd have taken the safe route and bypassed the door by breaching the wall, but this was supposed to be a sneak and peek operation. If we could figure out how to use the door, we had to try it. If a few of us got blown up in the process, well, that was what we got paid for. Besides, as Fetterman would have reminded us, it'd be our own fault for missing something.

When the instruments couldn't tell us anything more, Linda Zalaznik and I got the questionable privilege of going over the door with our fingertips and eyeballs. As far as we could tell—and supposedly we were the experts—it wasn't wired or hinged. After testing it carefully, we decided it was set in groves cut into the wall itself, designed to open by sliding straight up,

and secured from the other side by some sort of cruciform
locking bar. We could see three different ways of opening it.
Thermate, plastique, or a High Explosive grenade, all of which
were apt to be a bit messy and/or noisy.

The ventilator duct showed more promise, and after a scan
we pried the grating off with a couple of combat knives. We
moved into the ventilator system, and Gamma squad moved
in after us, leaving exit security up to the rangers. If all was
going according to plan, Delta and Epsilon squads would be
moving in too, two and a half clicks away on the other side of
the dome. Once all four squads were inside, we were supposed
to split up, Gamma working around to the right to recon and
link up with Delta, while we worked left until meeting with
Epsilon. Beta squad would remain outside the dome to act as
HQ and liaison with the rangers and the PAI maneuver battalion.

Our orders were simple enough. "Make a reconnaissance
of the southwest quarter of the interior of Lesser Dome 1-6.
Bring back any available enemy printed material. If possible,
effect the capture of a human intelligence resource, or if not,
kill one of the enemy and bring the body and personal equipment back for analysis. If possible, bring back enemy weapons
for analysis. Maintain radio silence. Do not engage the enemy
if contact can be avoided. Leave no trace of your passing."

The only possible fuzzy area was the "human intelligence
resource." We didn't know if the enemy was human or not.
Hell, we didn't even know if the enemy was here or not.

The ventilation system opened into what could best be described as a street lined with shops. It was more like a wide
corridor really, crisscrossed above with catwalks and elevated
roadways. We waited in the ventilators for fifteen minutes,
watching the street. Nothing moved.

Finally Patterson and Ehrlich dropped out of the ventilator
and sprinted for the building directly across the street. They
slid up against the wall on either side of the open doorway,
glanced both ways down the street, and dived into the shop.
Nothing happened. Five minutes later Mary appeared in the
doorway and shrugged her shoulders.

Mark and Wendy went next, taking the building across the
intersection from the shop. It was an instant replay of the first

venture. Thirty minutes and ten shops later we began to get
scared. No, that isn't the right word—Fetterman wouldn't have
approved if he'd been there. Cautious. That was the word.
"Become afraid, and you'll make mistakes. Make mistakes,
and you'll die. Never let your fear control you. You control it.
When you realize you're starting to fear, become cautious.
Concentrate on being cautious, and you won't make a mistake.
Don't make any mistakes, and you'll stay alive."

That's the way he'd put it. Well, right now we were being
cautious as hell.

Each squad put a sniper team up on the catwalks. Communication was becoming a problem so we punched up the
shortcom on the helmet radios, but didn't use them. We'd
transmit only in an emergency. With a power setting of .25,
nobody over 250 meters should be able to hear the transmission
anyway.

We searched the shops again, thoroughly this time. There
wasn't any question of what had happened to the enemy. The
only question was when the enemy would happen to us.

The shops provided few clues. They were a combination of
the vaguely recognizable and the totally incomprehensible. One
might have been a barber shop or a beauty salon, or both.
Another appeared to be some sort of jewelry shop. It held a
number of assorted stones, crystals, and pieces of quartz of
various sizes, shapes, and colors, in addition to what could
have passed for bracelets, necklaces, and even whole belts of
different kinds of shaped, hammered, and engraved or inlaid
metal. It was our first real indication that the indigenous population possessed a knowledge of metallurgy. It was a bit more
primitive than one might have suspected from a race capable
of knocking down our space probes. At least it seemed primitive
by our standards.

A lot of the shops seemed oriented toward craft-type production. They didn't seem to be shops in the sense of a place
you'd go to buy finished goods made at some distant factory.
Most of the goods appeared to have been made right in the
shops themselves, sort of like the old neighborhood tailor shops.
There weren't any tailor shops, however. There really didn't
seem to be any clothing stores at all.

One of the shops was full of various sizes and shapes of

edged weapons. They ranged from a little, clean, straight one—
about the size of a large pocketknife—up to some that could
best be described as a broadsword. They were double- and
single-edged, serrated, some with a large blade and as many
as five or six smaller ones. None of them had folding blades
though. A few seemed to come with sheaths, mostly of hammered metal. Patterson and Ehrlich got into an argument over
whether the place was a sporting goods store or a museum.
Mary said it wasn't a sporting goods store because it didn't
have a cash register. Richard countered by saying that that was
stupid because we didn't know what Tau currency looked like,
or even if they used currency. Besides, the place was too small
for a museum. Mary reminded him it might not be, since we
didn't know how big the Taus were. Richard pointed out that
a pygmy wouldn't likely use a broadsword. Susan broke up
the bickering by telling us we'd been sent to do a recon, and
since the locals weren't going to obligingly present themselves,
it was time to go take a look around.

We moved out in a modified, standard search formation—
two-man point trailed at a discreet distance by a two-man fire
team, three-man command element, and two-man rear security.
We only had one man on the left flank however, since it was
mostly taken up by locked storerooms. That left two men on
the right flank and one on the overhead catwalks.

We advanced slowly, checking each shop or building, being
alert for alarm wires and booby traps. We found neither. A lot
of the shops seemed geared toward food production. The dome
itself had been more or less surrounded by irrigated fields fed
by a system of unknown origin. One large building seemed to
be a sort of mess hall. It had a number of long tables with
benches made out of some type of fairly heavy stone, not too
unlike concrete.

Our rate of progress was steady, but not rapid. We'd been
in one of the enemy's cities for over two hours, on a street that
appeared to have seen frequent and recent use, and yet we'd
seen no sign of any living creature. We might be green troops
when it came to combat, but we weren't total fools. You can
train some pretty mean people in five years time, and we'd
trained in conditions just this side of hell. SCAF PAI had lost
seven percent of its total troop strength to training fatalities,

and had another fifteen percent injured. Most of those had recovered and were duty fit, but those figures didn't even count the small shit like broken ankles and sutures under five stitches. What I'm trying to say is, even though it was a recon, which normally implies a certain amount of speed, we had the entire night to work with, and we were on *their* home ground. We didn't want to make any mistakes. We couldn't afford them.

We reached the appointed rendezvous point with Epsilon squad and still hadn't sighted the enemy. We didn't recognize the rendezvous point's appearance, of course, since no one had ever seen it before, but out of twelve sets of calculations from the twelve members of the squad, we all agreed we'd come the proper distance, and Marquette concurred.

Physically the terrain was a T-shaped intersection, the tail pointing in toward the center of the dome. We searched the buildings for 250 meters around, then deployed in a U-shaped defensive perimeter about the intersection. If anything went wrong, and we got cut off or came under fire, we'd blow one of the grain hatches, make our way through the bin, and breach the outer dome wall at ground level with rifle grenades. Then we'd extract through the breach with ropes and grapnels.

O'Rourke and I were stationed on top of a hardware store that seemed to feature the production of agricultural tools. I say seemed to because they differed sufficiently from shovels and hoes to make a positive identification impossible, but given the irrigated fields and the grain bins, and the general shape of the tools, it seemed the most reasonable explanation.

I flipped up my night-vision filters and snapped down the clear visor on my helmet. Though there didn't appear to be any streetlights, the entire area was softly illuminated, and the light was of just the right intensity to make it questionable whether you could see better with your own eyes or with the filters. Dan and I were positioned at a corner where I could watch up the tail of the T and he could see back the way we'd come, along the street and past the bins. We were fairly close together, with our feet touching—an old Special Forces trick— so that to a certain extent we covered each other and could be sure the other was still there, not taken out by someone sneaking up from behind.

Perspiration had soaked my uniform as thoroughly as if I

were emersed in a bathtub, but as I scanned the street below, I shivered slightly. At first I attributed it to a reflex reaction to the situation we were in—plenty of evidence that the enemy was around, but no sign of him. After a while, though, I began to realize that the air temperature was somewhat cooler than it had been outside the dome. It must have been close to 30 Centigrade, but that was still enough of a difference for my body to notice it. It could only mean that the dome was air-conditioned, a logical enough fact—but why 30 instead of 20, one could only guess. Perhaps it was simply the temperature at which the locals were most comfortable. Just because we'd prefer 20 degrees didn't mean they'd have to. It struck me suddenly that it was possible they could have just as easily preferred 40 or 50 below or a hundred above. We might have been quick-frozen or broiled the instant we breached the outer dome wall. Well, being a soldier always did have its risks. It would be nice, however, if the brass would occasionally tell us about them in advance. Maybe they figured if we knew, we wouldn't play the game anymore. I don't know why they worried. Go AWOL? Twelve light-years from home? Not likely! In all fairness to SCAF command's intellect, though, maybe they just hadn't thought of that contingency.

We waited until Epsilon squad was ninety minutes overdue. There were four possibilities: one, they hadn't been able to gain access to the dome, which was improbable, given their thermate; two, they had reached the rendezvous point before us and left before the appointed time, but then their TAC advisor would have shot them; three, they'd gotten lost and hadn't been able to find the RP, but they'd have to be complete fools, and fools didn't get to be pathfinders; four, they'd run into trouble.

We couldn't wait any longer. We pushed in toward the center of the city, keeping to the rooftops and catwalks as much as possible, staying in whatever shadows we could find. We didn't check every building anymore. Susan and Marquette figured the risk of bypassing someone was outweighed by the risk of running into booby traps or an ambush if we moved up the street checking every building. The apparent absence of the enemy had put the operation into a different light. Absence could mean ambush; stealth became the best security.

About halfway in toward the center we came to the compound. Unlike most of the buildings, which were butted up against each other, the compound was set off by a roadlike circle of open space running around the outside of it and a high wall topped with what looked to be broken glass. There was a heavy gate similar to the doors of the grain bins, and what looked like watchtowers at each point of the pentagon-shaped outer wall. The place was crisscrossed by catwalks, and the area below was compartmented into five-sided chambers and narrow corridors. Steve said it looked like a zoo because of all the bars over the tops of the chambers and corridors, but I knew the only kind of animals that had ever been kept in those cages had been the kind with two legs, assuming the enemy had legs. I'd seen pictures of Alcatraz before.

The cages were empty now, as empty as the streets below, and we moved on past the compound, toward the center of the dome. The mission seemed to have taken on a quiet urgency now. Too much had gone wrong. We were here because an Earth ship had been attacked and destroyed nearly thirty years before, and we'd lost a recon vessel coming in, but there was still no sign of enemy activity, no planes or tanks or soldiers other than our own. We'd landed unopposed and now were pushing in toward the middle of a dome-protected city that must have had a population in excess of fifty thousand, and we couldn't even find a dog alive. Not that we expected to find a dog, but something should be living here. There were plenty of signs of recent habitation, but no inhabitants. I think we all wanted to get the mission over with and get the hell out.

We were near the center of the city when we came to the park. It was a large circular area, with grass that was more blue than green, and trees. There were a lot of the low scraggly bushes and scrawny trees, like we'd seen outside, and about a dozen that were more like real trees. They looked sort of like a spruce or pine and had large pinkish-white flowers. In one area there was a sort of amphitheater with a walkway running out among the rows of benches. Near the edge of the park we found the monument.

It must have stood fifteen meters high, and looked like it was made of obsidian. It had two eyes made of some kind of red crystal which seemed to have a light of their own, and it stood atop a huge cube of cut stone which might have been marble. The figure had a head like the big cat we'd killed the day before, wings like an eagle, and a body that was almost, but not quite human. There was a row of triangular plates running down the back and along the top of a dragon's tail. It had a belt like one of those we'd seen in the jewelry shop, with a broadsword hanging from it. The hands were four-fingered with a thumb, but were webbed. One held a massive rectangular shield, and the other held something that looked more like an old-fashioned sidewinder missile with a handle on it than anything else. I didn't think a shield and broadsword would be much of a match for assault rifles and grenades, but that missile thing bothered me. I had a feeling that if this was what the enemy really looked like, we could be in for a rather unpleasant time.

After the monument we moved quickly. Our primary concern now was getting out safely. Nobody knew how much bigger than life the monument was, and recon or no, nobody really wanted to find out, at least not this deep into the city's interior. We paused only to check the buildings that seemed the most interesting from the outside. We found one that seemed to be a bakery. It didn't have any cakes or cookies or doughnuts, and the loaves on the shelves were off-colored and funny shaped, but the smell of fresh bread was unmistakable. Equally unmistakable was the fact that some of the loaves were still warm to the touch.

At least after the bakery we were sure of one thing: Wherever the enemy had gone, they hadn't been gone long. The warm bread made us more cautious, and we started checking each building again. Two buildings down from the bakery, on the other side of the corridor, we found a curious sort of shop. It had a lot of cylinders, of various sizes and diameters, which seemed to be rolled out of leaves of some kind. They varied in color from light through dark brown, and from a pale green to almost a yellow. We took several of most of the types as samples and a couple of whole leaves from the back room.

We were near the rim of the dome when we found the factory. Only it wasn't a factory. It was a power station. But, of course, we didn't know that until we got inside. We stopped to check it out for two reasons. First, it was easily the largest structure we'd seen, except for the compound. Second, we could hear the hum of dynamos even from the outside. All of which implied a technical order somewhat higher than anything else we'd seen, and for that reason we stopped. It was a good thing we did.

All the steam turbines and pipes and regulators without any boilers suggested the application of geothermal energy. It seemed kind of a waste, with all the sunshine the place had, but maybe the locals had never bothered inventing the solar cell.

We'd completed our search of the ground floor and were working our way toward the rear of the second level when a flash of golden movement caught my eye. It was back near the far wall, in among a maze of pipes and generators, and I couldn't see it clearly. I just caught a glimpse, and then it was gone. The color had been about right for the cat we'd shot, and remembering the head on the monument, I wondered briefly if we'd already killed one of the enemy and didn't know it yet. I keyed the mike for the shortcom.

"Masterson. There's something moving in back of floor two. Bearing zero-four-three degrees."

"Damn it, Masterson, you'd better be sure."

"I am."

"Okay. Hold until we're deployed. Marchetti and Martinez, secure second-floor exits to ground. Patterson and Ehrlich, secure outside exit. O'Rourke, take McAllif and Zalaznik and move on line with Masterson and Korsumaki. Noonan and Desoto form on me for the cover element."

There was a brief pause of about five seconds while I must have sweated off five pounds and aged five years, then the shortcom crackled again.

"Okay, Lara, we're set. Move it when you're ready."

I glanced to my right, where O'Rourke had filled in. He gave me the okay with his thumb and fingers, and I motioned Linna Korsumaki forward with my left arm.

We moved slowly toward the rear wall, weapons ready. Nothing happened. We were almost to the rear now, and I was beginning to sweat—no, to get nervous. I'd been sweating ever since I blasted out of the shuttle. There was no doubt in my mind that I had seen someone or something moving back here, but if we didn't find them, him, or it, I'd be lucky to get away with a thorough ass-chewing for breaking radio silence. I needn't have worried. From the left came the sharp clatter of the bolt going full auto on Korsumaki's silenced submachine gun. Almost immediately I could hear the slugs screaming and pinging off the rear wall. I glanced toward Linna, but couldn't see what he was shooting at. Then I heard the deeper, flatter clanking of an assault rifle firing semiautomatically, and ahead of me, a pipe exploded in a cloud of steam. From the other side of the cloud I heard a scream, then silence. I flipped the selector on my rifle from semi to full, sidestepped the steam, and slid cautiously around the edge of the generator. Flat on her back in a little pool of blood lay what seemed to be a human female, stark naked, with a bullet hole between her breasts.

It was so unexpected that for a second or two I just stood there, then the training took over. She'd been tall—almost two meters, and her skin was a rich golden color, almost the same shade as the cat's. She had thick black hair long enough to hang below the waist, full black eyebrows, and very long lashes. I said she was naked—well, not quite. She was wearing some kind of wristlets made out of shiny metal, and sandal-like shoes with straps that crisscrossed their way up her calves and shins and fastened under her knees with a metal pin. She had a plain metal belt, like those in the shops, and a knife in a metal sheath hung on it, next to a little pouch made out of the same stuff as the sandals. It might have been leather, but it had a pebbly grain to it more like lizard- or snakeskin. I took the knife and covered her with my rifle until Dan and Linna got there. I was pretty sure she was dead, but I checked for pulse, breath, and heartbeat while they covered. She didn't have any.

I shook my head. "Nothing. She's dead." I looked at the knife. It was about eighteen centimeters overall, with an edge on the bottom and halfway up the top. It wasn't really a fighting dagger, the blade was too thick and broad, but it could have made a passable combat or utility knife. "Who shot her?"

Linda stepped up. "I did. Guess I should have tried to get her alive, but she was heading for that ladder, and I was afraid she'd get away. She'd seen me, and I didn't want her telling anyone we were here."

"You did the right thing," said O'Rourke. "Wonder why she was running around nude?"

I looked at the sandals and the belt. "Maybe they don't wear clothes, or maybe—"

"Damn!"

I heard a loud whang, followed by a clatter. I looked up sharply, to see who was swearing. It wasn't any of us. Then we all heard scuffling coming from the other side of a circuitry box. It was cut short by three quick, muffled cracks.

We slipped around both sides of the box, weapons leveled. Steve was leaning against some pipes, holding his pistol in his right hand, his left palm pressed against his side, blood coming from between his fingers. A meter and a half away on the floor lay another female, naked as the first, with a knife just beyond her fingers.

"Steve, you okay? Here, let me look at that."

"Nothing a bottle of peroxide and five or six stitches won't take care of. I don't think she got deep enough to hit anything important, but I don't ever want to try again."

He gestured at something that looked a little like a pipe wrench lying on the floor. "She took a swing at my head with that thing, missed fortunately, but she got my Stoner. Then she made a pass at me with the knife and I shot her. She dead?"

Dan grunted. "Definitely. When SCAF promises you an expanding boat-tail bullet, they deliver substantial results. Did you have to shoot her so many times?"

"It seemed a good idea at the time."

O'Rourke keyed his mike. "O'Rourke. Two dead enemy, possibly civilian. We've got one wounded." He looked at me.

"Not serious," I said, shaking out a dressing and applying it to Steve's wound.

"McAllif's the casualty. Not serious, but we'd better get him to a doctor."

"Roger," said Susan. "Let's get the hell out of here before anyone else shows up. Can you transport the bodies?"

Dan looked at the mangled body on the floor and shrugged. "If they don't fall apart. It'll slow us down some. They're a pretty good size."

"Better bring them along for the Intell boys. We can always ditch them if we run into trouble."

"Understood."

"My Stoner okay?"

I picked up the sawed-off machine gun with the grenade launcher under the barrel. "Seems all right, Steve. I'll carry it for you."

"Give me my weapon back. I'm not an invalid, just wounded a little."

"Don't be an ass," I said, slinging the Stoner. "Here, 'wounded,' lean on my shoulder."

"I can walk," he said. But he couldn't. He took about two steps before his legs sagged under him. I caught him just in time. "Guess maybe I'm a little more hurt than I thought."

"You'll live."

Linda and I got on either side of him and put his arms over our shoulders. Dan picked up the woman and tossed her over his shoulder in a fireman's carry. Linna got the other one, and we took Susan's advice—we got the hell out.

We didn't encounter anyone else on the way, and we extracted through our original entrance to the dome. We had to take Steve and the two bodies out in basket litters, which was a little tricky, but some clever person had sent for a rope ladder, which saved us from having to hand over hand it.

There was a dust-off waiting to evac wounded, and we loaded Steve and the two bodies aboard. It wasn't really a medivac, but it wasn't really a gunship either. Oh, it had Gatlings and rocket pods hung on it, but there was a cargo hold plenty big enough for the three stretchers and a medic. They carry wounded, and the troops—when we don't have to walk—and provide about all the close air support we get. So far we'd walked and hadn't needed any close air support. They don't fly well inside domes.

After we had Steve on his way back to the hospital, we hunted up Platoon Sergeant Bocker to make our initial report before going back to be debriefed by Intelligence at the airhead. Bocker got good news, bad news, and no news. The good news came from our squad and from Gamma. Both had made a good recon, come back with valuable tactical information, seen no military equipment or soldiers. We'd brought back two bodies for the Intell boys to study, and that was the best news of all. The bad news came from Delta. They encountered "insurmountable obstacles" and had to terminate their recon. Translation: A short way into the interior they'd run into a solid wall dividing the dome. Thermate wouldn't burn it, and they couldn't use plastique without risking the whole mission. Attempts to bypass the wall were futile. Three times they withdrew from the dome and reentered from another location, but their entire quadrant was honeycombed into cells, each surrounded by the same sort of stuff as the wall. The no news came from Epsilon. They hadn't kept their rendezvous with us, and they hadn't extracted with Delta. They hadn't been heard from, which could have been the worst news of all.

Bocker was content to leave the analysis of most of the stuff we'd found up to Intell, but when we showed him the cylinders of wrapped leaves we'd found, he sniffed them carefully, examined them, then tucked eight or nine of the largest dark-brown ones in his map case.

"Guess I'll wait until Intell has analyzed the others before I smoke one of these, just in case they've poisoned them, but I just can't see letting the rear echelon commandos get all the good stuff."

Zalaznik looked at him questioningly. "Why would you want to have the flyboys lay down a smoke screen on those things, Sergeant?"

Bocker laughed. "No, not smoke them, *smoke* them. You ignite one end and place the other end in your mouth. Then you suck in on it, and then exhale, and it sort of relaxes you."

We all looked at him with faces ranging from horror to disgust.

"They're made out of tobacco," he said. "People called them cigars. They used to be quite common back, oh, a hundred and fifty or so years ago. Some people didn't like them, and they were called antismokers or nonsmokers. People who used them were called smokers. The antismokers got pretty powerful in Congress and Parliament and the other old governing bodies we used to have, and tried to get them outlawed, but they didn't have quite enough votes or influence. Then the Exchange came along, and after the various world dictatorships and juntas seized power, people were forbidden to grow tobacco because what arable land was left was needed for growing food. Only the rich and powerful could afford bootleg tobacco."

"I remember reading about the tobacco once in a history book," said O'Rourke.

Bocker sighed, "Ah, those were the days. Havana cigars, Beam's Choice whiskey, medium-rare steaks." He spoke as though he'd actually tried them all.

"Steaks?" I said. "You mean those thick slices of dead cow people used to eat?"

"The very thing. Though I think they came from steers. People got milk from cows. My grandfather told me all about them. When he died I found a metal can in his trunk in the attic. It had never been opened, and it had twenty-five cigars in it. They were called Dutch Masters cigars. My mother wanted to give them to a museum, but I took them instead and ran away to join the army. Smoked the last one of them nearly twenty years ago. Longer than that, if you count Earth time. You kids can all be thankful the governments decided to permit the production of alcohol to continue. Couldn't really stop it, I guess. As long as there's grain, there's going to be booze.

"Norton, you take the squads back and debrief with Intell, then have them shower and get some breakfast and rest. I'll keep Beta here for another hour or so, in case we hear from Epsilon, and then come on back. You people take my advice— don't smoke any of those things until part of them have been checked out, but don't give up all of them either. You've lucked into a once in a lifetime chance to smoke a cigar. You probably won't get another. Here, let me see those leaves again. Just as I thought. I can't be positive, but I'd say the green-looking ones are marijuana. They're supposed to have an effect like alcohol. I've never had one, but I intend to try one soon. Give me a couple of those."

Bocker tucked three of the marijuana cigars into his map case and sauntered off toward the ranger HQ. For a second or two we all stared after him, sure he must have snapped over losing Epsilon and gone nuts, then Susan was telling us to form up and get moving back to the airhead, and all I could think about was how good that shower and a few hours of sleep were going to feel.

16

Kadrmas, Karen
Major, First Armored Corps, SCAF

We were ready for a fight the moment we rolled down the tailgate of the transport shuttle. Notice I do not say we were spoiling for a fight, or we were looking for a fight. I said we were ready for a fight. There is a subtle, but definite distinction. It really doesn't matter though, because at that precise moment we were smack in the middle of the SCAF airhead, which by this stage of the game had been named Zech Combined Arms Base in honor of the hapless captain of the *Star Explorer,* and the only thing around to fight was the heat, which the air-conditioning was doing a rather nice job on.

The traffic was heavy enough that MP's were running all over the place trying to keep things going smoothly. It took us nearly twelve minutes to make the six hundred meters from the shuttle to the quick-set concrete revetments of the tank park. I sent Anjanette, one of my weapon systems specialists, over to Base Housing to find out where we were supposed to be billeted, and then walked over to Armor HQ to find out what was supposed to be going on when. The combat engineers had been busy fortifying everything in sight since the initial landing, not so much for protection against air attack—that's what the Point Air Defense Systems were for—as for protection against ground attack. I found Armor HQ seven-eighths buried in a sandbagged concrete and impervium bunker a good five hundred meters from the tank park.

Armored Corps is composed mostly of Israelis, for the simple reason we've got more combat experience in armor than any other country around. About twenty percent of the combat arm is made up of West Germans and South Africans, who are supposed to be more adept at armored operations in forests and bush country than we are, and about ten percent are Russians, who are supposed to be the cold weather experts. But desert has always been the traditional battlefield of armor, and from the looks of things, this op was going to be pretty much our show. The best brains of seven countries had designed our tanks for us, and had we been going up against any army back home, I'd have almost felt sorry for their tankers. Since nobody seemed to know exactly what we were up against here, I was a little less arrogant.

The two MP's at the door asked me to check my weapons before going in, and I smiled sweetly and told them to go to hell. They got rather surly after that, and I decided that rather than kill them over something so trivial, I'd play their stupid little game. I handed over my Kalan, my four hand grenades hung on my web gear, and my SCAF-issued pistol. Apparently they didn't consider my combat knife a dangerous weapon, though I had no doubt I could take out both these clowns with it. They stood there looking smug because they'd won their little victory, and I flipped them both the finger and walked on down the steps into the bunker. I still had a grenade in each of the side pockets of my nomex suit, and great-grandfather's Browning was tucked securely next to my skin in an orthopedic shoulder holster under my left armpit.

When I'd cracked the hatch on my cupola and crawled out of *Haifa Hannie*, the heat had just about bowled me over. By the time I found the command bunker, my nomex was soaked through, and when I finally opened the door at the bottom of the stairs and stepped into HQ, the air-conditioning damned near drove me into shock.

Colonel Levinson, the brigade commander, was in conference with Brigadier Shapiro, the Corps chief of staff, and I
had to wait about fifteen minutes until he came out. An orderly
brought me some coffee I didn't really want, but after I'd gotten
used to the air-conditioning, I decided to drink the stuff anyhow.
At least it was warm, and after walking into this refrigerator
from outside, I needed to get my heart started again.

Levinson finally came out of the meeting and waved me
into his office as he pushed past me.

"Can I get you a drink, Karen?"

"Not if it's coffee. I just had some, and it's even worse than
the stuff they serve aboard ship."

He smiled. "How about a Coke then?"

"I could do a Coke." I watched him walk over to a small
refrigerator in the corner and open it. It must have held about
three cases of Coke, and little if anything else. Levinson was
a teetotaler, he didn't drink beer or alcohol, but he did drink
Coke. Know any Israelis who don't? He opened two of them
and handed me one of the moisture-beaded bottles.

"Come on over to the desk and have a look at the recon
photos. Intell got together with Army HQ and sent pathfinders
into all the lesser domes last night for a look-see. They all
report finding pretty much the same basic layout inside each
of the cities. We've used their photos and sketches to put together a series of composite photo maps and line drawings that
we believe represent a typical interior arrangement. We've got
to do this one pretty much cold, no help from handy libraries
or secret agents. That means no good maps and no tour guides.
Also we're not even positive that the major domes follow the
same layout as the lesser domes, because so far we haven't
been able to breach the dome wall on one of the major cities.
If you want my opinion, I think they're going to have to use
a nuke to crack it. One of the new, high-powered, relatively
clean tactical jobs ought to do it. Neither the engineers nor the
artillery boys are ready to admit defeat yet, but I'm willing to
bet Army HQ will approve helicopter emplacement of a Joshua
warhead sometime later tonight."

"Shapiro tell you that?"

"Let's just say it's in the air."

I looked at Levinson and saw him grin broadly. He had an

almost piratical look about him that was heightened by the black eye patch he wore over his right eye. I'd known him before, back in Israel, when as a young lieutenant I'd commanded my first tank platoon and he'd commanded another company in the same battalion. The eye patch, I knew, was more than just affectation. He'd lost that eye to a fragment from a terrorist bomb that had killed his wife and son and left his daughter a cripple. I wasn't all that surprised he'd been retained on the IDF Tzahal active roster, but I'd been mildly surprised to find he'd been brought into SCAF. I was also pleased. First, he was somebody I knew. Second, he was a damned good tanker. Third, he cared about his troops.

His smile dimmed, and he was suddenly serious.

"There is some bad news you should know about, I think. Not all of the pathfinder troops sent into the lesser domes last night have returned. As of this moment they are officially listed as missing in action. The unofficial line is, of course, that they are presumed to be lost to enemy action."

"How many?"

"Nine squads."

"And none of them reported being attacked?"

"Negative. They were operating under radio silence. They should have broken it in the event of attack, but no messages were received. We know only that whatever happened, it must have come very quickly. Whether the disaster that befell them was natural or the result of hostile troops we cannot say. We do, of course, assume the worst."

"Were they all lost in the same general area?"

"No. One each was lost in lesser domes 1-3, 1-4, and 1-6. Two were lost in Lesser Dome 3-9. The real disaster was in Lesser Dome 5-12, on the far side of the planet. The pathfinder platoon there lost everything but the headquarters squad."

"Damn. What about the squads that made it back okay? Did they take any casualities?"

"Only the group from Lesser Dome 1-6. I understand they had one man wounded, but not seriously."

"So at least we've got a look at the enemy then."

"Maybe, maybe not. We still can't tell for sure."

"You mean he didn't get a look at who or what hit him?"

"Oh, he got a look all right. It's just that the person who

attacked him may have been, probably was, a civilian."

"I take it by your use of the term *person*, that the hostile was human in appearance?"

"Indeed. The squad brought back two bodies. The locals seemed quite reluctant to come along quietly, and had to be neutralized. The bodies appear to be human females, could pass for identical twins, and ah . . . they don't seem to wear clothes."

"They run around naked?"

"It seems to be their preferred style. A helicopter pilot who got shot down this morning managed to wound and capture one before he was picked up. She could have been a sister to the first two, and was just as naked. The medicos patched her up, and Intelligence is trying to make some sense out of her now, but so far they can't even figure out how to get her to speak. She doesn't seem able to."

"Doesn't all this nudity strike you as just a little strange for a people advanced enough to be the folks we're looking for?"

"A bit of a puzzle, I'll agree, but let's not forget that they seem advanced enough to knock down a helicopter or build a dome we can't crack with conventional explosives. And, of course, there are the missing squads to consider."

"Yes," I said. "There is that."

"At any rate, Army HQ is planning a big push for zero-six-thirty tomorrow. Our cookie is Major Dome 1. Pathfinders will go in first to reconnoiter. They'll have an air umbrella provided by elements of the Twenty-first Close Support Wing. If all goes well, they'll be backed up by the Ninth PAI Division, and you won't have anything to do until resistance of sufficient magnitude is required to warrant your special skills. If all does not go well, you'll spearhead the infantry drive into the city. In the meantime other units will take Lesser Domes 1-3, 1-6, 7-8, and 4-12, and Major Domes 3 and 7. Army HQ has announced their intention to ignore the other domes unless they prove bothersome, and to nuke them if they cause us any headaches."

"What's the size and population particulars on our target?"

"About the same size as New York City, or to be more precise, about the same areas as Long Island, Manhattan, the

Bronx, and Queens put together. Population could run as high as seven or eight million."

"And we're supposed to take that with one crummy division and an armored brigade?"

"Those are the orders."

"They smell."

"Don't they always?"

We grinned at each other.

"So naturally I have decided to send your battalion in first," he said.

"Naturally. Is there any more good news I should know?"

"Only that the administration brass hats neglected to provide billets for the Armored Corps. I'm afraid your troops will have to sleep in their vehicles tonight."

"Terrific. They'll like that."

I picked up my gear from the MP's at the door and started back to give my troops the bad news. As I got close enough to identify individuals, I could see that Anjanette had already come back from Base Housing. I could also see, from the disgusted way the troops were knocking around ammo boxes, helmets, and anything else that wasn't bolted down, that she'd already broken the news to them. Zilikovski, my exec, strolled up to meet me.

"The troops aren't very happy about the housing situation, Major," he said.

"I know, Val, but they don't know the half of it yet. Have the company commanders meet me at my tank in fifteen minutes, will you? I've got some good news and some bad news. Some very bad news."

"We are going into a city? There is going to be street fighting?"

"Afraid so."

"The devil take their eyes. Do they not know what a tank is for? It is made for open ground, not for conducting bus tours!"

"They know all right. It's just that there's a shortage of infantry, and we've been elected to make up the difference."

"Which city are we going into?"

"Major Dome 1."

"That is the biggest. What other support will we have?"

"Just our brigade and the infantry."

"Humph! And you said there was a shortage of infantry. How much infantry is there to be?"

"One PAI Division and a pathfinder platoon."

"Holy Virgin, Mother of God. They *have* gone mad."

"I think that God is likely to have very little to do with it," I said.

"It smells," he said.

"Don't they always."

17

Masterson, Lara
Lance Corporal, First Pathfinder Brigade, SCAF

We had returned to the high ground outside Lesser Dome 1-6, and there still wasn't a cloud in the sky. I could feel the sunshine on my back, burning through my body armor and shirt. The whole sand dune had been baked for hours before our arrival, and I could feel the heat radiating up and through the front of my uniform, as if I were in a giant broiler oven.

As I stared at the hated dome, McAllif crawled up to tell me, "They've started in. So far no resistance, but they just breached Major Dome 1. We go in five minutes." He crawled off to alert the ranger platoon dug in behind us. Susan was in the middle of that formation with Fetterman, and as McAllif reached her, she raised her arm and signaled us forward. Using the standard combat techniques that had been drilled into us during our five years in space, we worked out way to the hole we'd made during the recon, moved fifteen meters to the left, and burned a new opening. We secured that until a squad of rangers joined us and the rest of their company filled the positions they vacated. Half of our squad dived through the opening, dropped to the grain, and tried to dig in.

Once we had secured the bin, which meant we were inside and no one had seen the enemy in there with us, Fetterman and his rangers came in behind us. We worked our way across the grain to the door or hatch or whatever, and when we failed to find an easy way to open it, Susan ordered us to stop fooling around. O'Rourke and Korsumaki started pressing thermate against the sides of it, and after lining the whole thing, they stepped back. O'Rourke ignited it without a word or waiting for further instructions, and it burned briefly before the door fell in.

I had expected to find the shops on the other side, as we had the day before, but all I saw was another huge bin of grain. Susan, O'Rourke, and Fetterman studied it for a long time while the rest of us tried to cover them and not look as if we expected the enemy at any moment. Finally Susan looked back and silently pointed to half of us. She waved to O'Rourke, nodded at the far door, waved us forward, and stayed behind to coordinate with Fetterman and the rangers. As we crawled through the door, we tried to spread out, for what little good it would do us in the confined space of the bin. When we reached the other side, the rest of the squad leaped in with us.

It was anticlimatic because all we found was another hatch which was a carbon copy of the one we'd just burned through. We couldn't open it either, and O'Rourke just shrugged as he pulled out his thermate and began patting it along the perimeter of the door.

As he lined the hatch, the rest of us formed a half circle around it, our weapons held at the ready. We didn't expect trouble because we hadn't found any trouble yet, but we couldn't be sure that this door wouldn't open onto a street full of Taus just waiting for us.

O'Rourke looked over his shoulder and said, "Ready?" to no one in particular. He didn't wait for an answer as he ignited the fuse. The door burned, and some of the molten remains fell into the bin, causing the grain to flare. Patterson tried to smother the flames by pushing a huge pile of grain into the fire. Smoke poured out and Patterson was forced to use his canteen, dribbling water into the smoke.

As last of the hatch collapsed into the bin. O'Rourke dived

through the opening, followed closely by McAllif and then Korsumaki. The corridor was as empty as it had been the last time.

I took a position near the door to the shop-lined street we'd found during our first recon. Most of the squad had taken places in the doorways on either side of the hole we'd made. Across the street I saw movement, but it was only Steve crashing into one of the shops, looking for Taus.

Once we secured the immediate area, I waved Fetterman and the rangers forward, into the second bin. Fetterman came through first, keeping low and diving to one side, as if it was the first time anyone had penetrated the bin. Then another ranger came through, leaping in the opposite direction. As the third man entered, Fetterman and the second ranger moved farther to the sides so they could cover the rest of the rangers.

When the first ranger squad was in the bin, Fetterman moved about halfway across the floor and they tried to dig in. Actually they forced their way into the grain so that they were partially protected by it. I suppose Fetterman was thinking he could move in any direction fastest from that position.

The second squad moved into the bin, following the same tactics. It was an amazing display of discipline. After watching us and then the first squad, they could be reasonably sure it was safe, but they still followed the manual.

After they were in, Fetterman and his people began moving toward us. I was about to shout for him to take his troops up the street, away from us, when the man in the middle of the bin screamed in surprise as he slipped from sight. Everyone turned toward the sound, and we could see the grain shifting and dropping. It looked like the center of an hourglass just after it had been turned upside down.

Fetterman took one step forward and I heard some of his rangers yell, "Get out! Get out!"

Another man disappeared, and a third struggled as the flow of the grain caught him and began to drag him away. He tried to swim free, and although he slowed himself, he was pulled relentlessly to the center.

Fetterman spun toward the door and fought to reach it. There was no sign of fear or panic on his face or in his eyes, only the strain of muscles as he tried to free himself from the trap.

Behind him the rangers were all trying to reach the closest door. One pulled a rope from his pack and threw it to the man in front of him. He tried to pull himself free, but the grain was irresistible and he was sucked under.

Fetterman hadn't made much progress, and was trying to locate his rope. A ranger near him threw her rope, but he missed it. She hauled it back and tried again. Just as Fetterman caught it, the grain swept over her and I saw the rope tighten. She hadn't let go, and as Fetterman tried to yank her free, the rope snapped.

I was amazed Fetterman even tried to save her, not because I didn't think he was brave, but because it looked impossible. After always saying that mistakes would kill in combat, Fetterman had just made the obvious mistake of trying to save someone who was beyond help. If he'd kept moving or had thrown his rope to me instead, we might have gotten him out. Now it seemed too late.

The grain around his feet was rushing toward the center and he lost his balance. He fell forward, toward the door, and tried to scramble to me, but the grain was sucking at him, trying to drag him into the center of the bin as a riptide would try to suck a swimmer out to sea. When it became obvious he wasn't going to get out, he looked me in the eye and shouted, "Well, shit!"

There wasn't a lot that I or anyone else could do except sit there and watch as the two squads disappeared into the grain. Since we were on solid ground, I wasn't worried about sinking out of sight, but I wondered how the rest of Fetterman's platoon felt. They were knee deep in grain in the first bin.

I activated the shortcom. "O'Rourke. Masterson. You'd better come back. We've lost two squads."

One at a time they fell back, forming a loose semicircle around the door. Without even looking at me, O'Rourke whispered, "What happened?"

I explained it quickly, as best I could, but he looked at me as if he was stupid. I ran through it again, adding a couple of details to make it clearer. He turned so he could stare into the grain bin, then turned his attention back to the street.

"I guess we'll want to find another route back."

"Easy enough. We'll use the ventilator like we did the last time."

O'Rourke looked through the door again. "Everything solid on the far side?"

"It was a minute ago. I'm sure they've pulled back."

O'Rourke centered himself on the hatch and touched the button for the shortcom. "Norton. O'Rourke."

"Go."

"Say instructions."

"Roger. Tie a lifeline to one person and have him explore the grain bin. We'll do the same at this end."

O'Rourke didn't say anything. He seemed to be waiting for something. Desoto finally shrugged and said, "I'll go. I'm the lightest."

"You sure you want to?"

She shrugged again. "Not really."

McAllif laughed, but there was very little mirth in his voice. He said, "I thought we taught you not to volunteer for anything."

She glared at him but didn't say anything.

O'Rourke pointed to Patterson and McAllif. "Take opposite ends of the street and keep watch." He turned to Korsumaki. "Take the shop just across from us. We'll put Desoto through in five minutes."

Desoto stripped her web gear and put down her assault rifle, but kept her knife and pistol, one in each hand. We tied two ropes around her waist because we weren't taking any unnecessary chances.

O'Rourke asked, "You ready, Lori?" When she nodded almost imperceptibly, he said on the shortcom, "We're going in."

He moved to one side of the door and I took a position on the other, so we could lower Desoto to the grain. She crouched there momentarily, probing with her foot, waiting for the grain to suck her under as it had the rangers. On the far side a ranger was lowered and went through the same motions. Both began to circle the perimeter of the bin, along the walls, walking carefully, as if they thought they would drop through the floor.

When Desoto reached the end of her rope, she swung back and began the process all over. When she'd checked out as much of the wall as she could, she walked toward the center, feeling her way carefully. Finally she headed back toward us, a look of relief on her face. Once she and the ranger were out of the bin, we withdrew through the ventilator, as I'd suggested, and then back to the ranger platoon.

It took them a little while to figure out what to do because most of the equipment they needed had been left with the fleet. No one expected us to need a pontoon bridge, given the geography of the planet, but we could have used one now. There were other things we needed, most of them at the airhead, which were going to be brought up as quickly as possible.

A helicopter flew in a pump. As they unloaded it, one of the ranger squads moved to the opening in the dome and a woman, using a grenade launcher, fired a hook carrying a length of rope through the first bin and into the second, or maybe through it. Two members of the squad shed part of their gear, buckled their D-rings to the rope, and started to crawl along it.

The plan called for them to burn a couple of holes in the metal walls above the grain and fasten ropes to it, forming an inverted triangle. When the bridge was ready, the rangers walked across the bin without coming close to the grain. Each carried a section of tubing, and once everything was connected and the end of the tube lowered, they began to suck the grain out of the bin. It took nearly an hour, but when they were done, they had found three bodies and the pointed bottom of the floor, with only a little grain left in it. The sloping sides carried the grain to the center of the bin, where the doors—when opened like the iris of a camera—let the grain fall through.

The ranger squad leader made her report and was told to drop several thermate grenades into the bin, to burn a hole through the floor. She said that it wouldn't work because they'd roll to the center, burning only a small hole.

Someone arrived with a flamethrower, and five minutes later we were crawling back into the bin, staying away from the cooling edges of the hole. We could see a floor only five or six meters below us. Susan had us circle it, and when it cooled enough, we dropped several ropes through it.

As the rangers entered the bin, several of us edged to the

hole and waited. Below we could see grain scattered on the floor, but no bodies or signs of life. Either Fetterman and his people had survived and moved off, been captured and forced off, or were dead, their bodies dragged off.

I watched Mario Marchetti and Wendy Martinez disappear through the floor of the bin. Two others followed immediately. Over the shortcom I heard Marchetti report, "Down. No enemy."

Susan nodded, and my group dropped from sight. As my feet touched the floor, I let go of the rope and moved toward the wall, trying to keep low. The walls of the tunnel were smooth and cool and seemed to glow with some kind of hazy blue light. About fifty meters down the tunnel, near a turn in it, I saw two of our people. I looked the other way and saw another two squad members.

Within seconds Susan was down, followed closely by the rangers, including their captain. Susan and the captain discussed the next move, then Susan called us together and said, "We're going to assume that Fetterman moved up, toward the surface. It's what we would do if we'd gotten down here. Mary, you have the point. Noonan, bring up the rear."

Mary trotted off to take her position, and when she waved, the rest of us began to advance. The tunnel floor was flat, with some kind of slot cut into the center of it, but because the incline was less than fifteen degrees, it was easy walking. There were no corners between the floor and walls, only a shallow arc that blended them together. The floor was littered with grain, as if the Taus loaded some kind of vehicle under the bin but were sloppy about it. They hadn't bothered to sweep the floor, and since everything else we'd seen had been so clean, I wondered why not. There were no doors leading from the tunnel, so we could only go either up or down. The air was slightly cooler than the air in the dome, which meant it was a lot cooler than the air outside.

It took thirty minutes to reach the end of the tunnel, which was sealed by a huge door. We examined it carefully but couldn't find any obvious way to open it. Susan became impatient and waved us forward with orders to burn it open.

As part of the door collapsed inward, nearly hitting O'Rourke and McAllif as they tried to dance out of the way, sunlight flooded in and we could see the rear of the ranger company. Outside we learned that the door was cleverly hidden in the sand and low bushes about a hundred meters from the edge of the dome. We could have searched for weeks without stumbling on it.

While the ranger company commander arranged his troops, scattering more of them around until his lines were fairly thin, we took a break. Steve and I tried to find some shade, but there wasn't much because there were almost no trees, and the few we saw were skinny, with only a few branches and fewer dried leaves.

"God, what an afternoon," he said.

"That seems to be an understatement," I replied, and then took a drink from my canteen. I was thirsty and had swallowed nearly half the lukewarm water before I realized that I shouldn't be gulping it down.

McAllif sat quietly, staring out across the sand at the dome. It looked like a giant silver bubble sitting under a cloudless, deep-blue sky. I could see sunlight shimmering on the surface of the bubble, and between us and it about a hundred men and women from Earth, trying to fight an enemy we really hadn't seen and didn't know.

"You know, Lara," he said, almost under his breath, so it was hard to hear him, "I sometimes think that this is all a mistake. I wonder if it's all worth it and just what the hell I'm supposed to be doing."

"You're supposed to be part of a—" I started to say.

"You know what I mean. Oh, hell, forget it."

Before I could begin to respond, Linda Zalaznik strolled over and sat down near us, without waiting for an invitation. She said, "I hear they're really catching it in the Major Dome. They've shot down all the helicopters and turned back the first infantry probes. The armor's moving in now."

"There you go, Steve," I said. "We've found you an enemy, a real enemy."

McAllif was quiet for a long time after that. He just stared at the dome as if it were something evil, waiting to kill us when it could draw us close enough to it. I wondered if the strain was beginning to get to him and I remembered the night, just after the voyage had begun, when he'd talked me into going to a movie with him. I'd been angry because he took me away from my studies, but it turned out that I had needed the rest. I wanted to return the favor if I could.

But before I could say anything to him, he turned slowly, so that he was no longer able to see the dome, and laughed once—a single sharp sound that didn't contain any amusement. He took a deep breath, and looked at Linda. "That all you hear?"

"Rangers had only gotten a brief sit-rep. HQ wanted us to know that resistance had been encountered and some of it was quite stiff."

"All the helicopters?" he asked.

"That's what I heard. Anyway, they're not going to use helicopters to recon anymore."

There didn't seem to be anything more to say to that. I watched a couple of people trying to eat their rations, but they didn't seem to have much in the way of appetites. Steve pulled his knife from its scabbard, wiped the blade on the cuff of his shorts, and began to sharpen it again. He inspected the blade carefully after a few seconds and said, "It's strange. We travel a dozen light-years from Earth, using the most advanced technology ever conceived by the human race, and here I sit, sweating like a fucking pig, cleaning a knife. We used these things to kill each other over six thousand years ago. We sure haven't managed to advance much."

I didn't like the sound of that—not the words, but the thoughts behind them—and wondered if Steve was beginning to lose his mind under the strain. But as the tanks appeared he slipped the knife back into his scabbard.

Susan came around and yelled at us, "We're about to go."

18

Fetterman, Anthony B.
Master Sergeant, Seventh Ranger Company, SCAF

I pulled my gas mask from the pouch worn at my hip and
snapped it over my head to keep the grain out of my nose and
mouth if I were buried. Instinctively I closed my eyes as the
grain washed over me. I was hot, drenched with sweat from
the heat of the day, and I could taste the bile in my throat. I
knew that throwing up would strangle me as surely as if I
wrapped a noose around my neck, so I forced myself to swallow
and to think of something else. I remembered stories of people
being buried in snow and surviving because they hadn't panicked, hadn't struggled uselessly, and I almost laughed as I
realized that I wouldn't starve, anyway.

For a few minutes I tried to relax, forcing the thoughts of
the grain and the shifting floor from my mind, then realized I
was slipping deeper, being dragged downward. I began falling
faster, and wondered how deep I would go. If it was more than
a couple of meters, the weight of the grain would crush instead
of suffocate.

Then, suddenly, I felt myself falling free of the grain, with cool air all around me. I hit bottom with a force that knocked the air from my lungs, and felt the grain cascading onto my body armor, but I was free of it. I rolled to my stomach and struggled to my hands and knees to crawl away. Seconds later I was leaning on the top of a hopperlike vehicle being loaded with the grain.

Most of the rangers were on the floor of the tunnel, their weapons drawn and ready, waiting for someone to take command. I climbed over the edge of the vehicle and dropped to the floor, drawing my pistol. I had lost my assault rifle somehow. The second squad leader, Sergeant Marvin, came over to me.

"Glad you could make it," he said with a mixture of sarcasm and relief.

"Situation?"

"I'm not sure," he said. "Apparently the grain was being loaded automatically, so the Taus won't be aware we penetrated the bin. I've posted people at both ends of the tunnel, or at least near the bends."

I nodded. "How many survived?"

"Most of second squad and about half of the first. Sara Jameson was killed, but we managed to recover her body. Donna Chilton has a compound fracture of the right arm."

"Have you tried to dig anyone out yet?"

"We were waiting for it to stop."

I looked up and saw that the flow had slowed to a trickle. "Have everyone climb aboard, and let's try to find the rest of our people."

Marvin turned and shouted, "Everyone back into the truck. Break out your entrenching tools."

The vehicle was like one of the giant grain hoppers used by trains on Earth. The floor of the tunnel was slotted, and it appeared that the cars were allowed to roll down the incline. I suspected that their weight was used to pull empty cars up another tunnel. I laughed at the simplicity of the system, and wondered why the geniuses on Earth who were worried about fuel shortages and energy conservation hadn't thought of such a system, which generated its own power.

As I climbed up into the car, the troops were already trying to dig through the grain, throwing it all over, most of it out of the hopper. It would leave a nice trail for the rescue party to follow, if they weren't smart enough to follow the tunnel down. Of course, it would leave a nice trail for the enemy too.

No one was surprised when we started to roll. I ordered, "Half of you put down the entrenching tools and stand guard. Let's be alert."

After five minutes the train slowed and stopped. There still was no one around. We found most of our lost weapons and all but three of the people who had been missing. Two were dead and one unconscious, but the others were able to function. I called a halt to the digging because it was obvious we wouldn't find the missing three. I waved the second squad leader over, and he whispered the command to his people. We all went over the side.

He posted his guards and trotted back to me. "Now what?"

"I suppose we start back up the hill."

"Then why in the hell did we ride down here in the first place?"

"Ask those people we dug out. Besides, without walking, it gave us a chance to do some of the recon we'll have to do later. Tell me you would rather walk down here." I was going to say more, but a burst of gunfire cut me off.

I spun toward the lower end of the tunnel and could see two of our people backing up slowly, their weapons held in front of them, the barrels pointing the way they had come. Both suddenly began firing on full automatic, and as they did, several squad members rushed forward and fell in with them. Everyone opened fire, and the tunnel reverberated with the sound.

Once they reached the front of the hopper, they stopped and took the little cover available to them. I could see the enemy flooding the tunnel, and was surprised to see it was an army of naked females, waving knives and short swords over their heads like some kind of perverse banners. They rushed toward us, but our rifle fire, though sporadic and uncoordinated, cut them down.

I saw a dozen, maybe two fall into bleeding, broken heaps before they broke and ran back the way they came. I moved as fast as possible then. At the front of the hopper, I yelled, "Let's get out of here. Come on! Move it! They're regrouping and there are going to be a lot more of them."

Up the tunnel I could see several people fanning out and a single man sprinting ahead to take the point. I turned back in time to see the enemy begin another assault. This time they weren't naked, but dressed in strange costumes that covered their chests. They also wore very brief skirts and skull-fitting helmets with two probes resembling the antennae of large insects.

They advanced carefully, slowly, looking as if they knew exactly what they were doing. It wasn't an uncoordinated rush that had left them disorganized and dead, but a planned fire and maneuver operation.

"Take it easy," I said. "Let's use our grenades to wake them up. Toss them over the first rank if you can."

We all let fly at the same time. The first rank of the females suddenly kneeled and opened fire with some type of bulky semi-automatic weapon. One of our women fell, a bullet through her head just below the rim of her helmet. It had smashed the visor and splattered her blood over one corner of the hopper and the man standing next to her. He dropped his rifle and began scrubbing at his clothes, trying to remove the gore.

Two more of my people dropped, one dead and one wounded. From behind I heard someone give the order to fire, and wondered why that was necessary. They all should have been shooting the moment we were taken under fire.

The explosion in their ranks surprised and frightened them. Those in the front broke toward us, to get away from whatever was happening behind them, and we cut them down easily. Several reached the front of the hopper, and for an instant it looked as if we were going to be overrun, but not enough of them had charged us. We managed to kill them as the others fled down the tunnel, away from us.

"Hey, a couple of them are alive," yelled a ranger.

I stepped over and looked. One was badly wounded, having been shot in the chest and legs, the bullets punching through the flimsy armor she was wearing. The other had a minor scalp wound. A bullet had dented her helmet, probably knocking her out momentarily.

"Leave the one," I said, "she's about had it. Tie the other's hands behind her and let's get the hell out of here."

Two of our women and one of the men were dead, and we

had three wounded. "Leave the bodies," I ordered.

Sheila Buller, from the second squad, protested. "We've never left ranger bodies in the field."

"Fine. You want to sacrifice the living for the dead, go ahead. I'm for getting the fuck out of here." I didn't bother to point out that they'd only been in training exercises, never in the field. This situation was a lot more fluid and dangerous than a training exercise on the simulator ship.

Before I moved, I took a couple of grenades and threw them as far as I could. Then I spun and trotted after the others. At the first bend, I came to the rest of the troops.

"Is there anyplace we can set up a defensive perimeter?" I asked.

Sergeant Marvin, who had been on the point, said, "About three hundred meters up-tunnel there's a series of rooms or compartments. We could maybe burn holes into the walls for gun ports."

We headed there. Since both sides of the tunnel were lined with rooms, all we had to do was occupy a couple on each side and we could catch the enemy in a crossfire. I didn't think we'd have to hold for long, because I was sure the people topside were trying to get down to us. I wouldn't have been, were the situation reversed, but they weren't me, so I expected a rescue party.

I nodded. "Okay, we'll hold here. A couple of you check out the rooms."

Buller was standing nearest the prisoner, so I said, "I want you to take our guest up to the Intell people so they'll have a source of information. You can brief them on what's happened here, and speed up the rescue."

We took four rooms in the center of a straight stretch of the tunnel so we would have a clear field of fire. The inside was just as Marvin had said—not much more than a compartment. The shortcom would let us communicate among ourselves. One man was detailed to keep watch near the bend in the tunnel.

Once in the room, I took time to examine it closely. There was something like a coffee table but no chairs. I had the feeling it hadn't been occupied recently, because there was a fine layer of dust on everything. I could see no evidence that anything

had been hung on the walls, and there were no doors leading
out, except for the one we'd used.

Julie Benton and John Metsuco were pressing wads of thermate onto the wall to make the gun ports. I walked around the
room, tapping the walls, but didn't hear anything that suggested
hiding places or hidden passages.

With the gun ports ready, there wasn't much to do. All six
of us sat down, except the one who kept watch. Benton and
Metsuco took their canteens and had a drink. I checked my
rifle again. The magazine was about half empty, so I switched
it since I didn't want to worry about switching while the enemy
stormed the doors.

It was the first time I'd had to relax since we had moved
into the dome. I took a deep breath, holding it for a moment.
I needed to relax, so I tried to drain everything from my mind,
and just concentrated on resting.

We hadn't done too badly, so far. We'd been completely
surprised, but had recovered nicely. As far as I knew, we'd
been the first to meet an armed force of the enemy, and we
had taken them. Well, maybe not taken them, but we'd beaten
them back with heavy losses. I didn't know if it was because
we had surprised them by being where we were, or if our
weapons were better than theirs, but we'd won the first skir-
mish.

"Sergeant, they're coming."

I opened my eyes and nodded. I touched the mike button
for the shortcom. "Let the lead element get between us, but
don't let it pass."

There was a series of rogers.

By pressing my face against the wall I could see down-
tunnel almost to the turn. I saw the point of their column and
said, "Let the point by. When the main group gets here, open
fire. We'll try to cut down the point."

This time no one said anything. The only problem was the
holes we had burned into the tunnel wall, because they were
visible from the outside. That might give us away, but as I
thought of it, I saw the first of the point element pass without
looking. They must have assumed we would flee to the surface
as quickly as we could run.

Unfortunately the separation of their elements was too great. The point passed us and we couldn't really see the rest of the column. We waited.

They were very good, indicating that they had done this before. They maintained enough interval so our ambush wouldn't kill too many of them. I should have anticipated that, but hadn't. As the lead element walked by, I aimed my rifle out the gun port and fired. The first three went down immediately in the loose-boned way that meant they were dead, and the others began to scramble backward when the rest of us began to shoot. Fifteen or twenty more of the females were hit before they could withdraw. I tried to find their point, but could no longer see it. That meant it was up-tunnel from us, probably waiting for us to make a break.

For ten minutes after springing the ambush we stood ready, sure they were going to counterattack. But they didn't. I saw a few of the people with me getting edgy, the first signs of panic beginning to show.

"Take it easy," I told them. "Relax."

"Take it easy," shouted Metsuco. "Take it easy? My God, they're going to kill us all, and you want to take it easy. Jesus Christ—"

"Knock it off, Metsuco," I warned him as calmly as I could. "Just relax and we'll be okay."

After another ten minutes passed I said, "Metsuco, Benton, and Pittman, take a break. Grab something to eat or take a drink of water, but don't gulp it because it's all you'll get for a while. The rest of us will keep watch."

As I started out, I remembered that none of the people with me—in this room at least—had ever been in combat. It was too bad they had to get their baptism in a small group, badly outnumbered and trapped. I didn't tell them we were holding on to give Buller a chance to get to the surface with the information and the prisoner. That was the important thing, and I wasn't sure all of us could have made it.

I heard a sound behind me and looked quickly. Metsuco had dropped his canteen. I watched the water bubble out and saw him stare at it as if it were something new and fascinating. He didn't move.

"Shit," he said in a voice that quivered. Dropping the canteen was a little thing, but his eyes were shiny, as if he were on the verge of collapse.

"Pittman, take my place." He moved to the wall as I sat on the coffee table and stared at Metsuco. He was so young, I thought, and saw that he was trying to grow a mustache, but his hair was so light and fine that there wasn't much to it. I reached down for the canteen and put the cap back on it.

"I'm sorry, Sergeant."

I handed it back. "Don't worry about it. We're not going to need it anyway. The rest of the company will be here soon."

"How do you know?"

I was happy to hear the defiance creeping into his voice. It meant the immediate crisis was about over. "Because they wouldn't throw away two squads of highly trained people."

"You left the bodies behind," he accused.

"That's right, and I brought the wounded with me, even though it slowed us down. What's the point?"

"They won't come."

"Why not?"

"Because they don't know where we are."

"Oh, but they do. Think about it, man." I stressed the last word. Sometimes in training we babied them, but not here. Not now. "We disappeared into the grain. There's only one place to look for us. Once they break through there, they have only two ways to go, and we sent them a guide."

"If the enemy doesn't kill her."

"Christ, Metsuco, you're a fucking pessimist if I've ever met one. Why don't you worry about them flooding the tunnel with gas, or setting us on fire. It makes no difference if Buller makes it or not. They'll know that we came down. If we'd gone up, we would have reached the surface." I let the anger creep into my voice to let him know I was tired with the discussion.

Metsuco didn't seem to care about that. He stood and faced me, his face nearly white with rage. "Then why in the hell did we come down? Why didn't we get out of here?"

I grabbed the front of his shirt and pulled him close, so our noses nearly touched. "Because, you dumb fuck," I whispered, "you and several of your friends were trapped in the hopper and we had to get you out. Now sit down and shut up. I've about had it with you." I gave him a shove, and he stumbled backward.

Pittman called, "I think they're advancing."

"Then fire," I snapped at him. "You don't need my permission to kill the enemy."

Pittman pushed his rifle through the port and lifted the butt. There was a rapid clatter as the bolt worked, but I couldn't hear the detonation of the rounds because he had one of the silenced weapons. From the tunnel I heard a scream.

"They're running away again." Pittman turned toward us just as we heard a high-pitched whine. Then a thousand screams began. Pittman didn't say anything. He toppled forward, and there was his blood on the back of his neck, running into the collar of his shirt.

Those on the wall started firing again. I sprang to the gun port, stepping over Pittman. One of the bullets had found its way through the port and caught him between the bottom edge of his helmet and the top of his body armor.

Firing erupted all over the tunnel, and dozens of the Taus fell. But there were always others to come forward, picking up the weapons dropped by the dead. They gained one room. They smashed through the door and swarmed inside for a few seconds, pouring back into the tunnel after killing everyone inside.

The door of another compartment exploded open, and I was afraid the defenders were about to be overwhelmed. But once inside, the attack broke. Someone began tossing grenades out the door, and the vibrations of the explosions shook all of us. The Taus who weren't incapacitated broke and scattered in both directions.

The tunnel was piled with dead, bodies stacked on top of bodies—so many that in some places the dead couldn't fall. There was some screaming and moaning, but not as much as I expected.

Over the shortcom I heard, "Fetterman? Synder. We've got to get out."

"Give me a quick commo check."

There were fewer than a squad left. Out of the twenty-five people who had entered the grain bins with me, nine were still alive. At least it was nine if Buller hadn't been killed.

"Roger," I said. "On three we move out. Keep close to the walls, and remember that some of the enemy have gotten in front of us."

I checked Pittman. He had died immediately, a bullet in the back of his head scrambling his brains. I glanced at the others, and they nodded. For a moment I stared at Metsuco, wondering about him, but he stared back defiantly.

I touched the helmet mike button. "One. Two. Three."

I went out the door low and rolled to one side, facing down-tunnel, protected by a pile of bodies. The blood had pooled, and my elbow rested in it. It was already sticky, and the coppery odor had spread throughout the tunnel. I wondered where the flies were. In Africa the flies would have been thick.

Behind me I heard the others fleeing. Benton said, "Okay, let's go," as she passed me.

I stood, watching down-tunnel, easing back, covering our retreat. I glanced toward my people and saw them at the corner. I sprinted toward it while they covered me.

"What now?"

"Let's scram."

We fanned out, following normal squad tactics, half guarding while half ran up-tunnel. At the first bend we ran into trouble. A large force of the enemy was waiting for us. Fortunately one of them was trigger-happy and fired too soon. She missed, and gave the ambush away. We were able to take cover in another room before they could react.

Now the eight of us were crowded into one of the cubicles. We couldn't advance to the surface, and we couldn't retreat. There was nothing to do but wait for those above to come and rescue us.

"Metsuco," I said, "make us some new gun ports. You and Carson can then take a stand at guard. Let me know if anything out there moves."

To myself, I thought, it could get bad in the next few minutes. I hoped help would arrive soon.

19

Kisov, Vasili
Captain, Third Aviation Battalion, SCAF

I dumped the nose of my helicopter and broke toward the major dome. Strung out to my right was the rest of the aviation unit, a dozen helicopters, searching for the ground elements we would lead into the battle. I glanced at lead, who began a lazy turn toward the city. Below, one of the pathfinder squads began to cautiously advance, and I knew that the real invasion had finally started. Just as I pulled the cyclic to the left stop and kicked the pedals to make a tight turn, I saw Karen leap on to her tank, look up, and wave quickly. Without responding, I rolled out of the turn, descended fifty meters, and headed north.

I flew across the city once, avoiding the large chunk of dome that still covered about a quarter of the metropolitan area, throwing shadows on a dozen tall buildings. I turned and started back slowly, nearly hovering over the remains. Quite a number of the buildings had been damaged by the shuttle bombing, the debris clogging some of the streets, but most were still intact. There was a park near the center of the city, evidence of fire in the blackened ground and denuded trees.

I increased my speed, suddenly afraid the enemy would open fire and knock me out of the sky. The fact that so little of the city had burned suggested that the Taus had good damage control, or rather, fire departments, which suggested a sophisticated society that could easily have sophisticated antiaircraft. I didn't want to be the one to discover that, so I broke my search pattern and headed to the south, where I was to provide close air support for one of the pathfinder squads. They had reached the outskirts and had taken up a defensive ring in the remains of the dome. Behind them, not more than a kilometer or so away, were the tanks.

I swooped low over the pathfinders, saw their leader wave to indicate they were ready to go, and climbed again. I tried to stay in a position to watch them and still be able to cut loose with the mini-guns if they needed help, but they were doing quite well without me.

They gained the first of the buildings, entering through the holes in the damaged walls, rather than the doors or windows. Three of them disappeared inside and a moment later one of them ran out onto the roof to wave at me. Across the street another group of three vanished. They worked their way down the street that way, those in the buildings trying to cover those running around below them. Once one building had been secured, those in the one before would vacate it, leapfrogging forward to the next.

They halted at an intersection. The structures on all four corners seemed to have come through the bombing with little or no damage. Six squad members secured the two buildings on two of the corners, while the other six began to sprint across the street. They made it nearly halfway.

The whole avenue seemed to come alive suddenly, with at least a hundred of the enemy pouring from the buildings to meet the pathfinders. I saw those in the intersection form a crude circle, because they had been completely surrounded in seconds. The first ranks of the enemy stumbled and fell in bloody heaps as the pathfinders used their automatic weapons, but there were always more of them who kept coming.

I rolled around so I could try to cover them if they broke free, and wondered why those in the buildings didn't give supporting fire. I glanced at one window and saw a pathfinder fall from it.

I lined up on the crowd in the intersection, but held my fire because I had no clear targets. The streets from one building to another were littered with bodies as the pathfinders tried to fight their way out of the open. The firing stopped abruptly and the enemy started to run for cover.

That could only mean the whole squad was dead. I dumped the nose, firing a short burst. Nearly everyone in front of me dropped, and I hauled back on the cyclic, kicked the pedals, and made a 180-turn.

The streets were almost deserted, but a few stragglers were still trying to find cover. I cut them down. Before the Taus in hiding could react, I jerked in an armload of pitch and climbed out steeply.

Using the sunshade on my helmet, I was able to see the street easily, and tried to hover over the intersection. I could pick out the bodies of the pathfinders because their khaki uniforms, although bloodstained and torn, made them distinctive. The enemy was no longer naked, as we had seen earlier, but as far as I could tell, they still didn't have much in the way of uniforms, and were all female.

About 1500 meters to the right I could see another of the helicopters orbiting, and I knew there was a squad of pathfinders under it. Since I was no longer needed where I was, I wondered if he could use help.

I made a last sweep through the area, but there was no sign of movement—either from the enemy, which had vanished as quickly as they'd appeared, or from the pathfinders, who were obviously dead. There were at least three hundred bodies in the intersection below me.

The other helicopter suddenly dipped toward the ground, and I could see that he was firing. For a moment he hung in the air, just above the buildings, then he flared brightly. There was a plume of black smoke, and most of the helicopter disappeared in a rain of flaming debris.

I rolled to the right and pushed the cyclic forward as far as I could. Seconds later I could see the remains of the helicopter. There were no pieces bigger than a computer monitor, and nearly all of them were blackened and smoking. Near the remains were dozens of bodies, but only two or three were our pathfinders. Farther down the street I could see a swarm of the enemy trying to attack one of the buildings, but they were unable to get very close because of the intense firing that kept the bodies piling up. I lined up to make a gun run, leaving everything in front of me either dead or dying.

At that moment I saw several pathfinders burst from a doorway. While one covered, the others sprinted down the street, toward the edge of the city. They ran about 150 meters, stopped, and started firing again. The one who'd covered them from behind, jumped up and began a sprint. He got halfway to them before being cut down. Six of the enemy tried to cross the street to the body, but the other squad members shot them.

Once again the squad took off at a dead run. They stopped near an intersection, posted two guards, and tried to cross. Two made it before the enemy rushed them. Everyone was firing as fast as they could pull triggers and reload. There were hundreds of Taus running for the intersection held by the pathfinders. I opened fire with my mini-guns, raking the whole street, but couldn't stop them. Just as it seemed they would overrun the pathfinders, the attack broke, the Taus scattering. In seconds the street was empty except for the surviving pathfinders and the dead. They regrouped quickly, then ran for the edge of the city. Once there, they crossed into the savannah and found a place to defend themselves until the armor or the infantry could catch up.

As the pathfinders reached safety, I was recalled, as were all the remaining helicopters. It had been decided that the armor would go in, with helicopters providing the recon. I returned to the armor column, landing in the designated area for refueling and rearming. While on the ground, I learned that the pathfinder casualties were running about sixty percent and that two other helicopters had been shot down. I was not thrilled to learn any of this.

In the air again, I caught the tanks at the edge of the city, where they had halted momentarily. Behind them a division of infantry had begun to dig in, a battalion of artillery behind them. About half the infantry would move into the city as the outskirts were cleared by the armor.

As I flew over the top of the lead tank, the armor began to

creep into the city, the barrels on them slowly sweeping from right to left, as if searching for targets to shoot at. I had expected them to meet resistance immediately, since I'd seen one squad of pathfinders chased all the way to the city's edge. But that didn't happen. The tanks rolled in, crushing everything in front of them, bursting through the walls of buildings, knocking decorative trees down, and running over the bodies of the enemy dead and wounded.

The armor moved forward slowly, barely faster than a walk, in order not to get too far ahead of the infantry. At each intersection they stopped to recon the streets in all directions, then crossed and began again, until they reached the point of farthest penetration. The infantry scampered forward to fill in and secure all the locations.

After hesitating for nearly fifteen minutes, the line started rolling again, and still there was nothing. I wondered where the enemy could have gone. One minute they had been trying to overrun the pathfinders, swarming over the area like ants on sugar, and the next they'd vanished. I knew they had to be around, but I couldn't see them.

The farther we moved from the point of entry, the more spread out we were. Tanks and infantry split from the main body to fill in the side streets, so we couldn't be flanked. Maybe the enemy had guessed our tactics and were waiting until we split into smaller groups.

They surprised me when they finally appeared. Thousands of them flooded into the streets while hundreds filled the roof-tops. Those on the tops of buildings carried a weapon that looked like a missile. They seemed to throw it at the armor, but it had a rocket motor and must have had some sort of guidance system, because they didn't seem to miss.

As the lead tank burst into flame and then flew apart in a building-shattering explosion, I turned so I could rake the roof-top with my mini-gun. In seconds it was covered with bodies, and I couldn't see anyone moving. The building across the street still had hundreds of the enemy on it, all of them female and wearing bizarre costumes which made them look like giant insects. They all also seemed to have long, black hair hanging down their backs. They had ignored me and were firing down into the street, throwing more of their missiles. One of them saw me and turned, tossing her missile at my helicopter. I was able to swerve, but I didn't know if the evasive maneuver worked or the shot had been wide.

From the street I could hear the infantry begin to fire, until the noise from both sides combined into a continuous roar that drowned out everything else. I turned to attack another roof, and saw thousands of Taus rushing past the first tank, which was little more than smoking ruins. They were waving swords, the sunlight twinkling and flashing on the blades, giving them an almost harmless toy-like look.

I cleared another rooftop using my mini-gun, but more of the enemy charged onto it, taking the places of the dead. Many of them turned their weapons on me, and I was taken under a concentrated fire from the bulky rifles. Some of the projectiles, which didn't seem to be real bullets, bounced off the armored glass of the windshield. They didn't have much penetrating power.

Having emptied my mini-gun and fired down a side street using the maxi-gun, I broke away from the rooftops. I pulled the trigger and watched as the building fronts caved in, billowing smoke and dust as the interiors collapsed. I knew I was ripping them up, but the smoke and dust obscured my vision.

As I rolled out of a firing run, I glimpsed the enemy retaking one of the rooftops I'd cleared. Two of the missiles were launched at me, but again they missed. I tried to turn so I could return fire, but didn't get around in time. Another missile exploded near the tail of the helicopter, and I felt the tail rotor linkage give. I dumped the nose to try to keep the aircraft streamlined, so it wouldn't spin, but the enemy kept firing. When the engine was shot out, I had to auto-rotate.

There wasn't any time to search for a safe landing zone, and I could see that more of the tanks were burning. Beside them, fighting next to the infantry, were the surviving crew members. I hadn't been sure which tank Karen was in, or even which column, but prayed she'd gotten out alive.

As I passed over the battle in my forced retreat, I saw it was beginning to thin farther back. Hundreds of the enemy had pushed through the front SCAF elements and were fighting hand to hand with our infantry in the rear.

I tried to keep the helicopter straight. Since the engine wasn't working, the torque problem was reduced, but it wasn't altogether removed. As the skids touched the street, the friction slowed me. I began a lazy, uncontrolled turn to the right. The aircraft was heading toward a building and there wasn't a thing I could do to stop it.

So this is the end, I thought. Hardly a fitting death. The helicopter continued to slow, bounced several times, then rammed the buildings, shattering a huge window. I saw the blades hit the wall and explode into fine dust, but it broke the forward momentum. I came to rest inside the building, the helicopter lying on its side.

I wasn't sure whether the enemy was going to spring from the floor or not. It was what they'd apparently done before. I ripped off the shoulder harness, dropped out of the seat while kicking at the canopy, and grabbed my assault rifle as I tumbled out.

On the street, I wasn't sure which way to turn. To the right I could hear the firing, and knew the battle was there. I debated about heading to the rear, then decided that the way the enemy seemed to come and go at will, it didn't make any difference which way I went. I decided to catch one of the infantry squads that were rushing into the battle.

20

McAllif, Steven M.
Private First Class, First Pathfinder Brigade, SCAF

The tanks slid up as some of the rangers were removing the remainder of the door that had hidden the tunnel. I leaned back against the tree and watched them work, glad I wasn't asked to help. When they were through, it was obvious that a tank would be able to roll right in.

Susan came around. "Okay, let's saddle up. We're going back in. Lara, want to take the point?"

I spoke up. "Why not let me?"

"Sure, Steve. Any particular reason?"

"Not really. I just wanted to make a decision."

"Knock yourself out."

We formed near the first tank, but didn't really pay much attention to it. We had a couple of classes about infantry support of armor, but this situation was one they hadn't thought of covering. Tanks don't maneuver well in tunnels and buildings and caverns.

Susan said, "We'll move in using normal squad tactics, McAllif on the point. We won't worry about a rear guard because we'll have three tanks there. Behind them will be the remainder of the rangers. As we move in, a PAI maneuver battalion will fill in. Any questions?"

There was only one I could think of. "Do we engage the enemy?"

"The best thing to do is fall back to the tanks and let them handle anything. However, we don't have to worry about making noise. If we see the enemy, we can engage him."

Patterson mumbled from the back, "Don't you mean her?"

"Right. Her."

We waited while the rangers assembled. The tanks fired up, and each tank commander nodded. Susan turned toward me and said, "Okay, then. This is it."

I walked to the tunnel, leaned against the side, and peered into the darkness. Compared to the outside, it was nearly black. I flipped the sun filter out of the way, stepped into the shadows, and lowered the night optics. I would only need them for a few minutes, while my eyes adjusted to the relative dimness of the interior.

Slowly I moved deeper into the tunnel. I had forgotten the grain bins were so close. I'd only gone about two hundred meters when I came to the first grain spill, and took a minute to examine my surroundings. I then walked past the two squads and paused near the second turn in the tunnel. It wasn't much of a turn, but it did provide some cover and hid what was deeper inside. I waited until I could see the majority of my squad and one of the tanks before I stepped around it.

I could see down this section for a long distance. I crept forward slowly, trying to take in everything around me, but there wasn't anything except the smooth, glowing walls of the tunnel and the strange slot in the floor. Behind me the rest of the squad began to catch up, so I moved faster. I tried to estimate the distance to the next bend, but tunnel distances were deceiving. It looked like five hundred meters, but it could easily have been twice that, or only half of it.

After half an hour I reached the third bend. Again I stopped. Although it was cool in the tunnel, and getting cooler the lower we went, I was covered with sweat. I would gladly have swapped this for the sun and heat of the surface.

In the distance I heard a rumble, and wondered if one of

the tanks was in trouble, then realized the sound had come from the wrong direction. I held my breath, straining to hear it again, but the pounding of my own heart filled my ears, and suddenly I couldn't hear anything. I breathed out and lay flat on my stomach on the floor with my ear near the corner.

I had about decided I'd imagined the sound, when it came again, and then twice more. I replayed it in my mind, trying to identify it, but the only thing I could think of was artillery or hand grenades. I decided to wait for instructions.

Susan pushed past the others and knelt near me. "What's happening?"

"I think I can hear some shooting down there . . . only occasionally, and then only some grenades, but I thought I better tell you."

Susan listened for a moment, impatience evident in her posture and on her face. Finally she waved the rest of the squad over and told them quickly, "We're changing tactics. Mary, I want you to take a point position on the wall opposite Steve. Patterson, I want you and Desoto to take a similar position about five meters behind them. The rest of us will follow about ten meters after that."

Before we'd gotten far, I heard the chatter of an automatic weapon and another series of explosions. Mary looked at me for instructions, then halted. I shrugged and waved her on. We advanced slowly, trying to sense the enemy.

The tunnel again turned, and as we approached the bend, I could hear some shouting and a wild burst of firing. Both of us dived for cover automatically, although there was nothing to hide behind. I glanced at Mary, who smiled awkwardly. "Tension," she said.

We let Richard and Lori catch us, then the rest of the squad filled in. Now everyone could hear the shooting.

Susan said, "Let's go. That's got to be Fetterman and his people. If we wait, they could be wiped out."

It didn't take the tanks long to catch us. Once again Mary and I took the point, but this time a tank was five meters behind us. Three squad members walked along each side of it, with the rest right behind.

As we approached the turn, the firing became louder. I was sure a battle was going on just around the corner. Mary stopped again and stared to the front. She crouched and ran across the tunnel to me.

"There's about fifty of them in the tunnel."

"Fifty of what?"

"The enemy, mostly standing around. I couldn't see too far, but I did see some bodies beyond them."

"Let's see what Susan has to say."

As we briefed her, one of the tank commanders dropped to the tunnel floor and came over. Susan said, "The only thing to do is check this out carefully, then let the tankers drive in with us right behind."

The tanker nodded. "I'll keep the hatch open and we'll use the mini-gun to hose them down. That should clear them out quickly."

Susan waved me forward again, and I got down and crawled along the wall so I could see down the tunnel. The fifty Taus Mary had seen were still there, maybe joined by another fifty, and they seemed to be grouping for an attack. About seventy meters in front of them I could see another seventy-five or a hundred dead females. Most were piled near one side of the tunnel, indicating that they were attacking at that point. I assumed that Fetterman, or members of his unit, were holed up inside.

As I watched, a stampede of Taus started up the tunnel from the other side of the dead bodies. Apparently they were making a coordinated attempt to overrun our people.

I slipped backward, stood up waving the tank forward, then flattened myself against the wall so it could pass. I saw one track lock, the other moving as it rounded the corner. The turret swung and the mini-gun began to fire down the tunnel with the sound of ripping cloth, which was amplified by the walls, floor, and ceiling.

The squad moved up and was firing too. Many of the Taus dropped, while the others turned, looked at us, then fled in terror down tunnel, trying to get away. I thought we had chased them and was about to start after them, but I couldn't see the SCAF troopers and was afraid we were too late.

Susan yelled something, but it was lost in the noise of the shooting and shouting. The Taus had broken the attack only long enough to change the direction of the assault. They swarmed up the tunnel, completely filling it, ignoring Fetterman's people in their desire to kill us.

We returned their fire, but they kept coming. The rangers filled in around us and the tank. I saw one man fall back, blood spurting from his throat. Then another was hit. Two on the other side of the tank were shot, toppling out of sight.

The tank commander was still sitting on top of the turret, firing his machine gun. As I looked up, he clutched his throat, blood suddenly seeping through his fingers and painting the front of his body armor crimson as he rolled backward. He pulled on the machine gun handles, aiming it at the ceiling as he fell, and that seemed to excite the Taus. They ran faster, and were almost to us.

Some of the rangers pushed past us and rushed to meet the attack, firing as fast as they could pull the trigger. Three of them were hit in the arms or legs or face, but there were others to take their places. I saw one ranger throw down her rifle, grab for her pistol, and with the other hand reach for her knife.

The tunnel was about fifteen meters in diameter, so not many could get into the hand to hand fight. As the rangers met the enemy and mixed with them, we had to stop shooting or we might have killed our own people. The lines surged and sagged, and soon the rangers and the Taus were fighting up and down the length of the tunnel. In the confined space the assault rifles were no longer practical. Most of the firing had died, except for ragged volleys from the rangers' pistols. Slowly they pushed the Taus back, but I wondered if they were giving ground only to suck the rangers deeper into the tunnels so they could surround and kill them.

Over the radio I heard the ranger commander order, "Fall back. Fall back."

The battle seemed to waver for an instant, then began to slide toward our position. We got ready to meet it. One of the tankers had popped out of the turret and was sitting behind the machine gun, waiting for her chance to use it. Three or four of our squad crawled onto the tank and took up firing positions, using the turret for protection. From there they could shoot over the heads of our people. They began trying to isolate a small group of enemy, so that we could disengage.

The Gatling opened fire, and as it did, the rattling of the

assault rifles started. The Taus in the rear began to drop, and for a second there was confusion among them, then they broke and ran. The ranger company commander pointed down the tunnel and sent half the rangers after the fleeing Taus. Susan signaled us, and we charged toward where we thought Fetterman and his people had held out. We didn't know if they were alive or dead, and wondered why they hadn't come out yet.

We moved carefully, watching the dead and wounded Taus so we wouldn't be surprised. When it became obvious that some of our people had survived the attacks, Susan waved to Patterson and me.

"You two go. They might be trigger-happy and react badly if they see more women coming at them."

We moved carefully, shouting, "SCAF soldiers! We're SCAF soldiers!"

Someone seemed to peer out of one of the holes burned in the wall. For an instant part of a face stayed there, then there was a whoop. A door flew open and four men and women came out. They stared at us as if they couldn't believe we were there.

Susan yelled, "Sergeant Fetterman!"

He spun. "You people took your own sweet time."

"We got here, didn't we?" she shot right back at him.

Patterson said, "Where's the rest of them?"

Fetterman waved a hand to indicate the few people with him, and said, "I'm afraid this is it. The others have been killed."

The ranger CO walked up. "Sergeant Fetterman, take your people and head toward the tank." He stepped passed me and yelled, "Lieutenant Hermanez, fall back."

Susan looked at him incredulously. "We're going to withdraw?"

"Yes. I don't have the people to pursue this any farther. They probably have thousands down here, and I only have about a hundred fifty. Besides, there isn't much of interest in an underground storage facility."

Some of the rangers checked the field for wounded, and near the center of the battle area they found Buller's body. Fifteen or twenty wounded people had been put on the tanks and the medics were trying to help them. We left the wounded

Taus, figuring that their own kind would come to their aid as soon as we got out. The ranger CO waved a hand, and the tanks started backing up the tunnel. A line of skirmishers formed to act as a rear guard.

It didn't take long to reach the tunnel entrance. Fetterman was riding on the first tank, but we didn't get a chance to talk to him because they put him on a medevac as soon as he came out.

Susan waved us toward the trees and told us to take a break. Nothing was going to happen until the officers had a chance to digest the information we had gathered. Admittedly it was sketchy, and most if it came in the heat of battle, but there was now so much more of it. The rangers and the PAI maneuver battalion were going to set up defensive perimeters near the opening in the dome so we could guard them.

We waited for hours. The sunset and the twilight twinkled until the moon came up, washing it out. Susan walked around and told us we were going to hold until the units at the Major Dome either occupied all of the city or the enemy disengaged. We were to become waiters while the battles went on all around us.

21

Kadrmas, Karen
Major, First Armored Corps, SCAF

It should have been a shooting gallery. Instead it was a disaster area. According to the SCAF master plan, they cracked open the Major Dome during the night. We just sat tight and waited for the place to cool down so we could push into the city. It was simpler to wait the five hours for the radiation to dissipate to safe levels than it was to try and send everybody in wearing antiradiation suits. The Geiger counters finally calmed enough to send in the pathfinders, protected by air cover. Twenty-five minutes later SCAF was short two more helicopters and about thirty-five pathfinders.

At first there had been no resistance, no sign of movement of any kind. Then, as the pathfinders pushed inward, the enemy came pouring out of the buildings as if someone was dumping them out of a bucket. The odds must have been about fifty to one. The enemy was reported by the survivors to be rather primitively armed, having about equal numbers of what could be classed as some type of crude firearm and various types of swords, spears, and a bola that seemed to be made of a weighted line resembling piano wire. The bola was quite capable of cutting off a soldier's arm, leg, or head.

I left Zilikovski to run the administrative aspects of the operation with the Headquarters Company at the rear of the battalion, and established my forward HQ with my command platoon behind Second Company. Once into the city, I planned to work a concave diamond formation with First Company on the left and Third Company on the right. I'd hold Fourth Company as a rear guard and reserve until I saw which way the battle was going to break.

Most smartasses who think they know everything there is to know about anything can quote to you, usually without attribution, the well-known philosophy that "You don't send a boy to do a man's job." You can recognize them by their one inherent trait. They have a very short life span. But the survivor-participant, he'll know the words of Sun Tzu, a wise old man who had lived so long because he was so wise. Sun Tzu said, "You don't use your best iron for horseshoes, and you don't use your best men for infantry." Or at any rate words to that effect. What he meant was, you do send a boy to do a man's job, if you have reason to suspect that the accomplishment of the job may produce terminal side effects. I myself, being a long time student of Sun Tzu, followed this sound advice. I sent the majority of the Light Armed Force Vehicles in first to find out where the enemy was, and held back on my heavy stuff.

Each armored platoon had an infantry platoon assigned to work with it, and we moved in slowly, checking the bodies. We did find a few of the enemy that had only been wounded. As for the pathfinders, there was no chance of any of them being left alive. One girl was found with over a hundred stab wounds. Most of our people had been hacked to pieces, some long after they were dead, from stab wounds or bullets. They were the lucky ones. One of the worst things I saw was a corporal who had been killed with a bola. There wasn't a mark on his body. But he didn't have a head anymore.

I had no doubt that the body armor our troops wore enabled them to take out a disproportionate number of the enemy, but it simply wasn't good enough to keep you alive against those kind of odds. Your arms and legs, and to a certain extent your head, were still vulnerable, and once the enemy got in close enough, there were areas that a sword could penetrate—under the armpit, at the back of the helmet, at the juncture of the upper and lower body protectors.

We moved to the point of farthest penetration made by the pathfinders and halted. The infantry poured in, securing the buildings we'd passed. I didn't like the quiet. The whole damned area had been a battlefield less than an hour ago, and now not a damned thing moved. I smelled an ambush, and so did my troops.

The remaining pathfinders advanced about two hundred meters ahead of my lead elements, looking for tank traps, mines and antitank guns. They didn't find any, and I punched up the freqs for First and Third companies, and keyed the medcom. I told Spelman and Ben Canin to send up a platoon of Light Armored Fighting Vehicles apiece, and look over the situation. The ten vehicles broke off from their companies and rolled up two parallel streets, their engine noise abaters activated, the electric drive units producing only a high-pitched hum. Their rubberized track-sound limiter pads squeaked on the hard-surfaced street as they jerked up short at the first intersections, nosed around the buildings, then cranked their turrets around, covering themselves as they crossed the perpendicular streets. They slowly moved up the streets another block, covering the buildings on either side, the lead tanks pointing their main armament straight ahead. At the second intersection, they halted again and repeated the crossing technique they'd used at the first. At the third intersection they linked with the pathfinders. Together they advanced another 150 meters.

When nothing happened and no enemy was sighted, I sent one platoon of LAFV's from Second Company down the middle. They advanced 350 meters along the street and halted when they made visual contact with the platoons from First and Third companies. The infantry platoon moving up behind them checked each building, finding nothing.

I fanned the three lead companies out through the streets, one tank platoon and one infantry platoon for every other street. The streets sandwiched in between were filled in by additional infantry platoons brought up from the rear. In this way I established a mobile front twenty-three streets wide.

We advanced slowly, continuing to utilize the concave diamond formation. I knew that sooner or later we were going to contact the enemy, and I still wanted Fourth Company held as a reserve. I wasn't quite as concerned about a rear guard now, because of all the infantry working their way in behind us, but if any of my lead companies ran into trouble, I wanted to have Fourth Company available to tip the scales and eliminate the opposition.

I still had the three platoons of LAFV's out ahead as scouting units. I had a reconnaissance platoon made up of five CVR-1's. They were supposed to be used for reconnaissance and scouting purposes, and would have been more maneuverable than the LAFV's in a built-up area like the city. But they were the most lightly armed vehicles I had, except for the tracks used to haul support equipment and infantry. So far as we knew, the enemy didn't have any antiarmor stuff, but they had managed to knock down a couple of helicopters with something. And if the enemy had stuff that could knock down a helicopter, it might be strong enough to do a number on the little combat cars. Besides, I thought I might find a use for them later, and didn't want to waste them by making them my advance elements in an area where our forces had contacted the enemy less than an hour before.

We'd moved inward about another three hundred meters when the enemy pulled the old Hollywood Indian trick. I don't know how. I only know that one minute the streets were clear except for our troops, and the next minute they were swarming with the enemy.

The assault by the Taus was preceeded by a bola and spear attack on the infantry accompanying the three armored platoons out front. The spears really didn't do much damage, but the bolas were another story. About a fourth of the infantry were dropped in the streets, either dead or dying, then about five hundred of the enemy flooded out of the buildings, swinging swords and firing those clumsy-looking semiautomatic rifles.

The LAFV's buttoned up and started raking the enemy with their mini-guns and Stoners. At first they couldn't do a proper job because there were too many friendlies in the way, but as the accompanying infantry found cover, the tanks began to take a heavy toll. The infantry in the side streets adjacent to the advance armor reported they were under heavy attack, and a couple of helicopters dropped down and started making gun passes on concentrations of the enemy.

There were a couple of loud explosions ahead, and I thought for a second that the LAFV's had opened up with their 105's. Then there was a dull crump followed by a tremendous whanging noise, and I could see a sheet of flame shoot up in the air, followed quickly by dense black smoke. I've seen enough of that sort of thing before to know when a tank has just blown sky-high.

The firing was beginning to get really heavy up there, and I could now clearly hear the crack-chug-boom of the LAFV's main guns. I keyed Second Company commander's freq and asked for a situation report. Spelman replied that his forward platoon had lost two vehicles to antitank missiles, and that the AT fire was coming from rooftops. The other three tanks were still holding, but there was too much enemy infantry to be contained and the Taus were starting to push past the LAFV's. The tanks were too busy trying to keep the antitank fire off their own backs to properly cover the accompanying infantry, so Spelman wanted to either pull them back or reinforce them at once. I told him to send up his other LAFV platoon to deal with the enemy infantry, and to run up one of his Heavy Armored Fighting Vehicle platoons to handle the AT fire, then checked in with my other company commanders.

Ben Canin and Reshev both reported their advance elements under heavy antitank fire. Ben Canin thought his platoon commander had been killed, since he couldn't raise him or his assistant. Reshev said his troops were holding okay. The infantry had gotten chopped up some, but the tankers had been alerted by the first explosion from Second Company and had dropped back about fifty meters just as the enemy opened up. The report from his platoon leader stated no losses.

I told both company commanders to reinforce their forward platoons and draw in tighter toward the center of the battalion. Until I had a better idea of exactly what we were up against, I didn't want to leave my command all strung out. Since the enemy troops seemed to be concentrated in the center of five streets anyway, I wanted to run some of the armor up the sides and see if we couldn't box them in. If it turned out we were facing a sizable force, I might have to rethink my plans, but it looked as though what we had to contend with was a fairly large, but local concentration of troops.

I could hear the firing intensify as the reinforcements moved to engage the enemy, then something spattered against the side of my tank, and I decided it was time to get my head inside and button up.

"Jordan Six, this is Negev Six. Be advised that we are taking small-arms fire. Kfir Six reports loss of One Alpha and One Beta to antitank missiles. Galil Six reports probable loss of One Six and One Five. Gabriel Six reports heavy small arms and antitank fire but no losses."

I still couldn't see anything to shoot at through the periscope, so as soon as I got an acknowledgment from Jordan Six, I keyed the shortcom to talk to the rest of the command platoon. "Negev, this is Six. We're taking small-arms fire. Anybody see where it's coming from?"

"Six, this is Gamma. I think the firing is coming from the rooftop of the third building on the right in the next block."

"Roger, Gamma. Can you mark with smoke?"

"Affirmative. Will mark with smoke."

"Understand." I cranked my periscope mount around in time to see the initial puff as the grenade hit and the column of yellow smoke billowed up.

"I.D. Yellow."

"Roger, yellow."

"Roger, Gamma, understand smoke on target. Drop a 105 on them and stand by the mini-gun. Six will follow suit." I keyed the intercom and told Sharon to put a HESH round on the smoke.

As I watched through the periscope, the yellow cloud vanished in a ball of flame that changed rapidly into a wispy column of gray-white. It took most of the building edifice at roof line with it, and tossed a couple of bodies off. The second round impacted less than a meter from the first, and about half of the building toppled groundward, spilling more bodies onto the street. None of them moved.

It was at that point I realized that all the bodies recognizable as to sex were female. In fact every Tau I'd seen so far had been female. I don't know why it hadn't dawned on me before, maybe because SCAF is a fully-integrated service, but I hadn't seen a male anywhere. What's more, the females I'd seen might have all been struck from the same mold. I wouldn't go so far as to say they could all have been twins, but they certainly could have been sisters. There seemed to be a marked family resemblance.

The situation ahead was steadily worsening. Reports indicated that the Taus were pushing past the lead tanks, surrounding them. Most of them constituted a serious threat only to the infantry accompanying the tanks, but a few had managed to get past with some of the antitank missiles. Ben Canin reported the loss of One Gamma. Spelman reported that One Five was heavily damaged and unable to move, but still firing on the enemy. Reshev said Gabriel One Six reported he was successfully holding at the intersection, but that One Beta had suffered track damage.

The Taus kept on coming. The forward platoons reported approximately four hundred Taus killed or wounded, and there were at least five times that many left. They were fierce warriors who stormed both infantry and tanks without hesitation, but mostly they didn't have modern weaponry. We'd lost fifty infantry and five tanks, with two more heavily damaged. It looked like we could handle their regular infantry, but those lousy antitank missiles were going to cause us some trouble.

The reinforcements reached the forward platoons, and the LAFV's waded in among the Tau infantry and started cutting them up. The biggest disadvantage the tanks had was the lack of maneuvering room, and the Taus were doing their best to exploit it, moving from rooftop to rooftop. A helicopter orbiting over Second Company dropped in low, made a couple of gun passes at the rooftops, then broke down one of the side streets, apparently strafing it with 35mm fire. He started to pull up, but there were suddenly a couple of dark red-black puffs near the end of the tail boom, and the helicopter bucked violently. I thought he was going to lose it for a second, but he seemed to get things under control and started heading out toward the rear, trailing smoke. He looked as if he were going down, but I couldn't be sure because of the intervening buildings. Anyway, he wasn't my concern.

The HAFV's sent to reinforce the forward platoons were

having a hard time maneuvering because of all the bodies, rubble, and other tanks clogging the streets. They chewed into the walls of the buildings on both sides, running in toward the city center with their maxi-guns, and crawled over the rubble and into the ground floors of the buildings. The HAFV's literally ate their way through the insides of the buildings until they bypassed the SCAF troops and tanks blocking the streets, then crawled out again in front of the burning LAFV's. Their 105's and maxi-guns knocked off the tops and caved in the fronts of buildings up and down both sides of the streets. One of them lost a tread to antitank fire, but the missiles didn't seem to be able to penetrate their heavier armor. There was about a minute and a half when the noise of the battle took on the characteristics of a naval bombardment, then the firing stopped except for an occasional burst of mini-gun or small-arms fire. Finally that petered out too, and the war momentarily grew silent.

The final score for the Taus was five LAFV's destroyed, two more heavily damaged, one slightly damaged with tread loss; one HAFV with tread loss; and about 175 SCAF soldiers killed or wounded. The Tau losses were about 750 dead and 1100 wounded. I guess the brass would have called it a clear tactical victory for SCAF, but considering all the armor I'd lost and the sum total of what I had to work with, I wasn't quite so sure.

I think the thing that bothered me the most about the first engagement was the condition of the enemy prisoners we took. Not a single one of them hadn't been shot up. That meant one of two things, both of which were bad news. Either the enemy was prepared to resist to the bitter end, or those that could still somehow walk had made it past our flanking elements and vanished without a trace.

I was pretty mad at the infantry for the way we'd been taken by surprise in the ambush. They were supposed to be checking the damned buildings. But I figured that anything I might wish to say to them about their performance would be superfluous, considering the way their lead elements got cut up. They'd look four or five times as hard for the enemy from now on.

The Taus hit us again after we'd advanced about another five hundred meters, and again another 650 meters after that.

The enemy seemed to be especially adept at combat in built-up areas, and was a master of concealment. The casualties they took were always heavier than ours, but they obviously had the people to suffer those kind of losses. We didn't. And everytime we did get hit, my battalion came up short another couple of tanks—either destroyed or temporarily knocked out for repairs. And the loss of each tank meant the loss of combat-experienced troops. It began to look like taking the city was going to be a long, slow, hard process. About three kilometers farther in, it became damned near impossible.

We pushed out of a built-up area into a broad belt of parkland that extended off in either direction as far as the flanking elements could see. It was cut by a stream approximately five hundred meters wide. There was a strip of open grassland, with a few scattered evergreens with pinkish blossoms, on either side of the water, and then buildings began again.

We could have crossed it easily enough. The tanks were capable of swimming it, and we could have brought up tracks to ferry the infantry across. The bank wasn't steep enough on the near side to constitute a serious problem. There was no way of knowing exactly what it was like on the other side. It didn't look steep, and it didn't look spongy, and the sensor scan didn't show any mines or gun emplacements, though we all knew that didn't mean a damned thing. It was just too perfect and too easy to be quite as simple a proposition as it looked. Then again, there were all those buildings on the far side, about three hundred meters from the stream bank, which might hold just about anything.

We sent a patrol across in rubber boats, to reconnoiter. They landed without incident and reported the bank to be both shallow and firm, then leapfrogged across the open strip in two elements until they reached the buildings. They worked their way slowly into the built-up area and disappeared. They did not reappear, did not radio, and did not return. They quietly vanished without firing a shot.

Well, like I said, it had looked like a good place to cross, so I'd suspected it at once. In combat the shortest distance between two points is often the quickest way to get killed. I was sorry we'd lost a dozen men and women proving that axiom, but it was better than losing my battalion. The time had come to get some use out of my CVR reconnaissance vehicles.

I didn't especially like the idea of staying in one place, but I could be fairly sure the area we now held was secure. I couldn't say the same for the rest of the city. Besides, the cardinal rule of warfare is, Don't divide your forces in enemy country. I figured to deploy where I was, keep an eye on the far side of the stream or river or whatever in the hell it was, and send my reconnaissance platoon out to scope out the terrain and try to find another way across.

I sent two of the CVR's around to the left, and three to the right. Both patrols worked their way along the edge of the strip of parkland.

I didn't expect them to find a bridge. The helicopters assigned to us had already reported the absence of any such structures. What I did expect them to find was the reason why there weren't any bridges. It was a little too much to expect that the Taus would be so inefficient as to construct an artificial river through their city without having some way of getting material and people from one side to the other. If they didn't have bridges, then they had to have something else—fords, ferries, tunnels, something. If I could find that something, I could reasonably expect it to be heavily defended. So much the better. I could then launch a diversionary strike against the obvious target, and while the Taus made themselves busy defending it, I could cross the main body of my forces a suitably discreet distance away, outflank and isolate the Taus, and eliminate them. It was, I told myself, a sound idea. It should work well.

The CVR's were each equipped with three television cameras—one locked to the driver's periscope, one set to track coaxially with the 35mm gun mounted in the turret, and one mounted in a bullet-resistant induraplast bubble atop the turret with 360-degree traverse and 180-degree vertical axis, which can also be dismounted and hand held. The cameras are provided with a telecom link to the battalion commander's tank, making possible instantaneous battlefield intelligence from distant units. The only problem, as I was finding out, was that the telecom transmitters didn't work very effectively in built-up areas. At least they weren't working very well now. As long as we had line of sight communication along the edge of the

stream, they were fine, but as the stream followed the curvature
of the basic city layout, the intervening buildings began to
scramble the picture. The equipment had supposedly been tested
on Earth. I didn't know if I'd been lied to about the testing or
nobody had thought of testing it in the city. At least the radios
were functioning . . . some of the time.

Second Lieutenant Bernstein had taken the three CVR's
around to the right. After we lost the telecom pictures from his
units, he made three regularly scheduled longcom checks. His
section missed the fourth and the fifth checks, and every one
thereafter.

Sergeant First Class Rafferty had taken the two CVR's to
the left. His section missed the fourth and fifth longcom checks
also.

As the sixth commo check rolled around, I tried everything
I could think of to reestablish communications with my scouting
parties. I ran the Very Long Range commo mast up to max
height, boosted power to the transmitters and receivers or both,
tried several alternate frequencies, and tested all the circuits.
Nothing. As a final act of what should have been futile hope,
I switched on the telecom circuits and ran through the settings
for each camera. When I keyed in the lines for the bubble
mount on Rafferty's CVR, I got an erratic but definite incoming
transmission tone over my headset. I tied the telecom circuits
into the VLR mast and boosted the receivers up to maximum.
It took a little bit, but I finally got a picture clear enough to
see. It was still pretty fuzzy, and I couldn't hold it for very
long at a time, but I could tell what it was. Somebody had
stuck a photo map in front of the camera lens turret, and printed
on its acetate overlay in red grease pencil was a message.

CAN RECEIVE NOT TRANSMIT
LOST 1 CVR TO ENEMY
MANY TAUS HERE
FUCK COLLINS RADIO
RAFFERTY

There was an arrow pointing to an area circled on the photo
map, and a set of coordinates followed by a question mark. I
jotted down the coordinates and found and marked the circled

area on my own photo map, then keyed Rafferty's frequency on the longcom.

"Snoopy Five, this is Negev Six. Understand you able to receive but not transmit. Have coordinates and location marked on map. What is your situation?" I saw a hand reach in front of the camera and remove the photo map. After about half a minute the hand came back and left a new message.

```
SNOOPY GAMMA HIT BY AN AT MISSILE
NO SURVIVORS
TAUS AT LEAST BATTALION STRENGTH
BELIEVE THEM GUARDING TUNNEL BENEATH
    STREAM
THINK LOCATION MARKED X
FIVE HIDING IN VACANT STORE MARKED O
OCCASIONAL TAU MOVEMENT IN STREETS
TAUS HEAVILY ARMED
CANNOT MOVE
```

"Specify how enemy is armed, Snoopy Five. Give exact Tau positions, if possible. Are you damaged or cut off?"

```
TAUS ARMED WITH AT MISSILES RIFLES
AND AUTOMATIC WEAPONS ALSO USUAL SWORDS
    ETC
SOME AW'S CREW SERVED BELIEVE TWO HEAVY
    GUNS EMPLACED EACH
SIDE TUNNEL ENTRANCE EXACT NATURE UN-
    KNOWN
SUGGEST LOW LEVEL PASS BY HIGH SPEED DRONE
    FOR PHOTO RECON AS CANNOT GIVE SPECIFICS
TAU DISPOSITION OPPOSITE SHORE UNKNOWN
BELIEVE HOSTILE
```

"Thanks for the information, Snoopy Five. Have you any casualities?"

```
ALL OKAY HERE BUT PATROLS FIND SOON WILL
    LOSE TELECOM
```

LINK WHEN MOVE TRANS FROM EMERGENCY ANT
 FIXED TO ROOF
AND HELD ALOFT BY HYDROGEN FILLED CONDOM
MEERIAM'S IDEA
REGULAR COM ANT DAMAGED

I glanced over at Anjanette, who was wearing a puzzled
face. "Does that thing really say hydrogen-filled condom?"
"That's what it looks like," I said. "I suppose they bled the
hydrogen off from one of the fuel cells."
"This has got to be some kind of first."
I keyed the mike again. "Understand, Snoopy Five. Will
request photo recon and see what we can do about getting you
some help. Continue transmitting as long as possible. All additional information will be appreciated."

ROGER BE ADVISED THAT SOME TAUS NOW WEAR-
 ING SKIRTS WITH
HELMET AND CHEST PROTECTOR PROBABLY OF
 METAL
BALLISTIC RESISTANCE UNKNOWN
WILL ADVISE OF ANY NEW DEVELOPMENTS

I acknowledged Rafferty's message and keyed the brigade
freq. I filled Levinson in on the situation and asked him to
request the recon from air. Ten minutes later he informed me
that a drone-carrying helicopter would be dispatched as soon
as possible. ASAP turned out to be an hour and forty-five
minutes later. It took another twenty minutes for the helicopter
to get into position, and about ten minutes to launch the drone,
but in less than five minutes after that I had the first photofax
printouts dropping out of the bottom of the telecom box, and
fifteen minutes later I had the revised photofax that had been
updated and computer-enhanced by Intell.
The enhanced maps marked off the location of twelve light
and nine heavy crew-served weapons believed to be machine
guns. The photos also showed camouflaged emplacements
around the mouth of the tunnel entrance, which according to
the magnetic aberration detection systems, concealed four large
metal objects that might or might not be field pieces. Estimated

total strength of the Tau forces on this side of the stream was four hundred.

The other side showed only about half a dozen emplacements thought to be automatic weapons pits, two emplacements thought to contain more heavy guns, and a good deal of traffic in and out of some of the buildings. Estimated strength was about 250.

I planned to send First Company well around the Taus at the tunnel and have them force their way across the stream to take the enemy on the opposite shore by their upper flank once the fighting thickened. Third Company I intended to send across downstream of the tunnel, to cut off the enemy's escape route. Second Company would assault the tunnel defenses, with Fourth Company acting as security. Simple plans are nearly always the best, and this one was simple enough to work out successfully. Almost from the first it went wrong.

To begin with, the operation was delayed almost two hours while a sufficient number of tracks were brought up to ferry across the infantry and necessary supplies. Ben Canin's troops ran into a company of Taus while he was trying to sneak his tanks and accompanying infantry around the tunnel defenses, and a brief but fierce battle ensued that was sure to have tipped off the Taus that we were trying to push an armored company and infantry battalion past their position. Reshev's troops were ambushed twice by platoon-sized groups of Taus as they moved into their crossing positions, and Spelman discovered that the Taus had mined the principal routes of approach to the tunnel entrance by launching those damned antitank missiles from a large boxlike device which was triggered when a tank moving up the street broke the beam from a simple photocell.

The Taus were beginning to look like increasingly clever people with each passing minute, and I was starting to wonder what kind of equipment they could be planning on bringing up that made keeping the tunnel open so damned important to them.

For Second and Fourth companies it was a long, slow, hard process. The armor couldn't advance up the streets or along the strip of parkland because of all the mines and antitank fire, and the infantry couldn't clear the tank traps because of all the Taus. By the time we'd reached the main body of the enemy, the four hundred Taus had become more like seven hundred, and everytime we killed one, she was replaced by two more. It was fast becoming a losing proposition.

The chest protectors most of the enemy were now wearing would stop a pistol or submachine gun slug, but only at ranges of over two hundred meters or so, which was about max effective of the latter and way beyond that of the former. Our assault rifles seemed to have little difficulty with them. Of course, they'd also deflect a bayonet in hand to hand fighting, and that seemed to be the Taus preferred mode of warfare, failing a good ambush. SCAF had spent five years training its personnel in how to use almost every conceivable weapon ever developed by man. Unfortunately none of the training instructors had ever conceived of finding it necessary to go up against a horde of sword-wielding, armor-protected fanatics who didn't care whether they lived or died.

But the plan was working at least partially. The increasing numbers of Tau soldiers was pretty good evidence that the Taus were being reinforced from the far side of the tunnel, which indicated that the enemy must be massing his, or her, forces on the far shore. I thought the pincer movement by First and Third companies ought to work out well, despite all the setbacks. I fully anticipated that not only would they chop up the Taus over there, but would isolate those on this side from any help. Further, I expected them to secure our first permanent bridge head, or in this case tunnelhead, across what I now thought of as the canal. Since the Taus apparently didn't have a lot in the way of motor vehicle transportation, I was betting that the fact that our tanks and tracks were amphibious would come as a rather unpleasant surprise for them.

The minute things started to go wrong, I should have suspected the worst. The advance on the Tau tunnelhead was held up repeatedly by a combination of antitank booby traps and direct antitank fire. Our infantry had its hands full just trying to cope with the Tau infantry.

I had to give the Taus credit. They seemed to have done one hell of a job mobilizing their forces against a surprise invasion of their planet. For the most part they lacked technical parity with us, but every single Tau was armed. As I sorted out the gun- and missile-toting body-armor wearers from the

sword- and bola-swinging nudes, I made the connection that
the more heavily armed ones were the militia, and the others
regular citizens. Considering the use the "public" had managed
to make of their rather primitive weapons, I was thankful they
hadn't all had guns in their homes. If the entire population had
been equipped with firearms, even the rather crude types the
militia were using, they might have stomped our ass right off
their planet. Sure we could have nuked them, but you can't
blow up somebody and then extract retribution from them, and
after all, that's why we were here.

The fighting got heavier as we neared the tunnel mouth.
The crew-served weapons the Taus had emplaced around the
area were much more effective than their rifles. Instead of a
slug, they fired a short metal dart with stubby, triangular fins.
The fins were razor sharp, and the needle-nosed darts traveled
at a velocity that would penetrate body armor at ranges closer
than seventy-five or 150 meters, depending on whether they
were fired from a "light" or a "heavy" Tau machine gun. The
weapon fired between three and five hundred rounds a minute,
and was described by our weapons specialists as a light-gas
gun, a concept developed on Earth toward the end of the twen-
tieth century, but never made practical. It employed a small
explosive charge to rapidly compress a gas of low molecular
weight. This compressed "light gas" was then used to squirt
the projectile down a directional tube. The problem the twentieth-
century Earth scientists hadn't been able to overcome was how
to achieve multiple shot capability in a tactical situation. The
Taus didn't seem to be having any trouble doing that at all.

The advance by Second and Fourth companies finally ground
so near to a halt that effecting the canal crossing now became
more a matter of necessity than of offensive strategy. If we
didn't cut off the continuous flow of Tau reinforcements, our
drive on the tunnel seemed likely to bog down completely.

First and Third companies started taking heavy fire halfway
across the canal. The Taus were salvo launching those damned
missiles of theirs from large catapult arrangements which tossed
out ten to twenty of the things at once. Once airborne, the
rocket motors would kick in and carry the missiles on toward
their target. We'd lost so many of the helicopters to ground
fire already that we weren't getting proper air cover, and the

smoke screen laid down by the tanks' 105mm guns wasn't helping all that much. The LAFV's were wallowing pretty badly in the choppy water kicked up by the exploding missiles, and a couple of tracks carrying the infantry had been capsized by water spouts and a few more had taken direct hits. Most of the troops made it across, however, and engaged the enemy.

Ben Canin's armor spearheaded the drive on the Taus from the upper end, forcing a narrow path parallel to the canal. The PAI battalion accompanying the tanks had a simple duty—hold the left flank. Seizing the tunnel itself and spiking the Tau guns was left up to the ranger company and the combat engineers platoon.

At first Ben Canin's troops made good progress, but about two kilometers from their objective the Tau resistance thickened and the SCAF troops encountered Dragon's Teeth and missile tank traps, along with heavy automatic weapons and the Taus version of barbed-wire entanglements—a sort of metal web fired from a catapult and covered with barbs coated with a sticky, milkish-white substance that stuck like glue and produced death if absorbed into the bloodstream. The advance was held up as the HAFV's used their lasers to deal with the obstacles, blasting the tank traps into a fine, powdery rubble, and fusing the webs into steel-wool clumps.

On the lower end, Reshev's armor punched through the Tau canal defenses and lasered and shelled the missile launchers while raking the Tau infantry and fortifications with mini-gun and 35mm fire. Casualties to his accompanying infantry were light, and the two PAI battalions deployed in a semicircle to cut the Tau line of retreat and provide security while the combat engineers got busy emplacing their claymores and fougasses.

On this side of the canal problems kept piling up. What had started out as a reinforced battalion of Tau infantry had now grown to brigade size. I was, I decided, getting damned tired of all the faulty intelligence I was getting. It didn't seem to matter if the originating source was Intell, Air, the infantry boys, or my own troops. The buildings and locations they could get right, but the numbers were always wrong.

The Taus finally unlimbered their artillery as our advance units got within sight of the tunnel mouth. By the grace of God, for those who still believe in that sort of thing—or the fortunes of war, for those who don't—the enemy evidently didn't have any high explosive for their field pieces, and I was thankful for that. I wasn't sure our infantry would have agreed with me though. No HE meant the Tau gunners ignored our armor and concentrated on our grunts, and the Tau fire was pretty nasty stuff.

The guns chucked out at low velocity, a large sleeve of lightweight metal that deployed a drogue parachute as it flew through the air. The contents of the sleeve would continue, spreading out in a cone-shaped pattern. A slightly different variant used a large chute to lower itself over a body of troops. The sleeve would then split open, scattering several hundreds of small glass balls which exploded on impact, throwing needle-like shards for several meters. Death rarely resulted, but a soldier can't fight very well with dozens of glass splinters in him. It didn't take much cover to protect against injury from the damned things, but you had to have a roof over your head as well as a wall around you. Anybody caught in the open was out of luck.

The helicopters really couldn't do much about taking the guns out. The smoke over the battle was so dense from burning this and burning that and all the firing going on, that the pilots couldn't see their targets. They tried radar bombing, but there was too much ground clutter to get adequate target definition, and they couldn't bomb blind without risking collapsing the tunnel, which the brass hats thought it would be awfully nice for us to keep. I wondered if they were really that stupid, or nobody had told them the damned thing was probably mined so the Taus could blow it if we did somehow manage to take it. I'd thought it would be a nice piece of work to take it intact too, but only as long as we had a reasonable chance of hitting both ends at once with a fair amount of surprise. It was my experience that that was the only way to get a bridge without having it blow up in your face, and even then you had no guarantees. I figured a tunnel couldn't be that much different from a bridge, and that any chance we had of taking it by surprise had run out a long time ago.

There were just enough Taus running around with those missiles of theirs to make the notion of bringing up the tanks to deal with the guns one of the stupidest ideas I'd ever heard

of, and our infantry couldn't do anything about the missiles as
long as the guns kept them pinned down. After five hours of
heavy fighting we finally cleared the Taus from enough of the
buildings to send some HAFV's up through the insides. They
broke through the final walls and lasered the gun positions,
turning the cannon into pools of liquid metal.

Since it didn't seem likely we could do anything else to
improve the odds, we made the final push for the tunnel. Ben
Canin drove down hard on the opposite bank at the same time.
He took heavy losses, but also took the far end of the tunnel.
The Tau resistance on this side broke, and they retreated back
down the tunnel, not knowing that we now held the far end.
Reshev reported that part of the Taus had fallen back as expected and his troops had chopped them up like a vegamatic,
but that either we'd killed more of them than we thought or
he'd somehow missed the main body.

A few of Spelman's LAFV's and about half a company of
infantry pursued the Taus down the tunnel, trying to squeeze
them up against the ranger company at the far end. Most of
them drowned when the Taus flooded the tunnel.

They didn't collapse it, they just opened up a bunch of one-
meter valves and let in the canal. We didn't find out how until
much later, when we had the chance to send in some divers.
At the time all we knew was that we'd lost 430 men and women,
seven more tanks, eleven Armored Personnel Carriers, and one
more scout car for a God damned tunnel that was now full of
bodies and water.

We found Sergeant Rafferty and his crew about five blocks
from the tunnel. They'd been incinerated in a flash fire when
one of the Tau missiles ruptured their fuel cells. The missile
had apparently malfunctioned and passed through the CVR
without detonating, but its exhaust had ignited the hydrogen
leaking from the cells, and the ruptured oxidizer tanks fed the
fire. The whole thing probably burned itself out in less than
six seconds.

Judging from the Tau bodies heaped about the intersection,
Rafferty and his gunner and driver had given a good account
of themselves before the end. I decided to put all three of them
in for the Silver Star. I wasn't sure if they'd get it or not, and
it really didn't matter much because they would never know,

but I wanted to do something for them besides bury the charred bones.

When I first heard what happened, I wondered why they hadn't been able to get out, but once I saw the burned-out hulk of the recon car, I knew that the best nomex suit ever made wouldn't have helped them through *that*. Maybe they were even better off having gone the way they did. At least it was quicker than bleeding to death with a broadsword through your guts.

The infantry was still checking the Tau bodies, and I almost stepped on a wounded warrior as I was climbing down from the CVR's turret. I should have checked her for weapons and called a medic over, but I didn't. I pulled out my pistol and shot her once through the head, then walked back to my tank.

Word came down from brigade to hold where we were until further orders. The brass hats wanted a chance to evac the wounded, give Intell a shot at interrogating prisoners, and have the engineers put a couple of pontoon bridges across the canal. I interpreted the orders to suit myself and put my tanks across to beef up our defenses on the far bank. One of the infantry commanders did the same and had his tracks ferry his battalion over.

Since the Taus had flooded the tunnel, we didn't know whether to expect a counterattack or not. So far we'd done most of the attacking, and the Taus had done most of the defending. We dug in anyway and put out one hell of a batch of nasty stuff for perimeter defenses.

Flooding the tunnel, in a way, proved to be their undoing. When the engineers finally put on their aqualungs and went to have a look at the damage in the tunnel, they discovered a very curious thing. Most of the SCAF troops were drowning victims, but almost none of the Taus had drowned. They'd all been shot up. That didn't seem quite right, and since they hadn't come out past the rangers holding the far end, somebody got to wondering where all the Taus went.

They had to wait until the water-inlet valves had been hermetically sealed and the tunnel pumped dry. But they already knew what they were looking for, and they finally found it: a hidden door so cleverly engineered that it blended perfectly with the wall of the tunnel. Behind it was another tunnel, which branched into two tunnels, which branched into more tunnels, and so on. The engineers lost ten men removing all the booby traps they found in the first three hundred meters.

For the first time we had a clear picture of what we were really up against, of how the Tau's could appear and disappear almost at will. It should have taken us at most six or seven days to secure Major Dome 1; instead it took us almost a month before we could be reasonably certain the ground wouldn't open up and swallow us, and that was only after the infantry had cleared the tunnels down to the sixth or seventh levels with flamethrowers, grenades, and a whole lot of SCAF blood.

For the most part the Taus didn't use massed troops in the tunnels after the first few encounters with flamethrowers. They simply left the upper levels to us and moved lower into the tunnel complex. Of course, they always left their calling card. Sometimes it was a crossbow rigged to a trip wire, or a pressure plate that might throw anything from a spear to an antitank missile. Sometimes it was a pit full of spears coated with a poison that caused agonizing death, as if being impaled on fifteen or twenty spears wasn't enough. The Tau barbed-wire web, coated with the same stuff as the spears, was a favorite trick, as was their antipersonnel artillery shell rigged to a concealed triggering mechanism or a delay timer made from a variety of clock pieces of outstanding simplicity. Most of the time though, they just opened up a drain pipe somewhere and flooded the tunnel. Usually they flooded it with water, but after a couple of months they got pretty adept at flooding it with ultrasonics. When that happened, all we could do was back off and let them have the damned thing. You can't fight a war in a microwave oven, and the transmissions aren't that easy to jam.

Six months after the invasion we were still fighting in the tunnels beneath the city, or at least the infantry was. In quite a few places the tunnels had to be enlarged before a tank could get through. We had by now established that there was an elaborate tunnel complex under each city, and that the major dome complexes interconnected with the surrounding minor dome complexes. The fighting under what we now referred to as City Complex 1 showed every indication of continuing until hell froze over.

22

McAllif, Steven M.
PFC, First Pathfinder Brigade, SCAF

Masterson, Lara
LCpl., First Pathfinder Brigade, SCAF

The tunnel narrowed the deeper we went. It was still fairly bright, the blue light radiating from everywhere. In front of me I watched as two of the squad members kicked in a door and rushed inside. Seconds later they reappeared, shaking their heads to tell us they hadn't found anything.

Marchetti and Zalaznik moved forward then and did the same thing. We leapfrogged down the tunnel that way, to make sure no enemy got behind us. Lara was directly in front of me. She worked her way around Ehrlich and took up a position beside the door. Patterson followed her, stepped in front, and when she nodded once, he kicked.

As the door collapsed inward, Lara leaped to one side, trying not to silhouette herself against the light in the tunnel. Just as she disappeared, Patterson dived in from the other side. A few minutes later they both emerged and shook their heads. Still nothing.

The tunnel itself gave no evidence that it had been cut through rock, but appeared as if melted into solid stone. It implied a technology far above anything we had observed on the planet, but that was nothing new. Everything we'd seen contradicted everything else we had seen.

Susan signaled us, and we moved to a ninety-degree turn in the tunnel. As she stepped to the corner, Patterson walked along the opposite wall so he could see beyond the turn. He crept forward slowly, ready to jump backward at the first hint of trouble, but there wasn't anything ahead of us. The tunnel remained empty.

For a moment we hesitated where we were. Finally Susan tapped Mary on the shoulder and nodded. Mary was to take the point about a hundred meters away. Another squad member was sent the other way so we'd have a rear guard. The rest of us gathered around Susan, to be able to hear her.

I leaned against the wall, which was cool and smooth, thankful for the momentary break. Although we were still dressed for the outside, the tunnels weren't hot, and if it hadn't been for the body armor and the knee socks, I would have been cold. I took the time to close my eyes and rest them. They were burning from a lack of sleep and the constant strain of searching for the enemy.

Susan checked her odometer, an electronic device that measured the distance she had moved, and tried to use her compass. "I think we've come about as far as we were supposed to," she said. She shook her head as if she weren't very sure.

Patterson looked down-tunnel and then pulled back. "We still haven't found anything. All the rooms we've been in suggest living quarters, but there's never anyone living in them."

Susan sighed. "I know that. You sure that there aren't any other entrances to those rooms?"

"We've checked carefully. If they can get in from another direction, it isn't obvious. It would seem the enemy heard we were coming and pulled out."

I opened my eyes briefly. "That's no wonder. Those PAI's made enough noise to wake the dead. The Taus probably pulled everyone out when they heard the infantry."

Susan checked her watch, then looked at the compass again. I watched her as she tried to plot our location on her computer-generated map. It was a surface chart, and we were supposed to try to keep a record of where we were as we moved along.

The problem was, we didn't know how much of an angle the tunnel took or if the compass was giving an accurate reading, and we figured the odometer wasn't much good either—just another piece of electronic junk that SCAF engineers had dreamed up for us to tote around.

"Why not move to the next bend or until we see some signs of recent activity?" Patterson asked as he tried to look over Susan's shoulder.

"The thing to do, I suppose, is keep going," she answered.

We worked our way farther along. For the first few hundred meters we didn't see any doors, but we soon found where they started again. We operated the same way—with two people searching each room and the next two leapfrogging forward.

I stood close to a door while Martinez kicked at it. She had to hit it twice before it gave, and the instant it buckled, I went in. The interior was like all the rest. The inside was dark for the first few seconds, but it began to brighten almost as I hit the floor. In the first few rooms we searched, the automatic lighting had given us some bad moments. Before it was light, Wendy was in with me, covering the other side of the door.

Like all the others, it was empty, meaning there were no living creatures of any kind in it. On one side, near the wall, there was a piece of furniture similar to a cot. It was about half a meter high, two meters long, a meter wide and had a solid and uncomfortable look. I called it a cot but it really looked more like a coffee table. I didn't think the Taus would furnish a room only with a coffee table.

There wasn't anything else—no pictures or paintings or decorations on the walls, and no carpeting on the floor. Everything was the same antiseptic color. The walls blended with the ceiling and the floor, and there was no sign of an entrance other than the one we'd used.

I stood up and automatically brushed the nonexistent dirt from my chest. It was a reflex action. I walked to the cot and pushed it to one side, but there wasn't anything to see under it or behind it.

"I don't get it, Wendy," I said. "No one and no thing. This is worse than a prison. At least a prison has some variety."

Outside everyone was grouped near the door. Susan had her compass and her odometer out again. "I think this is as far as we go for a while. We should give the infantry a chance to catch us."

She sent the point and rear guard out again, and we spread along the tunnel. I was standing near the door of one of the rooms we'd already searched. I looked in once more, but there still wasn't anything to see. From far above us I thought I could hear the occasional sound of shooting or the rumbling of a tank, but it was so faint that I couldn't be sure.

I was straining to hear something else when I was pushed from behind. I stumbled forward, then felt a sharp pain near my right kidney. There was a white-hot burning that penetrated upward, and I lost sight of everyone in the tunnel. I knew that something was happening because I could hear shouting and a burst of gunfire from an assault rifle, but I couldn't see anything. I fell to my knees and put out my hands to break the fall, but I—

I turned to say something to Steve, and saw him begin to topple toward me. I put up my hands to catch him, and behind him there was a Tau warrior wearing the short, leather skirt and the molded chest plate that seemed to hide her shape. She shoved Steve, but he fought to keep his balance, and avoided colliding with me. The Tau turned to run, and I could see the blood-dripping short sword she carried. I raised my rifle, squeezing the trigger as the barrel reached toward the Tau's spine. The burst caught her in the small of the back, ripping through the bare skin, blowing holes through the armor in front as it threw her against the wall of the tunnel. She bounced off it and slid to the floor, smearing a bloody trail as she fell, then didn't move. I knew she was dead, but I didn't care. I kept pumping bullets into her until the magazine was empty and the bolt locked back; she was no longer recognizable as anything vaguely humanoid.

For a moment I stared at the heap of body parts and entrails, but finally tore my eyes away. Steve was lying on his back, almost at my feet. I set my rifle down carefully, trying to avoid the blood pooling on the floor, and crouched so I could talk to him. I tried to raise his head so he could talk to me, and when I felt his side, my hand came back covered in blood.

"Steve! It's me, Lara! Can you hear me?"

He didn't move, although I could swear he was breathing. There seemed to be no life in his eyes, and he stared at the ceiling with an intensity that was frightening. As I watched, his face paled and lost its expression.

"Steve!" I shouted. "It's me."

I thought I saw his lips move once, but there was no sound. From the amount of blood that he'd already lost, I could tell there was no hope. I looked up and saw some of the others staring down at me.

"He'll be okay," I yelled at them, not believing a word I was saying.

Susan knelt beside me. "Lara," she said, "we've got to get moving."

I didn't want to leave, but she pulled me up anyway. Steve just lay there and didn't seem to care about anything. I tried to get him to say something, but he wouldn't talk. I felt my eyes begin to burn, and couldn't see well. Suddenly I was mad. It wasn't fair, because we had checked the room. They hadn't given him a chance. They'd sneaked out of hiding, stabbed him in the back, and left him to die before any of us could do anything about it.

I pulled a grenade from my web gear and tossed the pin as far down the tunnel as I could. I leaned against the wall, glanced into the room, and let the safety lever fly off while I counted quickly. At three I threw it inside, and a second later there was an explosion. With my weapon ready, I dived through the door and rolled to one side. Near the bunk there seemed to be a crack in the wall. When I examined it closely, I saw part of another door, set flush with the wall. The explosion had forced the closet partially open and riddled it with shrapnel. I pulled it all the way open; there was no one in it. All I found was an old, rusty knife and a frayed pair of sandals.

Soon after that I heard another explosion and then a third. I stepped into the tunnel and saw smoke curling out of one of the rooms we'd searched earlier. Everyone had realized that the enemy could be hiding in any one of them, and we were no longer taking any chances. It was what we should have done in the first place.

Down-tunnel I saw a flash of bronzed hide as a Tau ran toward the point man with her knife held high. I swung around to fire, but before I could move very far, Zalaznik cut her down with a single well-placed shot to the head, splattering brains and blood. The Tau sprawled forward, sliding several meters on the smooth, blue floor.

As that happened, several of the enemy sprinted from their hiding places. Patterson tried to stop one of them by grabbing her around the waist, but the Tau turned on him with such fury that he had to shoot her. The others scattered both ways.

Two of them tried to jump Mary, but she was too quick for them. She ducked as one tried to stab her in the chest, and hit the Tau in the back with the butt of her rifle. The other took one step, and Mary shot her. The first started to get up, and Mary struck her on the point of the chin with her rifle butt. The female fell back and didn't move. She was our first prisoner.

We didn't worry about the enemy that had run up-tunnel because we figured the infantry behind us would catch them or kill them. Susan waved us forward and we started down-tunnel, to try and capture the three Taus who'd escaped. Not far away we came to another corner and paused.

About that time four more females broke from the cover of the rooms and came sprinting toward us, brandishing knives and swords. All of us opened fire at the same time, and the Taus collapsed into tumbling bags of ripped flesh and broken bones. When they were dead, Susan told Patterson to stay at the corner as a guard, to make sure the Taus didn't surprise us with a counterattack.

I looked back up-tunnel. The floor was littered with the bodies of the females we had shot. About seventy-five meters away was Steve's body, four of the enemy near it. We had evened the score; more than evened it.

Mary had tied the Tau she captured, so she couldn't move. Her hands were behind her back and roped to her ankles. Two of us grabbed the Tau and dragged her to the corner guarded by Patterson. We worked our way around the corner, then left Mary there to cover our rear and her prisoner. Instead of kicking in the doors and then checking the rooms, we were using our flamethrower to clear them.

A ranger platoon was following us about five hundred meters back. As we waited for them, we checked the rooms we'd

grenaded. In every other one we found a body. We were working our way along slowly, so the rangers could catch us, when
a dozen enemy broke from several rooms in a coordinated
attack. All at once they were swarming over us. I didn't have
time to look around or think, I could only react. I slashed with
my bayonet, stopping one of the enemy with a fatal wound
from her breast to the opposite hip. Another swung her short
sword, and I tried to block the blow with my rifle. She twisted
the blade and jerked the rifle from my hands. It hit the wall
about a meter away and slid to the floor, out of reach.

The Tau stepped closer and made a thrust at my chest. I
used my forearm to push the flat of her blade, but she jerked
around so that I lost my balance, falling on my back. The
impact drove the air from my lungs, and I wanted to close my
eyes as I tried to breathe. The Tau stood over me, raising her
sword, holding the hilt in both hands, the blade pointed at my
stomach. I struggled with the strap on my holster and the Tau
hesitated just long enough for me to draw. The instant the barrel
was clear, I fired. The first round hit her low, in her thigh, and
she staggered backward, falling. I shot her again, in the ab-
domen. She clutched at her stomach, surprised by the blood
pouring through the hole in the armor, then collapsed and died.

I got to my knees and looked around. All the enemy were
now dead, lying in bloody heaps around us, and we didn't have
any more casualties. Behind us, up-tunnel, I heard a noise and
saw the ranger platoon appear, trotting toward us in formation
and in step.

Together with the rangers we continued to explore the tunnel. Mary followed us, now that a couple of the rangers had
taken her prisoner to the surface for Intell. We had only gone
about a hundred fifty meters when we came to a large set of
double doors which seemed to be inlaid with silver and gold.
I wasn't sure it actually was silver and gold, but it looked
enough like it to impress me. The tunnel widened slightly, and
we halted on the up-tunnel side while Susan and the ranger
platoon leader studied the doors.

A minute later Martinez, O'Rourke, and I were sticking
thermate on the hinges. When Susan nodded, I touched the
fuse. There was a hissing as the metal melted, burning with a
cloud of blue smoke, but nothing else happened. Patterson

stepped to the center and stood with hands on hips, looking at the doors, then kicked at one of them. It toppled slowly inward, hitting with a loud metallic clang that reverberated through the tunnel.

The enemy was on him immediately. Dozens broke through the doorway, turning in both directions, attacking us with swords, knives, and oversized pistols. There were a few wild shots from us, and someone screamed, "You're shooting us!"

But that made no difference because firing then erupted all over the tunnel. As quickly as it started, it stopped because we were fighting hand to hand and no one could get a clear shot at anyone else. I bayoneted one female, put my foot on her chest and yanked the blade from her body. As the bayonet came free I used the momentum to carry the rifle butt around and hit another Tau in the side of the head, staggering her away from me. She was killed by Susan with a single thrust to the throat.

A third stepped up to me and attempted to shove her sword through my stomach. I parried and tried to get her with my rifle butt as she ducked. She had both hands on the hilt of her sword, swinging it like a bat, intending to smash my head. I had one hand on the stock, the other on the barrel, and threw the rifle over my head, blocking her blow. She swung the sword away and then back, to catch me in the ribs, but I blocked that blow too. I pushed her sword toward the tunnel wall, hoping to break the blade, but she pulled free. She thrust again, and I parried, swinging the rifle butt as she ducked again. I tried to hit her in the throat with the bayonet, but she blocked me, knocking the rifle lower. The point of the bayonet slashed her on the thigh and she jumped back as if burned. The wound seemed little more than a scratch, but it gave me the opening I needed. I fired a single shot into her chest, dropping her.

The rangers caught up to us, rushed forward, and with their help we began pushing the Taus back into the room. I ran through the doors and two females jumped me, but collided with each other. As they stumbled, I swung my rifle, slugging one in the stomach. She crumbled, her arms wrapped around her midriff, her ineffective armor failing to stop my blade. The other tried to chop me, but I was faster, firing once; she fell backward.

To my left I saw that Susan was surrounded for a moment.

She was on one knee, firing single shots as fast as she could pull the trigger. Patterson was behind her, trying to get to her, using his knife. I saw him grab one of the enemy to stop her thrust, and cut her throat, blood cascading down her chest. Another stabbed him in the chest, but his body armor stopped her blade. He cut her down with his own knife.

Not far away I saw five of the enemy pounce on Marchetti. He collapsed under their weight, and they all stabbed at him. He managed to fire once, and one of the Taus toppled. Before he could do anything else, one of them hit something vital under his body armor, or above it, and he stiffened, kicked, and died.

I spun toward them and fired a five-shot burst. It caught them all about chest high, and they fell. Susan and Patterson were withdrawing, working their way back to the giant doors. From the tunnel I heard several bursts from assault rifles and even the chugging of a heavier weapon, and realized we were surrounded, but that help was close.

Part of the ranger platoon had hacked toward the center of the great hall where we were now fighting. It was hard to see them because there were so many people in the room. Hundreds of the enemy were there, swinging their swords, chopping at people as if they were clearing vines from a jungle trail.

I backed against a wall. In front of me several Taus were fighting with the rangers. One of them swung her sword at a ranger's leg. The ranger fell, holding her thigh, blood running onto the floor. The Tau tried to sever her head, but I stopped that with my bayonet.

I was now standing with a small group of rangers. The enemy came at us from three sides. Some of the rangers were firing their weapons on full automatic, worried only about killing the Taus before the Taus killed them. I was afraid that they were shooting our own people while taking a heavy toll of the enemy.

One of the Taus made an attempt to get to us from the flank, but I clubbed her with the butt of my rifle and she went down like a rag doll. Another jumped in front of me, and I thrust at her. She forced my bayonet to the wall, breaking it. I dropped my rifle, and she sidestepped as I drew my pistol. I shot her through the head.

To my left I saw the last of the rangers in my group drop

out of sight, apparently dead. I turned and fired rapidly, killing five or six of the enemy standing over the bodies and mutilating them. Before any more could get to me, I threw away my pistol and picked up one of the ranger's rifles, flipping the selector to the five-shot burst position.

All at once, above the noise of the firing, the clanking of metal swords against rifles and bayonets, and the screaming of the wounded and dying, I heard a single voice clearly shouting, "Use your fucking grenades!" I didn't hesitate. I jerked one from my web gear and tossed it over the heads of everyone near me, trying for the rear of the hall, where there would be only enemy soldiers. There was a series of explosions, and the sound in the great hall died away slowly. One or two of the enemy made halfhearted efforts to stab the remaining rangers, but all the fight seemed to drain out of them.

For the first time since Patterson had kicked in the door, I had a chance to really look around. I was standing in a pile of bodies, mostly the enemy, but at least seven SCAF rangers. The rest of the force that had fought its way into the room were in groups of two or three. Twenty-five to thirty of our people had been killed.

The room was indeed huge, like an auditorium or a ballroom. At the far end, on a slightly raised platform, was an ornate chair riddled with holes from shrapnel. A large pile of Tau dead were scattered around it, as if they had been protecting it. I couldn't really see that much because of the smoke caused by the grenades. I stood there, gasping for breath, a rifle held loosely in one hand. I was slowly realizing how close the fight had been.

Although the ranger platoon had taken quite a beating, most of my squad had survived. We regrouped near the doors, drawing away from the enemy. The Taus didn't try to stop us. They were milling around, bumping into each other and the walls, stumbling over the dead and into us. Most had dropped their weapons and no longer seemed conscious of their surroundings. It was the most extraordinary thing I had ever seen.

I heard Susan practically shout, "What the shit is this?"

After several minutes we pushed our way deeper into the room. The ranger I had seen go down with the wound on her thigh was trying to wrap a bandage around it. I pushed her blood-smeared hands away, so I could do it myself. I helped her to her feet and we moved toward the raised area. She sat on one of the steps. Her face was pale, and I knew she'd need real medical aid soon because she had lost a lot of blood.

O'Rourke yelled, "Hey! Over here."

He was standing near the body of one of the enemy which appeared to be a lot bigger than the rest. I stood up and received another shock as Susan said in a surprised voice, "It's a male!"

We knew that Intell would want to know about this as quickly as possible, but when the rangers found the radioman's body, they also found that his equipment had been hacked into useless spare parts. One of the NCO's asked Susan about our short-coms.

"I can contact part of your company, I think," she said.

"Have them relay a message up to Intell. They'll want to see this. And then see if we can't get some medical aid down here."

I looked away from the male's body. I wasn't that interested in it. A moment later I felt Susan's hand on my shoulder, stared up at her and said, "Shouldn't we bring Steve's body down here?"

"Don't worry about it, Lara," she replied. "O'Rourke and a couple of others just went up for it."

"I wonder why the Taus stopped fighting?"

Susan shook her head. "I haven't the faintest idea."

Just after the scientists from Intell came down with the ranger company, Mary walked over to me. I was sitting on one of the steps to the raised area of the huge chair. Mary sat down, took her canteen from its pouch with deliberate slowness, and unscrewed the top. "Resistance in the areas closest to us has ceased completely," she said, "but I heard on the radio that they're still fighting in the other cities." She finally took a drink.

I looked toward the enemy we'd captured. They were all sitting quietly in a lopsided circle, none of them moving or talking. We had never heard them talking. Sometimes, when excited, they would scream, but the sound was unintelligible.

Now they just sat. The covered bodies of the people we had lost were near the doors. Steve was under one of the ponchos and I wished we had destroyed the resistance thirty minutes sooner. Steve might still be alive if we had.

I wondered if it was my fault. I'd been the closest to him when he died. I felt the tears sting my eyes, and knew I was only trying to make myself feel worse. It wasn't my fault that Steve was dead. He'd been the last person to check the room, and he hadn't seen anything. He had made the mistake that killed him.

I took a deep breath and let it out slowly. I tried to blink the tears away, and wished Steve was there to laugh at me and tell me that it wasn't important. Slowly I turned toward the enemy we'd captured and swung my rifle around. My grip tightened on the trigger and I considered shooting them, but hesitated because I knew it wouldn't bring Steve back.

I heard Mary say, "Lara! Lara! What's wrong with you?"

I shook my head, then wiped my eyes. "Nothing," I said calmly, quietly. "Nothing at all."

Then I found myself drifting toward the poncho-covered bodies. I knelt and lifted one corner so I could look at Steve. His face was strangely pale, almost a bleached-out white. His eyes were staring upward—dusty, hollow, lifeless. I brushed the hair off his forehead, stared into his eyes, and felt mine fill again.

I laid the poncho back, covering his face, then jerked it down to his waist. I could see the wet, ragged stain on his side. Quickly I reached down and pulled his knife from the scabbard. I put mine with his body and kept his. At least I would have something to remember him by. I took one more look, and gently replaced the poncho.

"Lara? You all right?"

I turned and saw Susan standing behind me, studying me. "I'm fine," I said. "I was just saying good-bye to Steve."

We were still confused about the sudden evaporation of resistance in our sector. Susan said she wasn't sure what happened, and seemed on the verge of saying more when there was a burst of shouting. A dozen laughing, backslapping rangers spilled into the hall. The linkup had finally taken place, and as far as we could tell, we controlled everything from the surface right down to where I stood.

The biggest surprise had to be the man who followed some of the combat troops into the hall. I had seen him before, but for a moment couldn't remember where. The flaming red mustache and stocky build were unforgettable, and the second he opened his mouth to speak, the Scottish accent gave him away. It was Peterson, the Intelligence officer who had briefed us about this place.

He walked over to the prisoners and stared at them. None of them moved or even looked up at him. They remained where they were, seemingly unconcerned. Peterson circled the group slowly, apparently studying them. He told one of the guards to untie those whose hands were bound. Even that didn't get any response. The Taus just sat where they were. It seemed they'd stopped doing everything, including breathing.

Peterson tried to talk to them. He used a variety of Old Earth languages, and when that didn't work, he looked around self-consciously. "We'd look pretty stupid," he said, "if they spoke a variety of German or Russian or something like that, and no one bothered to ask because we all assumed it wouldn't work."

Peterson continued his study of the prisoners. For minutes he would stand completely motionless, as if turned to stone, watching the Taus. Then he would shift slightly, stop again, and I felt I could see the lights flashing in his head. I'd never seen anyone focus so much of themselves into a task. Nothing made an impression on him while he was examining them.

After nearly an hour Peterson gave up. He had tried nearly everything, and nothing had produced any kind of response. He'd talked quietly, shouted, taken swings at them, and even hit a few. They did nothing. If they happened to be facing him, they watched, but if they weren't, they didn't bother to look around.

Peterson walked to the raised platform, stopped in front of the chair, and slowly studied the rest of the hall. There was nothing extraordinary about it, except that it was larger than any other room we had found in the tunnels, and it contained the platform, chair, and dead male.

Peterson checked it all carefully as he stepped to the doors

in the rear and peered behind them. He didn't need a flashlight
because the walls glowed with the same radiance that flooded
the rest of the tunnels. Once again there was nothing extraordinary.

The only thing that really set the hall off from the rest of
the tunnels and rooms was the body of the male, now being
slowly and painstakingly examined by half a dozen scientists.
Peterson had stared at it for a long time. Finally he turned his
attention to the prisoners, watched them for another thirty seconds, looked toward the chair and the male body lying near it,
then moved straight to it. He turned so he was facing the Taus,
seemed to wink at them with a slight smile, and sat down.

The reaction was immediate. All of them leaped to their
feet as if they'd received a telepathic command. Later we would
learn how close to the truth that was. But now they swarmed
toward Peterson as the guards tried to stop them. Peterson
shouted, "Let them be. They will no be doing a thing."

The guards halted, but fell in behind the Taus, who kneeled
in front of Peterson, their heads momentarily bowed. A dozen
of them made strange waving motions with their fingers. Peterson went into a trance, oblivious to everything around him
except the dancing of the prisoners' fingers.

For moments everything hung that way. Everyone sat still,
watching Peterson, who was sitting and staring. Nobody spoke,
including the Taus, who were watching Peterson intently while
wiggling their fingers at him. Slowly they gave up, until only
one of them was trying to get his attention with her fingers.
She too eventually quit and sat down, facing away from Peterson, as if he had disappointed her in some way.

Peterson waited for only a second, then he wiggled his
fingers at the Taus. All of them stood, even those facing away
from him, and they nearly rushed him again. The guards tried
to separate them, but Peterson repeated that it was all right.
They wiggled at him, and he wiggled back at them.

From the side of the hall, one of the rangers asked, "What
in the hell is he doing?"

Still moving his fingers in a complex and unintelligible
manner, Peterson said, "I'm talking to them, I think."

"How did you—"

Peterson shook his head and said, "Hush now, whilst I figure out just what I'm doing here." He looked around, saw one of the ranger officers, and suggested that everyone vacate the hall, leaving Peterson and the Taus alone for a while, so he could try to determine more about the situation. Peterson told the captain to set up to defend the tunnel, although he expected no counterattack in the near future. Peterson said that when he was finished, all of us, including the Taus, would move back to the surface.

Once outside, Susan told us to spread out and take five. The infantry captain wanted his company to guard both ends of the tunnel, so we set up near the huge double doors leading into the hall. I leaned against the wall and slid to the floor, setting my rifle beside me, within easy reach.

Mary and Richard sat down near me. I heard Mary mumble something before asking me, "How are you?"

I looked at her as if she was crazy. "What the hell do you mean, how am I? I'm fine. How the hell should I be?"

She shrugged. "I just wondered how you felt, that's all. I mean, after Steve was killed and all."

I felt myself getting angry—not because she'd been concerned, but because my behavior had been so transparent. Soldiers don't get upset when other soldiers die. Steve had made a mistake, as Fetterman would have said, and it was his fault he got himself killed.

Suddenly I realized that I wasn't going to stop missing him. Soldiers weren't supposed to have emotions, but I knew that was wrong. Soldiers had to feel things, otherwise they wouldn't stop killing because someone else ordered it. They would kill whenever it became convenient.

I shook myself and took a deep breath, letting it out slowly. "I'm fine," I said. "I'm tired. It's been a rough week."

Mary smiled. "I guess you could call it rough."

For a few minutes we didn't say anything. I looked at the rest of the squad. Most had gone to sleep, letting the infantry guard the perimeter. Susan had slipped, her shoulders and head resting on the wall, the rest of her body sprawled on the floor. I knew she was going to have a stiff neck when she woke up, and thought about waking her, but before I could move, I'd fallen asleep too.

Peterson roused us a couple of hours later. He was surrounded by the enemy, who seemed to be protecting him. He grinned, then said to Susan, "Ah, now lass, would ye be good enough to escort me and me entourage to the surface?"

"Sure. What about the prisoners?"

"They no longer be prisoners. They be our allies now."

Most of us had climbed to our feet and stood staring at Peterson as if he had lost his mind. He went on to say, "I will no tell ye all the details until I have a chance to brief the high command, but let me say this. 'Twas a king ruled them, and I may have the job now."

He explained a little of their social structure to us, claiming that each city dome was like a state, with the minor domes like the cities in it. The head of every dome, whether major or minor, ruled much like a king, and when he died, things were thrown into turmoil. Peterson had managed to end some of the confusion by a process that he didn't really understand, except he seemed to be the new ruler in the one dome and all its tunnels.

"How can you be sure they'll be loyal to you?"

Wanting to end the conversation, Peterson said, "That's something I should discuss with the high command first."

The infantry was left where they were so we'd have a rear guard, although Peterson claimed it wasn't necessary. We controlled the whole city and there would be no counterattacks for the moment. From that point on there were so many of our own troops around that they couldn't have counterattacked us.

Peterson and the Taus walked right out of the tunnel and kept moving toward the headquarters, but we all stopped as soon as we stepped into the sunlight. We'd been below the surface for so long, and our eyes had adjusted so well, that the sudden bright light hurt. We all stood blinking, eyes filling with tears and grabbing for our sunfilters as we tried to see where Peterson and the Taus were going. He hadn't even broken stride.

Finally we were able to continue. Only once did I look back, wondering if they would bring Steve to the surface or bury him where he was, if they could find a way to do it. I didn't think that they could, but they might try something like that.

Susan left us near the camouflaged entrance to the tunnel

system. A tent city had been thrown up close by, because we hadn't wanted to occupy the buildings. With all the tunnels and secret entrances, it hadn't been safe, at least until now. We were told to have some chow and relax.

Late in the afternoon Susan came to round us up. We were going to have a brief memorial service for those of the squad who had died fighting in the tunnels. I wasn't sure I wanted to attend, but felt it was my duty. I was certain it would make things harder on me. After managing to shove it all from my mind, it was now all going to be dug up in painful detail.

The chapel, like so much else on the planet, was a surprise. From the outside it looked like another tent, but the inside was much different. There was a hint of stained glass, an obvious illusion but one that was well done. The air was cool, the flooring soft, and the atmosphere sweet.

The only people there were members of the squad. The chaplin entered from the side and took his place in the front. He folded his hands, looked at us, and bowed his head. "Let us have a moment of silent prayer," he ordered.

I watched as the others bowed their heads. I was surprised so many of them went along.

The chaplain looked up then, and moved to the side. He glanced at a book and said, "Today we honor the memories of two fine soldiers, Steven McAllif and Mario Marchetti."

He misprounced Marchetti's name, but no one seemed to notice. Most of us mispronounced it too.

"Both these fine young men died in the service of their planet, defending humanity from the enemy here, on Tau Ceti Four. They did it without complaint, without reservation, giving all they could for all of us."

I wanted to plug my ears. I remembered Steve complaining constantly about the heat here, and how he hated everything about it. I stared at the chaplain and thought that he'd probably memorized the speech, changing only the names of the dead. It seemed to be a parody of what it should be, and I tried to tune him out.

Around me the others were listening closely. Several were crying. I hadn't known they were so close to either of the men killed, and I couldn't believe they were going to participate in this charade. The whole thing was making me sick to my stomach.

Steve hadn't died for the glory of his planet or because he believed in the cause or because God was on our side. He died because some unknown bureaucrat on Earth had moved an unseen key on a computer and Steve's name had popped out. The creatures here hadn't killed him, it was the ones on Earth who had conceived this monstrosity.

For a moment I believed, really believed, that the Tau Cetians hadn't destroyed the *Star Explorer*. It had been programmed to self-destruct so we would have an excuse, a motive, for putting together this fleet and this invasion. For a moment I believed it had been planned so that we could reduce the population of Earth by removing a portion of it from its surface.

Then I realized that it was all crap. I was angry because the government had taken my family from me six years ago—or was it twenty-six?—and they had now taken Steve. They hadn't killed him, only put him in a position to be killed. I felt the tears start again, and I couldn't stop them. I didn't care anymore. What I wanted was for something permanent. I wanted Steve, and I wanted a place to live with him. All I had now was my web gear and a tent, and the tent wasn't even mine.

Everyone stood, and I followed them. The chaplain was almost shouting something in a strange language. His arms were uplifted and his head thrown back, as if he were calling to God with every fiber of his being. I guessed he had to shout because we were so far from home.

When the service ended minutes later, the chaplain put out the candles and left the way he had come in. Susan moved to the front. She said, "I suppose there are a few more things that normally get said at a time like this, but I guess we all know what they are already so I'm not going to say them. We lost some friends, and words won't change any of that. Let's just get the hell out of here."

23

Fetterman, Anthony B.
First Lieutenant, Seventh Ranger Company, SCAF

Peterson moved to the center of the stage, in front of General Overton and his Imperial General Staff, and pulled a pointer off its hook. He spun it like a baton for a few seconds and then snapped it against the screen so it sounded as if a shot had been fired in the auditorium. When he had everyone's attention, he said, "I be sure that most of ye are now familiar with the tunnel system that we have found under each of the domes. For the unenlightened, I will take a few minutes to elaborate, for this might provide ye an insight into the society that we've found here."

Using a series of slides to demonstrate, Peterson showed a simplified schematic of a tunnel system. Then he projected an actual system, but it looked as if a child had taken a crayon and scribbled on a piece of paper. Peterson said, "So ye can see the problem that we're having with the taking of the tunnels."

He elaborated on that point for a few minutes. Then he said, "As ye know, we have taken City Complex 1. Most of the resistance has ceased, and the enemy there is now more or less aligned with us. There are some subtle and psychological reasons for that alignment, as well as the problems with it, but now is not the time to go into that."

Then, almost as if to contradict himself, he said, "It all boils down to the fact that everyone inside one of the complexes is related to everyone else, each male producing literally thousands of offspring."

Before anyone in the audience could react to the information, Peterson added, "These creatures are amazingly fertile. Almost every instance of sex results in a pregnancy. The gestation period seems to be shorter than the nine months required of human females, and there is an extremely high incidence of multiple births, so it is easily possible for one male to father thousands. And the vast majority of the Tau births are of females, the few males occupying a supervisory role, with the Tau kings at the very top."

Peterson then introduced a social anthropologist who explained that the Taus had a highly structured society resembling great extended families, with the dominant male at the apex of each family unit guiding all his children in some mystical fashion that wasn't fully understood. It was known that if the male died, there was a momentary confusion before his successor was chosen. When Peterson had sat on the throne in the giant hall, he'd added to that confusion, the throne being the symbol of a particular king, uniting several hundred family units.

"The key to the campaign then," said the anthropologist, "is find the ruling male of each major city-dome complex and kill him. In the reigning confusion, we might be able to overwhelm the enemy and deal them a crippling blow."

Then it was my turn. All I could say in the twenty minutes alloted me was that I had bad news. The tunnel fighting could continue for years, because the Taus had used the tunnels for centuries and knew everything about them. Given our finite resources—imposed by a twelve light-year supply line—it seemed we would eventually be overwhelmed.

When I finished, Peterson took over again. "As I'm sure that ye all now realize, we have found a way to shorten this war. During the last five days the Imperial General Staff has been studying the situation and has recommended a plan of action. I'll go over their recommendation in a few minutes. First, however, there are some additional facts that ye need.

"If we were fighting a conventional enemy, one tied to the planetary surface, we would be able to employ our thermonuclear and high-energy-beam weapons technology to neutralize the enemy's war-making capability. Our ground forces would then be able to control and govern the civilian population.

"We are not, however, dealing with a conventional enemy, and while we could control the planet's surface, we are quite incapable of subjugating the terrain beneath its face.

"We could," he continued, "using our thermonuclear devices, collapse the majority of the tunnels, but that would destroy the economic basis of the entire planet, thus negating the purpose of our mission."

There was an uneasy murmur from the room, but Peterson ignored it and went on.

"The upshot of all this, laddies and lasses, is that we are losing the war, and we are certain to continue to lose it unless we can remove the rulers of each of the remaining six cities in such a way as to create the most confusion among the various populations."

Peterson paused to let what he'd said sink in. The room seemed stunned by the enormity of the problem. Since I'd already heard most of it, I wasn't stunned. Impressed, yes, but not stunned. The thing that most impressed me was that the linguistics and semantic specialists in Intelligence had been able to figure out the Tau language at all. Not only was it completely new and foreign, but the method of communication was different. We used oral expressions and vocal gestures. The Taus used hand gestures and body postures. It explained why all the spies we sent in never returned.

"We have received absolutely reliable information," said Peterson, "that the male rulers of the remaining six city-domes will be meeting in three days time. If we can get into that meeting and remove the leaders, the entire population of Tau Ceti Four could be in our hands by Monday."

There was a stirring and rustling in the audience that slowly grew into a general pandemonium. The situation got so out of hand that Overton himself had to quiet them down.

Peterson moved to center stage again. "Our information is that each of the six leaders will be at the meeting, and that each will bring a personal bodyguard of two thousand warriors. That makes twelve thousand enemy soldiers, not to mention an estimated twenty-four hundred Tau scientists and technicians who work in the area, and another sixteen hundred security personnel. A force of nearly sixteen thousand."

He went on to detail the specifics of the raid, who would hit what targets, who would create the necessary diversions, who would search out the hiding places of the kings, and who would have the task of taking the thrones to prevent one of the lesser males from assuming command.

Peterson also mentioned a communications center to be eliminated, and I wondered exactly how they could communicate if they weren't in sight of one another. Peterson seemed to anticipate my question by telling us that the Taus employed a combination of cable and wireless communication links using a keyboard and printer system with a hundred twenty-seven character alphabet. We hadn't managed to figure all of it out. They also used a line of sight system like the heliograph.

When Peterson paused, as if to catch his breath, a captain stood up and asked, "How many of our people will be going on the raid?"

Peterson laid his pointer across the rostrum, leaned forward, and said evenly, "Two ranger battalions and a company of pathfinders."

"Jesus Christ!" someone said.

"Begging your pardon, sir," said the captain, "but a battalion is only about sixteen hundred troops. We'll be outnumbered eight or ten to one."

Peterson's only response was, "Thank you for that information, but we already know how many men and women make up a battalion. With the fighting in the other cities it's all we can spare. Anything else?"

A lieutenant colonel near the back stood and said, "I could be wrong, but isn't it a little unusual to find such a large force of Taus above the surface? What are they doing up here, and what's to prevent them from escaping when we arrive?"

"Let me answer the latter part of the question first. We have every reason to believe that the Taus would attempt to hold this area until reinforcements arrive. Second, we have been able to obtain a partial schematic of the tunnel complex in the area. We will use this knowledge to flood the tunnels in the immediate vicinity with neurone gas. That way, should the rulers make it into the tunnels, they won't go very far. As for what they're doing there, they've established a research and manufacturing facility that requires large sums of electric power, which they can best obtain through hydroelectric facilities at the dam."

"I'm afraid I didn't make myself clear," said the lieutenant colonel. "I was wondering what all the Tau rulers were doing in this one area."

"As I said, the Taus have established a research and manufacturing facility here, and it appears the rulers are coming for a demonstration of the first finished product."

The lieutenant colonel looked pretty put out. "For God's sake man, are you going to tell what they're building up there or not?"

Peterson looked toward Overton, who nodded slowly. "Go ahead, Major," he said. "They'll find out sooner or later anyway, and I guess they've got the right to know."

"Let me begin by saying that we have learned since our initial contact with the Taus almost eleven months ago that they are highly intelligent, imitative, and extremely logical creatures who have chosen to live a depersonalized and socialized lifestyle that is a very old one by Earth standards. If their weaponry was a bit primitive at first, it is only because their society did not demand sophisticated weapons before our arrival. I would remind ye that in recent months they have produced increasingly modernized weapons, some of them designs that Earth science would have trouble duplicating."

Now he detailed the specific buildings and the general purpose for each. There was a powder-billet manufacturing facility for beryllium. A building to produce lithium hydride. A plutonium facility and two structures that housed electromagnets for the separation of uranium 235 from its natural companion, uranium 238; and a reactor pile for transmutating uranium 238 into plutonium 239. And the lake contained an unusually high concentration of the deuterium isotope of hydrogen.

"In short, Colonel," said Peterson, looking directly at the

man who had asked the question, "what the Taus are doing up there is manufacturing a fusion bomb."

Nobody in the entire room said anything. It was almost as if the whole auditorium had stopped breathing. I could hear a hammering in my ears that I slowly realized was my own heart pounding in my chest. Peterson tucked the pointer under his left arm like a swagger stick and strode around the front of the rostrum to the very edge of the platform. His voice was clear and resonant. He no longer needed the microphone.

"I would like to point out that since the Taus have already exhibited a knowledge of rocketry, it is reasonable to assume that they will employ a missile delivery system for their bomb. And since they are well adapted to living in a tunnel environment, it will be relatively simple for them to render the surface of this planet useless to us while creating comparatively little danger to themselves. It is, of course, unknown how long it will be before they constitute a threat to the fleet. Based on the previous loss of one exploratory probe and a scout ship, it must be assumed that they have the capability of striking at the fleet now. We do not know why they have not chosen to do so.

"All this brings me to the final point of the briefing. Obviously we cannot risk having the Taus successfully complete construction of a fusion weapon. That is the reason for phase two of this operation. If the first phase is successful, the second will be cancelled. If, however, phase one fails, two hours and forty-five minutes after the commencement of phase one, phase two will begin. Phase two calls for the elimination of the Tau nuclear development facility by thermonuclear bombardment from the Strategic Fleet Air Arm. The raiding party must accomplish its task in two hours and forty-five minutes, or have withdrawn from the target area. Once the operation begins, unless the first phase is successful, the bombs will fall, whether our troops are clear of the area or not."

The room was suddenly as quiet as death; as quiet as the death of two battalions of SCAF troopers. Peterson didn't give the shock a chance to sink in and paralyze, but went right on. For the next hour he outlined the plan, the drop zones to be used by the raiding party, the specific objectives, and the weapons to be employed. When he finished, he looked at his watch.

"The names of those who will actually be going on the mission have already been selected by the Battle Planning Computer, and you will be notified within the hour. Training and armament phase will begin in four hours. Op Orders and other particulars, classified as Top Secret, will be distributed within the hour. Please read them carefully. There can be no margin for error."

Peterson nodded, and someone called the room to attention. The commanding general and his staff swept out, and the rest of the crowd started to file out of the auditorium in a stunned silence.

"Those going have already been selected by the Battle Planning Computer," he'd said. I looked up at Peterson, who'd walked over to where I sat.

"I have a very bad feeling about this," I said.

24

Masterson, Lara
Staff Sergeant, Second Special Operations Commando,
SCAF

For the raid the battle-dress design boys had mixed up a new
uniform that was supposed to make us invisible in the heavily
wooded terrain of the foothills. It was dark brown splotched
with forest green and daubed with patches of dull red and dull
yellow, with just enough black and battle gray and off-color
blue to be a camouflage expert's kaleidoscopic nightmare. It
looked like hell, and it worked like the devil. It was just about
the best set of no-see-me's I'd ever not seen.

They'd worked over the helmets and web gear too, and had
come up with a rubberized cover that fitted snugly over the
assault rifles and submachine guns without interfering with
the operation of the weapon. There were even new covers for
the body armor and a bunch of camouflage ski masks to cover
the face.

We'd studied every phase of the operation over and over
again, worked through it on models, and had so many rehearsals
in the simulator ships that we could have done the whole thing
blindfolded. And I'm not kidding. They made us do it blind-

folded nineteen times until we got it right. Just when I was beginning to think my elbows and knees couldn't take any more bruises, they called a halt and checked us out on the jet belts.

The belts weren't really new. We'd been trained in their use on the trip from Earth, but we hadn't yet had occasion to use them in battle. You strap into the thing like you would a parachute, and you can fly around all over the place at speeds up to 160 kilometers an hour or all the way down to a hover. They've got a range of about 240 kilometers at eighty percent power, and enough lifting capability for a fully-armed trooper to hook onto two wounded buddies and fly away with them. The controls are somewhat complex to explain but rather simple to work, and it flies hands-off so you can use your weapons.

I said the controls were simple to work. That's not quite true. There aren't any buttons to push or handles to play with, but you've got to learn to do something a whole lot trickier. You've got to learn a whole new way of thinking. There's a little nylon cap, sort of like an ancient flying helmet from the First World War, that goes on under your battle helmet. It's got a series of sensors in it that can pick up a certain brain-wave pattern and feed it into a computer-integrated control system that tells the belt what to do. You've got to be careful how you think once you've got it on because the computer works in strictly logical sentences and sometimes takes your thoughts a little too literally. People have gotten themselves killed in a flying belt by thinking the wrong think at the wrong time. Even so, it's a pretty good rig if your legs can hold up the twenty-five kilogram weight during landing, along with everything else a PAI trooper has got to carry. It only has two real faults: It burns an enhanced synthetic-triosene fuel, and there isn't a lot of that stuff to go around in the Retribution Army; and it *is* noisy. Even if you come in at top speed, the enemy is going to know you're coming a couple hundred meters away. Even if they're stone deaf.

The whole operation had been put together aboard the fleet for a number of reasons. First, the simulator ships could be set up to provide a close approximation of the target area; second, it made as good a staging area as any; and third, security. The top brass still didn't trust the Complex 1 Taus completely, and there were no Taus on board any of the ships, at least not any who were alive.

The brass had gotten so goddamn security conscious that they isolated us completely; we even had to sleep in the damned simulators on Thursday and Friday nights. I was so used to being screwed by SCAF by now that I only considered it a minor irritant, but it didn't set well with most of my squad. I really didn't give a shit, because I didn't know any of them. They were just eleven names that the Battle Planning Computer had chosen for the mission and said could do their jobs. I preferred it that way since I figured the odds were excellent that they'd all get killed. Not that it mattered much. Odds were I'd be just as dead as they were.

On Saturday we closed out the training at 1600 and were told that a party had been arranged in the auditorium in order to give everybody a chance to blow off some steam. Happy hour would start at 1730 and a super fancy dinner featuring a Tau reptile would follow. The history experts said the beast was supposed to be an excellent approximation of cattle, as far as taste was concerned—at least according to computer comparisons—and I was looking forward to my first taste of steak, even if it wasn't real cow. After dinner they'd crank up the band and there'd be more booze, in moderation, of course, and short-term, nonrecurring hallucinogens, uppers, and downers for those who preferred to get their kicks in a capsule. The best news was that we'd be permitted to sleep in a real bed for a change. The party would terminate at 2230, and Sunday wake up would be at 0530.

I checked my billet card and found out I'd been assigned to vacant NCO quarters. With so many empty rooms around— most of the army being on or below the planet's surface—few in the raiding party had more than one or two roommates.

I picked up my gear in the simulator and went off to find my room. Once I got my gear squared away and my weapons and equipment checked and laid out so they'd be ready in the morning, I took off my clothes and got in the shower. It was the first time in nearly six years that I'd had a shower all to myself, and I took my time and enjoyed it.

When I stepped out, I found a man shaving at the basin. His shirt was hung over the towel rack and I could see the

silver bar on the epaulet. He turned, saw me standing there
naked, and handed me a towel. Then he turned back to the
mirror, checked his watch, and washed the depilatory cream
from his face. He picked up his shirt and said, "You still
standing there holding that towel?"

"Fetterman?"

"Yes? We've met before?"

"Masterson," I said, tucking the towel around me. "You
were my TI when I first came in. Later you went to rangers
and I went to pathfinders. We worked together once, during
the start of the invasion."

"Oh, yes, I remember now. I didn't recognize you. Never
saw you with your clothes off. At least not since you filled
out. I hope you don't mind sharing your shower facility with
an officer, because they've billeted me next door. I guess being
only a first lieutenant, I wasn't important enough to rate real
officer country."

"I guess I don't mind too much," I said. "Sort of nice seeing
a familiar face again. I wonder why they put you in here?"

"The infinite wisdom of the Battle Planning Computer, I
suppose."

I looked at him sharply. "Are you going on the raid?"

He looked like he'd just let something slip he shouldn't
have, which he had. He shrugged. "Oh, hell. What difference
does it make? Yes, I am, and I assume you are too, or you
wouldn't know about it."

"At least now we know why they put you up in NCO country.
Probably want to keep the raiding party housed all together."

The situation got a little embarrassing after that, what with
me standing there wrapped up in a towel and Fetterman staring
at me. I suppose I should have felt silly about being embar-
rassed, I mean, after all, I was twenty years old and a combat
veteran. But I still felt awkward. What I'm trying to say is that
I guess I'd had sexual experience, but I wasn't really experienced sexually. Steve was the only guy I'd ever cared about,
and he was the only guy I'd ever had sex with. It wasn't that
there hadn't been other offers, it's just that I'd never accepted
them.

Fetterman finally said, "You a sergeant now?"

I automatically answered, "Yes, sir."

"Well, Sergeant 'Yes sir,' if you don't go get dressed, we're going to miss cocktails. Hurry up and I'll walk down to the auditorium with you."

Fetterman was so damned polite it was sickening. I don't really mean that. Actually, just talking to him as we walked down to the auditorium, he seemed almost human. It was hard to think of him as the rat bastard I remembered from training. I wondered if he'd changed his attitude because he was an "officer and gentleman" now, or because I was a sergeant and not just a dumb trainee. I finally decided that it wasn't so much that he'd changed as it was that I had. Being a combat veteran gives you a different outlook on life, especially when you're the only survivor of your squad.

That wasn't quite true, I reminded myself. Danny O'Rourke was still around, but he'd been given a rear area job while he got used to walking on his new legs. I guess next to Steve's, Susan's death hurt me the most. We'd been deep in Tau territory, in the tunnel complex under one of the minor domes, when she lost her balance on a ledge and fell, breaking her back. We couldn't move her, and we couldn't stay, because the Taus were closing in. We also couldn't leave her, because the Taus generally didn't take prisoners, and those that did get taken were invariably tortured to death. Danny had been hit already, and command of the squad fell to me. I'd put my hand over Susan's mouth and put Steve's knife up under her ribs. I hadn't liked doing it, but it was all I could do for her, and hoped that if I was ever in the same position, somebody would do it for me. It would have been easier on me if I could have put a slug through her head, but the Taus were too close, and we were too far into their territory. Even a silencer might have given us away.

At dinner, protocol demanded that Fetterman sit with the other junior officers, and I lost track of him. I hung around for a while and had a couple of drinks and smoked a Tau cigar, but I really wasn't in a partying mood. I didn't want to dance, and I don't do dope, and the orgy that was taking up the other half of the dance floor was a little too public for my taste. I wasn't worried about the mission. You're always afraid you might get killed, but you learn to live with your fear. I was just lonely and depressed, and I missed Steve. After about an hour I finally gave it up and went back to my room.

I noticed a light under Fetterman's door, knocked, and heard him say, "Enter!" He was sitting in the middle of a pile of equipment, reassembling his rifle. I noticed it was one of the sniper models.

"Didn't know you were on one of the take-out squads," I said. "Guards?"

"Kings."

"I'll be damned. My squad is spearhead for the Royal wrecking crew. We drew the bunker which also wins us the point for the battalion."

"Then I'll be riding down with you tomorrow," he said. "My platoon is security for the bunker operation. The sergeant in charge of my hit squad sicked out, and there wasn't time to train anyone else, so I get to do some of the long-range trigger work, if any. Would you care for a drink?" He fished a half-liter bottle of something out of his pack.

"What is it?"

"It's green."

"I can see that. What is it really?"

"Absinthe. Another name for liquid fire. Enjoy."

I tipped the bottle and nearly died. "Jesus. You weren't kidding. Where'd you get this, from the bottom of the fuel tank in your jet belt?"

"Had it ever since Earth. Been saving it for a special occasion, like my thirtieth birthday or something."

"Today your birthday?"

"Tomorrow."

"Some present."

"It will be," he said, his smile vanishing.

I don't think I ever did ask him what he meant. We sat there on the floor and talked for a while and drank from his bottle. But I don't blame the alcohol. It wasn't the alcohol. Maybe it was the loneliness. I don't know exactly how it happened, but I think I kissed him first. I'm almost sure I did.

I slept with him, and he was gentle, oh so gentle, not like the Fetterman I remembered at all, and he was very expert. I didn't love him and he didn't love me, and it was better that way. I needed him. It had been a long time since I'd been with a man, and for a while he filled an aching hollowness that I'd carried with me since Steve's death. I knew that for the night, at least, I also filled an emptiness in him.

At 0530 he woke me and we had breakfast together, got our gear, and walked down to the disembarkation bay.

"Tony," I said, "you got any idea why the Intell specialists didn't train with us?"

"Probably had to get them out of storage."

"What?"

He just smiled. "Never mind. You'll see."

I saw all right, when we found our shuttle in Berth 19, but I didn't understand. Standing quietly, split in two neat rows along either side of the corridor, stood Major Peterson. All fifty of him.

"I don't understand," I said.

"Neither did I for a long time. I found out for sure day before yesterday."

One of the Petersons detached himself from the group and walked over. Fetterman started to salute, but Peterson waved it away.

"Now, now, lad. We'll be having none of that. We've more important things to do, we do. This, I assume, is the lass who'll be finding us a safe route through any unexpected defenses the Taus may have set up." He grabbed my hand and pumped it furiously. "Me name's Peterson, or Pete if ye so prefer, and all of me answer to the same thing. It won't make any difference which one of us ye address either. We'll all be getting the message."

"I still don't understand," I said, looking past him at all the carbon copies.

"They're me twins," he said.

"All of them?"

"In a manner of speaking, lass, in a manner of speaking. We all spring from the same maker, if you take me meaning."

"I think I'm beginning to. You're not a clone?" He shook his head. "A machine?"

"Now, now lass. You've no call to be insulting. I'm a biomedically-engineered cybernetic with full heuristic and mnemonic capability and cross linked time-sharing, utilizing neuroskeletal and neuroeffector polysystems."

"The best General Motors can produce, I suppose."

"Now, lass, you're insulting me heritage. I'm the best British Leyland can produce. And I'd like to point out that the Peterson Series wouldn't be what it is by half if it weren't for me own truly amazing capabilities."

"All this and modest too."

"Aye. Now let's get ye strapped in good and proper. We got ourselves a few thousand Taus to kill before this day is over. Six at least, in any eventuality."

We did our best to make things difficult for the Taus. The drop was from ten thousand meters with a free fall to four hundred meters. Just before our chutes popped, a flight of helicopters rolled in over the DZ and dusted it with a particularly disgusting combination of nonlethal but thoroughly discouraging chemicals, then broke and laid smoke around the perimeter. We'd been told that there weren't enough helicopters left to fly us in for the mission. The way the Taus had knocked them down at the start of the invasion, I was amazed that they could even scrape up a whole flight to fly cover.

With all the extra equipment I had to carry, I hit hard, despite the oversized canopy. At least the wind wasn't going to drag me anywhere. I slipped the harness, gathered in the chute, and carried it over to my equipment container. I had most of my gear on, but the jet belt and about half of my extra ammunition and explosives were packed in the induraplast cylinder. I buckled into the jet belt harness, clipped on the munitions pouches, and stuffed my chute into the container.

I knew I had to get clear of the DZ before somebody from the next wave got dropped on top of me, but the smoke was so thick that I couldn't tell where the forest started and the dropping zone left off. I checked my wrist compass for a north heading, and started dragging my equipment container across the clearing. I didn't want some trooper breaking his leg when he landed on it. He might be the one who would keep me alive later. I hadn't heard any firing yet, and that was a good sign.

I finally almost bumped into a tree, and realized I'd reached the edge of the DZ. I pushed the equipment container up against the tree, unclipped my submachine gun from the belt, and found some cover behind a couple of trees with reasonably thick trunks.

I couldn't see a damned thing. The smoke was still pretty

thick, and after dragging the container across the DZ while
wearing forty-one kilos of equipment, I was sweating to beat
hell. The perspiration beaded itself up over my eyebrows until
it rolled down into my eyes and stung like you wouldn't believe.
There wasn't anything I could do about it. If I pulled off the
mask to wipe my eyes and clean the shatterproof lenses, I'd
be coughing and crying and puking inside of fifteen seconds,
to say nothing of developing the world's worst case of diarrhea.

I felt along my right forearm until I found the transponder
box, and keyed the squad circuit. As the fogged-up crystals in
the mask began to clear, I could vaguely make out the Heads
Up Display on my helmet visor through the left eyepiece. The
HUD showed eleven other marks beside my own, and gave
direction and distance readouts. I keyed the rally beacon and
cursed as another droplet ran down my closed eyelid and somehow found its way underneath.

I lay there shaking my head in a futile effort to keep the
sweat out of my eyes until Sergeant Brenner crawled up and
put his hand on my shoulder. He shoved the voicemitter on his
mask close to my ear so he could talk without keying the
shortcom, and told me everyone was here except Gaskell, who'd
managed to break his ankle on landing. He was out of the
game, and the medics had him in tow.

I wanted to get clear of the DZ as soon as possible so we
could lose the damned masks, so I keyed the transponder freqs
for Fetterman and Peterson. I wondered briefly which Peterson
would crawl up, then realized that it really wouldn't matter.
Probably whichever one was closest.

I told Brenner to take the squad fifty meters straight north
and then wait. As they stumbled off through the smoke I wondered if Brenner resented my being in command of the squad.
My permanent rank was the same as his, but I'd been made
an acting staff sergeant for this mission.

All in all the squad was pretty rank heavy. There were two
corporals, three lance corporals, and five PFC's—no, make
that four with Gaskell out. I figured that an army with that
many noncoms had to be in serious trouble, though I guess it
could have been that the Battle Planning Computer tried to pick
the best people for the job, regardless of rank. Still, I knew
I'd been promoted principally because I was a survivor. I lived

when others died, which in pathfinders is the real acid test of
bility. You could look at it either way. Either I had the cream
f the crop to work with, or I had the leavings after everybody
lse got killed. Either SCAF had given me a bunch of crack
allschirmjaeger to conquer Crete, or the Taus were on the
utskirts of Berlin and Herr Führer Overton had ordered the
olksgrenadier to win the war.

Fetterman and his platoon sergeant, a big bosomy blonde
ame Dessenko, crawled up with one of the Petersons, and I
riefed them on how I planned to run the op. I figured to run
y squad out about three hundred meters in front of their
latoons, keeping pretty much to a predetermined compass
earing and using the shortcom only when necessary to inform
em of deviation in the normal heading or of the presence of
au patrols or defenses. For the most part we'd just mark the
safe" route with the little wire-mounted flags we carried and
se the radios only if the situation got out of hand. We had
ive klicks to cover before we got into assault position, and
ot a lot of time to do it in.

The Tau base lay on the far side of the lake. It could be
ken only by surprise, stealth, and determination. The deter-
ination had been thoughtfully supplied by SCAF IGS in the
orm of five strategic shuttles being bombed-up somewhere
board the fleet. The stealth had been largely ruled out by the
ecessity of mounting the operation during daylight hours in
rder to ensure that the Tau rulers would be present for the
cheduled demonstration. That left only surprise to work with.

There were one or two suitable drop zones closer to the
arget, but they were too close. The DZ selection, the HALO
aradrop, everything, was designed to keep the Taus from
nowing we were coming. Even the chemical the DZ had been
moked with was designed to hang together, hug the ground,
nd break down chemically and dissipate without rising enough
o be visible to any Tau observers across the lake. When the
rmor under Lieutenant Colonel Kadrmas started the diversion,
ey'd be moving up what seemed the only possible route of
pproach after being brought into the general area in heavy
ansport shuttles. The Taus would throw everything they had
t them. They wouldn't expect two battalions to come flying
w and fast across the lake behind them in jet belts. At least

that's how it was supposed to work.

I found Brenner and the squad and we moved out. It wa.
pretty much a standard operation—a point, slack man, mai*
body, flankers, and trail. I almost laughed when I thought abou*
it. With all the city and tunnel fighting, it was just about th*
first "standard" patrol we'd run since the invasion, and ther*
wasn't anything standard about the mission.

I was thankful when we finally got far enough from the D*
to take off the gas masks and wipe our eyes and foreheads
The camouflage ski masks were much more comfortable t*
wear. They were made of a nylon derivative, and since the*
were designed to hide shiny faces and not keep out noxiou*
chemicals, the material "breathed" and helped keep your fac*
dry. I was glad for the small help.

According to the history tapes the Tau forests are more lik*
jungle. That really didn't bother me, since the only forest o*
jungle I'd ever seen had been made out of plastiform. The thin*
had trees, and that was good enough for me.

The air had a cool, wet smell to it, despite the heat, and a*
we moved through the thick growth I became aware of th*
insect life. I guess it struck me as funny because I hadn't see*
any Tau insects yet. They didn't seem to exist in the cit*
complexes, but here there was a multitude of shapes, sizes
and colors. I wondered how many of them could kill with *
bite or a sting, or perhaps even a touch if I stopped to take on*
in my hand. I knew that numerically the odds were against it
but those were Earth odds for Earth insects, and this was Ta*
Ceti Four.

The land roller-coasted along through the forest, all ridge*
and ravines that somehow managed to run mostly uphill. Th*
trees tended to be twenty-five to thirty centimeters in diamete*
and were close together. There was a lot of underbrush, but *
was well spread out and you could walk through it withou*
hacking your way along with a machete, which didn't exactl*
enhance my opinion of the fifty-centimeter, two-kilogram blad*
dangling from my web gear. I figured I had enough importan*
stuff to carry without lugging around some damned piece o*
nonessential equipment.

The ground here seemed to have a soft springiness, but *
didn't squish underfoot or feel damp, and the fallen leave*

rustled and cracked noisely on the forest floor when you forgot to be careful about where you stepped. Pathfinders aren't supposed to forget things like that, but they're not supposed to have to carry forty-one kilos through five kilometers of hilly forest, attack and defeat an enemy force with ten to one superiority, establish a new royal family, and do it all in less than two hours and forty-five minutes either. I've seen the manual, and it ain't in the job description.

I was startled out of my reverie by an abrupt snorting noise followed by the sounds of a large animal crashing loudly through the trees. After about a minute the crashing stopped and the forest got quiet, then slowly came the most inhuman snarling, crying scream I ever could have imagined in a month of horror movies. It finally died and everything was still again. I decided that whatever kind of creature I'd spooked into flight, I really didn't care to get close enough to find out.

I was mad at myself for having startled whatever it was. Pathfinders are supposed to be able to walk around in the wilds without disturbing the aborigines. Perhaps I would have been able to if this had been a normal pathfinder operation, but it wasn't in the cards. When you're trying to do this kind of job in a hurry, you make mistakes. That's what killed Corporal Olson.

I know some would say it was the snake that killed him, but it wasn't really. The trapdoor over the snake's hole was mostly dead vegetation. It really didn't blend that well with the surrounding flora. Olson should have seen it—maybe he did, but he didn't observe it. If he'd observed it, he would have avoided it. He walked right past it and the snake just stuck its head out and swallowed him, jet belt and all.

Olson had been the point man. We'd probably never have known what happened to him if Glenn, who had the slack, hadn't come upon the snake lying outside its hole with Olson's boots still sticking out of its mouth. Glenn emptied a full magazine into the snake from her submachine gun, but finally had to finish it off by shooting it in the head with her pistol. She ripped the snake open with her knife, but it was too late for Olson. I couldn't really tell if it had been suffocation or just shock that killed him. He had some broken ribs, but it didn't really look like he'd been crushed. Even the fang wounds weren't through anything vital. I suppose it could have been poison, but I don't think it was. Something that big doesn't need poison.

I should have chewed out Glenn for firing her weapons, but if there'd been any Taus around to hear the silenced firing, they'd have been close enough to hear Olson being eaten, so there was really no point. There was also the fact that she'd done everything she could to help Olson, and although it was too late for him, and was probably the wrong thing to do even if it hadn't been too late, I wasn't so sure I'd see everything in such an objective light if one of those monsters decided I might make a good snack.

We didn't have time to bury Olson and we couldn't risk the smoke from cremation. We hid the body and the snake's, picked up his weapons and ammunition, and went on.

We made about another kilometer before Murphy fell into the spider nest. They were gray hairy things about the size of a dinner plate. There must have been fifty of them in that pit, and they were all over her. They picked her apart like ants. It pissed me off, and I dropped a White Phosphorus grenade down the hole and barbecued the little bastards. I shouldn't have done it, but right then I didn't care. We've got an unwritten rule in SCAF. Nobody dies for nothing.

If I hadn't already figured out that it was going to be a rough day on point men, I knew it when we found Blakeslee. She was lying on her back in a little clearing with the bodies of about half a dozen Taus around her. Blakeslee had a Tau short sword through her chest armpit to armpit and three or four stab wounds. The Taus had faired even less well. Three of them had been all but cut in half by submachine gun fire. One had Blakeslee's knife sticking out of her kidney, one had a broken neck and a smashed windpipe, and two had pistol shots—one through the chest and the other through the back of her head.

"Well goddamn it, that tears it. They know we're coming now," said Brenner.

"No they don't," I said.

"What the hell do you mean, they don't?"

I pointed to the one Tau who had a rifle lying just beyond her fingertips. "Except for this one, who was probably an NCO, all the Taus were armed with swords."

"So?"

"So nobody picked up the rifle or any of Blakeslee's weapons. Rather inefficient, wouldn't you say? And if there's one thing that I've got to give the father-fucking Taus, its that they're one efficient bunch of bitches." I smashed the Tau rifle against a tree and it broke in half. "Come on. We don't have time to waste here. Blakeslee got all of them before any got away. That's what matters."

We were about a kilometer from the lakeshore when we lost Wysoske. He stepped on a mine. It was an ultrasonic one, a Tau copy of the kind that we use, and it fricasseed him like a Southern fried. He never knew what hit him, and we wouldn't have either if we hadn't seen the flash when the fuel in his jet belt went up. You don't hear an ultrasonic mine go off. If you're close enough to hear it, you don't get the chance to tell anybody about it.

Fortunately for us the mine hadn't been tied to an alarm wire. There were plenty of alarm wires and other mines in the area, not all of them as quiet as the ultrasonic ones, but they were all laid down in the standard overlapping sawtooth pattern the Taus used, and it didn't take us all that long to find a safe passage through them.

We made the edge of the forest at the lakeshore with five minutes to spare, and I slipped out of my jet belt and web gear and scrambled up one of the sturdier looking trees so I could get a peek across the lake. The surface was smooth as glass and I thought I could just barely make out where the opposite shore melted into the mirror-finished water.

I flipped down the range finder on my helmet and punched the image multiplier up to 20x. I scanned the shore until I found the camp, and started picking out the different buildings. There was one big one that I couldn't identify, and I was trying to puzzle it out when it moved.

I hiked the multiplier up to 40x and took another look. It wasn't a building. It was a formation of troops. I studied them for a few seconds, and then it dawned on me. The father-fucking Taus were having a goddamn parade.

I scanned the area until I found what I was looking for, then ran the multiplier on up to 50x. There they sat in a neat little row at the front edge of the reviewing stand—the remaining six Tau kings.

I keyed the freq for commando HQ, bypassing the normal channels, and broke radio silence. "Black Jack Six, this is Spearhead One-six with a priority communication for the operational commander."

"Spearhead One-six from Black Jack. Maintain radio silence."

"Screw the radio silence. Listen you idiot, if you don't put me through to Six right now, we're going to blow the whole show."

"Didn't you hear me, soldier? I said maintain radio silence."

"And I said put the goddamn general on the blower you motherfucking switchboard operator."

"All right trooper, that's it. What's your name?"

"General Robert E. Overton, SCAF's commanding general," I shouted, "and if you don't get General Ander on the phone in the next five seconds, I will personally bust you all the way to civilian!"

There was a long pause, but it didn't work. "Very funny trooper, but you used the wrong call sign. We'll talk about the court-martial later. Now get off the air."

Brass-hatted bureaucrat. I keyed the platoon freq and got Fetterman on the shortcom. "I haven't time to explain," I said. "Put one of the Petersons on the line or this whole deal is going to turn into the biggest fiasco since the Little Big Horn."

There was a brief pause and then I heard Peterson's Scottish brogue booming, "Go ahead with ye."

"Peterson, this is Masterson. Didn't you tell me you had a data cross link throughout the Peterson series?"

"I don't believe those were me exact words, but ye have the gist of it."

"So is there a Peterson with Commando HQ?"

"Aye."

"Then for God sakes tell him to get to Major General Ander and call off the tanks. I can see the encampment, and the Taus are having a parade. All the kings are on the reviewing stand. If we can get a sniper team across the lake right now, we can catch them in the open."

I tried to make it clear, but under the circumstances I guess it would have been confusing to anybody. But Peterson wasn't an anybody, he was an anything, a Norwegian-surnamed, Scottish-speaking, self-appointed Englishman who just happened to be something more than a machine, and he understood.

"Aye. By the beard of me maker, I take yer point. Hang loose, lass. I'll be getting back to ye."

I slipped down the tree and got back into my web gear and jet belt. Then there was nothing to do but watch the seconds run out on the left stopwatch of my chronometer and pray. It was the first time I'd prayed in six years—make that twenty-six.

The stopwatch said triple zero, but the harassing fire the tanks were supposed to rain on the Tau camp didn't come, and I watched the digital readout count up plus one, plus two, plus three, then heard the sweet music of Peterson's brogue inside my head again.

"I've got 'em stopped lass, now tell me, what do you suggest we do now?"

"I suggest," I said, "that since we have very little time before the bombers show up and vaporize this neck of the woods, and since the Tau kings are at this moment all in one spot and we know which one, that we get a team across at once with sniper rifles and take them out at long range. Even if we only get some of them, the loss of leadership ought to pretty well disrupt the Taus.

"After we take out the kings, the tankers can lay down a heavy blanket of antipersonnel stuff on the parade ground. That ought to reduce resistance even further. When the barrage lifts, we can jump the ranger battalions right on top of them and proceed with the operation pretty much as we originally planned, except that we run a couple of sappers and a weapons squad straight for the reviewing stand. They'll be in the thick of it, but most of the Taus probably won't be fully armed for a parade. Our troops ought to be able to secure the reviewing stand and eliminate any remaining kings."

"'Tis a sound plan. I'd not of done better meself. How large a sniping party do ye figure on, and how do ye plan on getting them across the way?"

"As to how large, I'm not really sure. The party ought to be small enough to have a reasonable chance of escaping detection and big enough to take out the kings and get themselves out of trouble. One hit squad and one security squad ought to do it.

"As for getting across, the Taus will be making a fair amount of noise with their parade. We'll have to hope it's enough to cover the jet belts. I'd swing well to the southwest, cross the valley beneath the dam, and come up on the left plateau from behind. If there's anybody around, we'll have to push our way across and take the best shot we can get. If the top is clear, I'd leave the belts at the northwest rim and cross the mesa on foot, make less noise that way. We'd probably have to run it, time's getting too short.

"Once the snipers get to the south edge, they ought to have an unobstructed field of fire and about a fifteen-hundred-meter shot. That'll be kind of tough, especially after the run, but not impossible with the equipment we've got."

"Tis a sound plan. Perhaps the best we could have hoped for. Since ye have already looked the area over, would ye be considering taking your squad across as the security team?"

"Might as well. If this doesn't work, the bombers are going to kill us anyway."

"Aye, and so they are. I'm thinking that I'll give Fetterman here and his troopies a shot at ending the war, and just so there won't be any more communication problems with headquarters, I'm thinking I'll be for coming along meself and bringing one or two of me twins with me. Why don't ye break the good news to yer troops, and we'll be along in a minute or so and get this show on the road, soon as I let Ander know what we're about."

We crossed the valley in a tight little formation about four clicks below the dam and turned sharply up a steep, rock-strewn ravine. The rule book says you cross open areas like roads or valleys one at a time and stay out of ravines, but the rule book wasn't written for soldiers in jet belts. The more you string out crossing an open area, the greater the chance that one of you will be seen. This was an all or nothing proposition, and we crossed in mass. If we lost everybody here and now, or fifty-five minutes later when the bombers came over, it wouldn't make much difference.

We followed the ravine about halfway around the plateau,

staying well clear of the walls and about ten meters below the lip. When we ran out of ravine there really wasn't much we could do except dump the power on and head for the mesa. If anybody saw or heard us coming up the cliffs, they at least didn't shoot at us.

The mesa was too broken and rocky for the Taus to worry about our using it as an LZ or DZ, and they apparently hadn't thought it necessary to mine or defend it. Their evaluation of its military potential was accurate. You couldn't have landed a flight of helicopters, and a company of paratroopers would have wound up with about sixty or seventy broken legs, backs, and assorted appendages. But it didn't really pose a problem for twenty-two people in jet belts.

There was a problem though. On the way in we had noticed a Tau observation post located on the southern rim of the mesa, at exactly the point that would be most advantageous for our snipers to fire from. I'd picked it up at extreme range on 50x magnification while scouting out the firing site. If the sentries had noted our approach, they showed no signs of it.

We hid the belts in a recess beneath a rock overhang and covered them with brush. I assigned Corporal Kerr and Private Trent to keep an eye on our equipment. Since we'd be needing the belts to get off the mesa, I didn't want any curious Taus walking off with them if they somehow managed to find them. Then the rest of us picked up our weapons and ran.

We ran until our lungs ached and our legs ached and our heads ached and our guts ached. At least mine did. I hadn't hurt so much in so many places since the first run around the outside corridor of the *Erwin Rommel* when we started basic. How long ago was that again? Six years or twenty-six, it really didn't matter. It had been a lifetime, a hundred lifetimes, and I'd been running since before the Exchange, since before Christ, since before the dawn of man.

I tripped over something and flew forward. The ground came up to meet me and I hit like an overfull equipment container on a streamer. I shook my head to clear it, then decided that was a bad idea. I didn't want it to fall off. I looked to see what rock or log had dared to lay itself in my path, and discovered that it was Krilnikov. He'd tripped over a rock and I'd tripped over him.

A pair of hands reached down and grabbed us both by the shoulder, and Peterson hauled us erect. "Be ye okay?"

"Terrific," I gasped.

"I think I twisted my ankle," said Krilnikov.

"Can ye run?" Peterson said to me. I nodded, and he tossed Krilnikov over one shoulder and started off with him. Look at him, he isn't even breathing hard, I thought stupidly; doesn't need to, doesn't breathe. But you've got to breathe, breathe and run. Do it now! I started after them.

It was almost two clicks from where we'd landed in the jet belts to the Tau OP, and we ran the first sixteen hundred meters in under four minutes. I don't give a damn if it is impossible. I know what my stopwatch said. Then we collapsed in individual heaps and caught our breath, long enough to know we were already dead but that our bodies hadn't quite figured it out yet. Then we started working our way through the last four hundred meters to the watch tower.

Since the tower overlooked the Tau camp, it didn't have much of a view of the mesa itself, and we'd been well hidden during the run by all the rocks and trees. The thing was designed to serve as an OP for the valley below the dam, not for the plateau, maybe the Taus in it were all busy watching the parade. There was a strip of chest-high grass about three hundred meters wide, extending from the edge of the wood, and an area of bare ground beyond that, running right up to the cliff. The tower sat about fifteen meters back from the edge.

We couldn't take out the guards at long range because the snipers couldn't get clear shots at them in the tower, and if we missed, or only wounded one of them, she might get off a warning and spoil the whole show. Grenades were also temporarily out of the question. The tower was within range of the tube launchers on the two Stoners we had, but they weren't set up to handle ultrasonic grenades, and the conventional rounds were both noisy and far more uncertain than the ultrasonics. All of which meant that we had to do things the tough way.

Krilnikov had sprained his ankle all right. It wasn't bad. He could stand on it, and even walk a little, but he wasn't going to be dancing for a couple of weeks. Fetterman, one of the Petersons, and I talked it over and decided to leave him and one of Fetterman's men behind at the treeline with one of the Stoners to provide covering fire in case things went sour. Then we split up the remaining troops into two four-man fire elements and two five-man maneuver elements, and started crawling through the grass.

We ran into a couple of trip wires attached to parachute flares, but they were simple random sets and easy to avoid. We planned to hit the tower from the left and the right at the same time, with our fire teams separate but more or less in the middle. We didn't have all that many silenced weapons, since the original mission had called for strong-arm tactics rather than covert operations, so the majority of the silenced sub-machine guns and sniper rifles had been delegated to the fire teams, one of which had the other Stoner. Unlike the one we had left with Krilnikov, that one was silenced. The idea was for the maneuver elements to assault the tower and take it out, using ultrasonic hand grenades.

We were about three fourths of the way through the grass when I thought I heard something and motioned everyone down. It couldn't have been more than three seconds before a Tau pushed through the grass right on top of us. She was facing the wrong way and didn't see me, but she did see Brenner. Her mouth was open in surprise, but she didn't scream, just slipped that heavy-looking rifle off her shoulder and started swinging the muzzle toward Brenner. He started to shoot her with his Kalan, remembered it wasn't silenced, and dug frantically for his pistol as he got up on one knee to rush her.

I jerked my knife from its leg sheath, pushed myself up off the ground, and leaped high on the Tau's back, wrapping my legs around her arms so she couldn't use the rifle and slapping my left hand over her nose and mouth, pulling her head sharply to the left, spinning her off balance. The knife was in my right fist, blade downward, which is the wrong way to hold a knife for anything except what I was doing, and even then it's right only if it has a double edge. The stroke drew the blade across the neck directly above the carotid artery, toward the Tau's left shoulder. As she started to fall I unwrapped my legs to lower the body quietly to the ground, flipped my wrist, and made the second stroke across her larynx just under the Adam's apple. I pivoted my hips, my left leg keeping downward pressure across the Tau's back as she hit, and drove in an overhand ice-pick strike at the juncture of the neck and shoulder so the blade slipped in along the collarbone.

Brenner, who had finally got his pistol out, grabbed the Tau's hair and pulled her head around to check my handiwork. "Nice," he said, grinning at me. "Thanks. I'd never have made it in time." I grinned back and told him to forget it.

I never did figure out why the Tau was out wandering around in the grass by herself—maybe she was just looking for a place to squat—but I did find out where she came from. There was a sandbagged pit just at the edge of the open ground, with a light gas gun in it and three Taus sitting around it, drinking the local equivalent of coffee and smoking little cigars. We took careful aim and dropped them all with a single muffled pistol shot apiece. Glenn and the ranger who was with us slipped into the pit, checked the bodies, and cranked the gun around to cover the tower.

My earlier guess had been right. The Taus in the tower were so damned busy watching the parade that they hadn't seen us take out the gun crew. It seemed a shame to waste that kind of break, so I let the other teams know what the situation was over the shortcom, and Brenner, MacLean, and I hunched over and ran like hell for the tower. Nobody saw or heard us coming, and we pulled up short under it. We'd swapped the weapons around again, and I had the silenced submachine gun and MacLean the suppressed assault rifle. Brenner had the Kalan slung over his shoulder, his silenced pistol in one hand and an ultrasonic grenade in the other.

We just got beneath the tower when a trapdoor opened in the bottom and a Tau started backing down the ladder. She closed the door and kept backing. Brenner stuffed the grenade in his pocket and shoved his pistol back in its holster. He pulled his commando garrote—a piece of piano wire with a finger loop at each end—out of his pocket, and we moved around behind the Tau.

Just as she stepped off the last rung, Brenner dropped the garrote over her, driving his knee into her back and pulling sharply on the rings. Then he pivoted his hips beneath her, crossing his wrists to pull the garrote into a circle, and flipped her over his shoulder, stomping on her windpipe after she hit the ground. It made a lot less noise than it sounds like, and it just about severed the Tau's head.

MacLean and I covered the door and Brenner started up the ladder with his pistol drawn. When he got to the top, he dug the grenade back out of his pocket, pulled the pin, and tried the door. It wouldn't budge. He looked down at me and shrugged. I made a knocking motion with my fist. He caught on, and tapped at the door with his silencer. When a Tau opened it, he shot her in the head and slid the grenade under the door before it could fall shut.

Brenner dropped from the ladder like he'd been hit, did a perfect PLF, rolled and came up running. We took about seven quick strides, threw ourselves forward, rolled when we hit, and covered our faces. I felt the heat wash over me and knew we had barely missed being too damned close.

I shoved myself up, saw that Brenner was helping MacLean to her feet, and ran back for the tower. I climbed the ladder and tried the door. It moved but didn't open. There was something lying on it. I shoved hard and it gave. I pushed the snout of my Kalan over the hatchway and poked up enough of my head for a look. The only thing in front of me was a bunch of smouldering Tau bodies. I shoved the door wide open and looked behind me. Nothing moved. I climbed into the tower and checked the corpses. There were no wounded.

I signaled the other parties on the shortcom and crawled back down. Brenner and MacLean were crouched near one of the corner posts covering the door, and I waved a deprecating gesture at them.

"No survivors," I said.

MacLean had a nasty burn on her leg, right around the boot top. Her blousing elastic had slipped up and some floater microwaves from the grenade had toasted the exposed skin. It was only a first-degree burn, but it was a dandy, and placed just right to be constantly irritated by her boot. I rubbed some burn ointment on a dressing and wrapped it around her calf. I finished tying it off as the other teams came up.

Fetterman looked the situation over and positioned three of his long-range experts along the cliff edge. He put the other two up in the tower and joined them. His short-range specialists had nothing to do, so they joined the rest of my squad in securing a perimeter around the clearing. One of the Petersons took a position with the snipers along the cliff, and another with the snipers in the tower.

I climbed up in the OP myself, because it was the best place to direct security operations from, and tried to stay toward the back, out of the snipers' way. I studied the perimeter defenses and decided I really couldn't improve on them much without setting out trip wires and claymores, and we didn't plan on staying long enough to make them worthwhile.

The third Peterson ambled lazily over to the corner where I was standing and leaned against the wall with the bored look of a sidewalk superintendent watching a new Holidrome Inn going up. It struck me as completely out of place, compared to the frantic activity of the snipers, but beneath that placid veneer there could have been half a thousand thoughts clicking through the microcircuitry he called a brain. With Peterson you can never tell for sure.

The snipers were taking no chances. They had ART scopes on their rifles, but they checked the distance with the optical range finders on the battle helmets and again with a handheld laser range finder. The readings all gelled to within plus or minus half a meter. They made allowances for wind drift based on meteorological data from Weather Section, and took local and estimated target readouts with a scanning anemometry sensor. I suppose it all took less time than it takes to tell, but it seemed like forever.

Finally, just when I was beginning to think the parade would end and the kings get away before they were ready, Fetterman told them to load with Velex and stand by to shoot. I wanted to see this, and nothing was happening around the perimeter, so I flipped the shortcom to the freq the snipers were using, stepped forward a little so I could see better, and hiked the image multiplier up to 50x.

The receiver cracked and I heard a voice say, "Team B ready." Fetterman answered with "Team A ready. Start shoot sequence count." Then the automatic sequencer broke in for a five count, *"Beep . . . Beep . . . Beep . . . Beep . . . Beeeeeeeeep."*

There was a ragged clatter of bolts and a tight series of dull pops as they fired. The rounds impacted the target area just over a second later; it only seemed like forever. A Velex round is made up of a recessed discriminating impact fuse in an explosive compound projectile. It doesn't just expand on entry, it goes off. All the expanding was done by three of the Tau kings. They came apart like they'd been hit with two cannon shells apiece instead of two rifle bullets, and I guess in a way they had.

Almost immediately Fetterman fired again. Someone down at the cliff edge must have fired also because a fourth Tau king and a warrior standing next to him blew apart. Things were happening fast down on the reviewing stand now as bodyguards attempted to shove the other two remaining kings off the platform and shield them with their bodies. One of them was hit in the leg and most of it came off, but it looked like he was still alive. The other had vanished under a pile of bodies somewhere. I didn't know if he'd been hit or not.

"Targets of opportunity," yelled Fetterman, and the snipers began firing at anything that moved.

"If ye be ready for it, I'll be calling in the artillery from the tanks now," said the Peterson nearest him.

"Do it," said Fetterman.

The Peterson stared straight ahead and said to no one in particular, "Shoot, over," and the Peterson behind me stared idly out the back of the tower and said, "Shoot, out."

Neither of them did anything after that, at least not anything visible, and I glanced back toward the Tau camp in time to see the first explosion shred about a dozen Taus with flechettes. The entire encampment was in a state of confusion. The whole scene was suddenly obliterated by the gray-white smoke of 105mm shells as close to a hundred antipersonnel rounds erupted all over the parade ground.

I got Kerr and Trent on the medcom, and a few minutes later they dropped. Each had a jet belt clipped to either side of his or her own and a third one held in his arms. We distributed the six belts then sent back all eight troops to pick up the rest of the belts and collect Krilnikov and the ranger we'd left with him.

The rest of the SCAF force that had been waiting across the lake jumped before the barrage lifted and landed in the Tau encampment as the last of the artillery fire was walking off the edge of the parade ground.

By the time we got organized and down off the plateau and

into the camp, SCAF was pretty well in control of the battle. But the war wasn't over yet. Rangers had secured the base perimeter and most of the Taus had stopped fighting, but two of the kings had gotten away and there were still close to four thousand Taus who weren't ready to quit.

Most of the resistance was from surviving bodyguards of the two kings who had slipped away, but there were also close to a thousand base security personnel who had apparently been selected from the domain of one or both of the surviving kings, or had been conditioned to function without their divine guidance because they were still putting up a hell of a fight.

The bodyguards and security forces were both elite units, and for the most part their equipment and troops were nearly as good as our own. The chief advantage we had was in the superior maneuverability afforded by the jet belts. We were left with some nasty mop-up operations to handle with time running out. The bombers were due in nineteen minutes, and they wouldn't stop unless we wrapped up the whole show.

The action was still reported hot and heavy around the reviewing stand, though the rangers there were holding nicely and the sappers had blown up all six of the thrones.

We proceeded to our original target—the weapons test-control bunker—and found it ringed by a series of pillboxes which weren't supposed to be there. The rest of Fetterman's platoon had already engaged the enemy and were trading the Taus' M-219's for light gas-gun fire. They'd already taken out three of the pillboxes, but ran out of missiles as we arrived.

Fetterman sent two of his troops off to find some more 219's, then decided we couldn't wait. The Stoners weren't any good because the pillbox walls were about a meter thick and steeply sloped, and the H.E. stuff kept bouncing off before it exploded. We couldn't get a round inside because the guns were mounted in power turrets and the vision blocks had been glazed over with armored glass. I don't think it would have mattered much if they hadn't been. It isn't that easy to put a grenade round inside a view slit when somebody on the other side of it is shooting at you. The only vulnerable point seemed to be the ventilators on top of the pillboxes.

We layed down all the smoke we could in front of the last pillbox and about half a dozen of us rushed it. We lost a couple of people, but three of us made it. I grabbed hold of a light gas gun barrel sticking out of one of the turrets and used it to haul myself up on top. The barrel was hot and scorched my glove. I rolled across the roof to one of the ventilators, and my heart sank as I saw that it was covered by a heavy metal grid. I couldn't see any way to get it off, and a grenade sure as hell wasn't going to fit through it.

The guy checking the other ventilator made a mistake then. When he found the grill over it, he sat up, slapped his fist down on the ventilator cowl, and said, "Shit!" He took a stray round right through the visor. It looked like his head exploded.

I was too busy trying to figure out how in the hell I was going to get off the goddamn pillbox without being killed to feel sorry for the stupid bastard, when I heard a familiar voice say, "Perhaps I can be of assistance to ye."

"Peterson?" I said, squinting up at him while I tried to burrow into the concrete roof. "I didn't think you'd be stupid enough to come, too."

"Normally I'm not, lass, me being such an expensive piece of machinery and all—'tis not logical to risk meself in such a manner. However, after the majority of the bunch of ye had already started forward, me, being somewhat more observant than the rest of ye, and having a might superior eyesight, noticed the grids over the ventilators and figured ye might be needing an assist. Besides, me heuristic center hasn't been getting much of a workout lately, and I thought it might be an educational experience."

"You're nuts."

"Tush, lass, just curious."

"Bring any thermate with you? Maybe we can burn the grids off."

"Afraid not."

"Well what the hell good are you, then? For such a smartass machine, you sure are stupid."

"Lassie, I am good for anything any other man is good for, and whatever it is, I can do it better than most, but this is hardly the place or time to be discussing that sort of thing. Now if ye would be so kind as to move a might, I'll open the grid for you."

He made it look so simple. He just hooked his fingers under

the top of the rolled steel plate of the ventilator cowl and peeled it back like he was opening a can of sardines with a key, then he ripped the top off the other one.

"Now if ye would be of a mind to loan me a grenade, I'll chuck it down this here shaft while ye spike the other one. Normally I'm programmed to be a regular pacifist—I think somebody was afraid if I knew how to kill I'd likely do in a few of the brass hats who think up stupid wars like this one— but I learn real fast, and I think maybe just this one time we could make an exception, for education's sake."

"Here's to higher learning," I said, handing him a frag. "You do know how to use it?"

"Sergeant Masterson," he said, "really!"

"Okay. So stuff it down their throats and let's get on with it."

We dropped in the frags and sat, or rather lay, on top of the pillbox until they hatched. That's not my idea of playing it safe, but we couldn't crawl down the thing without getting shot up by the turrets. Anyway, it worked.

There was still some heavy fire coming from the bunker itself, but that cut off abruptly as the door blew inward and two SCAF troopers dropped down on jet belts and torched their way inside with a flamethrower. When they backed out of the inferno, I could see that it was the two rangers Fetterman had sent off to find some more missiles.

"Couldn't find any more 219's, Lieutenant," yelled one of them, "so we picked up some HEAT grenades and a blow torch."

"You did all right, Kowalski," Fetterman shouted back at him.

That's when I noticed the firing had stopped. Everywhere. I didn't know if the remaining Tau kings had been in the bunker, or if they'd been killed by someone else or gotten away. I only knew that the battle was finally over.

"Excuse me a moment," said Peterson, "but I do believe I ought to have a few words with me twin who's flyin' with the wing commander. We won't be needin' the bombers now."

I stared at him for a minute, then let out a whoop. It was as if I already knew it, but needed confirmation, and Peterson's word was as good as Overton's. I ran over and wrapped my arms around Fetterman and kissed him. He hugged me and tossed me up in the air and kissed me back. It was over. It was really all finally over. And I was still alive, and Tony was alive, and Petersons never die, and by God, we'd won!

25

Masterson, Lara
First Lieutenant, 358th Training Company, SCAF

We gathered up our gear and flew over to the parade ground, since the reviewing stand was originally our planned rendezvous point. There were about a thousand Taus who were mostly sitting on the ground looking dejected, and about fifteen hundred SCAF, some of whom were nervously guarding the Taus, but most of whom were smoking and laughing and beating each other on the back. I saw Captain Bocker, formerly Senior Platoon Sergeant Bocker, our company commander, passing out Tau cigars to everyone in his general vicinity. He had two lit ones in his mouth, one sticking out of each corner. He said they'd found a wounded Tau king at the hospital. The other one had tried to escape into the tunnel system and the neurone gas had gotten him. He'd had his mask on, but the best mask ever made won't do you any good against something you absorb through the pores in your skin.

There wasn't much to do for the next few hours. The upper-echelon brass had been so confident of our victory that they hadn't bothered to allocate shuttles to pick us up. There's no point in picking up radioactive ash. Someone did get cute though, and while the retrieval force was being organized, a shuttle flew over and LAPES'ed a bunch of 255-liter drums of beer.

Fetterman and I found some shade in the shadow of the remains of a Tau barracks where we could stretch out and sip the beer from our canteen cups. He pushed his equipment up in a pile next to his jet belt, took off his upper body protector, and leaned his back against the junk.

"Aren't you getting just a bit too casual?" I said.

"Relax, kid, the war is as good as over. All that's left now is mopping up, collecting the medals and back pay, and drinking toasts to the dear departed."

"I suppose you're right,' I said, following suit. "It's just that I've worn this damned body armor so long I feel like it's a permanent appendage." Stretched out next to him, I took a pull at the canteen cup and asked, "So what are you going to do now, Tony?"

"Well, depends on whether they ship us back home or keep us here as an occupation force. Whatever it is will be okay, I guess, so long as it's soldiering. Hope it's back home though. Somehow I don't think there's going to be much more action here, and if there's one thing that bores me, it's life in a peace-time army."

"You really love it, don't you? I mean war."

"Love it? War? Hell, no. You out of your mind? Nobody hates war more than a soldier. He hates it more than the pacifist, more than the priest, maybe more than he hates the pacifist and the priest."

"I don't understand. I thought . . . I mean, well, why do you do it then?"

"Because I'm so good at it. It's what I do best."

"There has to be more to it than that."

"You want a goddamn philosophy lesson? All right. It has to do with a lot of things. First, I believe that every living thing ought to serve some useful purpose in life, ought to serve some function. There's no particular logical, theological, or philo-sophical reason for that point of view, it's just that I fancy myself a practicalist. I'm a better soldier than anything else, so being practical and needing something to do, I soldier. Second there's the being apart. It has to do with standing outside of things and seeing them as no one else does. It's not letting your hair grow long and espousing a political point of philosophy your parents can't or won't understand, and knowing you're right and everyone else is wrong, and passing out leaflets on the University of Iowa Pentacrest. It's something that only Shakespeare and soldiers can understand."

"I don't follow you. What's this Shakespeare guy got to do with it?"

"You never heard of William Shakespeare?"

"I don't think so."

"The English author and playwright?"

"No, I don't place him. Has he written anything good?"

"Not for about five hundred fifty years. He died in 1616."

"And he said?"

"Not him. One of his characters in a play called *King Henry V*. The whole quotation is a bit wordy, but the gist of it runs like this:

> 'He which hath no stomach to this fight,
> Let him depart.
> But we in it shall be remembered;
> for he today that sheds his blood with me
> shall be my brother.'

"What he meant was that you've never lived until you've almost died, and for those who fight for it, life has a flavor the protected will never know."

"I think I can understand that."

"I think you can too. I wasn't sure about you until I saw you operate this morning, first on that Tau that tried to shoot your sergeant, then at the tower, and finally at the pillbox. You're okay, Masterson. You're a soldier. I'm glad for you, and proud of you, but you realize what goes with it, don't you?"

"Yeah," I said. "I won't fit into a peacetime army or as a civilian any better than you would."

"Come with me, Lara, when we get back home. I'll find us a war. There's always a little one somewhere. It won't be like Tau Ceti Four—the business isn't what it used to be, but then, it never is."

"I appreciate the offer, Tony, and I might accept, but by itself it just isn't enough. I'm not a very good loner. I need more than brothers-in-arms. I need a family too, and I'm not likely to find much left of mine when I get back to Earth. I want you to be my family, Tony. Just you. That would be enough. I don't need children—I don't think I'd want any, or be a good mother—but I do need someone. Will you be my family, Tony?"

"You know what you're asking? I've got ten years on you."

"I'd never have guessed it from your performance last night."

He grinned, remembering, and I grinned back. "Beware of wartime romances," he said.

"What the hell. Some days you've just got to say, 'What the fuck?'"

"You'd better if you're going to be a soldier. As for the rest of it, well, we'll have to find out, won't we? Here, give me your cup and I'll get us both another beer."

He'd walked about seventy-five meters when one of the rangers guarding a Tau work party yelled at him. The ranger was only about fifty meters away and I could hear him clearly.

"Yo, Lieutenant!" he called. "I wouldn't go that way if I was you. The party that hit the barracks put out some mines in that area beforehand, and I don't think the engineer platoon has gotten to clearing it yet."

Fetterman waved at him and started back. He took about three steps when the mine went off behind him. I knew from the way it blew that it was a geophone sensor model.

I remember screaming, but I don't remember what.

I ran to him. The guard got in my way and tried to hold me back, but I knocked him down. I knelt next to Tony and screamed at the guard to get a medic, but I already knew it wouldn't do any good. There was blood coming from his mouth. When they're like that it usually means they've taken some shrapnel in the lungs and they're filling up with blood.

"Oh! God damn you, Fetterman," I cried. "Why the fucking hell did you have to go and step on a goddamned mine? One of our own fucking mines, for Christ's sake."

"Made a mistake," he coughed, choking on the blood. "My fault."

"Shut up, damn you. Save your fucking strength. I'm not going to let you die on me now. Oh, Jesus, not now."

"Guess you'll have to find your own war after all, kid."

"Shut up, you idiot. Didn't you hear me tell you to save your strength? Why in the hell did you have to go and take off your body armor?" I shook out a field dressing, but one look at his back told me it wasn't worth the effort. "Why'd you have to pick today to turn stupid?"

"It's my birthday," he said.

"I told you to keep your mouth closed."

"Lara, promise you'll bake me a cake. Never had a birthday cake. Not even as a child. Parents died. No cakes at the orphanage."

"Sure, Tony, sure. Now shut up and save your strength, or you won't be able to eat any of it."

"Medic!" I screamed, turning away from him for a moment. "Medic! For Christ's sake, somebody get some help over here. Jesus. Everything I touches turns to shit!"

"Lara," he whispered, "I want you to know . . ."

I didn't find out what he wanted me to know. I'd like to be able to say that the medics got to him in time, that he wasn't hurt as bad as I thought, that he got well and I baked him the birthday cake and we found us a nice little war and lived happily ever after, but that sort of thing only happens in movie romances. I'd like to be able to say he said he loved me, then closed his eyes and went quietly while I held him. It would make a sweeter if somewhat maudlin ending, but people don't die that way in the real world, at least not the Fettermans in it. He fought for life until long after it should have been gone, and then he coughed his blood out on the ground, clawing at the dirt with his fingers until he was still.

I vaguely remember walking back to our gear to get Tony's bush jacket to cover him, and telling the medic he was too fucking late, but they put him on a stretcher and ran away with him anyway. I don't remember much else, except that somebody helped me gather up his gear and my own and took me over to the aid station near the reviewing stand. I guess I was pretty well shot. It was a while before I realized not all of the blood covering my fatigues belonged to Tony. Apparently I had taken a few fragments of shrapnel from the mine as well.

The doctor kept calling me lieutenant, and I couldn't figure out why until I finally realized I'd covered Tony with the wrong jacket and had his on.

I seem to remember sitting out in front of the aid tent smoking a Tau cigarette, drinking coffee, and staring at the sky with tears in my eyes, but I'm not sure anymore. I think that's what I was doing when half a dozen white, triangle-shaped ships with red markings, each at least twice as big as anything in the Retribution Fleet, cut across the heavens, splitting the air over the camp into a hundred thousand thunderstorms that sent troops and Taus scurrying for cover as one of the ships opened up and rained a shower of parachutes down from the sky.

Hung beneath the closest canopy was a lone figure in a leather jumpsuit, the sun flashing off the metal of chest armor. It did a perfect PLF, rolled over, and popped the quick release ring as it came up off the ground, leaving the canopy behind it. The figure carried a strange-looking weapon in its gloved hand. It was about the size of one of our Stoners, but had no barrel, and the thing in the jumpsuit and body armor handled it like it couldn't have weighed more than one of Captain Bocker's cigars. Since the weapon didn't seem to be pointed at me, I glanced at the figure's head. It peeled its insect-looking face off, and the top of its head came with it.

I found myself looking at the biggest, meanest, black-haired, black-eyed woman I had ever seen in my life. And I remember thnking, It's not fair. We already won. The Taus aren't supposed to have any ships.

The woman stared straight at my throat with those hard black eyes and said, "I suppose we're too fucking late to stop this fucking debacle from taking place. My name's St. Croix. What the fuck's yours, Lieutenant?"

All that took place a week and a half ago. I was now sitting in the dimly lighted officer's club aboard one of those big white ships, getting drunk with that same woman.

The keel of the ship, *Jaroslaw Pelinski*, hadn't been laid until ten years after we left the Earth, and the SCAF Relief Force hadn't spaced until almost thirteen years after we did. They'd done their best to get here in time, and with the new antigravity engines to eliminate acceleration and deceleration problems, they'd made the trip in just under thirteen years instead of the twenty-five it had taken us. But they'd still arrived eleven months and three days too late to prevent a war being fought on the wrong planet.

It seems the politicians and corporate presidents had learned the truth before we ever left Earth, but had suppressed it because an interstellar war was good for the economy. Probably the truth would never have come out if the Republican and American Independent Coalition hadn't come to power in a coup just after President Putnam suffered a coronary.

The *Star Explorer* had been destroyed all right, but the only connection that the Taus had with it was that the fight had occurred in the general area of their planet. The real bad guys hadn't even come from the same star system, and the scout ship the fleet had lost had blown itself up because of a faulty reactor baffle plate on the main drive pile. We'd killed several million people and conquered a few hundred million more for no good reason at all.

The table was a big nine-sided affair in the back corner of the club, and there was a hand-lettered sign in the middle of it saying, RESERVED FOR SURVIVOR-PARTICIPANTS, TAU CETI FOUR WAR GAMES.

Lieutenant Colonel Kadrmas, who'd led the armor during the raid, was there with a helicopter pilot named Kisov. Kisov had crashed his helicopter into a building and got to sit out most of the war in a SCAF hospital recovering from a bunch of wounds afterward, I'd heard. I'd also heard that he and Kadrmas had gotten real friendly during his recuperation. She was a good-looking woman in her mid-thirties with a black patch over her left eye. I gathered she'd lost the eye four or five months back. I suppose anybody else would have had a plastic replacement put in, but the Israelis seem to have an affinity for eye patches that almost equals their thirst for Coke. She was kidding Kisov a lot about finally making major and having picked up his fifth Purple Heart in the raid. He kept insisting it didn't count because it was only a flesh wound, and saying he really didn't need the sling. I'd come to the party at Peterson's invitation, God only knows which one he was, and because SCAF had decided to make me a real first lieutenant.

Someone had thoughtlessly invited a lieutenant commander who was the ship's liaison officer for Relief Force–Retribution Fleet relations, and he'd dragged along some Relief Force major who didn't know his ass from a hot rock. The creep wasn't even jump qualified, and he kept trying to play up to me. I ignored him, first, because he was a creep; second, because he wasn't rated; third, because he hadn't seen combat since he came out of the academy; and fourth, because I was well on my way to finding out if a person could turn into an alcoholic in one night, and didn't want to be bothered.

The creep kept yammering about how lucky we were to have seen so much action and cover ourselves with so much glory, and how good that would look on our records at promotion time, until finally I told him to shut up and go to hell. He got real huffy then, and I think he was going to threaten to put me on report. That's usually about all his kind can come up with for a comeback, but Kadrmas cooled him down.

"All I was trying to do was make conversation," he said. "That's no reason for the lieutenant to get insubordinate."

"And all that Lieutenant Masterson was trying to do, Major," said Kadrmas, "was explain to you in nice, simple terms that you could understand, that there is no glory in war, only death."

The lieutenant commander, I decided, was basically a nice guy for a fleet type, because he mumbled something about having to go somewhere, and tried to get the major to go with him. But the creep wasn't having any of it, and the lieutenant commander shrugged and shook his head at us.

Fortunately St. Croix came to my rescue. St. Croix is my warrant officer, a W-2. If there'd been anybody like her twenty-six years ago, SCAF would probably have settled for calling her a senior platoon sergeant. St. Croix said to me, "Lieutenant, I'm sorry to interrupt, but it's almost twenty thirty-five. You said you wanted to welcome the new trainees tonight."

I stood up and said I'd be back in about an hour. Once we were outside the Officers Club, St. Croix helped me get my beret on straight and asked if I was sure I wanted to talk to the troops. I told her I didn't think I was that drunk yet, but that I'd pass if she thought I might fall off the stage. She said, "Just don't breathe on anyone."

The troops were in the assembly hall, and the platoon sergeants had them all formed up nice and neat. St. Croix bellowed attention, and they snapped to as we came in. The two of us walked to the podium and I stepped to the mike. St. Croix stood off to the right.

"At ease," I said. "My name is Masterson and I am your

training company commander. For the next eighteen months plus the duration I will remain your company commander unless you are either reassigned or make a mistake. If you are reassigned, you will have a new company commander. If you make a mistake, you will be dead. Remember what we teach you and stay alive.

"Your battalion commander is Major Simms, and she'll be talking to you tomorrow morning. For your information SCAF has a shortage of combat-rated officers, so you'll soon find that Warrant Officer St. Croix and myself are the only two in the company. Warrant Officer St. Croix got her experience in a series of police actions in Latin America back on Earth. I got mine here, on Tau Ceti Four. All your noncoms, however, are combat veterans who have passed the acid test of warfare. They have survived. Listen to what they tell you, do what they tell you, and you might live to see Earth again.

"I understand that most of you have received at least some fundamental training before you left Earth. That will help, but it won't make the job much easier. My group had five years ship's time to train before we went into combat. You will only have eighteen months, plus the month ship's time you already spent in transit to Tau Ceti. After that they tell me the cryonics experts are going to put us all to sleep for a few hundred years. When we finally reach our destination, you will have the task of destroying the enemy on the ground and occupying his territory.

"I take it that, from what has transpired since I left Earth, you all understand why this new war must be fought. We'll be fighting an enemy that constitutes a clear and present danger to the Empire of Sol. If you still have questions as to whether it's morally right or just, take them up with the chaplain, not with me. This is a lawful war, whether it's either of the other things, and a soldier is duty bound to carry out lawful orders. Your orders are to seek out and destroy the enemy."

I paused for a second, looking out into the sea of young faces, and thought briefly that I had nothing in common with them. Then I remembered that it didn't matter. I once had.

"All right," I said. "Now before I turn you back over to your noncoms, I want to say just two more things. Remember them. Etch them into your brains. Don't ever forget them.

"First, there is no such thing as a dangerous weapon, only dangerous men and women. Anything and everything can become a weapon in the right hands, and the most deadly weapon of all is a well-trained and inventive mind.

"Second, the only way to get killed in combat is to make a mistake. Remember what we teach you and stay alive.

"That is all."

They were good words. Tony Fetterman would have approved.

FETTERMAN, Anthony B., First Lieutenant, Seventh Ranger Company, SCAF.

KADRMAS, Karen, Lieutenant Colonel, First Armored Corps, SCAF.

KISOV, Vasili Illiyavich, Major, Third Aviation Company, SCAF.

MASTERSON, Lara, First Lieutenant, 358th Training Company, SCAF.

*MCALLIF, Steven M., Private First Class, First Pathfinder Brigade, SCAF.

*Denotes killed in action during the Tau Ceti Four Campaign

ENDIT
TELEX